PRAISE FO
S
AND HER

TOUGH CUSTOMER

"Entertaining . . . a must-read for anyone who appreciates a tough guy hero with a heart of gold."

—*Publishers Weekly*

"Sandra Brown charges her characters and their relationships with electricity. . . . *Tough Customer* is a page-turner."

—*San Francisco Book Review*

"Brace yourself for exhilarating twists and turns in this gripping tale of obsession, murder, and the fragile nature of relationships. . . ."

—Fresh Fiction

"Brown doesn't disappoint . . . a steamy tale of obsession, love, and terror."

—*The Dallas Morning News*

"The draw here is the appealing Dodge, a character Brown fans will have no problems rooting for."

—*Booklist*

SMASH CUT

"Brown's dialogue snaps, crackles, and pops. . . ."

—*St. Louis Post-Dispatch*

"Superlative."

—*Publishers Weekly* (starred review)

"One of Brown's best books—a terrific setup that grabs you in the first chapter, an extremely cunning villain, and a plot that contains one surprise after another."

—*Connecticut News*

"Packed with surprises and the kind of propulsive plot for which Brown is justly famous. . . ."

—*Kirkus Reviews*

"A taut, satisfying page-turner."

—*Booklist*

SMOKE SCREEN

"Gripping and elegantly structured. . . . A true master of suspense."

—*The Providence Journal* (RI)

"Scorching . . . with a solid action-filled plot."

—*Publishers Weekly*

"Excellent . . . the characters are finely drawn."

—*The Dallas Morning News*

PLAY DIRTY

"A masterpiece."

—*The Providence Journal* (RI)

"A thriller with more twists and turns than a Cowboys wide receiver trying to lose his marker. . . . Great story, well told."

—*Herald Sun* (Australia)

"Full of steamy sex, intrigue and greedy secret plots."

—*The Washington Post*

RICOCHET

"No one does steamy suspense like Brown. . . . A stand-out thriller."

—*Publishers Weekly* (starred review)

"[A] taut Southern thriller . . . delectable."

—*Life* magazine

"Lots of surprising twists and turns, credibly flawed characters and a love affair that's as steamy as a Savannah summer."

—Lisa Scottoline, *The Washington Post*

CHILL FACTOR

"Races along with the passion and verve that are the hallmarks of a Brown novel."

—*Orlando Sentinel*

"Lust, jealousy, and murder suffuse Brown's crisp thriller."

—*Publishers Weekly*

WHITE HOT

"Family conflict, murder, and romance are ablaze in bestselling Brown's latest romantic thriller. . . . Exciting."

—*Publishers Weekly*

"Brown's writing lures readers with haunting, sultry seduction, redolent with secrets as deep as hot, breath-snagging Southern nights."

—*BookPage*

HELLO, DARKNESS

"Will keep you up past your bedtime."

—*Pittsburgh Post-Gazette*

"Strong characters, crisp dialogue . . . the suspense builds in Ms. Brown's capable hands."

—*Richmond Times-Dispatch* (VA)

These titles are also available as ebooks

By the same author

Rainwater
Smash Cut
Smoke Screen
Play Dirty
Chill Factor
Ricochet
White Hot
Hello, Darkness
The Crush
Envy
The Switch
Standoff
The Alibi
Unspeakable
Fat Tuesday
Exclusive
The Witness
Charade
Where There's Smoke
French Silk
Breath of Scandal
Mirror Image
Best Kept Secrets
Slow Heat in Heaven

SANDRA BROWN

TOUGH CUSTOMER

POCKET STAR BOOKS
New York London Toronto Sydney

Pocket Star Books
A Division of Simon & Schuster, Inc.
1230 Avenue of the Americas
New York, NY 10020

This book is a work of fiction. Names, characters, places, and incidents either are products of the author's imagination or are used fictitiously. Any resemblance to actual events or locales or persons, living or dead, is entirely coincidental.

This Pocket Star Books paperback edition July 2011

POCKET STAR BOOKS and colophon are registered trademarks of Simon & Schuster, Inc.

Manufactured in the United States of America

10 9 8 7 6 5 4 3 2 1

ISBN 978-1-4516-5485-1
ISBN 978-1-4165-6322-8 (ebook)

TOUGH CUSTOMER

PROLOGUE

HE WAS OUT OF THE TRUCK WHILE DUST AROUND THE TIRES was still rising.

The ambulance's emergency lights sent pulsing shafts of color into the surrounding forest. The doors of the ambulance had been left open by the EMTs, who, he assumed, were already inside.

His boots crunched in the gravel as he covered the distance to the porch in three long strides. He entered the house through the open front door, stepping into a wide foyer. His eyes swept the main room on his left. Nobody in it. Nothing apparently disturbed. Two empty wineglasses were on the coffee table in front of a slip-covered sofa. Traces of lipstick were on one of the glasses but not on the other.

The sofa faced a stone fireplace, where a leafy fern had been placed in the grate for the summer. Rocking chair with woven cane seat. Patchwork quilt folded over the arm of an upholstered easy chair. Magazines and books in shelves and stacked on various tables. Reading lamps.

It was as homey, cozy, and placid a setting as could possibly be.

He registered it all within seconds. Beyond the living room was a dining area rimmed by a bay window, but he left off exploration when noises from above drew his gaze up to the gallery that ran the width of the house. Taking the stairs two at a time, he rounded the landing, making sure not to touch the newel post, and proceeded up to the second floor.

He walked along the gallery, which led him into a short hallway and to an open bedroom door. Again he assessed the room in a glance. Matching lamps on either side of an unmade queen-size bed cast disks of light onto the pale, peach-colored wall. A ceiling fan with blades made of palm leaves circulated overhead. There were three wide windows. Through the louvers of the shutters he could see the continued play of the colored emergency lights on upper tree branches.

The EMTs were kneeling on either side of a prone figure, a man, judging by the bare feet and hairy legs, which was all of him that could be seen from this vantage point. Under the man, blood had soaked into the rug.

One of the EMTs glanced over his shoulder and bobbed his head in greeting. "Hey, Ski. We've been expecting you."

He walked into the room. "What have you got?"

"Messy GSW to the lower left torso."

"Is he gonna make it?"

"Don't know yet."

Until she spoke, Ski hadn't realized that the second EMT was a woman.

"A good sign, though," she added. "The lady said he was conscious right up till we got here."

"Lady?" Ski asked.

The first EMT nodded into an open doorway, which they were presently blocking. "She called in the 911."

"Name?"

"Hers? Uh . . ." He was distracted by situating the IV bag. The name escaped him.

The female EMT supplied it. "King."

"*Caroline* King? The realtor?" Ski asked with surprise. "This is her house?"

The woman EMT shrugged. "That's the name in our database."

"So who's the guy that got shot?"

"Lady said his name is Ben Lofland."

"Are they the only two in the house?"

"Appear to be. The front door was standing open when we got here. We followed her shouts upstairs. Found him lying here as you see him. She was kneeling beside him, clutching his hand, crying. We haven't seen anybody else. She's shaken up pretty bad."

"Did she shoot him?"

"That's your job," the woman EMT replied.

Satisfied that the shooting victim was stabilized enough to transport, the two competently placed him on the stretcher they'd carried up with them, affording Ski a better look at him. He appeared to be in his mid-thirties. He had even features and the trim build of a runner or tennis player. No facial hair, visible tattoos, or distinguishing scars.

He was wearing nothing except a pair of gray knit underwear. It had been cut away on the left side, where there was now a large bandage. The woman EMT threw a blanket over him. The guy was out cold, but he groaned as they strapped him down.

Hearing the clomping of footsteps, Ski turned just as another deputy barged into the room, then drew up short. "I got here as soon as I could," he huffed. His wide-eyed gaze moved past Ski to the dark, wet bloodstain on the rug, then to the victim on the stretcher.

He was younger than Ski by more than a decade, nearly a foot shorter, soft around the middle. His apple-cheeked face was flushed, and he was out of breath, either from excitement or from running up the stairs. He was a rookie. This was his first shooting. To him, it must represent the Big Time.

Ski said, "Give them a hand, will you, Andy? Getting that stretcher around the landing might be tricky. Don't touch anything in the process unless you put on gloves."

"Right."

"Hal's on his way to help secure the house."

"He's got some miles to cover."

"And until he gets here," Ski said sternly, "it's up to you not to let anybody else inside, and that includes our own men. I'm counting on you. Got it?"

"Got it." The younger deputy hiked up his slipping gun belt and accompanied the EMTs out.

Ski crossed the room and went to the open door that had been blocked by the fallen victim.

He looked into a bathroom, where a woman was sitting on the rim of the tub, rocking back and forth, her elbows on her knees, her head in her hands. He had a bird's-eye view of the center part in her hair. Ski thought it might be auburn, but it was hard to tell because it was wet. It formed a heavy curtain on both sides of her face.

A summer-weight cotton robe had been carelessly tied at her waist. The wide sleeves had fallen back to reveal slender arms sprinkled with pale freckles. The skirt of the robe had separated above her knees, leaving her legs bare. Her toes were curled into the deep pile of the bath mat.

She wasn't Caroline King.

Inside the bathtub, the porcelain was wet. Three of the pewter rings holding the shower curtain had been detached from the rod, leaving the wet curtain hanging unevenly. A bottle of shampoo in the corner of the tub was uncapped.

She must have been interrupted while taking a shower, which explained the damp patches where her robe was stuck to her skin.

Lying on the floor a few inches from her feet, incongruous with the vulnerability of her pink, bare toes, was a .38 revolver, a standard Saturday night special. The base of the commode would have kept it from being seen by the EMTs. Ski wondered if that had been deliberate.

He removed a pair of latex gloves from the hip pocket of his jeans and worked his right hand into one of them, then cautiously walked forward and bent down to pick up the revolver by the trigger guard. He thumbed the latch, and the cylinder swung out. There was an unspent bullet in each of the six chambers. He sniffed the barrel. It hadn't been fired recently.

As though only then realizing that he was there, the woman lowered her hands from her face and looked up at him. Her light brown eyes remained disconnected and vague. The whites of them were streaked with red from crying. Her skin was very pale, her lips practically colorless.

She swallowed noisily. "Is he all right?"

"Not really."

Whimpering, she looked past Ski to the bloodstain just beyond the threshold. "Oh, God." She pressed trembling fingers against her lips. "I can't believe this happened."

"What did happen?"

"He's *got* to be all right. I should be with him. I must go."

She tried to stand, but Ski placed his hand on her shoulder and pushed her back down. "Not now."

For the first time since he'd come into the room, she focused on him. "Are you . . . Who are you?"

He unsnapped the leather wallet on his belt and opened it to show her his ID. "Deputy Ski Nyland, Merritt County S.O."

"I see." But Ski didn't believe she actually did. She'd barely glanced at his ID. Her watery gaze was imploring. "Please tell me he's going to be okay."

"What's your name?"

She seemed to have to think about it. Then she hooked her wet hair behind her ears and answered in a husky voice. "Berry Malone."

Ski noted that her last name wasn't the same as that of the man who'd been shot. Neither of them was named King.

He said, "The wounded man, Ben Lofland . . . is that right?"

She gave an abrupt nod.

"He's on his way to the ER."

"He's not dead?"

"Wasn't when they left with him."

"He bled a lot."

"He did, yeah."

"He can't die."

"Unfortunately, he can."

She made a choking sound and whispered, "I must call his wife."

"His *wife*?"

She stared at Ski for several seconds, then covered her face with her hands and began to cry in loud, wracking sobs.

Ski planted his feet wider on the bathroom floor tiles. "What happened here tonight, Ms. Malone?"

She moaned into her hands and shook her head.

"Is this your pistol? Did you shoot Lofland with it?" He didn't believe she had, at least not using the pistol now in his possession. But he wanted to see what kind of reaction he'd get by asking.

She dropped her hands from her face and gaped at him. "What?"

"Did you—"

"No!" She surged to her feet, reeled slightly, then steadied herself by placing a hand on the edge of the pedestal sink. "I didn't get out the pistol until after I'd called 911."

"*After* you'd called 911?"

Her head bobbed an affirmation. She gulped a breath. "I was afraid . . . afraid he would come back."

"Who?"

Before she could answer, sounds of a commotion downstairs reached them. A door slammed. Voices were raised. Ski heard Andy telling someone that they couldn't come in. Just as insistently, a female voice, ordered him out of her way. Apparently Berry Malone recognized the woman's voice, because suddenly she gave a sharp cry and slipped past Ski through the bathroom door.

"Hey!" He was careful to hurdle the bloodstain on the rug as he chased after her. Midway across the bedroom, he made a grab for her arm but came up with only a handful of cotton fabric. She whirled around and yanked it from his grip, but not before he got an eyeful.

Then in a flash of bare skin and printed textile, she vanished through the bedroom door.

Ski went after her, crossed the gallery in a run, and bolted down the stairs, hot on her heels.

CHAPTER 1

When his cell phone's jingle pulled him from a deep sleep, Dodge figured the caller was Derek. Likely his employer had had one of his famous middle-of-the-night brainstorms and wanted Dodge to act upon it immediately.

Dodge couldn't think of what might be so crucial that it couldn't keep till daylight, but Derek paid him to be on twenty-four-hour call, if for no other reason than to act as a sounding board.

He fumbled for his phone in the dark and, without even opening his eyes, figuring he was about to be sent out on an errand he wasn't in the mood for, answered with an unfriendly and unenthusiastic "Yeah?"

"Dodge?"

Surprised to hear a woman's voice, he sat up and swung his feet to the floor. He reached through the darkness for the lamp switch and turned it on. Using his lips, he pulled a cigarette from the pack, then flicked on his lighter. As he took his first inhale, he wondered which woman, among the vast number with whom he was acquainted, he had pissed off this time. He didn't remember getting on anyone's fighting side recently, but maybe that was his transgression—disremembering.

Since he hadn't yet responded to his name, his caller asked with uncertainty, "Have I reached Dodge Hanley?"

He was reluctant to confirm it before he knew who was asking. He preferred keeping a low profile. He had a driver's license because it was a necessity. He carried a single credit card, but it had been issued in Derek's name. Dodge used it only when doing business for the law firm. Privately, he operated strictly on a cash basis, and not even Derek knew his home address.

"Dodge? Is that you?"

He replied with a sound that was half word, half dry cough. "Yeah."

"This is Caroline."

His lighter slid from his fingers and fell to the floor.

"Caroline King."

As if she needed to specify which Caroline. As if she needed to jog his memory.

After a long moment, she said, "Are you still there?"

He sucked tobacco smoke into his lungs and exhaled as he said, "Yeah. Yeah." To prove to himself that the call wasn't part of a dream, he stood up and took a few steps away from the bed. But because his legs were so shaky, he backed up and sat down again on the sagging mattress.

"Fair to say that you're surprised to hear from me?"

"Yeah." That seemed to be the only word he was capable of uttering. How many *Yeah*s did that make now? Four? Five?

"I apologize for the hour," she said. "It's late here, and I realize it's an hour later in Atlanta. I mean, I assume you're still in Atlanta."

"Yeah." Six.

"How are you? Are you well?"

"Yeah." *Shit!* Had he forgotten the language? Find some other words for crissake! "Uh, I'm okay. You know. Okay."

He was okay except for a total brain shutdown, a heart rate that had shot off the charts, and a sudden inability to breathe. He groped for the ashtray among the clutter on his nightstand and laid the cigarette in it.

"That's good," she said. "I'm glad to hear it."

Then neither of them said anything for so long that the silence began to hum.

Finally she said, "Dodge, I never would have bothered you if not for . . . I would never ask you for anything. I imagine you know that. But this is vitally important. Urgent."

Jesus. She was sick. She was dying. She needed a liver, a kidney, his heart.

Plowing his fingers up through his hair, he cupped his forehead in his palm and, dreading the answer, asked, "What's the matter? Are you sick?"

"Sick? No, no. Nothing like that."

Relief made him weak. Then he got angry, because—just like that—he'd become emotionally invested. To counter his stupid susceptibility, he asked impatiently, "Then why are you calling me?"

"I have a situation here that I don't know how to handle."

"Situation?"

"Trouble."

"What kind of trouble?"

"Can you come?"

"To Houston?" A place to which he swore he would never return. "What for?"

"It's complicated."

"What about your husband? Is it too complicated for him? Or is he the problem?"

A few seconds ticked by. Then, "He passed away, Dodge. Several years ago."

This news filled his ears, his head, with pressure. Her husband was dead. She was no longer married. He hadn't known, but then why would he? It wasn't like she would have sent him an announcement.

While his ears thrummed, he waited for her to say more about her husband's demise. When she didn't, he said, "You still haven't told me the nature of this trouble."

"The kind you specialize in."

"That covers a lot of ground."

"I don't want to go into it now, Dodge. Can I count on you to be here?"

"When do you need me?"

"As soon as you can get here. Will you come?"

Her stubborn refusal to be more specific pissed him off. "Probably not."

A hostile silence quivered between them. He picked up his cigarette again, inhaled deeply, blew it out. He wanted to hang up on her. Wished he would. Wished he could.

Quietly she said, "I understand your reluctance to become involved. Truly I do."

"Well, what did you expect, Caroline?"

"I don't know what I expected. I acted on impulse without thinking it through."

"You call me in the middle of the freakin' night. You tell me *shit,* but I'm supposed to drop everything and come running to get you out of some kind of unspecified trouble?" He paused for effect, then said, "Wait. Why is this sounding familiar to me? Is this sounding familiar to you?"

She responded exactly as he'd expected her to: with pique. "I'm not asking you to help *me,* Dodge."

"Well, good. Because—"

"It's Berry who's in trouble."

"Looks like somebody actually cooks in here now." Dodge sat down at Derek and Julie's breakfast table in their organized but well-used kitchen. "Didn't used to."

Derek laughed. "I don't recall ever turning on the oven before Julie and I got married." He lifted the coffeemaker carafe with an implied offer of some.

"Sure," Dodge said. "Two sugars. The real stuff."

Derek carried over the mug of coffee along with the sugar bowl, a spoon, and a cloth napkin. Dodge fingered the fringe on the napkin's hem and looked at his employer with raised brows.

"Julie insists on cloth."

Dodge snuffled as he scooped sugar into his mug. "She actually use all those gizmos?"

Derek followed Dodge's gaze to the ceramic jug that held some of Julie's cooking utensils. "Yep. They've got a gadget for everything. You wouldn't believe."

"Where is she?"

"Upstairs throwing up."

Dodge blew on his coffee and took a sip. "That sucks."

"No, she's actually glad about it."

"She enjoys puking?"

"Morning sickness is a good sign. It means the embryo has latched on to the lining of her uterus, which creates all kinds of hormonal chaos, which causes the nausea, which—"

"Thank you," Dodge grumbled into his coffee mug. "I don't want to know anything about Julie's uterus. In fact, I'd just as soon keep the mysteries of human reproduction mysterious."

"I thought I heard your voice." Julie entered the kitchen and smiled at Dodge. She looked the picture of health despite her bout of nausea. "It's awfully early for you to be up and about, isn't it? Especially on a Saturday."

"Sounds like you've had a rough morning."

"I don't mind so much. It'll pass soon, and the sickness is a good sign, the result of the embryo latching on."

Derek laughed. "We've been over that. Dodge doesn't want to hear any more."

"Fair enough." She asked if Derek had offered their guest something to eat to go with his coffee, and when he said no, she sliced him a piece of pound cake, which he accepted, knowing what a great cook she was.

Through his second bite, he mumbled, "If I'd married you, I'd have gained twenty pounds by now."

"Have you seen Derek naked lately?"

"Hey!" Her husband of six months smacked her on the fanny, then pulled her into his lap, bounced her on his knees, and nuzzled her neck, saying, "You're the one getting chubby." He splayed his hand on her abdomen, which as yet showed no signs of the pregnancy. She placed her hand over his, and they exchanged a warm, meaningful look.

Dodge cleared his throat. "Y'all need me to leave the room, or what?"

Julie slipped off her husband's lap and took a chair across the table from Dodge. "No, I'm glad you're here. Derek sees you nearly every day, but I don't get to."

Dodge ribbed his boss about his honeymoon giddiness, but he was glad about the marital happiness these two had found with each other. Derek and Julie Mitchell were among the very few people on the planet that Dodge had even a limited tolerance for. He'd go so far as to say he respected and liked them, although, as with everyone he knew, he kept them at arm's length, more for their sake than for his own. He wasn't good for people. Something in his makeup was destructive.

"What brings you by?"

Derek's question seemed innocuous enough, but Dodge knew better. Derek had razor-sharp instincts and uncanny intuition, which served him well in his chosen profession of defense attorney. Despite their easy chitchat, his boss had sensed that something was out of joint. When was the last time Dodge had come calling early on a Saturday morning? Never.

Dodge shrugged with feigned indifference and sipped his coffee, nursing a twinge of uneasiness about having to lie to this man who was the closest thing he had to a friend.

"How pissed would you be if I asked for some time off?" He kept his eyes fixed on the contents of his coffee mug but sensed the puzzled glance Derek exchanged with his wife.

"I wouldn't be pissed," Derek said. "You've earned the vacation time."

"Think before you speak, Counselor. Because I don't want to get somewhere and have you phoning me in the middle of the night, asking me to run down some lowlife that—"

"Dodge. You won't get an argument from me. You're past due a vacation. If something comes up while you're away, it can wait till you get back."

"Like hell it can. Even if you say it's okay for me to go, those hotshots you've got working for you would have a fit. They don't address me unless it's with 'Dodge, when . . . ?' As in, When can you get that background info for me? When can I expect the skinny on this guy? When can you track that down?"

Derek said, "Everyone in the office depends on you."

"See, that's what I'm talking about. If I left for a few days, the whole damn firm would collapse."

Dodge had been of considerable help solving the case in which Julie had been involved. The murder of Paul Wheeler had been a tragedy in every sense except that it had brought Julie and Derek together. Initially, Dodge had suspected Julie of being a liar, manipulator, and worse. She'd borne his hostility and suspicion with dignity and now seemed to hold no grudge. He thought she might even like him a little.

It was to her that he shifted his gaze now. But maybe that was a mistake, because she was regarding him with concern, which, in his present frame of mind, was almost more dangerous than her husband's incisiveness.

"I hope your reason for needing time away isn't health related," she said softly.

"Like what, dying of lung cancer? No, no, I'm not," he said when her concern was replaced by alarm. "Not that I know of. Not yet." He shifted in the seat of his chair and patted his shirt pocket, reassuring himself that the pack of cigarettes was there, even though he'd just as well pee on the *Mona Lisa* as light up in their kitchen.

Back to Derek, he said, "Forget it. I knew better than to ask." Placing his hand over his heart, he said, "The firm needs me, and, if I'm loyal to nothing else, I'm loyal to Mitchell and Associates."

"Cut the crap. What's going on?"

"Going on? Nothing. I got this notion to—"

"Take some time off, and I said okay. But now you're arguing with me for saying yes, fine, go. Why?"

"No *why* to it. It was a dumb idea, that's all. I thought of slipping off somewhere for a few days, but . . ."

"Did you have a destination in mind?" Derek grinned. "One of those tropical islands you're always talking about. *National Geographic*–type places where all the women go topless?"

"I wish."

"Then where?"

"Buttfuck, Texas."

Dodge could have kicked himself for blurting that out. He hadn't meant to.

Derek stared at him for several seconds, then deadpanned, "Does that have a zip code?"

Dodge rolled his shoulders. "Doesn't matter. I'm not going."

No one said anything for several moments, and Dodge sensed another mystified look pass between Derek and Julie. She asked, "What's in Texas?"

"Texans."

His droll reply didn't have the jocular effect he'd hoped for. He looked at Julie again, and he didn't know what the hell it was that was drawing him to her this morning. Sure, she was and always had been easy on the eyes, but that hormonal ruckus taking place inside her was inspiring in Dodge all kinds of sentimentality that went against his nature.

Typically when someone asked him a personal question, even something as innocuous as "What's in Texas?" he would tell them to stay out of his effin' life. But he found himself answering Julie simply. "Business."

Derek reacted with a start. "Business?"

"Relax, Counselor. I'm not looking into another job. This is business of a personal nature."

"A personal nature."

"Jesus, is there an echo in here?" he asked crossly. "Why are you making a big deal of it anyway? Business of a personal nature could be constipation."

"I've just never known you to have personal business of any kind, but especially not in Texas."

"Well, that just goes to show that you don't know everything, doesn't it? Besides, why are we still talking about it? I'm not going. I'd get down there, and this goddamn cell phone would start buzzing like a band saw. You'd be asking me how soon I could get back. Not worth it. Forget I asked." He tossed his fringed napkin on the table and stood up. "Look, thanks for the coffee. Tasty cake, Julie. I gotta be shoving off."

"Sit down."

"Excuse me?"

The set of Derek's jaw was resolute. "You're not leaving this house until you tell us what the hell is going on."

"I told you. I got this notion to—"

"This isn't about vacation time. Sit down."

Dodge dropped back into his chair. But with attitude. After several moments of hostile glaring, he raised his shoulders. "*What?*"

"Do you remember when I told you about Julie and me?" Derek asked.

"About the flight from Paris?"

"Precisely. I admitted to you why I was compromised and couldn't represent Creighton Wheeler. I bared my soul to you because I knew I could trust you with my deepest, darkest secret. With my career. My life."

"Okay. So?"

"So that trustworthiness works both ways, Dodge. You have our confidence. What's going on?" Derek waited, and when Dodge didn't say anything, he added, "Must be something really important, or you wouldn't have put on such a dog-and-pony show about vacation time. You're here because you wanted to tell us something and didn't know how to go about it."

"You're a shrink now, too? Being Georgia's hottest trial lawyer isn't enough for you anymore?"

Derek didn't flinch.

"What's in Texas, Dodge?" Julie asked again.

Her softness of voice got to him as Derek's badgering never could have. His shoulders slumped in defeat. "Not what. *Who.*"

"Okay, who's in Texas?"

He avoided looking at both of them as he picked up his mug and walked it over to the sink, where he poured the contents down the drain. "My daughter." He felt their astonishment even before he turned around and saw their shocked expressions.

Derek said, "You don't have a daughter."

"Yeah, I do."

"Since when?"

"Since thirty years ago," Dodge said.

Derek shook his head to clear it. "You specifically told me that you didn't have a daughter."

"No I didn't."

"Dodge, I remember the conversation. You were checking into Creighton Wheeler's background. You told me that, based on what you'd learned about him, you wouldn't want your daughter dating him. And I said, 'You don't have a daughter.' And you said, 'If I did.'"

"See? You're the one who said I didn't, not me."

"But you *implied* it."

"Sue me."

"This quarreling isn't very constructive, is it?" Julie divided her reproach between the two of them, landing on Dodge. "We're just surprised, Dodge. You've mentioned a couple of ex-wives, but never children."

"Not children. Child. One."

He looked down at his shoes, wondered when they'd last been shined. *If* they'd ever been shined. He really should have them buffed at least. Maybe, if he had time at the airport . . .

Airport? Airport, hell. He wasn't going.

"When did you last see her?" Julie asked.

"On her birthday."

"Her last birthday?"

He shook his head. "Her actual one. The day she was born."

Their stunned silence teemed with questions he didn't want to answer. But Derek had the tenacity of a bulldog. "So why are you considering going to see her now?"

"I'm not."

"For the sake of argument, let's assume you are."

Dodge chewed on his inner cheek with annoyance and indecision, then heard himself telling them that his daughter had got herself into a jam. "I don't know the details, but it's a police matter. And her . . . Somebody thought that maybe, with my background, I could help out. But I don't think so, and, anyway, why would I want to?"

Derek and Julie continued to look at him, their gazes admonishing and speaking volumes. Lowering his head, he dug into his eye sockets with his thumb and middle finger, then dropped his hand and sighed. "Shit, shit, and double shit."

CHAPTER 2

FOR NEARLY HALF AN HOUR, BERRY AND CAROLINE HAD BEEN sitting on hard, unforgiving wood benches, like church pews, just inside the entrance of the Merritt County Court House. When Ski Nyland approached them, he looked like a man with a purpose for which he was running late.

"Sorry to have kept you waiting. I got a call."

Caroline asked, "Something positive?"

"I'm afraid not, Ms. King. Oren Starks is still at large, and I've only got a few minutes before I need to get back to the hunt." He touched the cell phone attached to his belt as though to guarantee that his line of communication hadn't been cut. His gray gaze slid to Berry, acknowledging her for the first time since he'd joined them. "Ready?"

"I've been ready."

After a beat, he said, "I guess marketing adheres to a stricter timetable than law enforcement does."

Touché, Deputy, she thought. Her remark had been bitchy, and bitchiness was something she was striving to fix. However, given the stressful circumstances, she felt entitled to backslide.

Taking the edge off her tone, Berry said, "It's just that I thought you got everything you needed from me last night. I didn't expect to be summoned here again this morning."

"Sheriff Drummond asked for the meeting. Your lawyer is already up there."

"Then we should join them without further delay," Caroline said with a graciousness that Berry envied. She'd never mastered that special trait that seemed to come naturally to her mother.

Deputy Nyland gestured for them to precede him.

As they crossed the lobby, Berry wondered why he wasn't in uniform. He hadn't been wearing one last night, either, but she had figured he'd been off duty when her 911 had interrupted his Friday evening.

Today, except for his sport coat, he was dressed for a rodeo. Jeans and boots, crisp, white, western-cut shirt. He was also as laconic as any western-movie cowboy. She wondered if he envisioned himself as such. All he needed was a large white hat, a big tin star on his chest, and a six-shooter strapped to his thigh.

She assumed he was carrying a weapon somewhere. He might remove it when he was in the courthouse, but more than likely he kept it on, concealed from view, as were the emergency lights behind the grille of his tricked-out SUV, in which he'd driven her here last night to get her statement about what he'd referred to as "the shooting incident."

Now, as they waited for an elevator, Berry noticed how dwarfed her mother was by his height. Even Berry, who'd been taller than every boy in her class since seventh grade and had graduated high school with only a few of them having outgrown her, felt diminutive next to him.

They decided in favor of the stairs over waiting any longer for an elevator. As they walked up the one flight, Berry felt his stare like a physical pressure on the center of her spine.

The courthouse structure dated back to 1898, but it had been well maintained. The sheriff's office had original paneling and hand-carved molding around the plaster ceiling. The window glass was wavy but lent the room character. The wide desk was flanked by matching flagpoles. Between Old Glory and the Texas state flag hung a painting depicting Santa Anna's surrender to Sam Houston.

When they entered the office, the two men in it stood up. One was the lawyer her mother had summoned to the house last night. The other was Sheriff Tom Drummond.

He stepped from behind his desk and met them halfway to embrace Caroline, taking her shoulders between his hands and kissing her cheek. "Always a pleasure to see you, but I hate the circumstances of this meeting."

"So do I, Tom." She turned to indicate Berry. "I believe you met my daughter last year at the country club's Labor Day picnic."

"Of course. Ms. Malone."

"Berry, please."

He took her hand and patted it warmly. "I assure you, this case has the full attention of this office. Your mother's company has become important to this community by turning a stagnant real estate market active. Anything concerning her concerns me, especially your safety. We're going to catch this character. I give you my word."

"Thank you. I have every confidence in you."

The lawyer—his name was Carlisle Harris, Harris Carlisle, Berry couldn't remember which—was roughly the sheriff's age. He was a nice-looking, pleasant gentleman, but she felt sure her mother had chosen him more for the evident shrewdness behind his bright black eyes than for his cordiality.

He had shown up at the lake house last night as though Caroline had waved a magic wand to produce him. As soon as her mother had learned the nature of the emergency and Ski Nyland had begun posing questions about Berry's pistol, Caroline had politely asked him to hold off until she called her attorney. The deputy hadn't liked it, but he had complied, and Berry hadn't uttered another word until the lawyer got there.

He stepped forward now to shake hands with her and Caroline in turn.

The sheriff must have sensed Ski Nyland's impatience because he curtailed the pleasantries and suggested they all take seats. Berry and her mother sat side by side on a well-worn leather sofa. The men sat in armchairs that formed a semicircle facing them.

The sheriff began. "Ski has given me a rundown of what happened out at the lake house last night, and I have a copy of your official statement, Berry. Harry, you got a copy?"

"I did," said Harris Carlisle. "Thank you."

"Is there anything you'd care to add to it, Berry?" the sheriff asked. "Anything you've remembered between last night and now that could help us track this guy?"

She shook her head. "I was as comprehensive as I could be. To capsulize it, Oren Starks has been stalking me for months. Last night he came to the lake house, shot Ben, and threatened to kill me."

"You met Starks at your place of employment, is that correct?"

"Delray Marketing in Houston."

"I understand that he was fired from the company."

"Some months ago."

"Do you know why?"

"He wasn't a good fit," she replied. "At least that was the watercooler speculation for why he was let go."

"Did *you* think he was a good fit?"

She turned to Deputy Nyland, who'd posed the question, and answered coolly. "It isn't in my job description to evaluate co-workers."

"Candidly, did you think Oren Starks was a good fit?"

"No, I didn't."

"Why not? Wasn't he any good at what he did?"

Berry gave a half smile. "Oren wasn't *good* at his job, he was *exceptional*."

"I don't follow, Berry," the sheriff said. "Ski said you painted this guy as an oddball."

"His personality has no bearing on his skill," Berry said. "Marketing is about creativity, and strategy, and making dozens of components come together to form a harmonious whole. One wrong element throws the whole thing off. At Delray, Oren was our go-to guy when a campaign wasn't coming together the way it should. He had a knack for isolating the piece that didn't fit."

"Yet he was a misfit at the company," the sheriff said.

"Ironically, yes. He made people uncomfortable. Women in particular. I wasn't the first he focused his unwanted attention on."

"Were sexual harassment complaints filed against him?"

She shook her head. "None officially. Oren didn't do anything overt. No touching. No obscene e-mails or lewd texts. He's too intelligent, too sly to do something that could have trapped him.

"But he was very clever with innuendos implying an intimacy that didn't exist." As an afterthought, she added, "If you took issue with one of his remarks, he could make you feel as though you'd mistaken his meaning."

"Was this your experience?" the sheriff asked.

"Yes. At first. I began to think I was reading too much into the things he said and did. But after he was fired, he became more persistent and aggressive. To the point where I grew frightened of him. I thought that if I came here and stayed the summer in Mother's lake house—which she'd been trying to get me to do ever since she bought it—if I came here, essentially disappeared for a while, Oren would become discouraged or simply lose interest and leave me alone."

"When you say stalking . . ." The sheriff leaned forward, inviting her to elaborate.

"Calling several times a day. Constantly sending me text messages."

"Why didn't you change your phone number?" Deputy Nyland asked.

"Too many people have that number. Clients, co-workers, people who need to reach me for a quick solution to a time-sensitive problem. It would have been very inconvenient to change it."

"More inconvenient than being stalked?"

"You don't have to answer that, Berry," her lawyer said.

She didn't answer. Instead, she redirected her attention to the sheriff. "Oren would show up at my house uninvited. Sometimes he would be parked at the curb, or even sitting on the porch, waiting for me when I returned home. He would appear at restaurants where I was having dinner and would send flowers with enclosure cards that suggested a romantic relationship. I assure you there was none. He sent me small gifts that—"

"Like what?"

Flustered by the deputy's constant and skeptical interruptions, she had to think for a moment. "He once sent me a video game. A Dungeons & Dragons kind of game. Fantasy stuff with wizards, evil sorcerers, castles with mazes. You know the kind of thing."

"You're into that?"

"Not at all, Deputy Nyland. But Oren is. He loves puzzles of any kind, and he's good at them."

"Which made him good at working out solutions to marketing campaigns with problems," the deputy said.

"Exactly."

"What else? What other gifts?"

"A bestseller by an author he knows I like. He stood in line for hours—so he claimed—to have the book inscribed to me. He gave me a CD that he'd burned himself. The most personal gift was a silver charm bracelet. Thin chain. One charm. A heart."

"Did you return these gifts?" Nyland asked.

"At first I tried, but Oren refused to take them back. Eventually I just kept them."

"Why?"

"Because attempting to return them involved seeing him or talking to him, and that's what I was trying to avoid."

Harris Carlisle interceded. "I think we understand the concept of stalking, don't we, Tom? Ski? The man has pestered her beyond endurance, and last night his obsession turned violent."

The sheriff nodded. "Please, Berry, continue."

"I forgot where I was."

"You moved here for the summer."

"I hoped to be rid of Oren forever. I don't know how he discovered the location of Mother's lake house—the address isn't in the phone book. But he did," she said quietly. The reminder of what had taken place caused emotion to well up in her throat.

Quietly her mother asked if she'd like some water. She shook her head. Caroline took her hand and gave it an encouraging squeeze. The deputy shifted in his chair, making the old wood squeak, and looked toward the door as though anxious to adjourn.

Berry was tempted to ask if she was keeping him from something more important but then realized that of course she was. He was coordinating the search for Oren. The sooner he was done here, the sooner he could get back to it.

Without further delay, she picked up the story. "Last night Oren came to the house. He scared me out of my wits. I was in the shower. Suddenly the curtain was flung open and there he was, *Psycho* style. Except instead of a knife, he was pointing a gun at me."

The sheriff turned to Caroline. "You were out, I understand."

"I'd been away all day. I'd intentionally made myself scarce because Berry had told me that she and Mr. Lofland would be working on a very important project. I didn't want to be a distraction.

"After work, I went straight from the office to attend a dinner party hosted by former clients. Sort of a housewarming. I had told Berry not to wait up because I wasn't sure how late I'd be. Apparently I arrived shortly after Deputy Nyland got there. A deputy sheriff was standing guard at my front door. He forbade me to go inside.

"Berry had tried to call and alert me to the emergency, but my cell phone was in my handbag, and I'd silenced it during the party. I hadn't thought to check it before I left for home."

The sheriff looked across at Nyland. "When she got there, you two, you and Berry, were still upstairs?"

"We heard the argument between Andy and Ms. King at the front door. Came down. Ms. King called Mr. Carlisle."

"Which was my right to do."

The deputy conceded the point with a nod. "Soon as he got there, I continued interviewing Ms. Malone. First off, I asked if Starks had broken in. He hadn't."

"That's correct, Sheriff," Berry said. "All the doors to the house were unlocked. Ben and I had been in the pool, we'd cooked steaks on the outdoor grill for dinner, so we'd been going in and out all evening. I hadn't yet locked up for the night.

"Oren simply came through the front door; at least I assume he used the front door since that's the way he went out. The time between him yanking open the shower curtain and my placing the 911 call couldn't have been more than a few minutes. It all happened in a blur."

"In your statement you said the man was maniacal."

"She said he was unhinged."

Berry looked quickly at Deputy Nyland again, surprised that he recalled the exact word she'd used to describe Oren's state of mind. "That's right. He was wild-eyed. He was sputtering. 'I must kill you. You realize that, don't you? I've got to kill you.'"

Beside her, Caroline shuddered and gripped her hand tighter.

"The instant I saw him and the pistol, I screamed. That seemed to rattle him even more. He was shushing me and repeating, 'I don't have a choice. I've got to do it. Don't you see? Don't you understand?' He spoke in a sort of chant. He was . . ."

The four of them looked at her expectantly. As she searched for the word, she looked at each of them in turn, ending on the deputy, whose gray gaze remained unwavering.

"Unhinged," she said with a helpless shrug. "That's the best word to describe him."

"Well, he went there to kill you," the lawyer remarked. "One wouldn't expect him to be rational."

"No."

"Had you ever seen this side of him before?" the sheriff asked.

"Only once, when he became extremely angry at me for rejecting him. But last night he was more upset than even then." She wished for a moment to ponder that, but when Nyland shot another look toward the door, she plowed on. "Ben must have heard my screams and Oren's raving. He came running from the guest bedroom. When he reached the bathroom door, Oren heard him, spun around, and fired the gun."

She paused, reliving that horrifying moment: the jarring sound, the unbelievable sight of Ben falling backward, the wild expression on Oren's face when he turned back to her. Through it, she'd told herself that this couldn't be happening, that traumatic, violent events like this didn't happen to normal, nice people like her.

But it had happened. She'd lived it. However, now as she tried to describe the scene and her feelings about it, she knew her words would be inadequate to convey what she'd felt at the time.

"All I can say is that it was unreal, and yet it was reality taken to another dimension. Every sensation was overblown. After the gun blast, I remember experiencing a sense of timelessness, of suspended animation. But then Oren suddenly turned and ran. That galvanized me. I climbed out of the tub. I paused only long enough to bend down and tell Ben that I would get help, then I ran from the room to see what Oren was doing, where he'd gone."

"You weren't afraid that he would shoot you also?"

"She explained that to Ski last night."

"Calm down, Harry," the sheriff said, mildly rebuking the attorney. "I only ask because I'm curious."

Harris Carlisle signaled for her to continue.

"Honestly I didn't think about it, or I probably wouldn't have done it," she said. "I acted on instinct. I went after Oren, and by the time I reached the gallery, he was rushing down the stairs. At the landing he lost his footing and fell. He tumbled all the way to the ground floor and landed on his back.

"He saw me watching him from the gallery. He struggled to get up. He pointed the pistol at me, and that's when I thought for certain that I would soon be dead. I threw myself to the floor, trying to take cover behind the railing. He pulled the trigger until the pistol was empty."

Her mother placed her hand over her mouth to contain a small, distressed sound.

"Miraculously, his shots missed," Berry continued. "When he realized he had no more bullets, he struggled to stand up. He was yelling, 'I'll kill you. You must die.' Things like that over and over again. Then he turned and staggered through the front door."

After a short silence, Nyland asked, "He didn't reload?"

"No."

"He just ran away, vowing to kill you."

"That's right."

"Which is consistent with what she told you last night, Ski," the lawyer reminded him.

"Yeah, I know." He held Berry's gaze, and she could see wheels spinning behind the gray eyes. "Lofland was down. You were otherwise alone and defenseless."

"Yes."

"Starks had you in the bathtub, where he could have shot you at point-blank range. Instead, he made out like he was going to flee. Then you went after him, still defenseless, right?"

"Right."

"You didn't have your pistol yet?"

"No."

"Starks emptied his pistol from a dicey angle and at a distance of . . . what? Thirty feet?"

"I suppose. I don't know."

The sheriff leaned forward. "What are you driving at, Ski?"

He looked at his boss. "If Starks was that intent on killing her, saying he must, saying she had to die and so on, why didn't he shoot her in the bathtub? Why sputter threats against her life, then turn and run, when he could have popped her right then? Doesn't make sense to me."

"People do crazy things," the sheriff said. "He chickened out. He saw God. Who knows? When push came to shove, the best he could do was threaten her life, not actually take it."

"I guess," the deputy said, sounding unconvinced.

"I can only recount what happened, Deputy Nyland," Berry said. "I can't explain Oren's behavior. I don't know why he didn't seize his opportunity and shoot me dead. But I'm glad he didn't."

"Goes without saying," he mumbled.

"Please go on, Berry," the sheriff urged. "What happened next?"

"Once Oren was out of sight, I ran back into the bedroom and called 911 on Mother's landline. I hadn't heard a car engine, so I wasn't absolutely certain that Oren had left the premises. Because I was afraid he would come back, I took a pistol from the drawer of the nightstand. I had put it there the day I moved into the lake house."

"Even after leaving Houston, she feared for her safety against this guy," the lawyer said. "She bought the pistol as a precaution, Tom. It's registered to her, and she has a license to carry."

"I believe you, Harry," the sheriff said around an impatient sigh. "My wife keeps a twenty-two in her nightstand drawer except when the grandkids are visiting." He turned back to Berry.

"There's really nothing more," she said. "I stayed there in the bedroom with Ben until the paramedics arrived."

The sheriff expelled a long breath. "We're lucky you're with us today."

Caroline solemnly agreed.

"What's the latest on Ben Lofland's condition?" the sheriff asked.

"Fair," Nyland reported. "He's in surgical recovery. His wife's with him."

Berry knew he'd thrown in that last part just to embarrass her. She shot him a dirty look, but he was addressing the sheriff and didn't see it. "Houston PD and Harris County S.O. are assisting us in trying to run down Starks."

"You got the arrest warrant?"

"Right here," he said, patting his breast pocket. "I stopped at the DA's office on my way here." He glanced at Berry. "That's why I was late."

"Does Starks have any prior arrests?"

Nyland looked back at the sheriff and shook his head. "No criminal record. Clean as a whistle. Not even an outstanding parking ticket. He's not at his house, although the car registered to him is in his garage."

"He would have rented a car," Berry said.

"No record of that."

"Okay then, he'd've stolen one," she said, testily. "Or borrowed one. Or roller-skated. I don't know how he got here. I just know he's too smart to have used his own car if he came here with the intention of killing me."

Caroline intervened. "Deputy Nyland, we might feel better about the situation if you outlined for us the efforts being made to capture him."

His flinty eyes shifted to Caroline. "Yes, ma'am. While I was interviewing Ms. Malone last night, other deputies were notifying the sheriffs of surrounding counties. They dispatched their deputies immediately.

"But Merritt County alone has more than nine hundred square miles, and a lot of it is virgin territory. There are only twelve of us in this department, and that includes the court bailiff, a jailer, and a retired schoolteacher who comes in three days a week to help out with paperwork."

"He's right," the sheriff said. "And neighboring counties are of similar size and makeup and have even fewer personnel in their departments than we do."

Nyland said, "What we're saying is, there are a lot of good hiding places in this part of the state, and peace officers are spread thin."

Berry was certain her mother's intention hadn't been to question Deputy Nyland's competency, even by implication, but apparently Nyland was sensitive to criticism.

No one said anything for a moment, then Berry said, "I'm almost positive that Oren's leg was injured in his fall down the stairs. He was practically hopping on one foot when he left."

"I'm sure you've canvassed medical facilities in the area." Sheriff Drummond looked to his deputy for confirmation.

"Last night, sir, and it continues farther afield as we speak."

"DPS?"

"Last night I sent out a blanket e-mail. DPS, Texas Rangers, municipal police departments. I provided a description of Starks, but, unfortunately, we don't know what he's driving."

"I'm sorry," Berry said. "Maybe I should have followed Oren when he left the house. But at that point I didn't know if Ben was dead or alive. My first priority was to get medical attention for him."

"Understandably," the sheriff said.

Nyland turned to Berry. "Do you have any photos of him?"

"Of Oren? No."

"None were found at his house when it was searched."

"Not a single photograph? That's odd, don't you think?" Caroline asked them collectively.

"This whole thing is odd," the deputy said, almost under his breath. Then, "I'll ask Houston PD to go to that marketing outfit, see if they have a photo of Starks in their employee files. It would help to circulate one." He came to his feet. "Sorry, but I need to excuse myself and get back out there. Sir, you know how to reach me."

"I want to be kept up to speed, Ski. Don't go through the office lines. Call my cell."

"Yes, sir." He nodded in the attorney's direction. "Mr. Carlisle." To Berry and her mother, he doffed an imaginary hat. "Ladies."

Then he walked out. As soon as the door closed behind him, Sheriff Drummond said, "Ski's manner could use some polish, but you couldn't ask for a better man to be conducting this manhunt. His background is—"

He was interrupted by a soft beep. "Excuse me, Tom." Caroline took her cell phone from her handbag. As soon as she looked at the small screen, she shot to her feet. "I was expecting this call. I really should answer."

Without another word, she left the office. Berry stared after her, puzzled by her mother's uncharacteristic rudeness.

"Must be important," the sheriff observed out loud.

Berry echoed, "Must be."

CHAPTER 3

DODGE CURSED THE TOUCH-SCREEN KEYBOARD ON HIS CELL phone, wondering who in the hell had fingers small enough to actually type something on it. "Damn computer geeks," he muttered.

Of course it would help if, at the same time he was trying to peck out his message, he wasn't also driving an unfamiliar car and lighting a cigarette.

Finally he gave up on getting the text typo-free and sent it with only a few misspellings. The important thing was, Caroline would receive the message that he was on his way to Merritt.

He still couldn't quite believe that, after thirty years and counting, Caroline had contacted him. She'd called with a desperate plea for help. For Berry, not for herself. *I'm not asking you to help* me, *Dodge,* she had said.

Well, good, he'd said back. Because if she'd asked him for a personal favor, he would have hung up on her. He was certain he would have. Probably. Maybe.

But Caroline was too clever to take that approach. Instead,

she'd called him for their kid's sake. He would look like a real bastard if he didn't at least show up and check things out, wouldn't he?

Derek and Julie had thought so, and they'd told him as much. Insisting on driving him to the airport, they'd packed him into their car without further ado. They'd even ushered him through the ticket-purchasing process and seen him as far as the security checkpoint, mistrusting that he would follow through on his reluctant decision to go.

Throughout the flight, he'd told himself that he could always hook a U-turn at the Houston airport and fly right back to Georgia. Or he could go someplace else for a few days. Mexico sounded good. Tequila and brown-eyed ladies. Or a Caribbean island. Many to choose from. All had girls in string bikinis that matched the potent pastel drinks. Yeah, sand, surf, and getting tanked sounded good.

Instead, he had called Caroline as soon as he landed at Intercontinental, before the plane had even taxied to the gate.

When she answered, she'd sounded breathless—relieved?—and told him it wasn't convenient for her to talk just then but she would text him directions to their meeting place. With the text message, she'd added a postscript, asking that he text her when he was in his rental car and on his way.

Which he'd done, and now, he was ninety minutes away from seeing her.

The thought of it filled him with a sick anxiety that made him mad at himself. He would make it clear to her from the get-go that he wasn't about to get sucked into any mess not of his making. He had come only to listen, provide some advice if he could, and then leave. If at any point he determined that she was crying wolf, he would tell her to go to hell, that she was on her own, which was the way she had wanted it. Well, wasn't it?

He should have told her that last night the instant she identified herself. He should have hung up, finished his cigarette, then rolled over and gone back to sleep.

Instead he'd got up, showered, and dressed. He'd even packed a suitcase, on the outside chance he lost his senses and heeded her summons.

While waiting for daylight to come so he could go see Derek with the hope of being refused time off, he'd sat there in his shabby room, on his sad double bed, staring into the lonely darkness, wondering again if the call had been a dream.

Because before that, he hadn't dreamed about Caroline in . . . hmm . . . at least three, four nights.

He had never been to Merritt, wasn't even sure he'd ever heard of it before. He took the interstate north out of Houston, then exited onto a four-lane divided highway that angled slightly east for about seventy miles until he left it for a two-lane highway that cut due east, cleaving a pine forest like the straight and narrow shaft of an arrow.

It was beautiful country, the kind of forested terrain that most people didn't associate with Texas, which typically called to mind barren plains, tumbleweeds, and oil derricks silhouetted against an endless sky. There were plenty of oil and gas wells in East Texas, too, but the dense forests concealed them. In this part of the state, the sky looked smaller, closer.

Twenty miles outside of Merritt, he began seeing billboards advertising bait shops and taxidermy services, public piers, lake resort communities, cabins for rent, and RV campgrounds. A mile out, he spotted a pink and white sign for Mabel's Tearoom, and his stomach did a somersault.

Mabel's Tearoom. On your left as you approach town, just inside the city limit sign. 2:30. That had been Caroline's reply to his text.

He glanced at the dashboard clock and saw that he was just going to make it by the appointed time. Actually, he'd hoped to arrive early, so that he could already be there when she came in, and he would see her before she saw him.

Thirty years could do a lot of damage. He wondered how Caroline had withstood time. Her hair might have gone gray. She could be wrinkled, flabby, fat. If so, by comparison, he would look reasonably good.

But what he feared was that his manner of living for the past three decades was going to be glaringly apparent. She would see lines in his face that had been etched by vices, hard living, and a total disregard for his health.

Too late to worry about it, though. The damage had been done, and he was here.

Mabel's Tearoom had lacy curtains in the windows and pink geraniums in white wood planters on either side of the entrance. He wondered which of the three cars parked in front was Caroline's.

He was glad he'd taken time at the airport to get his shoes shined. Maybe he should have got a haircut, too, and a professional shave, but then he wouldn't have made it here by two-thirty.

He'd love another cigarette. Just one puff might sustain him through the next few seconds. But . . .

He pushed open the door and walked in. Announcing his arrival, a little bell above the door jangled, sounding to him as loud and portentous as Big Ben. The place was a single room. Three of the little tables were occupied. One by Caroline.

When he spotted her, his turncoat heart stuttered and stalled. Jesus, she was beautiful. Absolutely, positively, breathtakingly as beautiful to him as the last time he'd seen her.

Being the only person in the place with testicles, he felt about as agile and inconspicuous as a woolly mammoth as he walked toward her. She stood as he approached and stuck out her right hand.

Well, that was one question answered: There would be no hug. Not even a long time, no see one.

"Dodge, thank you for coming."

Even though he hadn't immediately recognized her voice on the telephone last night, probably because it would have been the last one he expected to hear, the years hadn't altered it. Though now it had a flutter, like maybe she was just as nervous to see him again as he was to see her.

"I was afraid you wouldn't," she said.

"I started not to."

She released his hand immediately after giving it one firm shake, then resumed her seat. He pulled out the chair across from her and sat down. Then for a time they just looked at each other.

Her hair was lighter than he remembered. Maybe she was using blond to cover up strands of gray. Whatever, he liked it. It was still that rich cinnamon color that he'd never seen on anyone before or since.

Sherry-colored eyes. Once, when he'd waxed poetic—poetic for him, anyway—about her coloring, she'd laughed. *Cinnamon and sherry? I think you read that in a recipe book.* And he'd replied, *Maybe so, because you look good enough to eat.*

He'd bet he could still encircle her waist with his hands. A strong wind could blow her away. Upon closer inspection, he saw a few fine lines at the corners of her eyes, and there was a slight softening of the skin along her jaw, but her complexion was flawless and appeared as soft as ever, and looking at her made him ache all over.

He sensed that this lengthy perusal was as painful for her as it was for him. Painful for him because he couldn't gobble up the sight of her fast enough, and painful for her because she was seeing in his face the corrosive effects of the life he'd lived since she'd last seen him.

She cleared her throat. "How was your drive?"

"Fine."

"Traffic?"

"Not too bad."

"No problem with my directions?"

"I got here." He tried to smile, but his lips felt stiff.

"Welcome to Mabel's. What can I get y'all?"

Dodge hadn't realized the waitress had approached. Feeling helpless, he looked across at Caroline for guidance. She said, "I'll have Darjeeling, please."

He had no idea in hell what that was. Forcing his lips to move, he asked if they had regular Coke, and when the lady said yes, he ordered one.

"Anything to eat? Our apricot scones are worth the calories."

"Nothing for me," Caroline said.

"Me neither, thanks."

She left to get their drinks. Dodge didn't know then, or remember later, what the server looked like, if she was young, old, tall, short, skinny, plump, if she was disappointed that they hadn't tried the apricot scones or if she didn't give a flip and only wanted her shift to be over so she could get out of there. He was functioning in a vacuum.

Caroline must have sensed his uneasiness. "I chose this place because I've never been here. I know a lot of people in town, and it's a friendly community. I thought our first meeting should be where it was unlikely we'd be interrupted."

He wanted to ask what would have been wrong about meeting at her house, but he already knew the answer. She would want to meet in a public place, where a scene was less likely to occur.

"This is fine. Just awfully . . ." He glanced around. "Frilly."

She smiled, and that made him relax a little.

"I don't know where to start," she said. "I don't know anything about your life in Atlanta."

"What do you want to know?"

"Why there?"

"That's where I ran out of gas. Thought it was as good a place as any."

"You joined the police force?"

"Fulton County Sheriff's Office. They had an immediate opening. I started as an investigator. Good job. Good benefits. Stayed with it for twenty-five years. But the city grew, mostly in self-importance. The office got very button-down. I was getting sick of all the rules and regulations.

"Then I solved a case and had to testify at trial. That's where I met Derek Mitchell, attorney at law. He cross-examined me. We were on opposing sides, but we impressed each other. He asked if I would be interested in working for him as his firm's investigator."

"Less button-down?"

He shrugged. "It's been all right so far."

"It was very generous of Mr. Mitchell to let you leave to come here on such short notice."

"As bosses go, he's okay."

She rearranged her legs beneath the table and took great care with smoothing the napkin in her lap, keeping her eyes down. "Do you have a family?"

"No."

She raised her head and looked across at him. "You never married?"

He replied with a guffaw. "Don't I wish."

She appeared on the verge of giving way to natural curiosity and asking about his marital status but didn't. Wisely, he thought.

Instead, she said, "You didn't know until last night that I was a widow."

"Nope."

"I'm still in real estate. Did you know that?"

"Figured as much."

"I thought you might have. . . . I mean, your being an investigator by trade, I thought you would have—"

"Kept track of you over the years?"

"Frankly, yes."

"Frankly, I did. For a while. Then I . . . stopped."

"Lost interest?"

"Lost hope."

He sounded pathetic even to his own ears. Practically growling, he said, "I don't suppose smoking is allowed in here."

Her head went back several inches. "You *smoke*?"

That caused him to laugh. "I don't actually smoke. I just inhale. Smoking takes too long to get the nicotine into my bloodstream."

"When did you start smoking?"

"Thirty years ago."

The significance of the time frame didn't escape her. She held his gaze for several beats, then said, "You should quit."

"What for?"

Their stare held until the waitress returned with her tea and his Coke, which was served in one of the vintage bottles accompanied by a slender glass of ice sitting on a little china plate with a white paper doily underneath it. They didn't have Coke in ordinary cans in Merritt, Texas? He didn't touch anything, afraid he'd break something.

Caroline thanked the waitress, spooned sugar into her cup, then poured steaming tea out of a little white pot with pink flowers painted on it. "It's still weak. I didn't let it steep long enough," she remarked.

Okay, enough of this bullshit. "You gonna talk to me, or what?"

She set her spoon in the saucer. It clinked against the cup as though her hand might not have been quite steady. She looked across at him. "Last night, in my house, a man was shot and seriously wounded. Berry was there."

Dodge placed his elbow on the edge of the table and cupped his mouth with his hand. For the next quarter hour, Caroline talked, pausing only occasionally to emphasize a point or to organize her thoughts. He listened without interrupting her. He would gladly have sat there looking into her face and listening to her voice until his vices caught up with him and his heart stopped.

But eventually, she paused and took a deep breath. "Around noon we had a brief meeting with the sheriff," she said. "Tom Drummond. He's a nice man. We're social friends. He's held the office for as long as anyone can remember. Berry talked through last night's event with him, although I think that meeting was more of a courtesy to me than anything. Tom's duties are basically administrative. He relies on Deputy Nyland for investigative work."

"Did you have a lawyer there during this meeting?"

"Yes. Last night, and again today."

"Good."

"He wasn't really necessary. Berry's under no suspicion. She hasn't deviated from her first account to Deputy Nyland."

"Do they believe her?"

The question took her aback. "Why wouldn't they?"

"Do they?"

"They seem to."

Dodge didn't comment. He asked, "So where do things stand now?"

"The official word is that Oren Starks is being sought for questioning, but Deputy Nyland secured a warrant for his arrest. As soon as I got the okay from him, I hired professionals to clean up the mess in the house. They're there now.

"I didn't want Berry to see those rooms again until everything was back to normal, so after our meeting at the courthouse, we went to lunch at the country club. Then I dropped her at the hospital. She wanted to check on her friend's condition. I came here to meet you."

She took her first sip of tea. It was no longer steaming. He watched her graceful hands, the way they handled the delicate cup and saucer. Her fingers were almost as translucent as the china. "That's everything up to the present."

Dodge waited for several seconds, then asked, "Does she know I'm here?"

Caroline shook her head.

"Does she know you called me?"

Another negative shake.

There were many unspoken questions on that subject hovering between them. For the moment it was better to let them hover. "This deputy. Nyland? Can he find his ass with both hands?"

She smiled. "Your vernacular is still colorful, I see."

"Sue me," he said, and she actually laughed. Music to his ears. Then her expression became serious again as she thoughtfully considered the answer to his question. In concentration, her forehead wrinkled just as he remembered. The lines were a little deeper.

"Tom speaks highly of him. He places a lot of trust in him."

"He would. Nyland's his deputy."

"From what little I've seen of him, he appears competent."

"What's he like?"

"Characteristically you mean? Serious. All business. Watchful. A man of few words. Even a bit brusque at times."

"I know a lot of button-up, by-the-book cops who've never solved a crime or found a fugitive," Dodge grumbled. "So, back to my original question."

"I don't know the level of his competency, Dodge," she replied with a trace of impatience. "That's partially why I called you."

He wanted to know what the other part of *partially* was, but again he saved that conversation for later. If there was a later. That was still a big *if.* So far this seemed Mickey Mouse. A bullet, a loss of blood, but not the earth-shattering, calamitous event he'd expected when he packed his suitcase last night.

"This whack job, Starks," he said. "What do you know about him?"

"Only what Berry has told me."

"I'll need a lot more than that, Caroline. I need to know what she hasn't told you or doesn't know herself."

"I figured that much. What I can tell you is that he's been pestering her for months. She was at her wit's end when I convinced her to get out of Houston for the summer. She agreed to, but it hasn't been easy for her."

"In what way has it been uneasy?"

"She's very focused and ambitious. She works as hard as ever from the lake house, but it's not the same as being in the office. I know because I've done it. There are inherent problems to working out of a satellite location. She hasn't talked to me in any detail about the difficulties posed by being away from her office, but I can tell when she's worried or—"

"You two are close?"

"Very, Dodge," she replied earnestly. "Very."

It knifed his heart to know how important they'd been to each other, and how dispensable he'd been to both. He hadn't done anything to make himself vital, though, had he? There were reasons for his being inessential to their lives.

Guilt was a parasite that would eat you alive, but only if you let it. So he forced self-flagellating thoughts from his mind and focused on what Caroline was telling him about the daughter he didn't know.

"Oren Starks had made her life hell or she wouldn't have moved to Merritt, even temporarily. She would be in Houston, at Delray, working. She thrives on it. She lives for it. Last year, someone else got a promotion she was hoping for, and she was crushed. Admirably, she used her disappointment to propel her, so that the next time a promotion comes along, she'll get it. Her career at Delray has been the focus of her life."

Her face became even more troubled. "She would never have imposed this exile on herself unless she felt she had no choice. Which should give you an indication of how much she'd come to fear this man. You called Oren Starks a whack job, but I think he's more dangerous than that, Dodge. And I believe Berry fears he is, too. Last night proves it."

"Yeah, let's talk some more about last night." Setting aside his timidity toward all things breakable, Dodge pushed away the glass of melting ice and took a drink of his Coke straight from the bottle. "Specifically, what about this Ben Lofland?"

"He'll survive the wound."

"That's not what I meant."

Caroline fiddled with her spoon, avoiding eye contact. "He and Berry are friends."

"He's married."

"Happily, Berry says." His silence caused her to lift her gaze back to his. "I believe her, Dodge. She's never lied to me. If she says their relationship is platonic, then that's what it is."

He took another swig of Coke, but his eyes stayed fixed on hers. "Okay. So, the guy caught in his undershorts recovers from his wound and lives happ'ly ever after with his oh-so-understanding wife. The competent veteran Sheriff Tom, who's your nice, social friend, along with his trusty, tight-assed deputy catch the bad guy and lock him behind bars. Berry returns to her Houston office. Then all's well and life goes on." He leaned forward. "Why'd you call me here? Come up with something more dire than this, or back to Atlanta I go."

"What's more dire than Berry's life being threatened?"

"That's *exactly* what I'm trying to get from you," he said in a tense whisper. "The death threats of a guy who's unhinged, sputtering, and chanting can't be taken as serious unless his motivation for being unhinged, sputtering, and chanting is. So, either cough up what you haven't told me yet, or I'm outta here."

Her eyes sparked. "You're still a bully, aren't you?"

"Yeah. And I still want to fuck you. Just like I did the first time I set eyes on you."

CHAPTER

4

Houston, Texas, 1978

DODGE SET TWO CAPPED FOAM CUPS OF COFFEE ON THE counter.

The cashier smiled at him. "Is that it?"

"How about throwing in those doughnuts, gratis?" He gestured to the clear acrylic box, which in the morning was filled with fresh bakery goods. At this hour of the night, all that remained were one glazed doughnut with sprinkles and one with chocolate icing.

"Un-uh, no way."

"You won't sell them. They're dried out. See the cracks in that chocolate?"

"The last time I gave you something for free—that Eskimo Pie, remember?—I got in serious trouble with the boss."

"Come on, Doris," Dodge wheedled. "He's not here." He winked at her. "I'm not gonna tell on you."

"He's an A-rab, you know," she said in an undertone. "He'll call it stealing and cut off my hand or something."

"Pretty please? With sugar on it?"

"Oh, shoot." She glanced at the security camera. "At least pretend to pay me for them."

"You're the best, Doris."

"And you're full of shit. I haven't forgotten that you promised to take me dancing."

Grinning, he said, "I'm taking lessons."

"My ass."

Out the corner of his eye, he caught the flash of headlights on the patrol car parked in front. "Gotta go. Don't bother sacking the doughnuts. Just set them on top of the coffees."

She did as he asked, and, as he backed out the door, balancing the cups and doughnuts, she said, "I'm holding you to that date."

Dodge's partner had kept the engine running. He reached across the front seat and pushed the passenger door open. "We're on."

Dodge tipped the doughnuts off the cups and onto the console. "You get the sprinkles, I get the chocolate."

"You got the chocolate last time."

"Sue me." Placing his coffee cup in the holder, he buckled his seat belt. "I'm the one stealing from the A-rab, and one of these days I may have to make good my promise to take Doris dancing. What've we got?" he asked as he fixed the plastic lid on the coffee cup so his partner could drink while he drove. He'd already sped from the 7-Eleven parking lot and turned on the emergency lights.

"Domestic."

"Damn!" Dodge, like most cops, hated responding to domestic disturbances because the offenders often turned their rage onto them. Cops got killed that way. He bit off half the stale chocolate doughnut. "Who called it in?"

"The alleged victim."

"That's good. Means he hasn't killed her."

"Not yet," Jimmy Gonzales returned grimly.

Gonzales looked more Anglo than Dodge did. When they'd become partners, Dodge had asked where the Hispanic name had come from. Gonzales had shrugged and said, "Dunno. Must've been a Spanish or Mexican gene in the deep end of the pool."

"Did the caller say her name?" Dodge asked him now.

"Nope. Disconnected after giving the address. No answer when the dispatcher called back. The house is a rental."

Gonzales was a good partner, reliable, always enjoyed a joke, but knew when it was time to shut up and focus on the job. As now, while they covered the short distance from the convenience store to a tidy house on a quiet street in a middle-class neighborhood.

He pulled the squad car into the driveway and left the lights on. He and Dodge alerted the dispatcher of their arrival and got out. They were watchful and wary as they approached the house. Dodge was particularly skittish about the windows overlooking the front yard and the exterior lighting, which seemed to him as bright as spotlights on him and Gonzales.

They made it to the porch without being shot at or threatened, and he counted that a good sign. When they reached the door, Gonzales stood aside, his hand on his holster. Dodge raised the brass knocker and tapped it loudly several times. "Police. Is there a problem in there?"

The door was pulled open immediately by a man who, Dodge would guess, was in his late twenties. His shirttail was hanging out, but his clothes looked expensive. He was good-looking and clean-shaven, although his black hair looked like it had been recently groomed with a gardening tool. His whole aspect was one of agitation.

He divided a look of disgust between the two officers. "I can't believe she called the police."

"Where is she?" Dodge growled.

"She's all right. She got upset—"

"Where is she?" Dodge asked with menace, emphasizing each word.

The man hitched his thumb over his shoulder. "Bathroom. End of the hall, right-hand side. She's locked herself in. Can you turn off those damn lights on your car?"

Dodge didn't deign to answer. He pushed past the man and crossed a neat living room, stepping into a dark hallway. He heard Gonzales telling the son of a bitch that the emergency lights stayed on and asking if an ambulance was needed. "Hell, no!" the guy exclaimed. "I didn't hurt her."

"Maybe I'll call one anyway," Gonzales said.

"I'm telling you, she's fine."

"What's your name?"

"Jesus."

"Are you cursing or being a smart-ass?"

That's all Dodge heard. He'd reached the end of the hall. He knocked on the bathroom door. "Ma'am? This is Police Officer Dodge Hanley. Would you open the door, please?" He tried the knob. It was locked. "Ma'am? Are you all right? Can you hear me?"

He heard the snick of the lock, then the door was opened. She was petite, reaching no higher than his collarbone. The guy who'd met them at the door was about Dodge's height, over six feet. Without even knowing the circumstances, Dodge already wanted to kill him.

The overhead light shone on reddish hair. Her head was bowed, and she was holding a folded, wet washcloth against the side of her face like a compress. She was fully dressed, but her clothes and hair were in disarray, as though she'd struggled.

"Ma'am, do you need an ambulance?"

She shook her head, then lowered the compress and tilted her face up.

When she did, Dodge felt his whole body expand and levitate as though it had suddenly been inflated like one of those Thanksgiving Day parade balloons. Then her eyes tethered him and slowly he resettled, but he still didn't return to normal. He retained that sense of buoyancy.

"I'm all right." Her eyes were the color of sherry, and if aged whiskey generated sound, it would be exactly like her voice. "I should have called back, told the operator there was no reason to dispatch the police, but Roger had taken the phone away from me, and I was afraid . . ."

"To leave the bathroom," Dodge stated, finishing for her when she foundered.

She lowered her head again and reapplied the compress.

"What's your name?"

"Caroline King."

"Is he your husband?"

"Boyfriend."

"Whose house is this?"

"Mine. I mean, I lease it."

"He live here, too?"

"No."

"Does he pay the rent?"

Her head came up quickly, and Dodge could tell that his implication had affronted her. "No. I do."

He was glad to know it and didn't apologize for asking. Instead, he gestured at her upper cheek. "Mind if I take a look?" She removed the washcloth. At the outside edge of her eye socket, the skin was red and beginning to swell. "We'll get you to the emergency room."

"There's no need for that. Really."

"Okay, but let's get some ice on it." He stepped aside.

She went past him, down the hall, and into the living room, where her abuser was seated on a sofa, being questioned by Gonzales. Upon seeing her, the guy shot to his feet. "Do you see, Caroline?" he shouted at her. "Are you enjoying my humiliation?"

"Okay, Mr. Campton. Calm down."

"Don't tell me what to do." He shoved Gonzales with both hands. "Do you know who I am?"

"I sure do." Before the offender could react, Gonzales spun him around and pushed him facedown on the sofa. In seconds the man's hands were shackled behind him. "You're the guy on his way to jail."

The cuffed man began screaming a litany of curses aimed at Gonzales. Unfazed by the insults to himself and his lineage, he asked Dodge, "She okay? Do we need an ambulance?"

"I don't think so. Just shut him up."

Caroline King had hastened from the room. Dodge followed and found her in a compact kitchen, where she had planted her hands on the edge of the counter to brace herself against it. "Will he be arrested?"

"Yes, ma'am."

"Will he go to jail?"

"Oh, yeah," Dodge said, relishing the thought.

She turned. "There'll be trouble over it. His family has money. Significant money. A battery of lawyers."

Dodge didn't give a rat's ass. "Have you got some ice in here?" Without waiting for an answer, he opened the freezer above the fridge and removed an ice tray. He shook cubes into a cup towel he'd found folded on the counter. He twisted the towel to hold the cubes inside, then passed the makeshift ice pack to her.

She took it and pressed it against her eye socket. "Thank you."

"You're welcome."

He pulled a chair out from under the dining table and remained standing beside it until she sat down, then he took the second chair. He removed a small spiral notebook and pen from the pocket of his uniform shirt. He wrote down her name. "What's his name?"

She hesitated, then said quietly, "Roger Campton."

Dodge wrote down the name and put a question mark beside it, wondering why it sounded familiar. She seemed to read his mind. "He's part of the Campton Industries family."

Holy shit. As she'd said, *Significant money*.

This kitchen, the house, the neighborhood itself, were strictly middle class. Pridefully well maintained, but hardly opulent. Again, his puzzled expression must have given away his thoughts.

She said, "You're wondering how Roger and I met."

He gave his head a noncommittal bob.

"He introduced himself to me at a Christmas party at his parents' house last year."

Dodge's eyebrows shot up. "You were a guest?"

"Server. I was working the holiday season for a caterer. It was a moonlighting job."

This told Dodge several things about her. She was a single working woman on a budget that required moonlighting to make ends meet. She paid her own way and wasn't too proud to admit it. Her slim prettiness had caught the rich boy's eye, which wasn't surprising. Nor was it surprising that she would want to hook up with a Campton heir, all that dough, and what it represented.

Right now it represented a black eye, which made Dodge's insides roil with anger. Why would a woman, who appeared to be self-sufficient otherwise, put up with that?

"Has he done this before?" Dodge asked.

"Never."

"Never to you, or never to anybody?"

"Never to me. I don't know about anybody else."

Dodge made himself a note to check on that. "What set him off?"

She raised her shoulders, and again Dodge was struck by how delicate her frame was. "We were having an ordinary quarrel, a difference of opinion, and he flew into a rage. I've never seen him like that before." She wet her lips. "But he's been under a lot of pressure lately."

"What kind of pressure?"

"Business. He and his father have been having disagreements. Roger takes them to heart."

"What did you do or say that caused him to slap you?"

"I said something to the effect that his father had more experience and that perhaps in this particular instance Roger should give him the benefit of the doubt."

"You took his old man's side against him."

She lowered her head, addressing the tabletop. "I guess that's how it sounded to Roger."

"Doesn't excuse him from slapping you."

"No."

"Are you going to stay with him?"

She raised her head and looked at him with surprise. "Of course."

Dodge watched her, said nothing.

She licked her lips. "I'm sure this was an isolated incident, Officer. Roger lost his temper. Flew off the handle. It could happen to anybody who's under stress."

He shook his head decisively. "Most people are stressed one way or another. They don't hit. Only somebody with a violent streak does that."

She set the ice pack on the table. The cubes were melting, dripping through the cloth. She stood up. "My cheek feels much better. The ice helped. I'll be all right. Don't let me keep you from your other duties."

Reluctantly Dodge replaced his pad and pen in his pocket and followed her back into the living room. Through the windows, they saw Gonzales pushing down Campton's head, none too gently, and guiding him into the backseat of the patrol car. "Will he be charged with a crime?" she asked.

"He'll be accused of assaulting a police officer," Dodge replied. "Whether or not the charge sticks isn't up to me or to Officer Gonzales." He paused, then added, "You've got a better shot at him. You could file an assault charge. I urge you to."

"I promise to think about it." Because she avoided his eyes when she said that, Dodge figured it was an empty promise. "Thank you for responding so quickly," she said.

"No need to thank me. That's what we're for."

"I know, but thank you anyway." She gave him a tremulous smile, and he knew that, as soon as he left, she'd start crying. She was barely holding it back. "Good night, Officer—" She gave her head a small shake. "I'm sorry."

"Hanley. Dodge Hanley. Good night, Ms. King." He tilted his head toward the police car, where Roger Campton sat fuming in the backseat. "He won't be out before morning at the earliest. We'll be slow to get the paperwork done. But keep the doors locked anyway."

"I will."

He hesitated on the threshold and looked at her for several moments, but he couldn't think of anything to add to what had already been said. He didn't have a valid excuse for sticking around any longer, so he bobbed his head good-bye and turned toward the patrol car.

• • •

"So what I was thinking," Gonzales was saying, "is that we ought to volunteer."

Dodge, who'd been woolgathering, brought his partner into focus. Their shift had ended a half hour earlier. Now they were seated on opposite sides of a booth at Denny's, where they were having breakfast before going home.

"What?"

"You haven't been listening, have you?" Gonzales used the handle of his fork to stir sugar into his coffee, then sucked it off before applying the tines to his huevos rancheros. "Your mind's still on that broad."

"What broad?"

His partner guffawed. "Don't play dumb. The little one? Red hair?"

Angrily Dodge speared a chunk of potato and put it in his mouth. "She wasn't a broad."

Gonzales grinned. "Sure are touchy about her."

"Drop it."

Gonzales shrugged good-naturedly and picked up the subject where he'd left off. "I was saying we should volunteer for that task force they're pulling together to catch that bank robber." He plopped a strawberry into his mouth and chewed vigorously. "What do you think?"

"You read my mind."

"Yeah?"

Dodge had been thinking about it for days, ever since he'd heard about the task force. For more than a year, an armed robber had been plaguing area banks. During the last robbery, a bank guard had been shot. He was still recovering from a serious wound. It was feared that, if the culprit weren't caught, someone would eventually be killed. The perp had grown bolder with each robbery, and now his holdups had taken on a taunting attitude, as though he was enjoying his celebrity, having a whale of a good time, and thumbing his nose at the police in the process.

Working with several law enforcement agencies, including the

FBI, Houston PD was determined to catch him. They had a list of possible suspects comprised of felons convicted of similar robberies who had served their sentences or were out on parole, but there was no evidence connecting any of them to the current crimes. The robber could be one of them or a new and clever crook on his debut crime spree.

Bottom line, the authorities really didn't have anything. Thus, the task force.

With the ink on his sheepskin from Texas Tech barely dry, Dodge had joined the HPD. His goal was to make detective and ultimately Homicide as soon as possible. He had the innate skills for crime solving. He just needed to pay his dues in the rank and file, get some seniority, and distinguish himself.

He'd been thinking that this task force might provide him an opportunity to prove himself a notch above the rest. If he got one of the coveted spots on it and impressed his superiors, it would speed his way toward achieving his goal.

"I put my name on the sign-up sheet yesterday afternoon."

Gonzales looked crestfallen. "You did? Oh."

Dodge smiled at him. "I put yours on there, too."

Gonzales beamed. "Good. Great. We'll both look more handsome out of these uniforms."

"Whoa. A lot of cops want on the task force. We haven't been selected yet."

"We will be. You for sure."

"Why me for sure?"

"It's bound to involve *undercover* work." Gonzales bobbed his eyebrows. "That's your speciality, partner."

Dodge cut into his rare steak. "Rumor."

Gonzales gave him an I-know-better look.

Dodge said, "All that gossip about me? It's bullshit."

Gonzales pushed aside his empty plate and leaned across the table. "That multiple murder at the strip club last month?"

"What about it?"

"There's nothing to the story that while the detectives were questioning the so-called eyewitnesses, you took the hostess of the club behind the building for a little one-on-one?"

"I was off duty. I just happened by. Got lucky."

"Lucky?" Gonzales scoffed. "I'll say. Within twenty minutes, she'd given up the shooter. You walked the detectives straight to where she told you he'd be hiding. There's no truth to that story?"

Dodge reached for his coffee cup. "I didn't take her behind the building."

"But you got her to give him up."

"Wasn't that hard to do." He grinned. "Not once I'd convinced her that a guy like that was no good for her, that she could do a lot better."

Gonzales was laughing, shaking his head in admiration. "Didn't you say that the solution to most mysteries could be found under a woman's skirt?"

"I never said that."

"You're quoted."

"Locker room talk." But Dodge's sly grin gave away the lie.

They finished their meal, divided the check, and paid out. As they separated outside the restaurant, Gonzales said, "Makes me feel a little better, knowing there's one woman you can't have. That redhead isn't gonna give up a superrich guy, even one who knocks her around now and then, for a street cop. You'll have to live without that one, Dodge."

Gonzales was proven right. When Dodge reported for duty that evening, he learned that Roger Campton had been released from lockdown before noon. His lawyers—plural—threatened a countercharge of police harassment, and Ms. Caroline King had declined to press charges. It was even said by the lawyers that she regretted having involved the police, that it was all an unfortunate misunderstanding, a mountain made of a molehill. Et cetera.

Dodge had figured that was the way it would shake out, but he didn't like it and couldn't leave it at that.

After his shift, he told Gonzales he didn't feel like breakfast and went instead to her house. He was parked at the curb in front of it when she came out to get her morning newspaper. He got out of his car and started up the walk.

"Ms. King?"

She shaded her eyes against the sun and regarded him warily.

"It's Officer Hanley."

She was dressed in shorts and a T-shirt, no shoes. Compared with his size twelves, her feet looked like a child's.

"Oh. Hello. I didn't recognize you without the uniform."

"I just got off duty, thought before I went home, I'd come by, see how you're doing."

"I'm fine."

"You've got a bruise."

She touched the edge of her eye. "Not surprising. My skin is so fair, I bruise if you look at me hard."

"He did more than look at you hard." The statement was out before he could stop it, and he'd sounded tougher and more dangerous than the guy who'd slapped her. But he didn't apologize for what he'd said.

She seemed embarrassed, even apprehensive. "I didn't press charges."

"I know. I checked."

"Roger was mortified by his behavior. He'd had a shouting match with his father and took his residual anger out on me. Both have apologized. Roger has sworn that it'll never happen again. I'm confident it won't."

Dodge wasn't, but he didn't tell her that. "Everything's okay then?"

"Everything's fine."

He stood there, feeling oafish, searching for something to say to prolong the conversation but thinking of nothing.

"I need to . . ." She gestured behind her toward the front door, which she'd left standing open. "I'll be late for work."

"Oh, sure, sorry. I just came by . . . you know, to check on . . . things."

"I appreciate the follow-up, Officer Hanley. Truly. Thank you."

"You're welcome."

"Good-bye."

"Bye."

He stood there until she went inside and closed the door.

Dodge and Gonzales were interviewed separately for the task force. Dodge was appointed to it. Gonzales wasn't.

"Hey, Dodge, don't worry about it, man."

"My partner isn't good enough for their task force, they can fuck themselves." His language had been as raw as his mood ever since that morning he'd gone to Caroline King's house and heard from her own lips that everything was hunky-dory between her and Roger Campton.

So rotten was his disposition, people had begun avoiding him. Even Doris, the night-shift clerk at the 7-Eleven, had sensed he wasn't open to bantering about their dancing date. Their recent transactions at the cash register had been uncommonly stilted.

Gonzales, however, seemed immune to his temper. In response to Dodge's opinion of the task force, he said, "Look, partner, I appreciate the level of your loyalty, but don't mess it up for yourself. You wanted on this task force, you got on it. Do yourself, and me, proud."

Dodge continued to grouse and protest, but Gonzales wouldn't hear of him letting the opportunity pass.

"You've got two years of service on me. I'll get my turn," the younger officer said with confidence. "Show 'em what you've got. Kick butt."

He slapped Dodge on the back and was about to walk away when he stopped, snapped his fingers, and turned. "Almost forgot. You see the Sunday paper? Your girlfriend and the rich boy made it official. They're engaged."

CHAPTER 5

PATRONS OF THE PINK AND WHITE TEAROOM PROBABLY DIDN'T drop the f-word that often. Dodge's saying it had shocked Caroline speechless. It didn't used to, but it had been thirty years since she'd been around him. Her ears had grown soft.

He'd used the word specifically to shock her. He was tired of beating around the bush about their daughter's involvement in a shooting, and sometimes shock therapy was the only way to get people to give up information they'd rather not disclose.

"Talk to me, Caroline."

She cleared her throat. "I think, I'm *afraid,* that Oren Starks meant exactly what he said when he threatened to kill Berry."

"He's not just a goof spouting off?"

"On the contrary, Berry says he's brilliant."

"Brilliant people go crackers all the time," he said. "Get mad, get jealous of competitors, say things they don't mean. *I'm gonna kill you!* They rarely follow through, Caroline. If all the people who said, 'I'm gonna—'"

"All right," she snapped. "I see your point."

He waited. She said nothing. He glanced over his shoulder. They were the only two customers left in the tearoom. The server hadn't reappeared since she'd brought their order. Coming back around, he said, "This is the last time I'm asking. What do you know that you haven't told me?"

"Nothing. I swear."

"Okay, then tell me what you *suspect.*"

Her back stiffened. "That's a policeman's word."

"A word that got a defensive reaction from you. Which indicates to me that I hit the nail on the head."

"You're that smart?"

He banged his fist on the table, softly, but with enough force to make the china rattle. "Apparently you think so, or you wouldn't have called me in the middle of the night, asking me to drop everything and haul ass down here, which I was stupid enough to do and am coming to regret."

Her eyes sparked angrily again. He was gifted in ways to make her angry. In a tight voice, she said, "Berry is a lot like me in many ways."

"Dandy. The world can be grateful for that. What's the problem?"

"The problem is . . ." She hesitated, then said the one thing that she knew would make him stay. "She's even more like you."

Berry was leaning against the wall of the hospital corridor, staring into near space, when out of the corner of her eye she saw Ski Nyland.

He was consulting with a nurse at the central desk. The nurse inclined her head in Berry's direction. He turned and, holding Berry's gaze, absently thanked the nurse and started toward her.

Every time he looked at her, she felt exposed and under scrutiny. What were those razor-sharp gray eyes looking at, looking for? Defensively, she fired the first volley.

When he was within earshot, she asked, "Any progress?"

"Like what?"

"Has Oren been spotted?"

"No, ma'am. At least no spottings have been reported."

She didn't miss his tongue-in-cheek tone, and it annoyed her. "Why do you do that?"

"What?"

"Patronize me."

He didn't deny it. In fact, he seemed about to answer when he changed his mind and motioned at the hospital room's closed door instead. "I'd asked them to notify me as soon as Lofland was moved from recovery into a regular room."

"They just brought him up." She called his attention to the empty metal bracket on the door. "They haven't even had time to get his name card in place."

"Have you talked to him?"

"Not yet. A nurse is helping him to get settled."

"Where's his wife?"

"Her name is Amanda. She's in there, too."

"Let's have a chat."

It wasn't a suggestion or an invitation but an order. However, Berry figured it best not to make an issue of it. He ushered her halfway down the corridor to a small waiting room. As she entered it, she remarked on his familiarity with the hospital.

"My mom was a patient here for a couple of weeks. I catnapped in this room the night she died."

Berry stopped and turned to face him. "I'm sorry," she said, meaning it.

"Thanks."

She looked into his face, expecting elaboration. None was forthcoming. He indicated a love seat that turned out to be as unyielding and uncomfortable as it looked. But it was the largest piece of furniture in the room, and she wondered if it was what he'd napped on that night.

He caught her looking at him speculatively. "What?"

"Nothing."

"You were going to say something."

"Just that . . . I'm sad for you."

"Sad?"

"I can't imagine life without my mother in it. Were you and yours close?"

"Yeah. She was great. But she was suffering." He coughed into his fist, an unnecessary, self-conscious gesture. For a moment his eyes lost some of their hard glint, leaving Berry to wonder if there wasn't a feeling human being behind them after all, if there was actually room for sentiment in their narrow gaze. Perhaps he wasn't as tough as he wanted everyone to believe.

He dragged a chair across the low pile carpeting and sat down facing her. When he did, he spread his knees wide to avoid touching hers, causing her to speculate further. Was he just being gentlemanly, or did that purposeful avoidance signify a vulnerability?

Which, of course, was a silly thing to think. He held all the advantages here. Why would he be reluctant to touch her, even accidentally?

He said, "Before I interview Lofland, I wanted to ask you some questions about Oren Starks."

The personal moment had passed, and he was down to business. As he should be. She said, "Mr. Carlisle would insist on being here."

"Call him if you want, but it's unnecessary. What I have to ask you is really background stuff on Starks. His character. Habits. Stuff like that."

Berry deliberated, then said, "All right. I'm happy to answer your questions if I can. I'm sure Ben will be equally cooperative when you talk to him."

"He doesn't have a choice. He's a material witness. I need to hear his version of what happened."

"His version? You think I'm lying?"

He remained unflappable. "I think two people can see the same incident from entirely different perspectives."

"Very diplomatically put, Deputy."

He shrugged. "Lofland may shed new light, give me some ideas as to where Starks might have gone."

"He could be miles from here by now."

"He could. But if he's hurt, he may not be up to traveling. He could be lying low, somewhere in the area, someplace close."

"Someone could be sheltering him."

"Like friends? Family? You tell me, Ms. Malone. Do you know of any?"

"Honestly, no."

"Well, we don't, either," he said. "Houston PD is helping with that angle, and nothing's turned up. He's not working anywhere. Since being fired from Delray, he's been drawing unemployment.

"His only known kin is his mother, who's elderly. She's in a facility for Alzheimer's patients, has been for several years, and she's in the final stages of the disease. For all practical purposes, she's . . . gone." He made a gesture to indicate that all the woman's cognition had been wiped clean.

"Neighbors say Starks is a loner. He doesn't host parties. No one remembers friends visiting his house. Asked if he had any outside interests—like a gym membership, an obvious hobby like tennis or golf, church affiliation—neighbors didn't know. Said he kept to himself."

He gave Berry a lazy once-over, the kind of which a woman can't mistake. "You seem to be his only passion." The suggestion underlying his tone was perturbing.

"That's not true. I told you earlier today about some of his passions."

"Right. Puzzles, games, problem solving. According to the officers who searched his house, his home computer had bookmarked several websites relating to that kind of thing. He routinely visits message boards and blogs but never posts on any." Again his eyes flicked over her suggestively. "Anyway, I doubt intricate mazes could hold a candle to you."

"Maybe it's a matter of degree," she said coolly.

"Maybe." A second or two ticked past before he continued. "He's now being sought all over southeast Texas and into Louisiana. We're checking hotels, but I doubt he'd go to one. Usually they require a credit card to check in. None of his has been used since last week. No ATM withdrawals since he took out two hundred dollars three days ago at a branch bank in Houston."

"He would know better than to leave a trail that's so easily followed."

"What I figured," he said, nodding. "But we checked anyway. We're canvassing motels, cabin rentals, like that. What worries me," he said, pulling his eyebrows into a frown, "is that there's a lot of territory around here to hide in."

"You mentioned that this morning."

"If he's holed up in the woods somewhere—"

"The woods?" Berry laughed. "He'd have to be crazy."

"You said he was."

"I said he was unhinged."

"Isn't that the same thing?"

"No."

"What's the difference?"

"Constancy. Crazy is a state of being. Unhinged is a reaction."

"Catching you with Lofland sent him over the edge."

"He didn't 'catch' me with Ben. He caught me in the shower. Alone."

"Right. When I got there, you were still wet." He kept his eyes fixed on hers for several beats before moving on. "You told Sheriff Drummond you'd seen Starks rattled like that only once before. When was that?"

"At the beginning of the summer. Just before I moved to Merritt."

"Starks wigged out on you, and that was the final straw?"

"Exactly. I got scared."

"Do you think he's sinking deeper into psychosis?"

"I have no idea. I'm not a psychiatrist. What I can tell you is that, ordinarily, Oren isn't a raving maniac."

He propped one booted foot on his opposite knee and crossed his arms over his wide chest. "Describe to me what he's like. Ordinarily."

"Well, one thing he's *not* is an outdoorsman. I can't see him taking cover in a well-protected campground, much less the woods. You can chalk that off your list."

"Okay, where do you think he ran to?"

She bent her head and rubbed her forehead. "I don't know, Deputy Nyland."

"Call me Ski."

She looked across at him but didn't address the topic of names. "Oren's persnickety. Orderly."

"Obsessive-compulsive?"

"Close," she said with an absent nod. "I used to tease him about his desk being the cleanest of any at Delray. Everything in its place. His mind works in an orderly fashion, too."

"For instance?"

"For instance, during a discussion over a project, I could jump around from point to point, but Oren wouldn't move from point A to point B until point A had been reviewed, discussed, and approved one hundred percent. He would go back to something a dozen times until it met with his satisfaction."

"What you're telling me is that he'll keep coming back until he gets it right."

"Yes," she said huskily. "Until I'm dead."

"I'll do my best to keep that from happening."

"Thank you."

"You don't have any idea where he might have fled?"

"None."

"Okay." He lowered his foot to the floor and leaned forward. "You've said that Starks made other women employees at Delray uncomfortable, not just you."

"That's right."

Removing a pad and pen from the breast pocket of his sport jacket, he asked if she could name a few. He jotted down the names as she enumerated them. "Sally Buckland in particular," she said. "She resigned from Delray at the beginning of the year. Oren factored largely into her decision."

"You know this for certain?"

"Absolutely. He had a terrible crush on her. She wasn't interested and tried everything to avoid him, but he was persistent. On several occasions she complained to me that he wouldn't take no for an answer."

"No to what?"

"To anything. The situation got so bad, it was beginning to affect her work, so I interceded on her behalf. I told Oren that Sally wasn't interested, that he was wasting his time on her."

"How'd he react?"

She smiled sadly. "He turned his attention to me."

"Was there ever a time when you were interested in him?"

"Romantically? Good Lord, no."

He arched one sun-bleached eyebrow.

"Absolutely not!" She chuckled. "When you see him, you'll understand. He's not at all my type."

"What's your type?"

His question checked her amusement, because the first word that sprang to mind was *You*. It startled her, rattled her right down to the soles of her feet. Because were it not for the fact that he was investigating a crime involving her, and seemed to harbor some mistrust of her that extended beyond a peace officer's instinctual mistrust of everybody, she would find the deputy sheriff attractive. His imposing bearing, his sheer physicality, even his damn gray eyes, were appealing.

But he seemed bent on trying to trip her up, to catch her in a lie, which made her dislike him intensely. Pulling herself up straight, she said, "Oren was my colleague. Bright. I'd even go so far as to say gifted. But he became a rejected suitor who stalked me, and who last night vowed to kill me. He said he must."

The deputy studied her for a moment longer, then replaced his notepad and pen in his pocket and stood up. "Maybe Lofland's settled in by now."

When Ski entered the hospital room, no one was happy to see him. Not the nurse, who told him the patient was still very weak and asked that Ski not take too long. Not Mrs. Lofland, who when he introduced himself was polite, but only because she had to be. Not the patient, who seemed the least happy of all that Ski was there.

Ben Lofland, fresh from the surgical recovery room, was attached to various lines and tubes and looked like warmed-over death. Oren Starks's bullet had gone clean through him, creating entry and exit wounds but, miraculously, doing only moderate damage to tissue on its passage. It had missed all his organs and the bowel. The worst of the injury had been the amount of blood lost. Either Lofland was living right or he had the devil's own luck.

Ski was betting on the latter.

His condition was far from critical, but he came across to Ski as a whiner. Once introductions were out of the way and the nurse had left the room, he said, "I really don't feel up to this right now."

"I'll be brief," Ski said.

"Why do you need to talk to Ben? Hasn't she told you what happened?"

Ski turned to Amanda Lofland, who'd placed hard emphasis on the *she,* making the pronoun sound like a word for something that smelled bad. "Ms. Malone gave a detailed statement last night and again this morning. But it might help us catch Starks—"

"You haven't caught him yet?"

Ski disliked the implication of incompetence that had underscored Lofland's question. "Ms. Malone didn't see his vehicle. She was busy trying to keep you from bleeding out on her bedroom floor."

Ski knew it was the mention of Berry Malone's bedroom and not pain that caused the guy to wince. Lofland shot a worried look at his wife, who was hugging herself as though at any moment she might fly apart.

Without further prompting from Ski, Lofland said, "I heard Berry scream. Heard their voices. I ran—"

"Were you asleep?" Ski removed his notepad and pen from his pocket.

"What?"

"Did her scream wake you up?"

"Uh, no. I hadn't gone to sleep yet." He cast another look at his wife, who had moved to the window and was looking through the blinds at the ventilation chutes on the roof.

"You were still awake," Ski stated.

"Right."

"But you hadn't heard Starks come into the house."

"No."

"Car engine? Boat motor?"

"You think he came by boat?"

"It's possible. We're checking it out."

"I didn't hear a boat motor."

"Anything?"

"No."

"Okay."

Lofland paused to see if Ski was going to ask something else, and when he didn't, Lofland continued. "I ran along the gallery to the other side of the house." He gave his wife another glance, as though to ensure she'd heard how far away from each other the two bedrooms were.

"When I got to Berry's room, I rushed over to the bathroom. That's where the voices were coming from. Oren was standing in front of the bathtub, his back to me. He must've heard me. He turned around and shot me."

"Did he say anything first?"

"No." Lofland grimaced with discomfort. "Can I have some water, please?"

Amanda went to the bed. She poured water from a carafe into a plastic cup, then leaned over him and guided the bent straw to his mouth. When he'd drunk, he looked up at her and touched her hand. "Thanks, sweetheart."

She gave him a lukewarm smile, returned the cup to the nightstand, and then resumed her study of the ventilation apparatus outside the window.

"He just spun around, saw you in your undershorts, and pulled the trigger," Ski said.

"Yes. He seemed completely unbalanced."

"Why do you think? Jealousy over the two of you being together in the lake house?"

"I don't know the cause for Oren's precarious mental state, Deputy."

Ski disliked his tone. To keep himself from knocking the sanctimonious jerk out of the bed, he scanned several of the sheets in his notepad. "What happened after Starks shot you?"

"I can't tell you. I blacked out."

"Ms. Malone says you were conscious right up till the paramedics got there."

"I was? If so, I don't remember. I must've gone into shock. I don't even remember feeling any pain until I regained consciousness in the recovery room this morning. I didn't know where I was. I was so disoriented, I freaked out. The nurse told me I'd been shot and had undergone surgery. Things began coming back to me then, but between Oren firing that pistol and my waking up in recovery, everything is blocked."

"How well do you know Starks?"

"Only as a co-worker."

"You hadn't seen him since he got fired?"

"No."

"You two ever hang out? Go for a beer after work?"

Lofland was shaking his head. "I never saw him socially."

"Mrs. Lofland?" When Ski spoke her name, she jumped and came around quickly. "What are your impressions of Oren Starks?"

"I don't have any."

"You never met him?"

"Well, yes. Ben introduced us at a company function."

"You only met him that once?"

"Once or twice. I don't remember."

"Nothing about him stood out to you?"

"They were casual introductions, Deputy. Insignificant. If I had known that one day he would try to kill my husband, I would have paid more attention."

In Ski's opinion, these two people deserved each other. One was as unlikable as the other. He returned his attention to Ben. "Did you and Starks get along okay in the office?"

"He was off-putting to some people, but I never had any issues with him."

"Did Ms. Malone?"

"Wouldn't you call stalking an issue?"

Again, his smart-aleck tone grated on Ski. He wanted to yank hard on the catheter draining Lofland's bladder, see what effect that would have on his sarcasm, but he settled on glaring at him coldly.

Lofland got the message. His smirk dissolved. "Berry told me Oren was stalking her."

"When?"

"When did she tell me? First I heard of it was when she decided to spend the summer here in Merritt. Naturally I was surprised."

"Why?"

"Berry's such a workaholic. Rarely even takes vacation days. First one in the office each morning, last one out in the evening. But Oren had become a real pest, she said. She wanted to disappear for a month or two, hoping he'd lose interest. She's been working from the lake house. She calls it the annex."

"How'd that go?"

"Not as well as when we're both in the office. We've been working as a team, almost exclusively, on a campaign for an important client." He gave his wife a quick look.

"A hundred miles isn't as convenient as next-door offices," Ski observed.

"No. The distance created a few efficiency problems. Here in the boonies the Internet connection isn't one hundred percent reliable, especially out toward the lake. But it's been okay. And if it helped her shake Oren, I was willing to put up with a few inconveniences and delays."

"Hmm." Ski pretended to think about that statement, give it importance. Then he said, "You brought some materials up here to her yesterday."

Amanda Lofland's shoulders raised and lowered on a deep breath.

Lofland sought a more comfortable position on the hospital bed. "How much more, Deputy?"

"Not much. You brought work up here yesterday."

"We had to put some finishing touches on our proposal before presenting it to the client next week. The mock-ups weren't coming through very well on the PDFs. Berry asked if I could run them up here, let her see them exactly as the client would. She had to sign off on a couple of other elements that had been added. So a trip up here seemed called for."

"Who knew you were coming?"

"Well, Amanda."

"Besides her. People at Delray?"

"I had to let people in the office know that I'd be out for the entire day, so yeah, I told a few."

"Three, four?"

With distinct impatience, he said, "The receptionist who answers the phone for our department. My immediate supervisor and his assistant. I can give you their names."

"Besides them, no one else knew?"

"Not unless one of them told somebody."

"Would they have told Oren Starks that you were spending the day with Berry?"

"I doubt that any of them kept in contact with Oren, but if you want to know, you'll have to ask them."

Ski smiled. "I have." Before Lofland could respond to that, Ski asked, "What time did you arrive yesterday morning?"

"Ten-thirtyish. We got right down to it and worked all day."

Ski flipped through several more pages in his notepad, then said idly, "You two get in the pool?"

Lofland shot a quick glance toward his wife where she still stood at the window, her back to the room. "After we knocked off, we each swam some laps to cool off, work out some kinks."

"You'd brought your swimsuit?"

Ski's question caught him off guard. "Uh, no. I had some gym shorts in my car."

"That was convenient." Lofland said nothing. Ski continued, "I guess the shorts are somewhere in the house?"

"I left them hanging on a towel bar in the guest bathroom."

"Okay." Ski let that reverberate for several moments, as though weighing its significance, when actually he'd found the gym shorts in the guest bathroom, exactly as Lofland had described. He just wanted to rattle him in front of his wife, see what shook loose when he did. Unnecessarily, he referred to his notepad again. "You and Ms. Malone grilled steaks for dinner."

"We didn't take a lunch break. We were hungry."

"It got late, you decided to stay over."

"Only after consulting Amanda," Lofland said hastily. "By the time Berry and I had finished dinner and I'd helped with the cleanup, it was well after dark, and it doesn't get dark till nine-thirty or better. That's when I called home."

"It was eleven oh three," Amanda said, keeping her back to them.

Lofland, looking sickly, said to Ski, "I didn't realize it was that late. But since it was, Amanda said she'd rather I not head back to Houston."

Ski nodded. "Probably best."

"Right. It would have been one o'clock or so before I got home."

"And you shouldn't have been driving after drinking."

Amanda turned suddenly and looked at her husband. His eyes moved from her back to Ski, looking both uneasy and resentful. "Berry and I had some red wine with our steaks."

"And beer."

Lofland pulled his lower lip through his teeth. "I had a couple while the steaks were cooking."

"And Ms. Malone?"

"She joined me for one."

"Huh." Ski looked over at Amanda Lofland's rigid back before returning to her husband. "You ate dinner in the living room?"

"No, in the dining area."

Ski shared a long look with the man, letting him know that he'd seen wineglasses on the living room coffee table in front of a very comfortable-looking sofa. He decided to let Lofland explain the significance of that question to his wife.

He closed his notepad and slid it and the pen back into his pocket. "I think that's everything for now."

"Good," Lofland said. "I feel like crap and would like to sleep."

Ski left them with the promise not to disturb his rest unless it was absolutely necessary and to keep the two of them updated on the manhunt for Oren Starks. As he left the room, he met a nurse going in with a phlebotomy kit. Ski held the door for her, then stepped into the corridor, where Berry Malone was still standing sentinel outside the room.

"They'll probably need a minute to draw blood," he said.

She nodded. "How is he?"

"Better than dead, which he could be."

That sparked her anger. "You're doing it again."

"Pardon?"

"You toss out these little editorial comments, most of them snide, when a simple statement would do."

He slid his hands into the seat pockets of his jeans but then realized that the position revealed the handgun holster attached to his belt, so he lowered his arms back to his sides. "Your friend is no doubt uncomfortable, but the surgeon—I talked to him by phone on my way here—said the wound is clean and that he'll be fine. He'll have bragging rights in the locker room."

The nurse emerged. There were several new vials of blood in her tray, so her mission had been accomplished, but still Berry seemed hesitant to go into the room. "What's Ben's state of mind? He must hate me."

"Why would he hate you?"

"For dragging him up here only to get shot! And poor Amanda."

"He says he called her."

"He did."

"She gave him permission to spend the night."

"It was late."

"*That* she knew." Gauging Berry's reaction, Ski added, "She didn't know about the cocktail hour and wine."

Berry raised her hands at her sides. "Are you going to make something of us having a couple of drinks?"

"No. I was just wondering—"

"What?"

"What kind of red wine goes with work?"

With exaggerated patience, she said, "The wine didn't come out until dinnertime, and Cabernet goes very well with filets mignons."

"When did you put the robe on?"

She looked at him for several seconds, then shook her head with puzzlement. "Excuse me?"

Ski took a step to bring himself nearer to her. "When I got there, all you had on was a robe."

A robe made of some soft, filmy stuff that had clung to her damp body, then seemed to dissolve within his grip. The imagery was strong, vivid, and way out of line. As was the irrational anger with which he asked, "At what point did you put on that robe? When you took off your wet swimsuit? Is that all you were wearing during your dinner hour with Lofland?"

He was leaning in close to her, unnecessarily close. Why? In order to intimidate a truthful answer out of her? Or for a reason totally unrelated to his investigation?

Amanda Lofland chose that moment to come out of her husband's room, and her displeasure upon seeing Berry there was glaringly obvious.

Ski hastily stepped back, placing appropriate space between Berry and himself.

"Hello, Amanda," Berry said.

Ski thought her apologetic, sympathetic tone sounded heartfelt.

"How is Ben?" she asked.

"Sleeping."

Amanda Lofland's curtness was in keeping with the anger

emanating from her. Ski noticed that her hands were fisted at her sides.

"I can't tell you how sorry I am," Berry said. "I would rather Oren have shot me than—"

Amanda's bitter laugh cut her off. "Oh, I doubt that."

"It's true." Berry's voice cracked. "I would never have thought Oren capable of doing something like this."

The other woman seemed not to have heard that. Her eyes were narrowed with hatred. "You had to prove it, didn't you?"

"Prove what?"

"That you could snap your fingers and Ben would come running."

"What are you talking about?"

"You can't stand the thought that he is happily married to *me*, so you lured him up here to—"

"Amanda, what—"

"I hated the idea of him spending a day here with you. But I pretended that it didn't bother me. It was for work, after all."

"It *was* for work. Our deadline to deliver that campaign is Monday. We are committed to meeting it."

"Exactly. So what kind of shrew would I have been to say, 'No, you can't go'? What kind of wife would I have been not to trust my husband?"

"You *can* trust him. Ben adores you. He called you several times throughout the day. I heard him."

"Oh, yes. He called periodically to assure me how hard the two of you were working."

"We were."

"In between dips in the pool and bottles of wine."

Berry groaned. "It wasn't like that. Please, Amanda, don't do this."

She extended her hands toward the other woman, but Amanda Lofland recoiled. "Do not touch me. And stay away from my husband!"

She sidestepped them and rushed past, blindly colliding with the couple who'd been standing only a few yards away and had overheard everything.

Ski hadn't noticed them until now. Caroline King was staring at her daughter with dismay. It was harder for Ski to define the expression of the tough-looking man with her, but his deeply shadowed eyes were also fixed on Berry.

CHAPTER 6

IT WAS JUST AS WELL THAT DODGE WASN'T IMMEDIATELY REQUIRED to speak, because he couldn't have if his life had depended on it.

He was world-wise and world-weary. Nothing much bothered him. He was hardened to the cruelty one person could inflict on another. Oh, if he saw pictures of starving babies in Africa, or American fighting men torn to bits in the name of some fanatic's god, he was moved, but more toward rage than toward sorrow. Sorrow had little place in the heart of a card-carrying cynic. The same went for all the softer emotions.

He'd thought he had prepared himself to see his daughter. After all, he didn't know her. It wasn't like he'd once had her in his life, had formed a strong attachment, and then had had her wrenched away. He didn't have photographs of the two of them together. He hadn't made memories with her like he'd made with Caroline.

He and his child had no common bond except for a shared bloodline. He figured that when he met her he might experience a few butterflies, maybe a slight dampening of his palms, but those would be the extent of his reactions, and they would be short-lived.

So he was completely unprepared for the profound physical

reaction he underwent when he and Caroline rounded the corner at the end of the hospital corridor and Caroline said, "There she is."

At first sight of the lanky, auburn-haired young woman, it was as though every cell in his body was slapped with an instinctual recognition factor, as though each stood at attention and declared, "I know *her.*"

His heart damn near stopped. He barely controlled the impulse to clutch his chest as he gasped for breath. The sound of rushing air filled his ears. He felt dizzy and uncoordinated to the point that he almost reached out to Caroline for support.

Even more surprising than these physical reactions was the emotional one. A sharp tug deep in his gut, a constriction around his heart, a piercing of his soul, all painful in their intensity.

This beautiful young woman with Caroline's coloring was his flesh and blood, his kid. The miracle of her being overwhelmed him . . . for the second time. But the first time, he'd been too young and stupid, too much in love with the mother, to fully appreciate the miracle of the child.

Along with these visceral and emotional reactions, another arose that was even more surprising but equally eruptive. Suddenly, he was Conan the Barbarian, proprietary and protective to a savage extent. God help anybody who laid a hand on his kid. He'd tear their throat out with his teeth.

Yeah, with all these new and explosive impulses running amok through him, it was a good thing that he didn't have to say anything right then. But God, or whoever was in charge and running this show, extended some mercy and let him survive the next several moments without making a fool of himself.

He managed to continue along the hallway at Caroline's side, his gait reasonably normal for a man whose knees seemed to have dissolved. Because he was overjoyed to be seeing Berry, but Caroline had admitted that even she couldn't predict how Berry would react when introduced to him.

He imagined she might be as nervous as he. Or she might spit in his face, or refuse to acknowledge him on any level, or fly into histrionics and rant, or scream and faint. Whatever she did, however she handled it, he'd have to live with it. He didn't expect the best, he deserved the worst, and he was braced for anything.

But the anticipated introduction wasn't imminent after all because Berry was otherwise occupied. Dodge and Caroline were close enough now to overhear the exchange taking place between her and a blond woman, whose pretty features were distorted by anger.

"Oh, yes. He called periodically to assure me how hard the two of you were working."

"We were."

"In between dips in the pool and bottles of wine."

Berry groaned. "It wasn't like that. Please, Amanda, don't do this."

Her placating gesture was rebuffed. After telling Berry not to touch her and to stay away from her husband, the blonde came barreling around a big dude in cowboy boots and ran flat into him and Caroline. She muttered an apology as she stumbled past.

Dodge placed his hand beneath Caroline's elbow. "She nearly knocked you down. You okay?"

She nodded absently and went quickly to their daughter. "Good Lord, Berry. What was that about?"

"Oh, Mother, this situation just keeps getting worse."

Caroline turned her aside, and the two began to speak in undertones. Having been shut out of the confidential conversation between mother and daughter, Dodge and the quasi cowboy sized each other up. Finally the cowboy said, "Ski Nyland."

Dodge shook the large hand extended to him. "The deputy sheriff."

"That's right."

He had cool gray eyes and the no-nonsense demeanor that Caroline had described. Dodge said, "I heard about you."

"Okay." Then after a beat, "Who're you?"

Under the strained circumstances, Dodge took no offense at his directness and answered in kind. "Friend of the family." He glanced over his shoulder in the direction the blonde had taken, but she had disappeared. Coming back around to Nyland, he asked, "Ben Lofland's wife?"

The deputy nodded. "And she's not a happy lady." His cell phone chirped. "Excuse me." He turned his back on Dodge to take the call.

Berry and Caroline were still conferring in whispers, leaving Dodge to his own devices. He decided to go and look for Ben Lofland's unhappy wife, who appeared to be in desperate need of someone to talk to.

And just like that, he realized he was in. Committed. This was his kid, his problem, his fight.

A half hour later, Dodge's cell phone rang. He saw the caller was Caroline. As soon as he answered, she asked, "Where'd you go?"

"Outside to smoke."

"We're on our way out."

"Have you told Berry—"

"No."

He digested that, then said, "I'll be in my car."

They disconnected. Dodge made his way along the landscaped pathways of the hospital campus to the parking lot where he and Caroline had left their cars in side-by-side slots. He finished his cigarette, got into his car, and started the motor so he could turn on the air conditioner.

Atlanta could have its humid days, but, *shit,* this air felt like a wet blanket. It clung to hair, clothes, skin. Its density congested nasal passages and bronchial tubes. The unrelenting humidity was one reason he hadn't been sad to abandon the coastal plains of Texas thirty years ago. The only reason.

He was watching the exit doors as the two women emerged. Berry was a full head taller than Caroline, but her limbs were as slender, and she moved as gracefully. When they reached the cars, Caroline bent down and spoke through his lowered passenger window. "Follow me."

He nodded and looked past her toward Berry. She opened the

passenger-side door of Caroline's car, then tipped her sunglasses down and regarded him curiously across the roof of the car. After a long moment, during which Dodge's heart acted like a jackhammer, she replaced her glasses and got in.

It was several minutes before his cardiac system settled down, but he continued to wonder how Caroline had identified him to Berry. What explanation had she given for his sudden presence in their lives?

Well, whatever, it wouldn't be long before he found out.

From the hospital parking lot, the drive to the lake house took seventeen minutes. Three of those minutes were spent at traffic lights on Bowie Street, which was the main drag through the center of Merritt.

Just past the high school football stadium on the outskirts of town, Caroline turned onto Lake Road, which was aptly named because, five miles beyond the turnoff, it ended at a three-way stop with the lake lying directly ahead, separated from the road by a bait shop/convenience store, a fishing pier, and a public boat ramp. The left and right extensions of the T were narrow roads lined on each side by forest, mostly pines.

Caroline turned left. The road followed the curves of the lakeshore. The occasional houses they passed were upscale and exclusive judging from what Dodge could see of them behind extravagant landscaping and estate walls. A few of the houses and several waterfront lots were advertised for sale. *Caroline King Realty,* the signs read. Her name was written in cursive white letters on a deep green background. A little gold crown was perched on top of the capital K.

Her house sat about a hundred yards off the road in a clearing that had been carved out of the surrounding woods. Pines and oaks gave way to cypresses nearer the lakeshore. The calm water reflected the sun like a mirror. A short pier jutted out over the water, but Dodge didn't see a boat.

The house itself was surprisingly modest, not nearly as grandiose as some they'd passed. The clapboard exterior was painted dove gray, accented by white window shutters and columns along the porch. There was a patch of yard in both front and back, the St. Augustine grass surrendering gracefully to the forest floor at the perimeter of the clearing. Well-tended flower beds provided patches of brilliant color, the plants neatly tucked under blankets of pine straw.

He pulled his rental car alongside Caroline's, cut the engine, and got out. Again, his knees felt unreliable.

Caroline said brightly, "Let's go inside to make introductions. Get out of this sun. Berry and I tend to freckle."

He was about to say, *I know.* He'd spent one whole night trying to get around to kissing each one of her freckles. But still clueless as to what Caroline had told Berry about him—certainly not that—he said nothing as he followed the two women up a set of back steps and through a door that opened directly into the kitchen.

As soon as they were inside, Caroline said, "I hope you don't mind coming in through the back, Mr. Hanley. We're informal around here and rarely use the front door." She sounded a bit breathless, like she had when she first shook hands with him at Mabel's Tearoom. "Berry, this is Dodge Hanley."

Berry removed her sunglasses, setting them and her purse on the kitchen table, then reaching across it to shake hands with him. "Hello."

He took her hand, touching her flesh for the first time. "Hi." For several seconds, that was all he could manage to articulate. Then he muttered, "Call me Dodge."

Still using that overly chipper voice, Caroline said, "How about some iced tea?"

Berry was still staring at him, taking his measure. Absently she said, "Sounds good."

He said, "Fine."

Caroline suggested they go into the living room and make themselves comfortable while she got the tea ready.

"This way," Berry said, disappearing through an open doorway.

Dodge shot Caroline a perturbed glance. She whispered, "Go on. It's fine."

He followed the younger woman from the kitchen, and when he reached the living area, she got directly to the point. "Mother tells me that you're a private investigator."

So, to some extent, Caroline had decided to be truthful. Truth was always helpful when you had to lie. "That's right."

"I've never actually met one before."

"It's not like on TV."

"How is it different?"

"Well, I've never had to leap off a tall building to avoid being shot, or been trapped by a bad guy in a dark, dead-end alley. Mostly I chase paper, not people."

She smiled like she didn't know whether or not to believe him. "You're from Atlanta?"

"I live there now. I work for an attorney. A defense lawyer. The best. Or worst," he added. "Depending on which side you're on."

"He's tough?"

"The toughest. I overheard an assistant DA accuse Derek of sprinkling ground glass over his Cheerios every morning."

She smiled again, but it quickly inverted into a frown. She went to a wall switch and turned on the overhead fan. "Mother had professional cleaners come in this morning. I can smell the solution they used. Can you?"

"No. My sense of smell is shot. Too much smoking."

"I tried it in high school. One cigarette, mind you. But Mother caught me. Those days, I was certain she had superpowers, eyes in the back of her head, amplified hearing. Anyway, she and Daddy had a fit, grounded me for two weeks and, worse, took away my phone for a month. I never lit up again."

He smiled, but an arrow went through his heart at the mention of "Daddy." "Good. That's good. It's a nasty habit."

She held his gaze for a long time, then motioned him toward a rocking chair. "I'm sorry. I'm forgetting my manners today. Have a seat."

She claimed a corner of the sofa just as Caroline came in with a tray bearing three tall glasses of iced tea. She set the tray on the coffee table.

Berry looked at it and murmured, "Our wineglasses."

Dodge took the glass of tea that Caroline passed him. Although there was a sugar bowl and spoons on the tray, Caroline didn't offer him any because she knew that, while he preferred his coffee with two spoonfuls, he drank his tea unsweetened. He wondered if Berry had noticed. She hadn't; she was still staring thoughtfully at the tray.

"What was that, dear?" Caroline asked as she spooned sugar into a glass before handing it to Berry.

Berry took the glass, sipped from it, then seemed to come out of her momentary trance. "Nothing."

She looked across at Dodge, who was trying to sit still in the rocker, because each time he moved, the cane seat squeaked. More like groaned.

She returned her glass of tea to the tray, rubbed her hands together to get rid of the condensation, cast a look in Caroline's direction, then addressed him again. "I'm not sure why Mother retained you."

"I told you why," Caroline said. "Mr. Hanley comes highly recommended."

"So you said, Mother. You learned of him through a friend of yours in Houston for whom he did some work." Looking back at him, she said, "But I don't know what you can do for me. For us."

"I don't know what I can do, either. But based on what your mother tells me, and on what I saw of that scene at the hospital, there's no question you're in a jam."

Caroline said, "Mr. Hanley—"

"Look, stop with the Mr. Hanley, okay?"

Caroline was momentarily silenced by his harsh tone.

If he'd sounded meaner than he'd intended, he was sorry, but her addressing him as Mr. Hanley was annoying the hell out of him. And wasn't it a little ridiculous that she wouldn't use his first name, especially when you took into account—

No, better not to take any of *that* into account.

"I'm sorry," Caroline said. "If you prefer being called by your first name—"

"I insist on it, Caroline."

"All right, Dodge."

"I guess that makes me Berry." Their daughter seemed amused and puzzled over the name debate. She divided a look between them, ending on Caroline. "You were saying, Mother?"

"I was saying that *Dodge* has years of experience with criminal investigations. I thought it would be helpful to have someone with his insight and skills on our side."

"To do what?" Berry asked.

"For starters, to find this asshole who's threatened your life." He caught himself. "Sorry for the language."

Berry made an impatient gesture that implied *Forget it.*

"I need to find this guy before he carries out his threat to kill you," he said.

"Isn't that up to the authorities?"

He made a scoffing sound. "Wild Bill Hickok?"

She smothered a laugh. "Referring to Deputy Nyland?"

"I like him," Caroline said staunchly.

Berry looked at her with surprise. "I thought you only met him last night."

"I did. But I like what I see."

Dodge's pang of jealousy was misplaced but undeniable. What was it that Caroline liked so well when she looked at the tall, rugged Deputy Nyland? His tanned face and sandy hair? His broad shoulders and flat belly? His stern mouth and cleft chin?

"Nyland's probably a stand-up guy," he grumbled. "Competent enough. But I don't have the confidence in the authorities that you do, Berry. I've found fugitives while the guys with badges were still trying to organize their search. I don't have to file paperwork. I don't have to get clearance from guys who're a lot dumber than me. I don't have to follow rules or fear demotion if the situation goes south."

Berry looked toward Caroline, who took her daughter's hand and pressed it between her own. "Dodge can keep his ear to the ground. Keep us informed. I don't want to be blindsided by anything, especially by the reappearance of Oren Starks."

"I'd rather avoid that, too." Addressing Dodge again, Berry

asked, "Aren't you required to have a license in the state where you're working?"

He shrugged. "I don't know. Maybe. Probably."

She laughed. "You don't care?"

"Do you?"

She looked at Caroline, who foundered. "We, uh, Dodge and I haven't had time to discuss all the particulars of his . . . uh . . . inclusion."

He jumped in. "I introduced myself to Nyland as a friend of the family. I'm not official."

"Until your bill comes due," Berry said drily. "What do you charge for keeping your ear to the ground?"

"A fair rate. I won't fleece you. That I promise. And as long as I'm not on retainer, we can honestly say to Nyland, or to anyone else who asks, that I'm operating in an unofficial capacity."

Obviously Berry still had misgivings. "It's a strange setup. *But* these are strange circumstances, at least for Mother and me. I don't suppose it can hurt to have someone working for us behind the scenes."

"I believe Dodge will be a tremendous help," Caroline said.

"Does Mr. Carlisle know about him?" Berry asked her.

"I'll inform our attorney when the time is right."

Berry withdrew her hand from her mother's clasp, stood up, and began to roam restlessly around the room. "I don't understand the need for a lawyer. I haven't done anything wrong."

"All the more reason to have an advocate," Dodge said. "Anytime Nyland wants to interview you, you don't say a word without a lawyer present."

"I already have."

Dodge cursed under his breath.

Caroline asked, "When was this, Berry?"

"At the hospital before you arrived. He and I talked."

"About what?"

"Oren's characteristics. Anything that might give Deputy Nyland a lead to follow. It was harmless."

Dodge had his doubts. “Don’t do it again. Understood? My boss would advise the same thing.”

“Of course he would. That’s how he makes his living.”

“True. And a damn good living. But I would trust him with my life. Lots of people have.”

“Guilty people.”

“Innocent people, too,” he returned calmly. “Including the woman he ultimately married.”

Caroline sat forward. “He married a client? I sense an interesting story.”

Dodge looked across at her. “Yeah. It’s a story about a woman in trouble, and the guy who came to her rescue. A very old-fashioned kind of story. Boy meets girl, and just like that, he’s in over his head.”

“Boy lost girl?” Berry asked.

“No,” Dodge said. “Lucky for Derek and Julie, their story had a happy ending.” His eyes remained locked with Caroline’s, and for several seconds the atmosphere was fraught with tension. She was the first to look away.

Dodge uncomfortably shifted his position in the squeaky chair and motioned down at the tray on the coffee table, calling Berry’s attention to it. “That seemed to spark a memory earlier. You mentioned wineglasses.”

She resumed her seat in the corner of the sofa and tucked her feet beneath her. “After dinner, Ben and I decided to split what was left in the bottle of wine. So before going upstairs, we sat in here to drink it. Deputy Nyland must have seen the glasses on the coffee table and jumped to the wrong conclusion about what they implied.”

“Wine-fueled hanky-panky?” Dodge said.

“Something like that.” A vertical frown line appeared between her eyebrows. “I wonder if he pawed through the trash to count the beer and wine bottles we’d consumed.”

“It was the happy hour that set Mrs. Lofland off,” Dodge remarked. Both women looked at him inquisitively. “I talked to her.”

“You talked to her?”

"When?"

They asked the questions simultaneously. Dodge explained. "After that ugly scene outside her husband's room. The two of you put your heads together for a private conversation. Nyland got a phone call. I thought I'd find the lady, see what was on her mind. She was in the hospital cafeteria, sitting alone, having a Coke. She was crying. I went up to her, told her I couldn't fail to notice that she was upset, asked if I could be of help."

He recounted to them almost verbatim the conversation he'd had with Ben's wife. It had been explanatory, enlightening, and, largely, troubling.

When he finished relating to them what had been said, neither Caroline nor Berry would look him in the eye. The thin bead chain dangling from the ceiling fan clinked against the metal casing. Dodge's breath soughed in and out of his overtaxed lungs. The cane seat of the rocking chair squeaked again, although he would have sworn he hadn't moved a muscle. Those sounds emphasized the silence of the two women.

Finally Dodge asked bluntly, "Is it true, Berry?"

She nodded.

He frowned and looked across at Caroline, who was staring at her hands, which she was clasping and unclasping where they lay in her lap. He cleared his throat and stood up. "I need to smoke."

He was almost out of the room when Berry, head lowered, said quietly, "When you come back, I'll explain."

"That would be helpful."

"What I don't get—"

"Yeah?"

She raised her head and looked at him. "Had you ever met Amanda Lofland?"

"Never laid eyes on the woman till I heard her telling you to stay away from her husband."

"Yet in half an hour's time she had poured out her heart to you. How did you gain her confidence that quickly?"

Softly Caroline said, "That's his speciality."

CHAPTER 7

Houston, Texas, 1978

THE TASK FORCE WAS A DUD.

At least in Dodge's opinion it was. Serving on it wasn't nearly as challenging as he'd been led to expect, nor as exciting as his fantasies had spun. He was glad to be out of uniform and off the night shift, but so far his task force duties had amounted largely to attending mandatory meetings conducted by egotistical windbags with nothing constructive or informative to say.

The group of elite police officers and FBI agents convened daily in what was called headquarters. Even in euphemistic terms, that lofty name hardly described the space. The unlabeled office was on the ground floor of an obscure office building on the outskirts of downtown. In an area where all the buildings were derelict, this was the worst of the lot. The only thing it had going for it was the cheap rent.

Here they met to review eyewitness accounts of the robberies, to watch the videos of the holdups from the banks' security cameras, to update one another on individual progress in tracking down leads, and to discuss strategy on how to proceed.

The premise that the group was elite was laughable. They'd reviewed the testimonies and watched the videos till they knew the contents by heart. They didn't have any leads, and, as for how to proceed with the investigation, nobody, especially the men in charge, had the least friggin' idea. These so-called high-level meetings usually evolved into swap fests of big fish stories.

Dirty jokes made the rounds. Cars were debated at length. Sporting events were argued over and gambled on. They drank gallons of high-octane coffee and snacked on empty calories. Those who smoked kept the room cloudy. They insulted one another, also one another's clothes, cars, alma maters, wives, mothers, and dogs. They held farting contests. They talked about women endlessly—who they'd laid and who they'd like to.

What they didn't do was capture the bank robber.

By the end of the second month, even the dirty jokes had turned stale, not to mention the snacks. Tempers were getting short, especially those of the higher-ranking HPD officers, who were feeling the heat of criticism from their superiors and the disdain of the feebs.

To address these issues, a meeting was called exclusively for HPD officers.

"Even the chief is catching hell from the mayor. He wants this guy caught before he comes up for reelection." The police captain presiding over this pep rally couldn't see his shoes for his overhanging gut. As he lectured on, Dodge's scorn increased. He wondered how many years it had been since this fat ass had covered a beat, tracked down a perp, made an arrest. He had his nerve to chew out subordinate officers when all Dodge had seen him do to distinguish himself was mooch coins for the cigarette vending machine and tell the stupidest jokes.

Because they had nothing else cooking, the task force members were discussing the viability of the suspects they had, based solely on their criminal profiles, not because any of them could be placed at or near one of the banks during a robbery.

One of these suspects had been arrested for drunk driving over the previous weekend. "He's in jail for parole violation. So if he's our man, he won't be holding up a bank anytime soon," the captain said.

"I don't think he's our robber anyhow," one officer remarked. "He's a punk. Cocky. Hotheaded. Hasn't got the coolness required to plan and execute these jobs."

Another cop said, "Last robbery, the guy flipped off the security camera."

"So?"

"So, if this guy is cocky, doesn't that sound like something he would do? Our robber is a smart-ass. He struts his stuff."

"From behind a disguise."

"Yeah, but you know what I'm saying."

A debate ensued. Dodge, who agreed with the first officer, had nothing to contribute, so he tuned out the argument and tried in vain to stifle his yawns.

Then, "Hanley!"

Dodge roused himself and sat up straighter. "Yes, sir?"

"How far have you got with Madison's girlfriend?"

Tommy Ray Madison, one of their suspects, was also on parole, having served his time for the armed robbery of a fast-food restaurant. He also had one botched bank holdup on his record. He fit the general height and weight description of their unidentified culprit.

Dodge replied, "In the way you mean, sir, I haven't even got to first base."

"First base?" Another officer chortled. "Admit it. You've struck out."

Dodge confirmed it with a weary nod. "I've struck out, Captain."

"How come? You're supposed to be the department's Romeo."

"The chemistry's off. The lady is knocked up."

"Aw hell. Who by? Madison?"

Dodge made a thumbs-up gesture. "She's four months along. She and Tommy Ray are in love. He's walking the straight and narrow, loves her, loves the baby to be, wants to get married."

"You said she was a sharp girl."

"That's how she strikes me."

"Madison is a goddamn felon!" the captain shouted. "She's falling for that hearts and flowers crap?"

Dodge shrugged. "That's love for ya. Besides, she says Tommy Ray found Jesus in prison."

"Jesus was in Huntsville?" another officer quipped.

"Always the last place you look," said another.

The captain squelched the responding laughter. He asked Dodge, "Who does she think you are?"

"Nobody except a regular customer who always orders the fajita combo. She brings me my Corona before I order it. Two limes. I tip her well, and I'm a good listener."

"You two talk a lot?"

"As much as I can swing without making her suspicious. I hang around till near closing. When the dinner crowd thins out, she dawdles at my table. I think I've won her confidence."

"What story did you give her?"

"I have nowhere else to go, and I hate spending my evenings in my empty apartment, where I live alone on account of my wife taking up with another guy and moving him into our house."

"I'm getting all choked up here." A cop pretended to be crying.

"Sounds like a sad country song."

The captain frowned over the interruptions and turned back to Dodge. "What's your take?"

Dodge had been giving Tommy Ray Madison and his girlfriend a lot of thought. Although his honest assessment wasn't what anyone in the room wanted to hear, he gave it to them straight.

"She's a nice girl. Too nice for Madison, but who can explain love? And maybe he did find Jesus and is now a changed man. On the other hand, if Tommy Ray was robbing banks, or even if she suspected him of parole violation, I think she'd dump him, baby or no baby. I think she'd turn him in for his own good. She's got this integrity thing going on, so I don't believe she'd harbor him if he was our perp."

"He's not our guy. That's what you're saying."

"I'm not positive of that, Captain, but he's not at the top of my list, no."

The other members of the task force, none joking now, took a moment to assimilate that, and it flattered Dodge that they gave such weight to his opinion. The captain ran his hand down his face, rearranging the fat folds. "Keep doing what you're doing. Watch for signs of a change in their relationship."

Dodge didn't need to be told that, but he nodded as though to say, *What a good idea, Captain. I certainly will.*

"What about the other one, Albright's squeeze?"

Franklin Albright was another parolee, but, beyond that, he and Tommy Ray Madison had little in common. Albright was scarier, meaner, and Dodge was almost positive he had never even looked for Jesus, much less found him and signed on.

Frowning, he replied to his captain's question. "The girl's name is Crystal, and this one's more difficult."

"How come?"

"Access. Albright is the jealous type. Watches her like a hawk. Drops her off at work every morning, picks her up at quitting time. She doesn't go out unless he's with her, not even on mundane errands. Supermarkets are usually good for accidentally-on-purpose bumping into someone and striking up a conversation, but Albright is always right there with her. He's alienated her from her friends and family. You see the problem? I haven't had an opportunity to get near the lady, much less become her confidant."

The captain stroked his chin thoughtfully. "Where does she work?"

"So now this fat jerk-off has got me working at her place of employment."

Gonzales laughed so abruptly he choked on his orange juice. After recovering his breath, he wheezed, "You're kidding."

"Swear to God. He adjourned the meeting, made some calls. Twelve hours later I reported for my first shift in the janitorial department."

"Oh, man."

"I've got a mop bucket, a push broom, a shirt with my name embroidered on the pocket. Can you believe it? But I have access to the whole place. I get to wander around, go everywhere, and nobody thinks anything about it. At least I'm not stuck in one spot all day."

He could be working on the assembly line of the tire manufacturing plant, making steel-belted radials instead of replacing burned-out fluorescent tubes and emptying trash cans. All in all, though, it sucked.

"A janitor, huh?" Gonzales could barely control his laughter. "Who knows? You may decide on a career change."

"Screw that, and screw you." Dodge doused his eggs liberally with Tabasco. The two had made a date for breakfast between the time Gonzales's night shift ended and when Dodge had to clock in at his new day job.

"You met your target yet?" Gonzales asked.

"We've made eye contact. She's a clerk in the payroll office."

"What's she look like?"

Dodge grinned. "Put it this way, it won't be hardship duty."

"Tits?"

"Two," Dodge said, then laughed at Gonzales's expression. "C cup at least. Good legs, too."

Gonzales gazed at him with a mix of admiration and envy. "And you're getting paid to put the moves on her."

Dodge glanced around. "That's not my official assignment, you understand." He pulled a somber expression. "HPD wouldn't condone an officer using—"

"Save it," Gonzales said. Then, leaning across the table, he whispered, "But we both know that's what they want you to do." He stuffed a three-ply wedge of syrupy pancakes into his mouth. "You live a charmed life, my friend."

"Don't forget that she's got a hard-case felon for a boyfriend. What I've heard of him, he'd probably slit my throat for taking a gander at her tits. Just for thinking about taking a gander at her tits."

"Bad one, huh?"

"Real bad. Series of armed robberies. Two assaults. One rape charge fell apart in pretrial, so he squeaked by there. He was suspected of a fatal stabbing in the prison shower, but the weapon didn't turn up, and, if there were any witnesses, they were too scared to come forward." Nodding somberly, Dodge said, "He's bad."

Gonzales frowned with concern. "Get the information from his old lady. Get the robber, get a medal, get detective. But don't get killed in the process, okay?"

"I'll do my best."

More than that Dodge couldn't say about his undercover work, not even to his trusted former partner. Gonzales understood that, of course, so when Dodge asked him about his new partner, he shifted subjects gracefully.

"He and I get along okay. Goes without saying, he's not you."

"Miss me?" Dodge teased.

"No. Hell no. When I said he wasn't you, I meant that he's *better* than you. But Doris at the 7-Eleven is pining. She's gone stingy with free doughnuts and ice cream bars."

They finished their meal and paid their tab. When they reached the parking lot, Gonzales paused and looked toward the freeway, where the rush-hour traffic was moving at a blistering five miles an hour. Then he studied the clouds scuttling in off the Gulf. He looked at just about everything except Dodge, who sensed Gonzales was struggling with indecision.

"What's on your mind, partner?"

"Nothing much." He glanced at Dodge, looked away again. "I just . . . Look, this is none of my business, okay? And it probably doesn't matter to you anyway."

"But?"

Finally he looked at Dodge directly. "Night before last, my partner and me responded to another call for help on Shadydale." He watched Dodge warily, to see if the street name rang any bells.

It did, of course. A couple of months had gone by since he'd come to Caroline King's rescue, but it seemed like yesterday. Dodge's whole system started humming with wrath, with dread. "Did he hurt her?"

"No. Didn't amount to anything, really. In fact it was the neighbor next door who called. Said she heard loud noises, shouting, abusive language. Campton had split by the time we got there. I talked to Ms. King. She was embarrassed. Hated that her neighbor had been disturbed. But Campton hadn't hit her this time."

Gonzales hesitated before continuing. "I didn't know if you still . . . you know." He bobbed his shoulders in a quick shrug. "The only reason I mentioned it is because . . . That night you and I were there? Seemed to me you were especially interested in this lady's welfare."

Dodge clenched his jaw and didn't say anything.

"They're still engaged," Gonzales continued. "I asked. And anyway, it was hard to miss the diamond on her hand."

Dodge nodded.

Gonzales made a sound of regret. "Hell, I'm out of line here. I shouldn't have said anything."

"No, I'm glad you did, Jimmy. Thanks for telling me."

Then, worried for a different reason, Gonzales asked, "You're not gonna do something stupid, are you?"

Dodge forced himself to smile. "Me? Hell no. I gotta make detective. I wouldn't do anything to jeopardize my shot at that."

Half an hour later, he reported for work at the tire plant. During his lunch break, he saw Crystal in the commissary and made a point of smiling at her. She smiled back, then shyly averted her head and didn't look at him again.

When his shift ended, he clocked out, then went looking for Roger Campton, and, when he found him, he beat the shit out of him. At least he tried his best.

It was after dark, but Dodge would have done the same thing in broad daylight. He caught up with Campton in the parking lot of the exclusive health club where he was a member. His hair was damp from his recent shower, and he smelled of Irish Spring. Dodge came up behind him, caught him in a headlock, and punched him in the right kidney.

Campton dropped his gym bag. Because of the pressure Dodge's forearm was applying to his larynx, the only sounds he made were guttural and unintelligible. After Dodge delivered several more hard blows, Campton's knees gave out beneath him. Dodge spun him around, hit him in the face with the heel of his hand, and felt his nose collapse with a crunching noise and a gush of blood and mucus.

He backed Campton into his Mercedes and bent him backward over the shiny hood. Shoving his hand beneath Campton's chin in order to keep him upright, he repeatedly drove his fist into the millionaire's belly and ribs with the impetus of a pile driver.

When he finally let him go and stepped back, Campton slid down the side of his sleek car and crumpled like a pile of dirty laundry onto the pavement. Dodge kicked him in the ribs and, out of sheer spite, in the testicles. The man screamed, then passed out.

Dodge went down on one knee and grabbed a handful of his hair. He slapped his bloody face until he came to. "Can you hear me?"

"Don't kill me," Campton whimpered. Because of his smashed nose, his mewling sounded almost comical.

"Not tonight. But I want you to listen to me, you motherfucking turd. Because of your daddy's money, you might think you can do anything you damn well please and get away with it. So far you have. But I'm telling you now that if you hurt Caroline King again, even a little, you die. Do you understand me?"

He relaxed his grip on Campton's hair to allow his head to wobble a nod of comprehension.

"You're not gonna forget what I'm telling you, are you, Roger?"

Campton shook his head.

"Because if you do, if you raise a hand to her tomorrow, or next week, or ten years from now, I'll kill you. You got it?"

Roger Campton had passed out again, and this time when Dodge released him, he left him where he lay, deeply regretting that he couldn't quite justify killing the son of a bitch right then and there.

• • •

It was twilight, and the air was muggy. Sunset had done little to relieve Houston of the steamy heat. Dodge was seated on a shaded concrete bench in the outdoor courtyard of an office park formed by four square, glass buildings, each six stories tall. He was waiting as requested, nervous as a whore in church, wondering why she'd asked for this meeting, hoping like hell it meant something good for him.

She came through the revolving door of Building Two five minutes after the appointed time. By then the back of his shirt was stuck to his skin, and streams of sweat were trickling down his ribs. As she approached, he stood up, praying his deodorant wouldn't fail him and wishing he'd chewed one extra breath mint.

She was dressed in black slacks and a sleeveless top the color of cream. The rosy hues of dusk made her hair look like molten copper. Her arms were impossibly slender, and her flat-heeled sandals added no height.

But her petiteness was incongruous with her combatant stride, and when she got close enough for him to read her expression, his hopes for this meeting turning out to be good for him were instantly dashed.

Every red hair on her head was bristling when, without preamble, she demanded to know, "Did you do it?"

Dodge didn't even pretend ignorance of what she was talking about, but he wasn't about to admit to an assault and battery, either. He motioned her toward the bench.

"No, thank you," she said stiffly. "I prefer to stand. And I insist on knowing if it was you who beat Roger to within an inch of his life. He'll be in the hospital for at least a week. He could have died."

"So I heard from Jimmy Gonzales."

His former partner had called his pager number the evening before, but Dodge hadn't been able to call him back until this morning. Gonzales had told him that Roger Campton had been hospitalized with serious injuries suffered in an attack by an unidentified assailant.

A long silence had followed.

Finally Dodge had asked if it had been a mugging, and Gonzales had told him that Campton's wallet was still on him when he was found, credit cards and several hundred dollars intact.

Gonzales hadn't asked if Dodge was responsible, because he didn't want his suspicion confirmed. Gonzales was as honest a cop as they came. Dodge could tell the guy was anguishing over his own complicity, which amounted only to his informing Dodge of the latest police summons to an address on Shadydale. But that would have been enough to eat at a man with Gonzales's integrity.

Dodge hated having put his partner and friend in such a compromising position, because he was also certain that Gonzales would never rat him out for anything short of cold-blooded murder.

Then Gonzales had dropped a bombshell. "She wants to see you." He'd told Dodge where to be and what time to be there.

So here he was, and here Caroline King was, glaring up at him with accusation. "You didn't need Officer Gonzales to tell you about Roger, though, did you? You knew because you were Roger's attacker."

"Why don't we sit down?" Dodge indicated the bench again, and this time she walked to it and sat down. He sat beside her, but kept as much distance as possible between them. He couldn't help but notice the diamond ring on her left hand. The stone was the size of a headlight. He supposed there were thousands of women who would put up with an occasional beating in exchange for a diamond like that.

But he couldn't believe this one would. She seemed way too strong, way too smart. He wondered what hidden quality Roger Campton possessed that made him worth the carats. Was his dick that magic? Or was it his trust fund that enticed Caroline King?

Quelling his resentment of both, Dodge said, "Gonzales told me that you were very upset when you called him."

"Wouldn't you be upset if someone you cared for was beaten like that?"

"Yeah," he returned quietly. "I would."

She turned her head, and their eyes connected, and he could

tell that his underlying message hadn't escaped her. Eventually she turned away and stared sightlessly at the building from which she'd exited.

"You work in there?" he asked.

She shook her head. "I work in the county tax assessor's office downtown. I attend classes here three nights a week."

"What kind of classes?"

"Real estate. I'm studying to get my license. We take a break at seven o'clock. That's why I asked Officer Gonzales if he could get a message to you to meet me here. He said he would try."

"Why didn't you call me directly?"

"I didn't know how to reach you. Officer Gonzales had given me his number the other night when . . ."

Her voice trailed off; Dodge picked up her sentence. "The other night when Gonzales responded to another domestic disturbance at your house."

"Nothing happened. My neighbor overreacted. It was a shouting match. That's all."

"This time."

His right hand was resting on his right thigh. She looked down at it, at the incriminating swollen knuckles, the bruises. Then her gaze moved across his body to his left hand, where scratch marks were still visible. Before Campton had collapsed, he'd made futile attempts to dislodge Dodge's arm from around his neck. His scratches had broken the skin on Dodge's forearm and the back of his hand. He made no attempt to hide this evidence from her. He wanted her to know how vicious the fight had been.

"You shouldn't have done it," she admonished softly. "You don't even know him. Or me. You're a police officer." She raised her head, her eyes now searching his. "Why did you?"

He said nothing for several moments, then turned the tables and asked a question of his own. "Why do you assume it was me?"

"I don't assume, I know. From the moment I heard about the attack, I knew it was you."

"Why would it even occur to you that it was me?"

He asked because he knew she would find the answer to her question in the answer to his. She'd known immediately that he was the culprit because she'd seen the way he'd looked at her. Bad taste in fiancés notwithstanding, she wasn't stupid. Or blind. Or deaf.

The night of the first incident, when they were alone together in her kitchen, she'd probably sensed that his care and concern went beyond those of a police officer. Any lingering doubts about the nature of his interest would have been dispelled the morning he showed up at her house again to check on her.

And right now she probably knew that he was aching to touch her hair, kiss her mouth, enfold her tiny body in his arms and hold her so close against him that he could feel her heartbeat. He willed her to comprehend the intensity of his feelings, but he must have gone too far, because she stood up quickly.

"You've overstepped your bounds, Mr. Hanley. You have nothing to do with my life. Your responsibility toward me ended when you performed your duties as a police officer that one night. I'm going to marry Roger."

Dodge stood up with her. "You'll regret it."

"If you insinuate yourself into our lives again, I'll have to report you. As for this violent attack, promise me that you'll never do anything like it again."

Dodge said nothing. He for sure as hell didn't make her a promise that would contradict the one he'd already made to Campton to kill him if he harmed her.

"All right. You've been warned." She gave him one last fulminating look, then turned away and started walking toward the building. But after covering only a short distance, she stopped and came back around. "Officer Gonzales told me you had been appointed to a special task force."

"That's right."

"Is it dangerous?"

"Not as dangerous as what you're getting yourself into."

She seemed on the verge of taking issue with that but must have thought better of it. "Take care of yourself."

Then she walked away from him.

When he got back to his car, he checked his pager, drove to the nearest pay phone, and placed a call to the task force hotline. It was answered brusquely. "This is Hanley. Somebody there page me?"

"Where the hell have you been? Captain's about to stroke out. He's paged you at least ten times."

"I've got a stomach bug. Came on this afternoon. Been in the crapper ever since I knocked off at the tire plant."

"Too bad. Get here. I'm talking sprout wings and fly."

"What's up?"

"Our guy waltzed into a bank just before closing, hit it for about thirty grand, and took out a guard."

"Took out as in a hostage?"

"No. Took out as in killed."

CHAPTER 8

"Ms. Buckland?"

"Yes?"

The voice was so faint Ski could barely hear her on his cell phone. He plugged his other ear with his index finger. "Sally Buckland?"

"Yes. This is . . . I'm Sally Buckland."

"My name's Ski Nyland. I'm a deputy sheriff in Merritt County." When she said nothing to that, he plowed on. "We had an incident here last night, Ms. Buckland, and some people you know were involved."

"Oren and Berry. I heard about it on the news."

Ski wasn't surprised that the Houston media had picked up the story of the shooting. Probably dozens of similar incidents had occurred last night, but Caroline King had been a large player in the Houston area real estate market before moving to Merritt. Her name was newsworthy. He was glad of it. Because of the news coverage, millions of people would be on the lookout for Oren Starks.

He confirmed with Ms. Buckland that Starks and Berry Malone had been her co-workers at Delray Marketing and that she was also acquainted with the shooting victim, Ben Lofland.

"They said Ben is in serious condition."

"That's been upgraded," Ski told her. "He's going to be fine."

Two deputies came into the squad room carrying Whataburger sacks. Others fell on the fast food like a pack of coyotes. Ski placed his hand over his phone and yelled at them to pipe down. His stomach rumbled, reminding him he hadn't had a proper meal today.

Back into the phone, he said, "I was wondering if you could answer some questions for me, Ms. Buckland."

"No."

Her abruptness took him aback. "I promise not to take up much of your time."

"Why did you call me?"

"Because I'm conducting an investigation, and you know the three principals involved. Oren Starks issued some serious threats, and he's still at large. Anything you can tell me would be greatly appreciated." She was silent for so long that Ski had to prod her. "Ms. Buckland?"

"I'm sorry, but I don't know anything."

Another deputy approached Ski, proffering a burger oozing melting cheese, but despite how mouthwatering it looked, Ski waved him off. "Ms. Malone has alleged that Oren Starks shot Mr. Lofland." Sally Buckland said nothing in response. "When you worked at Delray Marketing, were you aware of any hostility existing between Mr. Starks and Mr. Lofland?"

"No."

"No ill will of any kind, at any time?"

"No."

"Okay. What about—"

"This really is none of my business."

She sounded unreasonably upset. In Ski's experience, people—particularly people with nothing to hide—were flattered to have been contacted by the authorities. Typically they puffed up with self-importance and welcomed the chance to unload information even when it didn't pertain to the case.

"Please, Ms. Buckland, just a few more questions."

"But I don't know anything about this. I left Delray months ago and haven't seen these people since."

"Did you leave Delray on account of Oren Starks?"

"Who told you that?"

"Did you?"

"That's ridiculous."

"Starks didn't factor into your decision to leave the company?"

"Of course not."

Ski wanted to eliminate any confusion over this point. "Did Oren Starks persistently pursue a romantic relationship with you?"

"Heavens no."

"Did you quit your job in order to avoid his unwelcome advances?" She didn't respond, but he could hear her breathing. "Ms. Buckland?"

"None of that is true. If Berry led you to believe that Oren is a stalker, she's lying. Now I really must go."

She hung up before Ski could stop her.

"Very well done, Sally. Considering the disquieting circumstances and how nervous you are, you spoke exceptionally well and said exactly what I wanted the deputy to hear. Thank you."

Oren Starks covered her hand where it still gripped the landline telephone. "Let go, Sally," he said, laughing unctuously. "It's as though you're holding on to that phone for dear life."

She released the telephone and, without moving her head, cut her eyes far to the left so she could see him out of the corner of her eye—which had the barrel of a pistol pressed against it. "I did what you told me to, Oren."

"And I've said thank you."

"So you'll leave now?"

He smiled with feigned regret. "No, I'm afraid not."

"But you said—"

"What I said was that I would leave when you'd done what I asked you to."

"Which I did."

"But you're not finished yet, Sally." He stroked the pistol's barrel along her jawline, returning it to her temple. Her fearful whimper gave him enormous pleasure. "By throwing off that deputy sheriff, you made up for some of your meanness toward me. But not for all of it. You and I are still a long way from even."

"How did . . . how did you know he would call me?"

"You don't have to be a whiz kid to figure that out, Sally. It's Criminal Investigation 101. The first thing an investigator—in this case the deputy sheriff—would want to know is why I shot Ben Lofland last night. Berry would have told him that I am a spurned suitor. He would have asked if anyone could corroborate that, and she . . . would . . . have . . . named . . . *you.*"

He tapped the pistol against her head to emphasize each word. On the last, he pressed the barrel of it hard against her cheekbone. "Naturally the deputy would follow protocol and check out her story. What was his name again?"

"N-Nyland," Sally stammered. "I think that's what he said."

He shrugged with indifference. "Doesn't matter, really. What does matter is that you disputed Berry's allegations, leaving her with a lot to answer for."

"Despite what I said, this deputy might think she's telling the truth. Maybe I didn't throw him off track at all."

"Oh, I believe you did. You sounded very convincing to me, Sally."

"But law enforcement officers never take things at face value. He might have heard the nervousness in my voice. Even now, he could be—"

"Sally, Sally, you're getting your hopes up."

"My hopes up?"

"That you'll be rescued." He gave another sad smile. "Believe me, the Merritt County S.O. has more to do today than follow up with little, insignificant you."

Her lower lip began to tremble. He stroked it with the pad of his index finger. At his touch, she recoiled.

"Stop that!" He flicked his finger hard against her lip. Even though he had the upper hand, her rejection angered him. How dare she flinch when he touched her?

He was the one with the power now. Which she'd realized the instant she entered her house with a shopping bag of groceries. When she saw him standing in her kitchen, she'd given a startled cry, dropped the bag to the floor, and stumbled over it in her haste to escape.

He'd caught her and held on. To keep her quiet, he'd assured her that he meant her no harm. But of course she'd heard about what had happened in Merritt, so the implication of his ambush had been immediately clear. She'd struggled hysterically until he'd pressed the pistol to her head. That had made her considerably more cooperative, although she'd continued to blubber, asking what he wanted of her.

He'd told her that they would wait for some peace officer or another either to telephone or to appear at her door with questions about him. While waiting for that inevitability, he'd coached her on how to answer when those questions were put to her.

He'd promised that, if she complied with his request, she would live. If not, he'd shoot her in the head. Apparently she had believed him, because she'd answered the deputy's questions as though reading from a script written by Oren himself.

But now that the expected call had taken place, she seemed even more terrified of him than before. Probably because the deputy's questions had reminded her of how horribly she'd treated Oren. She'd rejected his affections and, adding insult to injury, had contributed to his dismissal from the job he'd loved and had been so well suited for.

No wonder then, was it, that she was trembling with fright.

He tapped the muzzle of the pistol against her temple, reminding her again that her fate lay entirely with him.

"Wh-what else do you want me to do, Oren?"

"I don't recall you stuttering like that before, Sally. You surely didn't stutter when you turned down my repeated invitations to dinner. Or when you returned my Valentine roses. You were articulate enough when you told our co-workers how you couldn't stand to be around me."

"I never—"

He struck her hard on the side of her head with the barrel of the pistol. Her cry of shock and pain was better than whispered sweet nothings. "Don't compound your cruel rejection by lying about it, Sally. Don't insult my intelligence."

She was crying in earnest now. Her face, which he'd always thought to be pretty, looked ugly, the features crumpled with pain and fear, snot dripping from her nose, tears streaming down her cheeks. "Please, Oren."

"Please what, Sally?" he asked silkily.

"Please don't hurt me."

"But you hurt *me*. You damaged me personally and professionally."

"I never meant to hurt you." Her voice cracked on the last two words. She was shivering as though she had a palsy.

"Now, Sally," he said in a soothing voice. "No need to fall apart on me. Didn't I tell you that you would come to no harm if you did everything I asked you to?"

"Yes."

"Didn't I promise not to hurt you if you discredited Berry?"

"Yes."

"Well then. So far, I've kept my promises, haven't I?"

She nodded.

Holding the pistol hard against her temple, he wrapped his hand around her biceps and steered her about. "Unfortunately, one chat with a deputy sheriff doesn't reparation make. So, into the bedroom we go."

Her footsteps faltered. "What for?"

"Use your imagination."

She sobbed. "Please, Oren. I'm sorry. For everything, I'm sorry. Don't hurt me. I'll do anything."

He laughed. "Oh, I'm counting on that."

• • •

While Ski was redialing Sally Buckland, he heard his call waiting chirp. The incoming call took precedence. He clicked over. "Nyland."

"It's Andy."

"What's up?"

"The night attendant at the bait shop?"

"At the three-way stop on Lake Road?" Earlier that day, Ski had questioned the man, who claimed not to have seen or heard anything out of the ordinary last night. Impatiently he asked, "What about him?"

"He watches a lot of TV during his long shift. Seen every episode of *Law & Order.* Reruns on cable, too. You know how they play several episodes back to back every night?"

"Okay."

"He doesn't miss. He pays attention to how the cops crack the case. So he's been doing some amateur sleuthing today."

Oh, Christ. Ski ran his fingers through his hair and wished he hadn't turned down the cheeseburger. It felt like his stomach was gnawing on his spine. Andy was still talking.

"He got out last night's sales receipts—"

"I went through those. None of the credit cards belonged to Starks, and he didn't fit the description of anyone paying with cash."

"Yeah, but this guy went *back* through his receipts, to see if something might've been overlooked. It's a slow day, he said. Anyhow, he ran down a guy who charged some gas for his bass boat late last night near the time of the shooting. And *that* guy, the bass boat guy, remembers seeing *another* guy while he was filling his gas can. Said he went into the men's room and it looked to him like the guy had a busted leg."

CHAPTER 9

"Allow me." Dodge clicked on his disposable lighter.

"Thanks." The woman smiled around the cigarette held between her lips and leaned forward to touch the end of it to the flame. She took a few drags while Dodge was lighting his cigarette. She exhaled. "Things have come to a sad pass when you can't smoke in a bar."

Dodge sighed. "I hear ya."

He'd been flirting with her through one beer, which he'd drunk slowly in order to give himself time to assess the place and its clientele. After gauging all the customers who'd come in for happy hour, he'd decided that the woman pouring the drinks was probably his best prospect.

She was forty-something and looked every day of it. Her face had lived through some hard times and harsh disappointments, and in her eyes was a sad resignation. But she had a naturally warm smile, and she was generous with it. Everyone who came in, men and women alike, addressed her by name, and she seemed to know their preferred drinks and everything else about them. He'd overheard her asking about a new job, a fishing expedition, elderly parents, a child in crisis, and a lame horse.

When she'd turned the bar over to a younger man so she could take a break, Dodge had followed her past the restrooms, down a short hallway, and out a back exit.

Now that their cigarettes were smoldering, she lifted the hair off the back of her neck and held it up, creating a provocative pose and extending an open invitation for Dodge to enjoy the view, which wasn't bad.

"I'm Grace."

"Dodge."

"Hi, Dodge."

"Hi, Grace."

They smiled at each other. She lowered her arm and let her hair fall back into place. "If you lived in Merritt, I'd know it."

"Atlanta."

"Texas?"

"Georgia."

"No fooling? You're a long way from home then. What do you do there?"

"A little of this, little of that."

She gave him a smile that said, *I've got your number.* "A man of mystery."

"Me? Shucks, no, ma'am."

She laughed at his b.s. "What brings you to southeast Texas?"

He embroidered a story about possibly relocating to Houston. "My brother is pressuring me to partner with him on a business deal. It's a good opportunity, and there's nothing keeping me in Atlanta, so I'm giving it serious consideration. But I can't take the city—or my brother, for that matter—all the time. I figure if I make the move, I'll need a getaway. Nothing fancy. Just a place to escape to on the weekends. Get in some fishing. Commune with nature." His smile would have melted butter. "This town looks like a good place for kicking back."

"Well, you're right about that. The population triples just about every weekend, but particularly in the spring and summer."

"What's the second-home market like? Is it favoring sellers or buyers?"

"Hell if I'd know," she said around a smoker's laugh. She dropped her cigarette butt to the pavement and ground it out with the toe of her shoe. "I can't afford a first home, much less a second."

"I've seen a lot of For Sale signs around. Green. Little crown."

"Caroline King. She's the big-shot realtor around here."

He held a light to her second cigarette. "A big shot sounds too rich for my blood."

She exhaled, shaking her head. "She handles big, small, whatever. Nice lady, too."

"You've done business with her?"

"Maybe if I won the lottery." She guffawed. "I know her to speak to, though. She comes into the bar occasionally. Sometimes with clients to have a glass of wine while talking over a contract. A few weeks ago she had a younger woman with her that she introduced as her daughter. I'd heard her daughter was staying with her for the summer, but that's the first time I'd seen her in town. Ms. King's house is out at the lake. They had some trouble out there last night."

"Trouble?"

"A shooting."

He pretended to choke on his smoke. "*Shooting?*"

"Some guy the daughter works with. Love triangle kind of thing is what people are saying."

"Wow. I thought this was a sleepy little town."

"We've got our scandals, believe me," she said, rolling her eyes. "But you could've knocked me over with a feather when I heard about that business with Ms. King. Neither she nor her daughter looks the type."

"What type is that?"

"Man-trouble type. But I guess it goes to show you never know what goes on behind closed doors."

"Isn't that a song?"

She grinned up at him, pleased. "You like country?"

By the time Dodge had finished his first cigarette and lit another, they'd exhausted the subject of country music, at least to the extent that he knew something about it. Trying to steer the topic back to Caroline, he frowned. "I guess this realtor will be too busy to take on any new clients, considering the mess her kid is in."

"I don't know. You can try. Ms. King is a businesswoman right down the line. I heard she made a killing in residential real estate in Houston. She moved to Merritt to retire."

"When was this?"

"Few years ago. Two or three."

"Her retirement didn't take?"

She laughed. "Guess not. She no more had settled in than she linked up with a property developer and—"

"Linked up?" He bobbed his eyebrows. "One of those closed-doors things?"

Grace nudged his arm, and somehow in the process his elbow made contact with her full bosom. "Ms. King is at least twenty years older than the developer."

"That's in fashion, isn't it? Older woman, younger man?"

"Maybe. But he's got a gorgeous wife and three perfect children. His partnership with Ms. King was strictly business. He enlisted her to sell the houses in his development. She sold them all in record time." Grace shrugged and dropped her second cigarette butt to the asphalt. "She decided retirement wasn't for her. Not yet, anyway. She's got even richer off all the development going on around here."

"She must have savvy."

Grace nodded. "And she works at it. She's got my respect and everybody else's. At least, I've never heard a bad word said against her. Of course the gossips will be all over what happened out at her place last night." She glanced at her wristwatch. "They're gonna think you kidnapped me." There was a trace of hopefulness in the smile she cast over her shoulder as she reentered the bar.

Dodge took one final drag on his cigarette, then dropped the butt and followed her inside. She'd been so unwittingly generous with information, he felt obliged to buy one more beer, but he didn't finish it before signaling her to tally up his tab.

"How long will you be in town, Dodge?"

He told her the unvarnished truth. "I don't know."

"Drop back by."

"I will."

"Do you have a wife?"

"Not lately."

She laughed. "Are you lying?"

"No."

She slid a small white card across the bar. "While you're here, if you need anything—directions, restaurant recommendations, a place to smoke—give me a call."

Before going into the bar, Dodge had parked parallel on Bowie Street, choosing a metered slot that had a shade tree growing beside it. The shade had helped. Nevertheless, the interior of the rental car felt like an oven when he got in. He cranked the motor so he could turn on the air conditioner.

He lit a cigarette, then took from the pocket of his jacket a slender pink cell telephone. Amanda Lofland's cell telephone. The cell phone she'd been careless enough to leave on the table while they were deeply involved in their conversation. The cell phone Dodge had pilfered while she was blotting her tearful eyes with a soggy Kleenex.

Most criminal investigators followed the money first. Dodge Hanley went after the scorned woman.

He tapped the phone's icon that accessed the log of recent calls and scrolled through it. All her calls yesterday and last night had come from one number. He called it. It was answered with a cheerful, "Hi, this is Ben, leave a message."

So, the couple had stayed in close contact yesterday while Ben was with Berry. Which came as somewhat of a disappointment, since it virtually disproved Dodge's theory of looking first at jealous females for possible suspects.

Or maybe not. Maybe Lofland had made all those calls to his wife as overcompensation for cheating on her, in his heart if not with his dick.

In any case, Dodge still considered Amanda Lofland worth looking at.

Next, he scrolled through the cell phone's menu, landing on her directory of contacts.

Sticking with protocol, Dodge entered the house through the back door. Caroline was at the stove stirring the contents of a pot. "Good. You're back," she said. "Dinner's almost ready."

"What are we having?"

"Spaghetti and meat sauce."

"One of your specialities."

She directed a worried glance toward the interior door that led to the rest of the house. "Be careful not to say things like that. How would you know it's one of my specialities?"

"Like how would you know that I drink my tea unsweetened?"

She thought for a moment, then said with chagrin, "This afternoon."

"Hmm."

"Habits die hard."

"And get you into trouble." The white card with Grace's phone number on it suddenly felt like a live coal inside his breast pocket. "Need any help?"

"No, thanks."

"I could set the table. I think I remember which side the fork goes on."

"Already done. Would you like something to drink?"

He shook his head. "I had a beer in town." She was about to ask him about that, but before she could pose a question he might not want to answer, he asked, "Where's Berry?"

"Still sleeping, last I checked."

They still hadn't addressed what he'd learned from his conversation with Amanda Lofland in the hospital cafeteria. After having recounted it to Caroline and Berry, he'd gone out for a cigarette. When he'd come back inside, Caroline had suggested that Berry walk him through the events of last night, showing him where everything had taken place. Actually, he'd been about to suggest that himself.

For the next hour, they'd moved from room to room while Berry related chronologically and in detail exactly what had taken place. In the bathroom, the shower curtain had been reattached to the rod. The blood-soaked rug had been removed from the bedroom and replaced by another to cover the bloodstain that had seeped into the hardwood. Despite these concealing measures, the room retained the feel of a place where something traumatic had occurred.

Dodge had knelt where Berry indicated Ben Lofland had fallen. He'd flipped back the replacement rug to examine the bloodstain. Then he'd gone into the bathroom. When he reached the tub, he'd turned back and estimated the distance to the bloodstain. "Starks was standing here when he fired?"

Berry nodded.

"Five feet, six at most. Lofland's lucky to be alive."

"Oren must be a lousy shot."

"Must be."

Out on the gallery, Dodge had inspected the holes in the wall, left by the bullets that Nyland or someone from the S.O. had removed. Then Dodge had had Berry show him exactly where Starks had landed after his fall down the stairs and the position from which he'd been wildly firing the pistol.

He'd laid down on his back on the floor and acted it out while she'd crouched behind the railing on the gallery above as she'd done the night before. Caroline had stood by, watching all this, hugging her elbows and chafing her upper arms.

"I can't believe how close you came to being killed," she'd said, tears in her voice.

Dodge had been equally shaken by the thought of how narrowly Berry had escaped a bullet. If she hadn't, Caroline's call to him last night would have been altogether different. Or maybe she wouldn't have bothered to notify him. It didn't bear thinking about.

After talking through it, Berry had told them she was exhausted and asked if they could postpone their conversation about her and Lofland until after she'd rested. "It's the elephant in the room. I know it must be explained, but can it keep until I've had a nap?"

He and Caroline had watched as she wearily climbed the stairs. When she reached the gallery, she'd gone into the guest room, Dodge supposed because being in her bedroom made the horrible memories too vivid for comfort.

As soon as she was out of earshot, Caroline had turned to him, her posture defensive. "What Amanda Lofland told you has no bearing on what happened here last night."

"I didn't say it did."

"You implied it."

"I did no such thing."

"I know how your mind works, Dodge. You're skeptical by nature. Why would you tend to believe Amanda Lofland over your own flesh and blood?"

Afraid that his angry voice might carry upstairs and through the guest room door, he'd propelled Caroline across the living area and into the kitchen. As soon as they'd reached it and he'd shut the door, he leaned toward her.

"You march out that flesh-and-blood connection whenever you want to make a point or to remind me that I should have blind loyalty toward Berry now. But you weren't so keen on her being my flesh and blood the day she was born."

"Do you blame me?"

"No, Caroline, and I never did. You were in the right. I was wrong. I admitted I was."

"It wasn't enough."

"How well I know." She'd tried to stare him down but failed, and he'd derived some satisfaction from her being the first to turn away. After a moment, he'd said quietly, "I think you should prepare yourself."

"For what?"

"For just in case Berry hasn't been quite as up-front with you as you think." When she would have spoken, he'd sliced the air with his hand. "That's what scares you, too, isn't it, Caroline? You said as much at the tearoom."

"I said—"

"I asked you what the problem was, and in reply you said that Berry is a lot like me. You knew that would be the one reason I'd stay on. Because we both know that the genes she got from me might not be pretty when they manifest themselves. If she's got herself into a mess, I'll help her get out of it, but the process might be disagreeable, to say the least." With that, he'd headed for the door.

"Where are you going?"

"To town."

"What for?"

"I need a place to stay. Once I've got a room and dumped my stuff, I want to nose around, see if I can find a grapevine to tap into."

"How long will you be gone?"

"Can't say."

"Be back in time for dinner."

He'd stopped on his way through the door and looked at her. She'd looked anxious, as though afraid that, despite what he'd said, he might not return. He'd been tempted to ask her if she cared whether or not he came back, and if so, how much.

But all he'd said was "Anything happens, you've got my cell number." Now he was back, and she hadn't called him during his absence, so he assumed that there had been nothing new to report.

While he'd been gone, she'd changed into a pair of white pants cropped at her ankles and a yellow T-shirt, through which he could see the outline of her bra. She'd always thought her breasts were too small. He'd thought they were downright perfect, and perfectly sensitive.

"Did you find a room?"

He dragged his gaze off her chest and onto more neutral territory. "Uh . . . yeah. Cypress Lodge."

"There's better available. I know of some houses that owners rent out when not in use. I should have thought of reserving you one before now, although I've been . . . My mind's been scattered. But I could call the office and—"

"The lodge is fine. My standards aren't that high. This room has all the comforts of home. In fact, it's several notches above my place in Atlanta."

She dipped a wooden spoon into the spaghetti sauce, blew on it, sipped a sample, then laid the spoon in a ceramic holder near the burner and replaced the lid on the simmering pot. Going to the small breakfast table, she sat down and motioned Dodge into the chair across from her. He sat.

"Mr. Mitchell doesn't pay you well?"

"Very well. A hell of a lot more than I'm worth." He paused, then added, "But not nearly as much as you make selling houses."

"I've been fortunate."

"You work your butt off."

She conceded the point with a small smile. "I've put in some long days. But I love the work."

"It's made you rich. In Houston. Then here."

She folded her arms across her middle and eyed him shrewdly. "Who'd you talk to? No, wait. Where did you go for your beer?"

"A place on Bowie Street."

"Chat and Chill?"

He coughed behind his fist, saying evasively, "I think that was it."

"Grace. You got your information from Grace." She held his gaze and asked softly, "What did it cost you?"

"Two beers and two cigarettes."

She smiled again, but this time it was a sad expression. "Nothing's changed."

"Everything's changed, Caroline. Thirty years ago we were making love while the spaghetti sauce simmered."

He saw from her expression that she remembered it as well as he did. They'd decided to fool around and had forgotten all about what was on the stove until the smell of scorched tomatoes had alerted them to the potential hazard. He'd told her to hold on and somehow had got them off the bed while still joined. Then he'd carried her into the kitchen, and, as soon as he'd turned off the burner beneath the pot, they'd resumed right there.

Her face became flushed, and she couldn't look him in the eye. "We were young."

"And a little crazy. Crazy in love."

"Don't, Dodge." Her whisper had a desperately pleading undertone.

"Don't what? Don't talk about it? Don't remember? I can't help remembering. That day the spaghetti sauce burned was one of our more rollicking fucks." It had been a combination of laughter and lust. He got hard now just thinking about it.

For Caroline's part, she set her elbows on the table and covered her face with her hands. He didn't know if she was hiding her shame or her delight. Tears, maybe. But when she finally lowered her hands, there were no tears in her eyes and her expression was impassive, giving him no clue as to her emotions.

She said, "If this lawyer pays you so well, why do you live in a place less appealing than your room at the Cypress Lodge?"

"Because a rathole comes with no responsibilities, and because I've got expenses that keep me on a tight budget despite hefty paychecks and bonuses." She gave him a questioning look, and he felt his shirt pocket for his pack of cigarettes, wishing he dared light up. "Alimony. Times two."

"You were married twice?"

"The first time to prove to myself that I could."

"Could what?"

"Forget you. The second divorce proved I couldn't."

She held his gaze for a long moment, then got up quickly and crossed the room to the sink, where she turned on the faucet, then immediately turned it off. "Stop saying things like that."

"Sue me."

She spun around, anger flashing in her eyes. "Don't be cute, Dodge. You can't flip off this crisis with one of your catchphrases. This situation—"

"Sucks," he said, coming to his feet and advancing on her. "That's what this situation does. Are you ashamed?"

"Ashamed?"

"Why haven't you told Berry who I am?"

"Why haven't *you*?"

That stopped him in his tracks. For the life of him, he couldn't think of a comeback. *"Shit."*

A long, taut silence stretched between them. Eventually she said quietly, "I shouldn't have called you. You should never have sent me your phone number."

Several years ago, on a night when he was particularly drunk, lonely, remorseful, and maudlin, he'd written his cell phone number on a postcard along with two words. *Sue me.* His catchphrase, she'd called it. He supposed it was, because he'd known that, when she read those two words, she would know immediately whose phone number it was. The postcard had a picture of Margaret Mitchell's house on it, so she would also know that it had come from Atlanta.

It did his old, thudding heart good to know that she hadn't fed the postcard into the office shredder, or torn it into tiny bits and flung them to the four winds. "Nobody forced you to keep my phone number, Caroline. I didn't even know that you'd received it until you called last night. When I mailed you the card, I didn't know if you still worked at that company. I addressed it to Caroline King, but I didn't know if you went by your name or his."

"I kept mine."

"Why?"

"Professional reasons."

"What did he think about that?"

"He didn't object."

Dodge's heart felt like it was in a goddamn vise, but he had to ask, had to know. "Why'd you marry him?"

"Dodge—"

"Tell me. Why?"

"Because I wanted to!"

"To spite me?"

"Don't flatter yourself."

"Did you love him?"

"Yes."

"You loved him."

"*Yes.*"

"After me, after *us,* was it that easy—"

He broke off when suddenly her eyes darted to a point behind him. He whipped around. Berry was standing in the open doorway, her gaze bouncing between them. "What's going on?"

Caroline was the first to speak. "As it turns out, our guest is very opinionated about how long spaghetti should boil." She smiled at Dodge, who forced a similar expression. Or tried. Caroline continued the charade. "In any case, it won't be long now. If you'd like to wash up, Dodge, there's a powder room, just . . ."

She motioned, and he mumbled, "Yeah, sure, thanks," and excused himself as he moved past Berry out of the steamy kitchen.

Through dinner, Caroline carried the conversation. He followed as well as he could, trying not to stumble, mindful that Berry was quiet but keenly observant. She watched him even when she was pretending not to.

Physically, she looked like Caroline, thank God. But she was his kid, too. If she'd inherited any of his deduction skills, this charade wasn't going to last long. He thought that he and Caroline were probably trying too hard to act normal, and that the effort was transparent. Or maybe he was just being paranoid.

Caroline pressed him into talking about some of the interesting cases he had worked on. He gave them a more detailed account of Derek and Julie Mitchell's romance.

"Wasn't conventional," he said. "Not by a long shot. The stakes were high for both of them, but they fell hard for each other, and that was all she wrote. Now, with the baby on the way, they're positively nauseating. Derek, a former man-about-town, has gone domestic. Uses fringed cloth napkins, for godsake! I'd accuse Julie of emasculating him, but I think she's rather partial to his balls."

Berry blurted a laugh. Caroline blinked with shock, then she, too, laughed. The sound of their laughter made his throat grow tight with emotion.

But the specter of his conversation with Amanda Lofland served as a centerpiece on the dining table. It loomed large. He was glad when the meal finally came to an end and he could excuse himself to go outside and smoke.

On his way out, he said to Berry, "One cigarette. Then we gotta talk about you and Lofland."

CHAPTER 10

SKI WAS ALMOST UPON THE MAN WHEN HE SPUN AROUND, PISTOL in hand, aimed straight at Ski's head. "Whoa!"

"Son of a bitch!" Dodge dropped his gun hand and gave the deputy a baleful look. "I almost shot you."

"That would have been bad for both of us."

"Worse for you." Dodge returned his revolver to its holster at the small of his back.

Ski asked, "Do you have a concealed handgun license?"

"In Georgia."

"This is Texas."

Dodge shrugged. "Doesn't GA have reciprocity with the Lone Star State?"

"Didn't you bother to check?"

"No. Does it?"

"Yes."

"Then what's the problem?"

Ski brushed past a sapling and closed the distance between himself and the tree stump where Dodge had been sitting when he came up behind him. The woods were noisy with the soprano choir of insects and the bass tones of bullfrogs on the lakeshore, which had helped cover the sound of his approach through the woods.

The night was hot, there was no breeze. The surrounding trees were stolid and still. Light spilling from the windows of Caroline King's house provided an ambient glow. The two men could see each other but little else.

Dodge returned to his seat on the stump and lit a cigarette. As he fanned out his match, he eyed Ski up and down. "You an Indian, or what? One of those Coushatta from around here?"

"Do I look like an Indian?"

"I didn't hear you till you were only a few yards away from me. Barely had time to get my pistol."

Ski crouched down at the base of a pine, sitting on the heels of his boots and putting his back to the rough bark. "Army. Special Forces. Covert missions."

"You're good."

"If I was good, I'd have slit your throat before you knew I was here."

"Did you think I might be Starks returning to the scene of the crime?"

Ski shook his head. "I smelled your tobacco smoke. He isn't a smoker."

The older man considered him for a moment. "How come you left the Army?"

"I got wounded."

"Iraq?"

"Afghanistan. Before it became the place to be," he said drily. "I got shot. Spent months recovering. By the time I was released from the hospital, my stint was almost over. I didn't re-up."

Dodge kept smoking, saying nothing. For reasons Ski couldn't explain, he would like to win this man's approval. Short of that, he'd like to alleviate the contempt with which Dodge Hanley seemed to regard him.

"I already had my degree, but I went back to UT, took courses in criminology, then brought my advanced degree back here to my hometown."

"Why this pissant burg? Why not a metropolitan department?"

"I like to ski."

Dodge's expression went blank. "I don't follow."

"Waterski. Boat. Fish. Hike. Big cities don't allow for much of that."

Dodge harrumphed. "Or, could be you're lazy and lack ambition."

"That's been said." He stated it frankly, without apology or contradiction.

Dodge kept his eyes on the deputy as he ground out his cigarette against the stump. "You like to ski. Is that how you got your nickname?"

Ski picked a chunk of pine bark off the ground and bounced it in his palm. "One summer night—I think between ninth and tenth grades—me and some buddies got a few bottles of rotgut whiskey, sneaked out a motorboat belonging to one of the guys' dads. I took a dare. Broke my arm, a few ribs, and my collarbone. From then on I was called Ski."

"What was the dare?"

"To slalom a half mile barefoot and blindfolded."

Dodge gurgled a laugh. "Jesus."

"I might have been sober enough to pull it off, but the guy driving the boat was wasted. Pulled me right into the shallows and a grove of cypresses." He caught himself chuckling over the reckless stunt, then sobered and assumed his professional demeanor. "Now, if I catch somebody driving a boat while drinking, I haul him to jail. No leniency, no excuses."

Dodge lit another cigarette.

After a time, Ski said, "Who are you? And don't tell me a friend of the family, because you've got cop written all over you."

"Former cop. Currently, an investigator for a law firm in Atlanta."

"Okay."

"What?"

"What are you doing here?"

"Freelance work."

"You came to Ms. King's aid on real short notice."

"I'd done some work for one of her friends in Houston, years back. She recommended me."

"You just dropped everything and came flying down here?"

"I was told Caroline King has lots of money, and I need the extra income. I've got two greedy, bloodsucking ex-wives."

Ski wondered what he'd done to make Dodge Hanley think he was stupid enough to swallow that bullshit. He considered revealing what he'd learned after making some fact-finding calls today, but, for the time being, he decided to play along and pretend to be as ignorant as the stump Dodge was sitting on.

Ski said, "Besides smoking, what were you doing out here?"

Angling the smoke away from Ski, Dodge exhaled and pointed toward the lake. "I thought maybe Starks came by boat. But I nosed around the dock and shoreline and didn't see any evidence of that." He came back to Ski with an arch look. "Nothing as solid as those fresh tire tracks you found."

Ski smiled wryly. "Who'd you torture?"

"No waterboarding necessary. You hang out at a county courthouse long enough, you hear things. Never knew one of them that didn't leak like a rusty pipe."

Ski considered the older man for a long moment, then, making a decision, stood up and angled his head back toward the woods. "Want to take a walk?"

Dodge came to his feet. "Lead on."

"Put out the cigarette. I don't want you burning down our forest."

Dodge sucked in a lungful of smoke and muttered a string of grousing swearwords as he exhaled. He ground out the cigarette, then fell in behind as Ski plowed through the underbrush, pushing aside tree limbs and adroitly sidestepping natural obstacles, retracing the way he'd come but without worrying about how much noise he was making. "I left my flashlight up here a ways. Can you see okay?"

"Don't worry about me," Dodge grumbled.

Ski ducked under a tree branch and hoped Dodge saw it in time to do the same. He hadn't planned to share any aspects of the case but found himself inviting the former cop's input. "The three-way stop where Lake Road dead-ends? The bait shop?"

"Yeah?"

"I talked to a guy who was there about midnight last night, pumping gas." Pride prevented him from telling the veteran investigator that a civilian had actually tracked down the bass fisherman.

"Kinda late to be pumping gas."

"He was getting his boat ready to take out first thing this morning. Wanted to have that chore done so he could get on the lake by daylight."

"That's one of the reasons I never fished. It starts too early."

"So," Ski continued, "he's at the pump filling his gas can when this guy pulls a Toyota up to the side of the building. Time roughly coincides with Ms. Malone's 911 call."

"Did the vehicle come from this direction?"

"It did."

"The fisherman is sure it was a Toyota?"

"Positive. His daughter has one like it. He said the driver got out and stumbled into the men's room."

"Exterior entrance?"

"Right."

"Stumbled?"

"He demonstrated it to me. Looked like limping. When the gas can is full, the fisherman thinks maybe he ought to check on the guy. So he moseys over to the men's room, knocks on the door, and says to the guy inside that he couldn't help but notice that he was limping and asks if everything's all right, does he need some help. The guy hollers through the door—"

"He doesn't open it?"

"No. He tells the fisherman that he's fine. He just came in to 'take a piss.' Those words. The fisherman is a die-hard evangelical and wanted to hear no more of—I quote—'that kind of filthy language.'"

"He sounds like a barrel of laughs."

Ski stopped to retrieve his flashlight from the crotch of a tree where he'd left it. He clicked it on and turned to check on Dodge, who'd been keeping up, but barely. The older man was huffing. "Are you all right?"

"I've got on city shoes."

His shoes weren't to blame for his wheezing like a malfunctioning bagpipe. "You need to lose the cigarettes."

"Walk."

Ski directed the beam of light to the ground, which made the trekking much easier. "The fisherman went on his way and didn't think any more about it."

"Not even when he heard there'd been a shooting in the vicinity around that time of night?"

"He was out on the lake all day. Didn't learn about the incident until he got home this afternoon, and by then we were contacting him."

"Did he describe the guy?"

"He got a fairly good look because there's a light above the restroom door. Oren Starks's general height, weight, and age. Receding hairline. The guy was wearing khaki slacks and a dark golf shirt. Ms. Malone said Starks had on khaki slacks and a navy golf shirt."

"No one coached the fisherman? He hadn't heard that description on TV or from his wife when he got home from his fishing trip?"

"He says no, and I don't think this guy would lie."

Dodge hawked up a wad of phlegm and spat. "Fuck no. Not if he takes exception to the word *piss.*"

Ski chuckled. "Plus, I showed him a faxed photo of Starks that I got from the marketing firm's employment records. Fisherman said he was ninety-five percent sure that was the guy."

"Not one hundred?"

"On account of it was dark and he was twenty or so yards away." Ski motioned forward. "It's just ahead."

The flashlight beam picked up the yellow tape that had been strung around a small area that appeared to be the cul-de-sac of an overgrown track. "My guess," Ski said, "is that when the house was being built, the construction crew pulled some of their vehicles off the road and parked them in here where it was shady, and to keep from cluttering up the area in front of the house.

"When the house was completed, the track and clearing became overgrown with disuse." He shone the light down on the tire tracks in the dirt. "Fresh. And they weren't made by heavy equipment. I discovered them just after daylight this morning, got a man out here pronto. He's no expert, mind you, but he made a pretty good cast."

"Lucky it didn't rain last night."

Ski nodded. "I'm rushing up the match, but I'm betting the tires will be standard-issue Toyota."

"Find anything besides the tracks?"

"Scuffed footprints." Ski shone the light onto the ground. "Unfortunately, nothing we could imprint."

"Candy wrapper, bottle cap, piece of cloth?"

"Nope. I've combed the area twice myself and had two other deputies do the same. Nothing. But, if you know what to look for, Starks left a clear trail to the house."

He showed Dodge a skinny branch that had recently been broken and was hanging limply from the trunk of the tree, also a patch of grass that had been trampled on. "Ms. Malone said he was no outdoorsman."

Dodge studied several broken limbs that Ski spotlighted. "He doesn't have your pathfinder skills, that's for sure."

The older man was thoughtfully gnawing the inside of his cheek, indicating to Ski there was more on his mind. He asked, "What are you thinking?"

"Why'd he stop at the bait shop and go to the men's room, risk being seen?"

"I hear ya. Sounds too careless for the controlled individual Ms. Malone described, doesn't it? But she also said that Starks was unhinged last night. He'd just shot somebody. He wasn't thinking straight. Or maybe he *was* being his orderly self and went into the restroom to assess the injury to his leg."

"In other words," Dodge said, "you don't have a clue."

Ski had the grace to smile. "I'm open to ideas."

"Who the hell knows why anybody does anything? I don't. The fact is, Starks made the stop. He was seen. What does that give you, Deputy?"

"Evidence that he was indeed here last night."

Dodge's eyes narrowed. "You doubted that?"

Ski gave a noncommittal shrug. "It confirms Ms. Malone's and Lofland's statements. It explains why neither heard the car either coming or going."

"Okay."

"Once we get a positive ID on these tire prints, we'll know the make and model of the car, and I can get an APB out on it. There's no Toyota registered to Oren Starks, but Ms. Malone said he would be too smart to drive his own car."

"But dumb enough to leave fresh tire tracks." Dodge had been musing out loud, but when Ski gave him the high sign to continue his thought, he said, "This guy's supposed to be a genius, right?"

Following his thought, Ski said, "Being smart doesn't necessarily make someone a good criminal."

"No, but it helps." Dodge motioned down at the incriminating tire tracks. "This is just plain stupid."

"Stupid like fleeing the scene of the crime and going directly to a place where he'd be exposed."

"Yeah, stupid like that," Dodge said. "I don't suppose the pious fisherman got the license plate number on the Toyota."

"We're not that lucky. He wasn't definite on the color, either. 'Dark,' that's all he could tell me."

"You're gonna piss off a lot of innocent Toyota drivers who'll be stopped."

"Can't be helped." Ski waited a beat, then asked, "Have you seen enough?"

"I may come back, take a look around. If it's okay."

"You're asking permission?"

"Not really."

"What I thought."

Ski followed the outlining tape to the other side of the clearing and then walked along the overgrown track till they reached the road. His SUV was parked partially in the ditch. He opened the driver's door and reached in for a bottle of water. He passed it to Dodge, who thanked him, uncapped it, and took a drink.

"Do you need a minute to catch your breath?" Ski asked.

Dodge recapped the water bottle and tossed it back into the SUV. "Any day of the week, son, I could still whip your butt."

"Not in a fair fight."

"I never fight fair. Fair gets you killed. Didn't the Army teach you anything?"

The two men sized each other up as they had the first time they'd laid eyes on each other in the hospital corridor. Finally Dodge seemed to reach a decision. He dug into his pants pocket, withdrew something, and, reaching for Ski's hand, slapped the object into his palm.

"Amanda Lofland's cell phone."

Ski looked at the phone in his hand, then back into the private investigator's implacable eyes.

"I found it," he said. "In the hospital cafeteria."

"They don't have a lost and found at the hospital?" Ski asked.

"I checked around. Didn't see one. I was in a hurry."

"So you had to turn on the phone in order to discover who it belonged to."

Dodge gave a half shrug, a very unapologetic half shrug.

Ski said, "I'll see that Mrs. Lofland gets it back."

"I'm sure she'll appreciate it."

They exchanged another long, assessing stare, then Ski motioned for Dodge to climb into the SUV. He went around the hood, and Ski heard him cursing as his city shoes sought purchase on the steep bank of the ditch.

As they drove past the car parked at the end of the lane leading to the house, Dodge remarked on it. "I noticed him there this afternoon. Security guard?"

"Reserve deputy. We've got a dozen men and women we can't

afford to keep on the payroll, but we use them in emergencies. There's another one watching the dock."

"Bumped into him earlier," Dodge said. "He looked me over good."

Ski smiled, thinking *I'll bet he did.* He said, "I don't want to take any chances that Starks will come back and carry out his threat to kill Ms. Malone."

"I'm sure you don't. Her mama is a town big shot. If something happened to Caroline King's daughter, your boss would have your ass."

Ski gave him a hard look. "That's a lousy thing to say."

"Sue me." Then, "Okay, okay, that was a potshot." After a moment, he asked, "What about the municipal police? Are they of any help to you?"

"Five-man operation. Mostly they break up fights at the high school football games and organize the Fourth of July parade."

"I figured."

"We of the sheriff's office are the main peace officers. It's up to us—"

"Up to *you.*"

Ski shrugged. "Up to me to find Starks."

"Well, he's not at the Cypress Lodge. I've already checked."

"Thanks," Ski said drily. "I'll mark it off my list." Then after a short pause, "I thought you might be bunking out here at Ms. King's house."

Dodge stayed stubbornly silent, ignoring Ski's bait and saying nothing as they approached the house. The headlights swept the front door just as Caroline came through it and stepped onto the porch. She looked relieved when she saw Dodge in the passenger seat.

As he alighted, she said, "I was beginning to think you'd fallen into the lake or that a gator had got you."

"You've got gators?"

She looked back and forth between Dodge and Ski, who came up the steps along with him. Obviously she was wondering where and how they had joined up. "What's going on?"

"I don't have Starks in custody yet," Ski said, "but there are a couple of things to report, and I've got a few more questions for Ms. Malone."

"She's inside."

Caroline led the two men into the entryway and motioned them toward the living area. "I'll get Berry." But before she was out of earshot, Ski's stomach rumbled noisily, bringing her up short.

"Sorry, ma'am."

She smiled at him. "No apology necessary."

Berry was just finishing the dinner cleanup when her mother came into the kitchen. "Have you already put the leftover spaghetti away?"

"Just now."

Caroline opened the refrigerator and took out the sealed container, handing it to Berry. "Would you please warm a plate of it for Deputy Nyland?"

"Sorry?"

Caroline took utensils from the flatware drawer. "He and Dodge just came in together."

Berry glanced through the kitchen window toward the back of the property, where the investigator had disappeared almost an hour ago, saying for her to be ready to discuss her relationship with Ben when he returned after having one cigarette. "How'd that happen?"

"I have no idea. But they're here, and Deputy Nyland admitted that he hasn't eaten all day. The least we can do is offer him some supper."

"The least we can do? Mother, he hates me."

"Don't be silly. And when you come, bring the tea pitcher, please."

Her mother left the kitchen, taking the flatware, a place mat, and a napkin with her.

Berry stared at the food container that had been thrust into her hand, and it felt as alien as all the other disruptive elements that had been thrust at her over the past twenty-four hours.

A violent act, something totally beyond her realm of experience.

A criminal investigation, which was foreign to her.

A deputy sheriff, who was blatantly skeptical of every word out of her mouth.

A private investigator, whose presence in her life was inexplicable.

She placed the food container in the microwave and set the timer. As she watched it count down, she puzzled over her mother's decision to retain the services of Dodge Hanley, a man who was rough around the edges, to say the least. He was the antithesis of Caroline's other acquaintances, who were generally prosperous businessmen, bankers, lawyers, doctors, cultured and refined men like Berry's dad had been.

Moreover, Caroline, who was ever a lady, seemed to take no exception to Dodge's off-color comments. That, to Berry, signaled a worry. There was only one explanation for Caroline's tolerance of his coarseness: she felt he was necessary to them. He was the kind of man you wanted at your back during a fight, which meant that her mother expected one.

Berry feared one, too. Oren wouldn't give up. That she knew. His obsession with her had caused her world to tilt. She had used the last two months to try to get it back on solid footing. But last night, it had been overturned and was now completely out of control. *Her* control. She seemed incapable of reclaiming command.

But she must. And in order for that to happen, she recognized that things would get worse before they got better.

The microwave dinged. She dumped the spaghetti onto a plate, added two slices of garlic bread, then put the plate and the iced tea pitcher on a tray and carried it into the dining area, where the other three were gathered around the table. Her mother had laid a place setting in front of the deputy, who stood up when Berry approached the table.

"I hope I didn't put you to any trouble."

"No trouble." She served him the plate of food and set the tea pitcher on the table. He didn't sit down until she'd taken a chair.

Then he didn't touch anything until her mother said, "Don't let it get cold." He put the napkin in his lap, picked up the fork, and dug in.

He was such a *presence*. In the semicircular dining area, he seemed exceptionally large, and not only because of his physical size. He was overbearing in intrinsic ways, too. Berry was aware of every blink, every motion. He robbed her of air. But she seemed the only one to be affected.

While he ate, Dodge, with Ski's permission, told them about Oren's coming to the house on foot from a hidden parking space nearer the main road, and his apparent stop at the bait shop restroom.

"That makes me feel a little better about failing to get his license plate number," Berry said.

"You couldn't have if you'd wanted to," her mother said.

Dodge asked her if Oren had ever driven a Toyota.

"I don't know. I never paid attention to his car."

"You never went anywhere with him?" Ski asked.

She hesitated and looked across at Dodge. "Should we wait until morning, when Mr. Carlisle can join us?"

Before Dodge could answer, Ski said, "I'm only after information about Starks. You're not a suspect."

Dodge's eyes narrowed on him as he forked spaghetti into his mouth. "Okay, Deputy, go ahead. But watch it. Berry, if you're uncomfortable answering a question, don't."

Ski looked at Berry and let his raised eyebrows repeat the question because his mouth was full. She said, "I never rode anywhere with Oren."

He held her gaze for several seconds, then blotted his mouth with his napkin. "Thanks, that was delicious."

There wasn't a morsel left on the plate. He'd used the bread to sop up the extra sauce. Since the thank-you had been directed at her, Berry said, "You're welcome. But all I did was warm it up. Mother actually made it. I'm a terrible cook."

He smiled across at her mother. "I'm glad my stomach growled in front of you."

Warmly, she returned his smile.

Dodge shifted in his seat, touched the pocket of his shirt where he kept his cigarettes, then folded his arms across his chest, looking surly and put out over something.

Ski pushed his plate aside and rested his forearms on the edge of the table. He turned toward Berry. "I talked to several of the female co-workers whose names you gave me."

"They told you about Oren's inappropriate flirting?"

"More like *inept* flirting. Teasing that fell flat, awkwardness in social situations, that sort of thing. They described more of a nuisance than a creep."

"He's a *creep,*" she said stubbornly. "Intelligent. Even genius. But as a human being, his ick factor is off the charts. He wasn't as persistent with the others as he was with me and Sally Buckland. Did you talk to her?"

"Yes."

"And?"

He divided a look between Dodge and Caroline before coming back to her. "Maybe we should wait on your lawyer after all."

On the surface, his statement seemed meant for her benefit. But it also had the undertones of a dare, from which Berry wouldn't back down. "Ask your questions."

"Berry."

"It's fine, Dodge."

"Not fine, it's damn foolish."

Ignoring him, she held Ski Nyland's stare. "Well?"

"Sally Buckland told me in no uncertain terms that Starks had nothing whatsoever to do with her resignation from Delray, and that to suggest such a thing was ridiculous. She also said that if you had called him a stalker you were lying."

Berry's breath slowly leaked from between her lips, which were parted in astonishment. "Why would Sally say that?" Then, her voice rising, she demanded, "Why would she say that?"

"Berry—"

"No, Mother," she said, cutting her off. "Something is terribly wrong here." She scraped back her chair, got up and rounded it, then leaned against it as she faced the other three.

"I'm telling you that Oren made Sally's work environment so miserable, she resigned. He redirected his attention to me. I have no idea why Sally is denying it now, but I'm telling you the truth."

"I believe you, Berry," her mother said. "In fact, no one here has disputed you. So please sit down and let's talk this out."

"Thank you, I prefer to stand. But I do want to talk this out." She shot a hard look at Ski, wishing that just once she could cause a disturbance in his steady gray gaze. "Well, what else?"

"Did you attend the office Christmas party with Starks?"

She dropped her head forward until her chin was resting on her chest. She sensed her mother's disbelief, Dodge's unspoken reproof, the deputy's condemnation. Then she brought her head up and shook back her hair in a small show of defiance.

"Yes, I agreed to be Oren's date to the Christmas party. I thought that if I went out with him once, he would stop pestering me. The party seemed a safer alternative than being alone with him for an entire evening. We would be surrounded by people we knew.

"I accepted his invitation on the condition that we meet there rather than his picking me up at home. I drove myself there and drove myself home. Alone. I told you the truth about being in Oren's car, Deputy Nyland. I never rode with him anywhere."

"What about the party?"

"Oren made certain that everyone knew we were paired for the evening. He didn't leave my side the entire night. He hovered. He treated me with familiarity, touching me constantly. The memory of it revolts me.

"I endured his manhandling, hoping that, once he could boast of having had a date with me, he would be satisfied and go away. But it didn't turn out that way."

She paused, stared into near space for a moment before focusing on the deputy again and continuing. "The last workday before the Christmas holiday, Oren received his dismissal notice. He turned to me for consolation, as though I was his lover, friend, champion."

She paused again and gave them each in turn a look. "That's when the stalking began."

Wanting to lance all the boils at once, she looked at Dodge. "During your tête-à-tête with Amanda Lofland this afternoon, she spilled the beans about Ben and me."

Dodge nodded unhappily.

Facing the deputy, she said, "There was a time when Ben and I had more than a working relationship." Noting his lack of reaction, she added, "But you don't seem surprised to learn that."

He tipped his head slightly. "Ms. Lofland called me late this afternoon, said maybe I ought to know that you'd attended the company Christmas party with Oren Starks and that you and her husband had been lovers."

"He wasn't her husband then," Berry said with asperity. "And until today, I didn't know that Amanda was even aware of it. In any case, it's ancient history and has no bearing on anything, especially what happened here last night." She pried her tight grip from the back of the chair and began to pace.

"Ben and I were working late one night, went for drinks afterward, felt like blowing off some steam, and one thing led to another. Being co-workers, seeing each other every day in the office, added a bit of spice to what would otherwise have been a rather bland attraction.

"Soon even that naughty element wasn't enough to make it worthwhile. We didn't want a pretend romance to damage our solid working relationship, and we realized how silly it was to continue when neither of us was emotionally invested in the affair. So we agreed to return to what we'd been before, platonic friends and co-workers.

"It was a fling that lasted less than a month. He hadn't even met Amanda yet. When he did, I was one of the first people he told about this 'amazing woman.' I was pleased for him. And when they got engaged, I threw them a party. Mother, you remember."

"You rented out the party room at the country club."

Berry nodded and looked at Ski. "That's it. That's the big, bad secret. Until that ugly encounter in the hospital, Amanda has always been cordial toward me. Maybe today's meltdown happened because she's upset and worried about Ben's medical condition. Maybe her outburst was a delayed reaction to the trauma of hearing that he'd been shot."

She raised her hands helplessly at her sides. "I don't know when Ben told her about us, whether it was before or after they married, or this morning when he woke up in the recovery room and realized that he'd been shot while wearing only his undershorts in my house. *I don't know.*

"What I *do* know is that my time with Ben was short-lived and forgettable. Nothing romantic has happened between us since it ended. Certainly nothing adulterous happened here yesterday."

Ski got up and rounded the table, coming to stand directly in front of her. "In the guest room, last night when I looked, the bed was still made."

"I can't account for that. Maybe Ben was sitting in the chair reading, maybe he was on the toilet, maybe he was . . . I don't know what he was doing because I didn't see him after we went upstairs, said goodnight, and retired to our separate rooms."

"On your bed, the covers had been pulled back."

"Nyland, what are you getting at?" Dodge asked.

Neither she nor Ski responded. She didn't know why this was such a sticking point, but she wanted to eliminate it as an issue between her and the deputy. "I turned down the bed before I went into the bathroom to shower."

Dodge said, "What's the deal with the beds? In fact, what difference does it make if she and Lofland were screwing their brains out? The important thing is that this jerk-off Starks—"

"I know what the important thing is." Ski angrily cut him off but without shifting his gaze away from Berry's.

Dodge fired back. "Then why are you harping on the sleeping arrangements?"

"Her relationship with Lofland might relate to Starks's motive."

"She's told you what their relationship is," Dodge argued. "Now can we move on?"

But Ski didn't look like he was prepared to move on, or to go anywhere, until he was completely satisfied on this point.

"Ben and I had a meaningless affair years ago," she said. "*Nothing happened* here yesterday or last night except what I've told you."

"Okay. Fine. Great. I'm glad that's cleared up," Dodge said. "Nyland, you happy now?"

Ski didn't flinch.

Berry took a deep breath. "In answer to your question of earlier today—"

"Berry."

"Dodge, sit down," Caroline said.

"She has rights. She doesn't have to say anything else."

"Maybe she wants to."

Berry heard them, but only with half an ear. Ski's focus was riveted on her, and she couldn't escape it. "In answer to your earlier question, I was fully clothed during dinner. I undressed only to get into the shower. It was that female EMT who suggested I might want to put something on. Before she called my attention to it, I hadn't realized that I was still naked."

CHAPTER 11

This was Davis Coldare's lucky night.

"But not here where somebody might walk past and see us." Lisa Arnold removed his hand from between her thighs, pushed him off her, and sat up, pulling her tank top back into place. "In fact, not in the backseat at all. That is *so* retro."

Davis, his erection throbbing, his brain foggy with lust, couldn't immediately think of a suitable place other than his car in which to have carnal knowledge of Lisa Arnold. "Uh . . . I don't—"

"A motel." Primly she readjusted her denim skirt to cover the area Davis had been exploring. It wasn't virgin territory.

"Motel?" he echoed stupidly. The concept didn't click because of the sensory clutter inside his head.

Lisa opened the car door and got out. "Just drive. I'll tell you where to go."

She had already switched to the passenger seat by the time Davis's cerebral synapses fired. Grimacing, he tucked himself back into his underwear, then, holding up his jeans with his left hand, got out of the backseat and into the front behind the wheel. He started the car and navigated it through the lanes of the drive-in theater, which was open only during the summer months, and where tonight a double feature of slasher movies was playing. Like Lisa and him, most people in the parked cars hadn't come to watch the films.

When the theater exit spilled them onto the highway, Lisa instructed that he turn left and reminded him to switch on his headlights. She reached across the console and slid her hand inside his jeans, squeezing him through his underwear. "Don't lose this before we get there."

"Not a chance," he panted. She began stroking him, and his eyes crossed, making it difficult to keep the center yellow stripe of the two-lane highway in focus.

"Do you have condoms?" she asked.

"Uh . . ."

"If you don't, I do. But from now on, it's your responsibility to bring them, okay?"

"Okay." He agreed—he would have agreed to anything—when actually all he heard was *from now on,* which implied a future of sexual encounters.

"Just up there on the right," she said. "I don't know the name of it, but it's got a raccoon on the sign."

He knew the place. The run-down motor court had been there for as long as he could remember, probably much longer than he'd been alive. He'd driven past it countless times without giving it a thought. Never in his wildest dreams would he have imagined he would be coming here with Lisa Arnold, the girl with the most promising put-out reputation in Merritt High School.

He pulled up to the lighted office, where a red neon Vacancy sign blinked off and on. Getting a room might cost him every penny he'd earned mowing lawns this week, but he shot one look across at Lisa and figured if it cost two weeks' income, it would be worth it to get on her. Guys who'd been with her said a blow job was practically guaranteed. But since she had insisted on someplace other than the backseat, maybe she was planning on doing more than her standard b.j. Thinking of the possibilities made his mind reel.

"Can you walk with this?" She tugged on him playfully, and

he moaned. If she made him come too soon, he'd die of mortification and then he'd kill her for spoiling it. Giggling at his obvious discomfort, she said, "Guess not. Give me forty bucks."

She released him. He raised his hips off the seat and braced his feet against the floorboard so he could wedge his hand into the pocket of his jeans to get his wallet. He pulled out two twenties, which she plucked from his hand. Shooting him a cheeky grin over her shoulder, she got out. As she walked toward the office, he watched her ass, barely covered by her skirt, covered not at all by her thong, as he'd recently discovered. He groaned with desire.

Working the check-in desk was a fat lady with stringy gray hair and a blue tattoo that covered the entirety of her flabby arm. Looking miffed for being drawn away from the magazine she'd been thumbing through, she grabbed Lisa's twenties and slapped a key onto the counter. The transaction took less than fifteen seconds.

Davis was glad Lisa hadn't been required to sign a register or anything. He was gonna go through with this no matter what, but he'd just as soon his parents never found out about it. Lisa was the kind of girl his dad—his mom, too, during one especially embarrassing conversation—had warned him to beware of.

As Lisa got back into the car, her short skirt rode up her thighs, flashing him a glimpse of the heaven that awaited and obliterating from his mind parental lectures about common sense and morality. Banished by her wink were warnings about fatal diseases and unwanted pregnancies, either of which could destroy plans for a college baseball scholarship and, by extension, his life.

"All set," she said. "Number eight. Straight ahead, on the end."

He got the impression she'd been here before.

He parked in front of room number eight. Lisa got out. As Davis alighted, he wondered if maybe he should pull his car around to the back of the building, where it couldn't be seen from the road. But his parents had gone to a card party at some friends' house tonight, and they lived on the opposite side of town. His parents wouldn't be driving past here on their way home.

Still holding up his jeans with one hand, he stumbled toward the door, where Lisa was waiting. She handed him the room key. "Be a gentleman."

"Yes, ma'am." He took the key from her and made several stabs at the doorknob, missing the keyhole each time.

Lisa moved close and sandwiched his biceps between her fantasy-inducing breasts. She licked the rim of his ear and whispered, "I hope your aim improves once we get inside."

He rammed the key into the slot and twisted it, unlocking the door. "Don't worry about my aim. I'll hit the target."

"Oooh. Are we talking G-spot?"

He pushed the door open and stepped into the room. He felt along the wall for the light switch. When he flipped it up and the light came on, the last thing Davis Coldare expected to see was the startled, disheveled man standing at the side of the bed.

Berry was lying on her back, staring at the ceiling of the guest bedroom, when Caroline tapped once on the door and asked permission to come in. As soon as she cleared the threshold, Berry asked, "Is he gone?"

Caroline gave her daughter a wry smile. "He passed on dessert and coffee. But he couldn't have stayed even if he'd wanted to. He got a call on his cell phone and tore out of here. Dodge went with him."

"They're a team now?"

"Not exactly." Caroline folded a chenille throw and laid it across the arm of a chair, avoiding direct eye contact with Berry. "Dodge wanted to know the nature of the call, and when Ski told him it was official, Dodge said, 'Fine. Don't tell me. It can be a surprise when I get there.'

"Ski pointed out that Dodge didn't know where he was going, and Dodge said he would after he followed him. I suppose Ski saw the futility of arguing. Dodge climbed into his SUV along with him, and away they went."

Berry sat up. "Maybe the call was to tell him that Oren has been apprehended."

"Let's hope." Caroline sat down on the edge of the bed and

reached for her daughter's hand. She placed it palm to palm with hers and linked their fingers. "You're not yourself, Berry."

"Me?" she exclaimed. "I've been thinking the same about you."

"Good try, but that tactic didn't work when you were in middle school, and it doesn't work now. You can't redirect this conversation."

"You've been onto my manipulation?"

"Since you were old enough to exercise it. But I'm not sure *manipulation* is the correct word. It denotes some mean purpose. You were never mean, just extremely clever."

"Not that clever. You caught on. And here I thought I was being so smart."

"Smart you are." Caroline's tone changed, became softer, more serious. "Also unshakable and in command of your emotions. It's unlike you to fly off the handle the way you did with Ski."

"'Ski'? 'Dodge'? I've never known you to get so chummy with men you've only just met. Although . . ."

"You're doing it again. This isn't about me. It's about *you*."

"Although," Berry continued stubbornly, "I believe you knew Dodge Hanley before today. And I'm not trying to divert the conversation away from me and my problems. We'll get to them, I promise.

"But first, I insist on being brought into the loop, because, up to this point, I've been left out." She lay back down and stacked her hands behind her head. "I'm listening. Who is this guy? You met him before today. I know you did. Otherwise you'd be put off by his manner and vocabulary."

Caroline sighed. "All right, I confess. I met Dodge in Houston a few years ago."

"How?"

"Through my friend, when she retained him to do some private investigating for her. She was uncomfortable with the whole idea. It seemed sordid, sleazy, a B-movie-type action to take. Dodge, being Dodge, made her even more apprehensive. So she wanted me to meet him and give her my honest opinion. Did he seem reputable? Worth his fee? That sort of thing. I had no experience in those matters, either, but she valued my judgment of people in general."

"Which friend? Do I know her?"

"Yes, but I can't tell you who it is."

"How come?"

"Because that would betray her confidence."

"Did Daddy ever meet him? Dodge, I mean."

Caroline laughed. "Goodness, no. Can you imagine the two of them even being in the same room?"

Berry smiled. Her dad had been a slender man, not very tall, but so dignified that his modest stature went unnoticed. He was tidy and compact, soft-spoken, cultured, and genteel. The polar opposite of Dodge Hanley.

Caroline was saying, "I didn't tell anyone, even Jim, about the straits my friend was in. It was a messy, humiliating situation."

"Cheating husband?"

"All I'll say is that she was desperate, or she would never have sought the services of a private investigator."

Berry mulled over her mother's wording, then asked softly, "Is that why you sought his services? Do you regard my current situation as desperate?"

"Not yet. He'll help keep it from becoming so."

"He's a street fighter."

"I'm sure."

"Irreverent, disrespectful of authority, and beyond the pale."

"I doubt he lets rules get in his way."

"He's unrefined."

"You should have seen him in Mabel's Tearoom."

Berry laughed. "You took him to a tearoom?"

"I had to meet him somewhere." She thought for a moment, then added, "Actually, he handled it with more aplomb than one would expect."

"He's kinda cute," Berry said. "If you're into scruffy."

"I hadn't thought of him in that way."

Berry gave her mother a playful nudge. "Come on. He's cute. Admit it."

"Some women might find him attractive."

Berry grinned at the evasion, mainly because her mother was working so hard at being evasive.

Following an acceptable period of grieving for her dad, Berry had encouraged her mother to start dating, especially when Caroline moved to Merritt, where no one had known her and her dad as a couple. The town had a large retirement-age population. There were a lot of unattached men of suitable age and means available.

Caroline would hear none of it.

"I'm done with that," she had said when Berry suggested she get back in circulation. "I had a good marriage. I had the love of my life. I will never have another."

But Berry continued to hold out the hope that her mother would meet a man who would change her mind. She was beautiful and smart, lovely and fun. She had much to offer, and Berry hated the thought of her living the rest of her life as a single.

"I like Dodge," Berry said now, almost expecting her mother to challenge the definitive statement.

But she didn't. In fact, Caroline was quite earnest when she asked, "Do you?"

"Yeah, I do. Warts and all. What I like best is that he makes no excuses for his warts."

"Then I'm glad I made the decision to retain him."

Worriedly, Berry pulled her lower lip through her teeth. "His purpose is damage control. Is that it?"

"Partially. His investigative skills could also be useful to Ski."

"If he'll use them."

Caroline nodded pensively. "Men are territorial. But Ski strikes me as someone too intelligent to decline help when and if he needs it."

Berry took one hand from behind her head and laid her forearm across her eyes. After a moment, she said, "The affair with Ben."

"You're a grown woman, Berry. Well past having to account to me about your relationships."

"Oh no?" Berry peered up at her from beneath her arm. "Isn't it you who's been giving me none too subtle hints that you'd like to have grandchildren before you're too old and decrepit to play with them?"

Caroline smiled. "I still wish for grandchildren. But," she added with emphasis, "I also understand how important your career is to you, because mine was to me. Simultaneously building a career and raising a family can cause conflicts."

"I haven't ruled out having a husband and children, Mother. My biological clock gongs whenever I see women my age with a toddler or two, husband smiling on with adoration. I'd like that very much.

"But let me assure you, Ben Lofland wasn't a prospective life partner. He and I spent a few harmless nights together. Our affair was hardly worth the federal case that Deputy Nyland made of it."

"He didn't make a federal case of it."

"Close."

"There must be a reason for his preoccupation with it."

"He told you the reason. Oren's motive."

Caroline settled an intuitive look on her, the kind that mothers specialize in.

"What?" Berry demanded.

"Nothing. Never mind."

"*What?*"

Caroline shook her head. "A wild thought. Groundless probably. Pardon the interruption. What were you saying?"

Exasperated, knowing there was more than her mother was willing to say at the moment, Berry tried to remember where she'd left off. "I refuse to wear a hair shirt because of those sleepovers."

"The affair would have taken on less significance if you'd been up front about it."

"I know," Berry admitted. "I should have come clean about it."

"Why didn't you?"

"Amanda. I didn't know if Ben had told her about us, but I was guessing that he hadn't. In which case, I didn't want to spring a past affair on her when she was having to cope with his getting shot, undergoing surgery, all that. I was afraid that, if I told Ski, it would open a can of worms, unnecessarily. I kept quiet to spare

Amanda's feelings and to spare Ben trouble with the wife whom he loves and adores. So much for my good intentions. They blew up in my face."

Caroline spoke quietly. "From here on, I advise you not to withhold anything from Ski."

Berry lowered her arm and looked straight into her mother's eyes. "For instance, you think I should tell him about the phone call I placed to Oren the day before yesterday?"

Caroline looked at her aghast. "Phone call?"

"Thursday afternoon. Oren and I talked for several minutes."

"I don't understand. You came here to *escape* him. Why on earth did you call him?"

"To make amends."

"For what, for heaven's sake?"

Berry worked her way to the other side of the bed and swung her feet to the floor. Moving to the window, she looked out toward the lake, although all she could really see was her own reflection in the windowpane.

"In order to explain, I have to back up," she said. "Do you remember— Of course you remember," she said ruefully. "The day of my big blowup?"

Caroline said nothing. Berry turned her head. Her mother was looking down at her hands. "You were upset, Berry. Justifiably upset. You didn't mean what you said."

"Don't excuse the inexcusable, Mother. At the time I meant it."

A co-worker had received a commendation from an account manager on the day the same manager had criticized some of Berry's work and had gone on to shoot down all her suggestions for correcting it.

Stung and angry, she'd sought out her mother at her real estate office and, for half an hour, had vented her outrage. She'd cited how unfair the criticism of her work had been, how lackluster the praised campaign was. "Which only goes to show how lousy this manager's taste is!" she had exclaimed. "And I have to answer to him. My position in the company is dependent upon this bozo's crummy opinion."

Caroline had tried to placate her, but Berry had refused to hear the reason behind her mother's observations. She'd discounted Caroline's advice to carry on and not to let this minor setback become a major self-fulfilling stall.

"You work harder than anyone I know," Caroline had told her. "You're the most dedicated employee that company has. You're talented. Eventually the right people will notice, and your labor, as well as your patience, will be rewarded."

The soft-spoken encouragement had only caused Berry to seethe. She'd gone to her mother for sympathy and got banalities instead. Seeing red, she'd sneered, "Or, in order to get to the top of my profession, I could skip all that kowtowing and do what you did. I could marry the boss."

Even as she spoke the words, she'd known them to be untrue. For years Caroline had worked diligently late into the evenings, on holidays, and over long weekends. Her success was well deserved, based on intuitiveness and hard work, not nepotism.

Berry had also known how wounding the words were and had regretted them the moment they were spoken. But she hadn't apologized. Instead she'd stormed out, leaving her mother reeling from the unexpected and unwarranted onslaught, the source of which was something deeper than anger and disappointment. With that outburst, Berry had revealed a long-harbored resentment of her mother's achievements.

"When I got home," she said now, "Oren was there waiting for me." She laughed drily. "I remember thinking that I probably deserved that for being so hateful to you. He'd brought me Chinese food. He admonished me for working too hard, too long, for not eating right, and for not taking care of myself properly.

"I was in no mood for more gentle chiding, especially his. So I lost it. I yelled at him, told him to take his moo goo gai pan and get the hell off my porch and out of my life. I told him that I'd had it, that if he bothered me again, I'd sic the police on him.

"At first, he responded weepily. How could I be so cruel as to break his heart, crush his spirit, destroy his dreams? I listened to a few minutes of that, and then I cut him off. I told him that he was a joke to everyone who knew him, but particularly to women. I told him that he was boring, that he was a pest, just *wrong,* and that I wasn't the only one who thought so. I told him that he was creepy and pathetic, and that I couldn't stomach the sight of him."

She rubbed her eyes, wishing she could rub out the memory, too. "I must have struck a chord. Several, in fact. Because he flipped out. Right before my eyes, he morphed into the Oren Starks rendition of Mr. Hyde. Outside a movie theater, I'd never witnessed such a dramatic transformation.

"His face became congested and red with fury like I'd never seen before, Mother. He shouted, 'You can't do this to me! I don't deserve *this*!' He threw the carton of food against my front door. It split open, splattered. He called me horrible names. Said awful, obscene things. He said it was no wonder that I didn't return his affection when Ben Lofland was fucking me."

She shuddered. "I can't even bring myself to repeat all he said, and you don't want to hear it. He ended with a chilling vow to make me sorry for rejecting him. In language more elaborate than that, but that was the gist of it.

"I went inside and bolted the door behind me. I had my cell phone in my hand ready to call 911—that's how afraid I was—but he drove away. I went into the bathroom and threw up. When I was done and was washing my face, I looked into the mirror above the sink."

She paused, then said slowly, "That's when I saw what I'd become. I barely recognized myself, Mother. I was as much a monster as Oren. I had been cruel, I'd said terrible things to him, I'd been horrible to you, the person I love and respect more than anyone in my life. And why? Because I was upset over a hand-slapping I'd received at work."

She turned to face Caroline. "I wanted to succeed at all costs. Ambition had consumed me. I'd lost all perspective. I was jeopardizing my relationships with co-workers, with friends, with *you.*"

Dashing tears off her cheeks, she continued. "Oren made me fear for my life that day. But I was just as scared of the person I'd become. I stayed up that entire night, with all the lights in the house on, afraid he would come back, also afraid that I would change my mind about doing what I had decided must be done. By morning I was packed. I came here, hoping that I would find some balance in my life, find the me that had somehow got lost."

She returned to the side of the bed and sat down beside her mother, who placed her hand between Berry's shoulder blades and began to massage the spot. "I'm proud of you."

Berry looked at her and sputtered a laugh. "*Proud?* After what I've just told you?"

"It's hard to be that brutally honest with oneself, and even harder to act on a self-realization." Caroline kissed her brow. "You called Oren on Thursday afternoon to apologize for the things you'd said to him that afternoon?"

"More or less. I also told him that Ben and I were about to put the finishing touches on the campaign he'd been working on when he was dismissed. It had turned out well. He could be proud of it."

"How did he react to all this?"

"Neutrally. I was actually surprised. He didn't issue dire threats, but he didn't say, 'Let bygones be bygones,' either. When I finished, he said 'Okay,' and hung up. I dusted my hands. I thought we were square. That is, until he ripped open the shower curtain."

"Surely you didn't tell him that you and Ben would be working here on Friday."

"Of course not. But I'm almost certain he's been watching my house, the office. He's smart enough to have figured out that I've been working from another location. He must have followed Ben when he left his house Friday morning to come here.

"Maybe Oren was sitting all day in his car near the road where they found those tire tracks, biding his time, waiting until dark, waiting until he thought he would catch us in bed together."

She raised her hands to her forehead and massaged it, pressing her fingertips hard against her scalp. "What haunts me, Mother, what I fear, is that, by making restitution with Oren, I unwittingly set Ben up to get shot."

"Berry? Sweetheart, wake up."

Berry turned onto her back, moaning for having been shaken out of a deep slumber. She pushed strands of hair off her face and opened her eyes. Her mother, wearing only a short cotton nightgown, was bending over her.

"What time is it?"

"Five-fifteen."

Berry groaned. The lengthy self-castigating conversation with her mother had left her too restless to sleep. After hours of tossing and turning, she'd relented and taken a nonprescription sleeping aid. Now, after less than three hours' sleep, her head was muzzy from the medication, her eyes dry and gritty.

But her mother's tone, her entire aspect, conveyed urgency. "Get up and get dressed. Dodge just called. He said we should come as soon as possible."

Berry threw off the covers. "Come where?"

"To the sheriff's office."

"Have they arrested Oren?"

"Dodge said he would explain when we got there." Caroline was already on her way out of the bedroom. "I'll meet you downstairs."

Berry put on a pair of old jeans and a T-shirt, brushed her teeth, pulled her hair into a ponytail, and, in under five minutes, met her mother at the back door. Caroline set the alarm as they left the house and told Berry that they would take her car and that she would drive.

When they reached the courthouse, they were surprised to find a deputy sheriff obviously waiting for them. He waved Caroline into a reserved parking space and touched the brim of his uniform hat as they hurriedly alighted.

"Ladies. I'm Deputy Stevens. Ski said for me to bring y'all right up."

He led them to an entrance on the ground level that was reserved for personnel only. He punched in a security code on a keypad. The door unlocked with a loud metallic click. He shepherded them inside, then into an elevator, also designated for official use. It whisked them up to the third floor.

The elevator opened directly into a large squad room. The first person they saw was Dodge, who apparently had also been on the lookout for them.

He wasted no time on greetings. "Hated to drag you out of bed. But Ski thought you should hear this, thought *you,*" he said, addressing Berry specifically, "might be able to help."

"Help how? With what?"

Dodge scowled. "Oren Starks has killed a kid."

CHAPTER 12

BEFORE BERRY AND CAROLINE COULD ABSORB DODGE'S shocking statement, their attention was drawn toward the sound of loud and uncontrollable sobbing. A middle-aged couple were seated on a bench against the wall. A younger man wearing a clerical collar was hunkered in front of them, speaking softly, his arms embracing their shoulders in a group hug.

Out of respect, Dodge spoke softly, but his voice vibrated with barely contained fury. "Mr. and Mrs. Coldare. Their sixteen-year-old son, their only child, was shot and killed a few hours ago. By Oren Starks."

Dizziness and nausea swept over Berry. She swayed. Dodge caught her arm. "Hey, steady."

"Sit down," her mother said.

Berry, looking at the grieving couple, gave her head a hard shake. "I'll be all right. They lost their son tonight."

Across the large room, Ski emerged from a smaller office. His and Berry's eyes connected immediately and held as he wove his way through the maze of desks. When he reached her, he said, "I owe you an apology."

"What for?"

"For not taking you seriously enough. I thought that too much was being made of Starks, his threats. I was wrong. I'm sorry."

Berry tamped down a surge of emotion, which would have to be dealt with later. But not now.

He continued, "Anyway, thank you for coming. I thought if you listened while the girl gave her—"

"Girl?"

"I haven't had time to fill in the details," Dodge informed him.

Ski bobbed his head once. "Davis Coldare was with a friend when he was shot. She's okay. Shaky, but uninjured. She picked Starks out of a group of pictures. No question, she said."

"He got away again?"

"The boy fell dead at the girl's feet. She ran for her life. Called 911 from the motel office."

"Motel?" Caroline asked.

"A hasty-tasty." Dodge compressed his lips with regret. "Coupla horny kids just looking for a mattress."

Ski said, "By the time the first responders arrived, Oren Starks was long gone."

"What provoked the shooting?" Berry asked.

"Not a damn thing."

"He just shot this boy for no reason?"

"Wrong place, wrong time for Davis Coldare." He spoke in a tight, angry tone similar to Dodge's.

"My God," Caroline whispered. Berry couldn't bring herself to say anything.

Ski said to her, "I thought if you listened to the girl—Lisa Arnold is her name—if you listened in while she gives us a recorded statement, you might pick up something about Starks. Hear something that might help us. I don't know. Worth a try."

"Of course. Whatever you think."

Apparently he thought she needed assistance walking, because as they retraced his path through the squad room, he kept his hand on the small of her back. "Get her some coffee, Andy," he said as they passed the wide-eyed deputy that Berry recognized as the one who'd been at the lake house the night of the shooting. "Do you take anything in it?" Ski asked her.

"Cream. Milk. Whatever."

"Some of that half-and-half stuff," he told the younger deputy. "Ms. King?"

"I'll get hers. I gotta go smoke anyway." Dodge peeled off with the deputy.

Ski escorted Caroline and Berry into a small room. She missed the warmth of his hand when it was withdrawn.

He motioned them toward a rectangular table that had brown metal legs and a chipped, particleboard top. "Sit there. Or you can watch through the window if you don't mind standing. The sound will be piped in, so you can hear her from anywhere in the room."

Caroline sat down at the table. Berry moved to the window. In the adjoining room, seated at a table identical to the one in this room, was a girl who appeared to be in late adolescence. With her was a woman, older by perhaps fifteen years. "Is that her mother?"

"Stepmother."

"Her father?"

"Split last year, whereabouts unknown. Neither seems very happy over having to live together, but they don't have options."

"Where's her real mother?"

"Nobody knows that, either."

Lisa Arnold had a voluptuous figure, made obvious by her braless tank top and short skirt. She wasn't the all-American, rosy-cheeked, and wholesome type but the kind of girl that was just as easily stereotyped.

Despite her hard-core appearance, however, there was an incongruous vulnerability that touched Berry. Although her eye makeup had been heavily applied, tears had left muddy tracks of it on her cheeks all the way down to her chin. Fresh tracks were being formed now as Berry watched her blubber, her whole body shaking as she wept.

The stepmother sat with her arms folded across her waist and stared into near space, looking bored, sleepy, or stoned, but definitely unmoved by her stepdaughter's distress.

Their general appearance, mode of dress, and body language were vastly different from those of the shattered couple who'd been praying with their minister.

Ski had come to stand beside Berry at the window. "You okay?" he asked in an undertone.

She nodded. "How did the two teenagers clash with Oren?"

"I'll let you hear it straight from the girl."

Dodge and the deputy came in bearing several foam cups of coffee, single servings of half-and-half, and packets of various sweeteners. Dodge tossed a handful of stir sticks onto the table, then reached into his jacket pocket and withdrew a stack of paper napkins, which he set in front of Caroline.

She smiled up at him. "Thank you for remembering."

He gave her a crooked grin and grunted an unintelligible reply.

Ski went to the door and opened it. Looking back at Berry, he said, "This shouldn't take too long. I'll come back as soon as we're done to get your read on it."

He left. Berry went to the table and fixed her coffee. By the time she had carried it to the window, Ski was already in the next room, along with the deputy who'd met Caroline and Berry upon their arrival. He was making adjustments to a tripod-mounted video camera.

Ski said something to the girl, then patted her on the shoulder before rounding the table and sitting down across from her. Berry saw him slip his hand beneath the table, and an instant later she heard the hiss of speakers as they were engaged.

"Whenever you're ready, Miss Arnold," he said, his voice amplified. "Tell me everything that happened in as much detail as you can remember. I won't interrupt you unless I need something clarified. All right?"

"Okay." She blew her nose into a tissue, shifted in her seat, crossed her legs, then uncrossed them. "Do you want me looking at you or at the camera?"

"You can talk to me if that's more comfortable for you."

"Sure. I mean, I guess. Where do you want me to start?"

"What was your relationship with Davis Coldare?"

"I only met him this week. I'd seen him at school, but we didn't have classes together or anything. We never, you know, talked or nothing. I went to the baseball game last Monday night. He plays. I mean played." Here she gave an emotional hiccup.

"I forget which position he played. Second base, I think. Anyway, after the game, a bunch of us sorta met up out at the lake. Me and Davis got together and, you know, messed around a little. He was sweet. He asked could we go out tonight."

"You had a date to go to the drive-in movie."

She bobbed her head.

"Start from when you left there."

She sniffed. "Well, things had got kinda hot, you know?"

Ski nodded.

"So we decided to go to this motel where we could, you know, be more comfortable."

Ski nodded.

"When we got there, I went into the office and gave ol' lady what's-her-name the money, and she gave me a key to room number eight. We drove to it, got out, went up to the door. I gave Davis the key and said 'Be a gentleman.' Meaning, you know, that he should open the door for me at least."

"Um-huh."

"But he had trouble getting the key into the lock because he was holding up his jeans with one hand. They were, uh, undone, see?"

Ski gave another nod.

The stepmother made a snorting sound and rolled her eyes. The girl looked at her with loathing. "Oh, like you're so pure and all."

Before the stepmother could form a comeback, Ski said, "Please continue, Miss Arnold." His voice was soft but carried a ring of authority that prevented an argument between the two women.

The girl returned her attention to him. "So . . . so Davis is having trouble getting the door unlocked. But then he does. He pushes it open and steps in and switches on the light. And there's this guy, standing beside the bed, looking as surprised to see us as we were to see him. We expected the room to be vacant, you know?"

Ski nodded.

"And then he just . . . he just . . ." Her lower lip began to tremble, and a new batch of tears flooded her eyes. "Shoots the gun."

"Did he reach for the gun?"

She shook her head. "He already had it."

"Did he say anything before he fired it?"

She shook her head again. Her throat was working with emotion.

Ski leaned forward across the table. "Do you need to take a moment, Miss Arnold?"

"Jesus," the stepmother hissed. "Just tell the man what happened so we can get outta here. Will you do that, please?"

Ignoring her, Ski kindly asked the girl again if she needed time to collect herself.

She said no, that she was okay. He moved a box of Kleenex across the table closer to her. She pulled one out, blew her nose, and wiped her eyes.

When she was more composed, Ski resumed. "He didn't speak to you?"

"No."

"Did you get a good look at him?"

"Well, yeah. Davis turned on the light, and there he was, facing the door, not six feet from us."

"You told me earlier that he was fully dressed."

"In khaki pants and a dark blue shirt."

"We found a pair of men's shoes on the floor beside the bed."

"I didn't notice his feet. But his hair was all messed up. I noticed it was standing on end. And his eyes were sorta, you know, bugged out. Like maybe he'd been asleep, and we'd startled him awake, and he'd jumped up off the bed suddenly. Then when Davis came in, he pulled the trigger."

"On impulse? A knee-jerk reaction?"

"Yeah. Like that."

"Don't let me put words in your mouth, Miss Arnold."

"I'm not. That's exactly what it was like."

"And you're sure it was this man?" He opened a manila folder he'd carried in with him and removed from it a blowup of Oren's employee photo from Delray Marketing. The girl nodded vigorously. "I'm positive."

Ski replaced the picture in the folder. "After he fired the shot at Davis, what happened?"

She began to cry in earnest again. "I don't know," she wailed. "I didn't even wait to see if Davis was okay. I just turned and ran. I ran to the office, where that sow was still looking through her stupid magazine. I yelled at her to call 911. I told her that Davis had been shot. The fat bitch says, 'I don't want no trouble.'"

Lisa Arnold spoke in a voice that was obviously an imitation of the motel owner. "I told her to get her fucking, fat—" She cut her eyes toward the video camera, then back to Ski. "Sorry."

"It's okay. Go ahead."

"Well, I told her to get her ass on the phone. But she just folded her fat arms over her big belly. So I grabbed the desk phone and called myself. I didn't even realize it then, but I'd dropped my purse when the gun went off. I didn't have my cell."

"The time between your 911 call and the first responder's arrival was less than five minutes," Ski told her.

"Five minutes?" she exclaimed. "Are you sure? It seemed like forever."

"What were you doing during that time?"

Her chin began to quiver, then her entire face collapsed. She sobbed into the tissue. "I should've gone back and checked on Davis. But I was too scared. I didn't know where that maniac was or what he was doing. I was afraid he'd come after me next.

"So I crouched behind the counter there in the motel office. That old bitch kept telling me that if her place got shut down on account of me, she was gonna kill me herself. I was screaming at her to shut up, to just *shut up,* but she kept cussing at me till that cop got there."

"You didn't see the man again?"

"No."

"His car? Which direction he went?"

"No." She wiped her face and took an uneven breath to steady herself. "I think you probably know everything else."

"Can we go now?" the stepmother asked.

Ski shot her a look that would have curdled milk, then to Lisa he said, "Thank you, Miss Arnold."

"Don't thank me. I feel awful for leaving Davis there."

"We'll have to wait for the medical examiner's official ruling, but I've seen a lot of gunshot wounds. It appeared to me that the bullet was fired directly into his heart. If so, he died instantly." Gently, he added, "There was nothing you could have done for him."

Ski attended to the business of seeing Miss Arnold and her stepmother out. He assigned a deputy to escort them home and to stay there on watch until further notice. He was afraid Oren Starks might decide to come after the eyewitness to Davis Coldare's slaying. He'd already told everyone within the sheriff's office that Lisa Arnold's name was not to be released.

Since the Merritt County S.O. didn't have a crime scene unit, they used that of the nearest office of the Texas Rangers. Ski called the ranger sent to investigate the motel room and asked for an update. He reported that he had finished his work there and was packing up his gear.

Ski said, "I'm having a man stay out there to guard that room. I don't trust the owner not to ignore the tape and go inside. She's got a rap sheet as long as my arm. I've arrested her twice for drug trafficking. She's partial to prescription drugs."

The ranger chuckled. "Yeah, she had some choice words about me messing up her swell place here."

"Let me know what you get."

"Sure will, Ski."

When he was finally able to return to the group in the interrogation room, their mood was somber. The coffee cups were empty. Caroline and Dodge glumly acknowledged him. Berry was sitting at the table, staring at the stir stick she was mechanically turning end over end. Ski pulled out a chair and sat down across from her.

"That boy died because of me," she said quietly.

"He died because Oren Starks shot him in the heart."

She let go of the stir stick, propped her elbows on the edge of the table, and buried her face in her hands. "I'll never forget the sound of his parents' weeping. And it's my fault, my fault."

"How is it your fault?"

She said nothing.

Caroline was staring at her, offering silent compassion and support.

Finally Dodge cleared his throat of a terrible rattle and said, "She, uh, she thinks it's her fault because—"

"I called him."

Ski turned toward her. "Excuse me?"

She took a shuddering breath and squared her shoulders. "I called Oren."

CHAPTER 13

SKI STARED AT HER FOR SEVERAL MOMENTS, THEN LOOKED AT Caroline, who purposefully avoided looking back. He settled on Dodge, who mumbled unintelligibly and patted his pocket in search of a cigarette.

Ski asked him, "What's she talking about, she called Starks?"

"They told me about it while you were . . ." He gestured to indicate Ski's business outside the small room, then, using his former cop's verbal shorthand, explained the nature of the telephone conversation as Caroline and Berry had described it to him.

Ski assimilated it, searched for the logic behind it, and came up dry. He wanted to ask Berry what the hell she'd been thinking but figured he should contain his incredulity and soften the language a bit.

"This call. Was it to his house or a cell phone?"

"House phone," she replied. "Why?"

"We hoped we might locate him using GPS to track his cell phone signal. But the phone has to be on. Each time we've called his number, we get a recording saying it isn't in use."

"He would know better than to leave his cell phone on."

"Right." He paused for a moment, then asked the question he really wanted the answer to. "Why did you feel an apology was necessary?"

"Dodge just told you."

"I want to hear it from you."

"I'd said horrible things to him. I'd told him he was pathetic. I'd called him a creep."

"He is a creep," Ski said.

"I know, but maybe if I hadn't been so cruel to him that day, he wouldn't't—"

"You are not responsible for his actions."

She didn't refute him, but nor was she convinced. "I wanted to make amends. I was trying to be nice."

Again Ski looked toward Caroline to gauge her reaction, but she averted her eyes. Dodge's opinion, however, was plain. He raised his shoulders and gave Ski a look that said, *Women. What can you do?*

When Ski came back to Berry, she was staring vacantly at a point in the center of his chest. "I never would have guessed that an apology could have such awful consequences." Her gaze moved up and connected with his.

The guilt and misery he read in her eyes twisted something deep inside him. He felt her pain, wished he could alleviate it, wished he didn't know what it felt like.

"If Oren was out for revenge," she continued, "why didn't he shoot me? Why not me instead of Ben? Why kill that innocent boy?"

She looked so haunted, Ski didn't have the heart to say what he was thinking: That she should have thought twice about being nice to a man who'd stalked her relentlessly. He imagined she now realized that better than anyone in the room. It would be needlessly cruel to underscore it.

Changing the subject, he asked, "Did you pick up on anything Miss Arnold told us?"

"Nothing that would help. I agree that it sounds as though

Oren was sleeping, probably with the pistol in his hand. They startled him awake. He fired the gun reflexively."

"His shot has improved a hell of a lot since he plugged Lofland," Dodge remarked.

"Why couldn't he have missed that boy?" Berry asked miserably, rhetorically.

Everyone would be asking that for a long time, and there would never be a satisfactory answer.

After a thoughtful silence, Ski continued. "Tire tracks matching those we found near the lake house were discovered behind the motel. He'd parked in a dense grove. The car wasn't visible from the highway or from the road behind the motel."

"After this, he'll ditch the car as soon as he can," Dodge said.

Ski nodded in agreement. "In the meantime, every peace officer in the state is on the lookout for a Toyota of that make and model. But still no definite color, no tag number. You heard me tell Lisa Arnold that we found a pair of shoes in the room. Apparently Starks left them when he fled. We've got shoe prints going toward the place, footprints going out.

"He used a towel, bar of soap, so we can get DNA and match it if he's ever caught. We can put him in that room, which is good if it comes to trial. But we've got to catch him first, and he's leaving us few clues. He didn't take anything into the room with him."

"He took the pistol," Dodge said.

"He took the pistol," Ski repeated grimly. "But no food wrappers, no empty drink cans, no extra clothing. Nothing was left in the trash cans. No sales receipts. No maps or brochures. Nothing that would point us in a direction."

He hesitated, then added, "The bullet's still in the body. Once it's removed, we'll match it to those we retrieved from the lake house and Ben Lofland. We must assume he still has the weapon."

No one spoke for a time.

Then Caroline said, "I thought all the motels and lodges had been canvassed. Was that one overlooked?"

Ski shook his head. "Checked but eliminated. Starks hadn't registered. He busted the bathroom window at the back of the building and crawled inside."

"How long had he been there?" Berry asked.

"No way of knowing," he said. "The room was cleaned—or so the owner says—three days ago. Hasn't been rented out since. Starks could've gone there straight from the bait shop Friday night and been there all day yesterday. Maybe he didn't get there till after dark last night. Anybody's guess. He needed shelter, a place to rest. He's got a bum leg."

Ski explained that the footprints bore that out. "One's deeper than the other. He's favoring his right leg. He needed a place to crash and took his chances on the room remaining vacant at least for last night."

"But it didn't." Berry's voice was almost inaudible. She hugged her elbows, and Ski noted goose bumps on her arms. She murmured, "I can't bear to think of what that boy's parents are going through."

"They're going through bloody hell, and you're right, Berry, it doesn't bear thinking about." Caroline stood up and retrieved her handbag. "What happened to their son could still happen to you. Oren Starks is aware that, if he's caught, he can be tried and convicted of killing Davis Coldare based on that girl's eyewitness testimony. He'll lay the blame for that mishap on you, and that makes him an even greater threat than he was before."

Dodge also came to his feet. "I agree."

"Then we're all on the same page," Ski said. "I'm going to double the number of men watching the lake house."

Dodge said, "I'm moving out there."

Caroline looked at him sharply. To her he said, "I'll stay in the room where Lofland was shot. Nobody else wants to sleep in it." He turned back to Ski. "Better swear me in as one of your reserve deputies."

"There's required training."

"Considered me trained."

"Can't do it, Dodge. I'm trusting you to—"

"Don't trust me to do a damn thing except kill that fucker if he shows up. He's upped his ante tonight. If I see him, his ass is fried."

Officially Ski wouldn't sanction vigilante law. But he'd been the one who'd had to break the news to the Coldares that their son was dead. He'd personally escorted them to the morgue to ID their boy's body. Friday night's crime at the lake house had been a grudge shooting, an act of jealousy, a personal vendetta that he had originally thought petty.

But now Oren Starks had killed an innocent kid in cold blood. Starks would receive his rights as guaranteed by law, but Ski would extend the man no mercy. Secretly he hoped, as Dodge did, that he was presented with an opportunity to take the killer out.

As Dodge and Caroline prepared to leave, she reminded him that his car was at the lake house. "You'll have to ride back with Berry and me. We'll stop at the Cypress Lodge on the way to pick up your things."

Ski said, "You two take care of that. I'll drive Berry home."

Once they were in his SUV and under way, Ski said, "I wanted to talk to you about Sally Buckland."

Berry sat stiffly in the passenger seat, staring forward, wondering if he realized that he had started using her first name. Another formality had also been dropped. It seemed to have been tacitly agreed that Harris Carlisle was no longer necessary. As they left the courthouse and went their separate ways, Dodge hadn't cautioned Berry against talking to Ski alone. With the fatal shooting of Davis Coldare, it was clear who the culprit was.

When she didn't respond to Ski's statement, he asked if the AC was all right.

"It's fine. What about Sally?"

"What's she like? As a person."

"Attractive, but in a modest, bookish sort of way. The librarian with distinct possibilities."

"I'm getting a mental image. What are her traits?"

"Character traits?"

Hoping to relieve her dull headache, she pulled the elastic band from her ponytail and shook out her hair. In addition to having the headache, she was exhausted. As a result of not sleeping long enough after taking the medication, she felt hungover and lethargic. Her eyes stung from an inadequate amount of sleep and the recent threat of tears. The sun was coming up, but it didn't lift her spirits. Rather, sunrise seemed like a mockery.

Ski was saying, "Is Ms. Buckland outgoing and talkative? Shy? What?"

"More toward an introvert, but not especially shy. She's conscientious. Anxious to please. That's why it was such a conflict for her to disappoint Oren."

"Is she a gossip?"

"I never knew her to be."

"A liar?"

"Again."

"Jealous? Malicious?"

"Not in my experience."

"Then why would she insist to me that you were lying about Oren Starks? There's no question now that everything you've said about him is true. In fact, you underestimated him."

"Unfortunately," she whispered.

"Don't beat yourself up."

"I can't help it. I shouldn't have called him."

He let that go for the moment, and she was glad. He had every right to rub in what an ill-advised move that had been.

Returning to the subject, he said, "If Sally Buckland's experience with Starks was similar to yours, why would she tell me the direct opposite? And this is what really puzzles me. She said you were lying before I'd even spoken the word *stalker.* She disputed the accusation before I made it."

"I'm sorry," Berry said, meaning it. "I can't fathom why Sally would lie, because it does seem entirely out of character. Perhaps to avoid involvement? I don't know. What I *do* know with certainty is that she left Delray because of Oren."

"Which brings me back to why she would lie about it." Looking frustrated, he ran his hand through his hair. "The whole conversation with her was . . ."

"What?"

"Off. But don't ask me how, because I don't know. It just was. I asked a Harris County deputy sheriff to go by her place, ask her some questions and get a read on her, but she wasn't at home. I've tried calling her again several times. No answer. Do you know where she's working now?"

"Last I heard she was freelancing from her house."

"Well, I want to talk to her again, first chance I get."

"You've been busy."

"I've been chasing my tail with nothing to show for it but a dead kid who was the light of his parents' life."

Urging him to let go of his guilt was pointless. She felt the same way. "As Dodge said, Oren upped his ante tonight. He has to be feeling the additional pressure."

"I hope. Stressed-out crooks get careless, make mistakes. My guess, he'll abandon that car soon if he hasn't already. Unless he's got a backup, he'll have to steal another. I'll be watching for reports of stolen vehicles. Also public transportation. Or," he said with a grim smile, "we might get lucky, and that Toyota will be stopped by a state trooper within the next five minutes, and Starks will come out with his hands in the air."

"I wouldn't bet on it."

"Me either."

She studied his profile for a moment and saw the fatigue in his face. "You're putting in long hours on this case."

"That's the job."

"What does your wife think of the overtime?"

He turned his head and looked at her.

Quickly she said, "I only ask because you seem to have been on the job since my 911 call."

"I won't go home except to shower and shave until we've got Oren Starks in custody."

"Where do you live?"

"On the lake. I've got a boat."

"Is your place near Mother's?"

He chuckled. "Hardly. That's the high-rent district. My house is half that size. Maybe less. The lot is only three quarters of an acre. It's nice, private, but nothing like your spread."

"It isn't mine. It's my mother's."

"Same as."

He waved to the reserve deputy as they turned in to the private lane. When they reached the house, he pulled around to the back.

Berry opened the passenger-side door. "Thanks for the ride." She could just as easily have ridden with her mother and Dodge. She hadn't answered many questions. Ski hadn't asked many, and what he'd asked, he could have done by telephone.

He got out when she did. She said, "You don't have to see me in."

"I'll feel better leaving you alone if I check the house."

"I won't be alone for long. Mother and Dodge are right behind us." She glanced toward the lake, where another deputy was stationed near the pier. "And with the two guards—"

"I'll feel better if I check."

Why argue? She turned and walked toward the back steps, retrieving the door key from beneath a pot of pink caladiums.

"That's not very safe."

"The alarm is set." She climbed the steps, unlocked the door, and pushed it open. The beeper went off. "See?" She punched in the code to disengage the alarm.

He reached beyond her and depressed the status button on the keypad. The LED showed that no interruptions had been made to the system since the alarm had been set. "Do all the doors and windows have contacts?"

"I think so."

"Glass breakage and motion detectors?"

"I assume. Mother is usually here by herself, so she's always cautious."

"Okay."

Berry set her handbag on the kitchen table. "Would you like some coffee?"

"Thanks, but I don't have time for it. I gotta shove off. You should get some sleep. You've had two short nights."

"I'd like to take a nap. Later I plan to go to the hospital to see Ben."

Ski's eyes narrowed fractionally.

Immediately she went on the defensive. "I haven't seen him since he was carried out of here on a gurney. Yesterday, I stayed out of his room because of the ugly scene with Amanda. But I'm entitled to go and see about my friend."

"I'm sure your *friend* will appreciate a visit. His wife won't."

The emphasis he'd placed on the word *friend* didn't escape her. "No, she probably won't. Because she, like you, can't get past the fact that I was naked when Ben was shot. In light of everything else, isn't it rather juvenile and ridiculous to be hung up on that?"

She stepped around him and headed for the door that led into the rest of the house. Over her shoulder she said, "You can see yourself out."

Before she'd taken two steps, he caught her shoulder with one hand and brought her around, pulling her against him. "I don't have a wife," he said in a low voice. "And the reason I can't get past you being naked is because I *saw* you naked."

Then he kissed her, hard and thoroughly, planting his tongue firmly inside her mouth. However, the kiss lasted for no more than a few seconds before it ended, and he set her away from him abruptly and decisively.

His chest inflated around a deep breath that he then expelled in a gust. His eyes skittered around the kitchen, stopping at random points before connecting with hers. Roughly, he said, "You could have the book thrown at me for that."

Berry's own breath was coming in short, insufficient gasps. She stared at him for several seconds, then reached up and linked her fingers behind his head. "To hell with the book."

She drew his head down as forcibly as he'd pulled hers to him moments earlier. She pressed her mouth against his, and, after the briefest hesitation on his part, the kiss resumed, hotter and hungrier than before. This is what they'd been moving toward. The mutual hostility had been a defense mechanism used by both in an unsuccessful attempt to deceive themselves. It had been about this from the start.

One of his arms curved around her waist while his other hand cupped her butt, and, using both, he pulled her high against him until she was on tiptoe, and he was fitted into the notch of her thighs, and, oh, my God, he was hard and solid, and it felt so good. Immediately her body grew warm and wanting, and when she inclined her hips to make the contact even more evocative, a growl vibrated from his throat.

The kiss intensified. It was that kiss you're lucky to experience once in a lifetime. That kiss that defies the rules, that banishes conscience, that is purely sexual. That kiss that makes you feel vibrantly alive and positively doomed. That I'm-going-to-die-if-I-don't-fuck-you kiss.

She thought he might.

She thought *she* might.

And they might have.

If they hadn't heard the car's approach.

The engine died. Doors closed. She and Ski released each other and sprang apart. She thought she probably should tug down her blouse, smooth down his hair, but there was no time because Caroline and Dodge were coming in through the back door.

Whatever Caroline was saying died on her lips as she cleared the doorway and drew up short, her eyes seesawing between Berry and Ski.

She had stopped so suddenly that Dodge ran into her back, crushing a grocery sack between them. Apparently sensing the electrically charged atmosphere, he took his turn looking back and forth between them.

Always the diplomat, her mother ignored the awkwardness of the moment. Pleasantly, she said, "We stopped at the supermarket and got some things so I could cook breakfast. I hope you'll join us, Ski."

"Thanks, but I can't."

Without another word or a backward glance, he squeezed past them and left.

Caroline and Dodge turned to watch his hasty retreat, then came back around to Berry. If they'd had question marks painted on their faces, they couldn't have looked more curious.

She backed away from them and through the connecting doorway. "I'm not hungry."

CHAPTER 14

Houston, Texas, 1978

THE MURDER OF THE BANK GUARD WAS THE LEAD NEWS STORY for several days, and the media milked it. The victim had been only twenty-four years old. It had been a case of overkill. He was down, bleeding, already mortally wounded, when the robber paused long enough to shoot him in the head before exiting the bank with his booty tucked under his arm.

The guard had been weeks away from marrying his high school sweetheart. He was buried in the suit that was to have been his wedding suit. His fiancée and parents were inconsolable. On camera, their testimonials were heart-wrenching. The young man was extolled by former teachers as the most outstanding student they'd ever had the privilege to teach. His scoutmaster praised his commitment and thoughtfulness toward others. His church conducted a worship service in his honor, not a dry eye in the overflow crowd.

The competence of those trying to nab the robber turned killer was called into question by the press, as well as by city officials who wanted to keep their elected positions, and by provocateurs who crawled out of the woodwork whenever given an opportunity to take potshots at the HPD.

The negative media coverage put everyone on the task force in a bad mood. Rather than strengthen their resolve and make them a more determined band of brothers, the public spanking eroded confidence and morale. It unraveled the fabric of their comradery. Their criticism of one another became vitriolic, causing friction between individuals, between cliques, between supervisors and subordinates.

To a man they wanted to catch the culprit by means of a spectacular police maneuver that would force their critics to eat crow till they choked on it. But each officer also had his own agenda, a self-serving purpose, a do-or-die reason for wanting to shine. On neither of these levels was failure an option, so, naturally, egos clashed.

Things got so bad, tension rose to such a level during their jam sessions, that Dodge began looking forward to his shift at the tire manufacturing plant. At least there he got a little relief from the constant pressure, bitching, and bickering. As long as he emptied all the trash cans within a reasonable amount of time, no one at the plant hassled him.

But he was still required to attend the task force briefings, which had turned into shouting matches. At the most recent one, he'd been reminded of his assignment by the screaming, red-faced captain, who'd just come from an ass-chewing in which his sizable behind had been the main course.

He'd stamped and sputtered and banged his fist on the table for five full minutes, citing all Dodge's failed attempts to establish a relationship with Franklin Albright's girlfriend, Crystal. He ended his tirade with a direct order. "Now get back to that fucking factory. Get in her face, get in her pants, I don't care, Hanley, just get something so we can either go after this bastard or chalk him off our list of suspects!"

Having been duly charged, Dodge doubled his efforts to make headway with Crystal. Gradually they began to yield results, providing incremental victories to report to his supervisor.

"I went to the payroll office yesterday, pretending to have a question about the taxes being withheld from my check. Crystal and I had locked eyeballs a few times before, but now we've actually chatted, and she knows my name."

"I time my lunch break to coincide with hers. On Monday, she was out of change, so I offered to buy her a package of Fritos from the vending machine, and after a lot of hemming and hawing and eyelash fluttering, she let me. On Tuesday, she paid me back. No, I didn't make a pass," he said, shooting a disparaging look toward the cop who'd asked. "I don't want to come across as a sleazeball and send her running in the opposite direction. Jeez. But that stupid question explains why *you* can't get a date."

"When Crystal went on her afternoon break, I loitered in the hall outside the ladies' room, fiddling with an electrical outlet. When she left the restroom, she stopped to chat, asked if I had any more questions about my check and said, if I did, to be sure to come by the payroll office and she'd help me out. Which I took as an invitation. I'll drop by there tomorrow."

"Crystal's girlfriend, the one she usually eats lunch with, quit to have a baby. So I insinuated myself into her place at the table where they always sat, and Crystal didn't object. I tried moving the conversation toward personal matters by remarking on her friend's pregnancy and asking if Crystal has kids of her own, and she said no, but she'd like to someday. Only she had to get married first, and that didn't seem likely any time soon, and I asked her why not, and she said because her boyfriend wasn't the marrying kind. First mention of Franklin."

"Today Crystal told me that Franklin is a great guy. Really, she said, stressing it. Except that he can get moody. In the past, he's been in trouble with the law, so her parents distrust and dislike him and told her that, as long as she was with him, they want nothing to do with her. Which sorta hurts her feelings, but she loves Franklin, so there you go."

"She and Franklin had a fight last night. He accused her of flirting with a salesclerk at Radio Shack, which she swears she wasn't.

Can she help it if the guy was ogling her? I said the poor guy probably couldn't help himself, and she laughed and swatted my hand. Well, yeah, that classifies as flirting. But at this stage, a little flirting is okay. Don't you know *anything* about women?"

"She wishes Franklin wasn't so jealous. For instance, if he knew we were eating lunch together every day, he wouldn't like it. *Not at all.* He'd never understand that we're just friends, she said. And I said, 'Is that all we are? Just friends?' And she got all flustered. Blushed a little. Did the bit with the eyelashes again. Swear to God, they're stiff and black like the legs of a dead cockroach. Where was I? Oh, right. I definitely think I'm making progress. One sure sign, her skirts are getting shorter and her blouses lower cut. Yeah, I gotta admit, the view would make you assholes drool."

"She put her hand on my thigh today. No, I'm not lying, jerk-face. She only did it to make a point of what she was saying, but still, it counts. How high up? Use your imagination. High enough to set my balls a-tingle. No, nothing about Franklin today, except that she said it probably wouldn't be a good idea if he saw us walking out of the plant together after our shift."

"This could be a major breakthrough, so everybody listen up. No, I didn't get to second base. Jesus, what are you? Fourth grade? Are you listening now? Okay then. Crystal told me that Franklin goes fishing periodically at Falcon Lake. He meets his cousin there. Any of you ignoramuses know the geography of Texas? Falcon Lake is right on the border with Mexico, where his cousin, ahem, has taken up residence.

"So what I'm thinking, is . . . Bingo, Captain. Franklin robs a bank, then drives on down to Falcon Lake, gets in a boat probably, and hands the loot over to his cousin in Old Meh-hee-co, where the cash is laundered. It reenters the US of A as squeaky clean legal tender.

"All I gotta do is get out of Crystal when Franklin's most recent fishing trip was and see if it corresponds with the date of the last robbery. If it does, Franklin moves up several notches on the suspect list. How am I gonna get the info out of Crystal? Don't you wish you knew?"

• • •

Caroline was trying hard to stay awake. She'd already been here two and a half hours, but with only thirty minutes to go, she was afraid she wouldn't make it without falling asleep from boredom.

She was on the verge of nodding off when a car pulled up at the curb and parked. A man got out and walked toward the house. Through the glass in the storm door, his silhouette showed up large, and she experienced a twinge of apprehension, as she always did when showing a house to a man alone.

He opened the door and stepped into the foyer.

When she recognized Dodge Hanley, her heart gave a bump of a different sort. The reaction startled and confused her. It had been two months since she'd told him not to interfere with her life and had warned him of serious consequences if he did. She'd thought she would never see him again. But here he was, and her involuntary excitement was unsettling.

She stood up.

He said, "Hi."

"Hi."

She'd been seated in a folding chair at a card table. Draped in a gold cloth, it served as a reception desk. Scattered across it were leaflets describing the house for sale and a goodly number of her business cards. She was unreasonably glad that the table was between her and the policeman, who was out of uniform, wearing a sport coat and slacks instead.

"What are you doing here?"

He raised the folded sheet of newspaper he'd carried in with him and pointed to an ad in the real estate section. "Open house. Sunday. Two till five. It's got a picture of this house, it gives the street address, and it's listed under your name as an agent for Jim Malone Realty."

"I know what the ad says. I proofread it before submitting it to the classifieds. That doesn't explain what you're doing here."

"It's an open house."

His obtuseness was irrationally disarming and made her want

to smile. Instead, she folded her arms across her middle, where she was still experiencing a flutter, and asked loftily, "Are you in the market for a home, Mr. Hanley?"

"Maybe." He gave the foyer a slow survey. "What's to recommend this house? Please don't tell me this wallpaper is its best feature."

She managed to keep her smile in check, but barely. "It's got a nice backyard. Fenced."

"Wood fence?"

"Cyclone."

He frowned.

"Large, native trees," she continued. "Very shady. And with a little repair, the patio—"

"Repair?"

"Minimal repair would return it to being, uh, usable."

"Huh." He glanced into the adjacent living room at the turquoise brocade divan. "Ugly furniture."

"The furniture isn't included in the sale."

"Lucky us."

"With new paint, wallpaper, and furniture, the house would look entirely different. You have to have an imagination."

"A *wild* imagination."

Knowing it was a game, she continued playing along. "It has three bedrooms, one down, two up. Two fireplaces, one in the formal living area, and one in the den, which used to be the garage. The owners converted it into a room when the house underwent a total renovation."

He looked up at a crack in the ceiling. "When was that?"

"Nineteen fifty-two."

He raised his eyebrows, and she could no longer contain her self-deprecating laughter. "The place is a disaster. But it's my first listing."

"Congratulations."

"Thank you."

They shared a grin, then he said, "Jim Malone Realty. He's a bigwig, right? His signs are all over Houston."

"I'm very fortunate to have been hired by his agency."

"He's fortunate to get you."

She accepted the compliment with a humble nod. "His company is very well established. I'm a newcomer. I've got a lot to learn."

"Is that why you pulled this detail?"

"I volunteered."

"You've got ambition, Ms. King."

"I don't want to go back to the tax assessor's office."

"Can't say I blame you for that." He smiled again and glanced down at the brochures on the table. "Have you had many people come by?"

"You're the third in nearly three hours."

"You've had to sit here for all that time by yourself?"

"Well, there's the cat, but he hissed at the first couple who came in, so I locked him in the pantry."

"Can you stick it out for"—he consulted his watch—"twenty-two more minutes?"

"I've been counting them down and trying to stay awake."

They exchanged another smile, then neither said anything, and the silence of the house pressed in around them. This man made her uneasy, and she couldn't account for it. Even when she was interviewed by Jim Malone himself, persuading him that she would be an asset to his agency despite her inexperience, she hadn't been as nervous as she was now. Around Dodge Hanley she became self-conscious, unsure, and at a loss for what to say and where to look.

Maybe it was a natural reaction to being in the company of a police officer. Drivers automatically tapped their brakes when they spotted a radar trap even when they weren't speeding. Perhaps it was Dodge's implied authority that intimidated her.

Or maybe she was still embarrassed over how he'd first seen her, with the effects of Roger's slap evident—the mark on her cheek fresh, the emotional impact of it equally raw. She'd been unable to hide her mortification then, and she couldn't now.

Perhaps her discomfiture had something to do not with *her* but with *him*. His strong features, tough bearing, and unmitigated masculinity hinted at the latent violent streak that she knew could be ferocious. After all, she'd seen the result of it. Roger had been hospitalized for ten days following the beating he took.

She didn't fear for her own safety, however. Dodge Hanley posed no threat to her, even by implication. In fact, his demeanor was protective, almost quaintly chivalrous. She felt a gravitational pull toward it that was entirely feminine.

It was that instinctual response to him that gave her butterflies. Being near him made her feel as if she was balancing on tiptoe at the end of a high diving board. By turns, it was exhilarating and terrifying.

All the time these thoughts were going through her mind, they'd been staring at each other. Needing to fill the dense silence, she asked, "Are you still on the task force?"

"They haven't kicked me off yet."

"So the crime remains unsolved?"

"We're working on it."

"Is it dangerous work?"

"Piece o' cake."

"I doubt that." Another silence descended while she stared at the cobweb in the corner just beyond his head, and he stared at her face. She could practically feel his eyes as they touched on each separate feature. "How's your partner?"

"Gonzales."

"Right, Officer Gonzales. Is he doing okay?"

"Yeah, he's good. I think he likes his new partner better than me, which kinda hurts my feelings."

"I doubt that, too."

"What? That he likes his new partner better, or that I can have my feelings hurt?"

"That he likes his new partner better."

He shrugged. "Maybe Gonzales is just trying to make me jealous." They smiled together. His faded first. "But I do have feelings, and they can get hurt."

"You wouldn't be human otherwise."

"Oh, I'm human. Real human. Very human." He looked down at her left hand, where, in the last few seconds, her engagement ring had taken on the weight of an anchor. "How are the wedding plans coming?"

The smile she flashed him felt artificial. "Great. Moving right along. Lots of details to see to."

"Parties to attend."

"Yes. There have been a few."

"Couple of weeks ago, I saw your picture in the society section of the *Chronicle*."

"You read the society section?"

"Didn't used to. I started scanning it a few months ago. Never read the Sunday real estate section, either. Now I never miss." He let those statements resonate for several seconds before continuing. "Anyway this picture showed you and Campton standing together under those"—he waggled his fingers above his head—"those whachamacallits hanging from the trees."

"Japanese lanterns."

"Yeah. Looked like a swell shindig. The article said the governor was there."

"Roger's parents are friends with him and his wife."

"Huh. Will they be at the wedding?"

"They're on the guest list."

"Who'll be there on your side? Your family?"

"I don't have a family. No brothers or sisters. My parents are deceased."

"Oh. Sorry."

"Don't be. I was a late-in-life child. They'd given up ever having a baby. I was a menopausal surprise."

"A good one, I'll bet."

She smiled wistfully. "Mom and Dad were very happy to have me, and I was fortunate to have them. They were middle-class wage earners and proud to be. My mother was a lady, my father a gentleman. Both had a strong work ethic. They loved God, and country, and me. They lived their life expectancy, but I was relatively young when I lost them. Being an orphan is no fun."

"It has its perks."

She looked at him with surprised puzzlement.

He rolled his shoulders as though his jacket had suddenly become too tight. "My mom was okay. She died when I was in seventh grade. My dad and I didn't get along that well, so we just tried to stay out of each other's way till I was old enough to leave home."

"How old were you?"

"Seventeen. Two days after my high school graduation, I split. Didn't even wait till the fall semester, enrolled at Texas Tech that summer."

"That must have made your father proud."

"Not really. When I told him I wanted to be a cop, he laughed, said I'd make a better criminal."

"I'm sure he changed his mind once you became an officer."

"He didn't live to see it. He died still thinking I wouldn't amount to much."

She could think of nothing to say that wouldn't sound banal, so she said nothing.

"So who's going to walk you down the aisle?" he asked.

"Roger's best man."

"That's handy."

"Um-huh."

"Got your dress?"

"The final fitting was last week."

"Pretty?"

"I think so."

"I'm sure you'll be a vision."

"I hope my groom thinks so."

"He'd have to be blind."

The conversation ended there, leaving Caroline to wonder how the entryway seemed to have shrunk over the course of their conversation. The air was thicker, the old house smelled mustier. And even though neither of them had moved, he seemed to be closer. She was even more grateful for the card table standing between her and this man who made her nervous.

She glanced at her wristwatch. "Nearly time. I can begin closing up shop."

"I'm sorry you didn't have any takers."

"Me, too. I'm going to urge the sellers to get more aggressive."

"More aggressive?"

"Lower their price."

He snuffled a laugh.

She expected him to tell her good-bye and good luck and leave. But he just stood there. She made a hand gesture and said, "Well . . ."

"I'll wait and walk you out. That cat might be really pissed off by now."

She freed the cat from the pantry. He was sulky for having been confined but not vicious. She turned out all the lights. She removed the cloth from the card table. Dodge insisted on folding up the chair and table and carrying them out to her car, where he stowed them in the trunk. He pocketed one of her business cards. Then they stood there at the curb facing each other.

Feeling awkward, she worried her car keys. "Thanks for stopping by."

"You're welcome."

"It helped to have company. Talking made that last half hour go faster."

"I kept you from falling asleep at least."

"And if you change your mind about the house . . ."

"I'll let you know."

She smiled.

He waited a beat, then said, "You wanna go get a cup of coffee or something?"

"Thank you, but I can't. Roger is expecting me."

"Oh. You don't want to keep Roger waiting."

The bitterness behind his words was unmistakable and prompted her to declare, "He's being very sweet."

"Good. That's good."

"When you and Officer Gonzales came to the house, that was an isolated incident."

"So you've said. A bunch of times."

"Well, it's true. Roger regrets that night. Deeply. He's sworn never to raise a hand to me again."

"A groom shouldn't have to swear to something like that, though, should he?"

"His contrition is sincere."

Dodge's expression remained skeptical, which compelled her to convince him.

"Roger thinks the beating outside his gym was a random, aborted mugging, and I've never told him differently."

Dodge didn't really give a damn if Campton knew he'd been the one to attack him, although he'd just as soon the department not get wind of it. But he figured Campton himself protected him from anybody in authority finding out. Even if the woman-beating asshole guessed, or learned through some other means, the identity of the man who'd jumped him, he wouldn't file a legal complaint against Dodge, knowing that if he did, his ill treatment of Caroline then would be made public. Nor was the millionaire likely to challenge him in private, because men who hit women were usually cowards.

It suited both men to leave it alone. But in a perverse way, Dodge wished he could rub the son of a bitch's nose in it.

"He remembers the mugger whispering something to him," Caroline continued. "But he was on the brink of unconsciousness and can't recall what the mugger said."

Dodge looked even more skeptical.

"He considers himself lucky to be alive."

"He is," Dodge said bluntly.

"Since the beating, and his painful recovery, he's been extremely sweet. I think the scare caused him to rearrange his priorities. In any event, he's gone back to being the Roger I first met. He can't do enough for me. He's charming and thoughtful. I've fallen in love with him all over again."

He said nothing, but his eyes turned stony.

"You're basing your low opinion of him on that one incident," she said with heat. "You've never seen the real Roger. The night he slapped me, he wasn't himself."

"No?"

"No. If you could see him now, compare the two, you'd realize that. I'd never seen him act that way before, and certainly not since you beat him up."

"So he changed his spots because of my attack, his brush with death? That's what you think?"

"Yes."

"Bullshit. A leopard never changes his spots. My old man was right about me. I'm a cop, and a damn good one, mostly because I think like a criminal. I have criminal impulses. My daddy knew it way back, and I own up to it now. People adjust their behavior to fit the society they live in. They integrate because they have to. But what they are on the inside doesn't change.

"So if Campton has gone back to being nice and sweet, it's not because he's seen the light and had a Pentecostal conversion. He's lying when he says he doesn't remember what his *mugger* said to him that night. If he's acting all lovey-dovey, it's because he's afraid I'll follow through on my promise to kill him if he ever hurts you again."

Her cheeks had grown hot with anger. "I'm marrying him."

"Because you love him?"

"Yes! Very much."

He took a step closer, forcing her to tilt her head back farther in order to look into his face. "You know what I think?"

"I don't care what you think."

"I think you're going through with the wedding not because you're so wildly in love but because you're stubborn. You don't want Caroline King's judgment questioned. You don't want to be proved wrong."

"You know nothing about me."

"I know one thing." He came nearer still. "I know you're all I goddamn think about."

She felt his words like a punch to a place low and deep inside her. They made her breath catch. They caused her heart to thump. They made her want to take that leap off the high board.

She was afraid he was going to kiss her. She was afraid he wasn't.

He didn't.

After countless tense moments, she turned and went to the driver's door of her car, opened it, and got in. He didn't try to stop her as she drove away.

For the third time, she left him staring after her. The first time she had retreated into her house, touched by the policeman's concern. The second time, she had returned to her real estate class inside the office building, upset over the beating he'd given Roger but acknowledging that Dodge's concern wasn't strictly professional.

This time was not so much a retreat as a full-fledged escape. From him, yes. But also from herself and the colossal mistake she was likely to make if she stayed.

Dodge arrived at the tire plant the following morning in a surly mood, cursing the rush-hour traffic, cursing the floors he'd have to mop today, cursing himself for making a mess of his visit with Caroline.

Things had been going real good. He would even go so far as to believe that she'd been glad to see him, and not just because she'd wasted a Sunday afternoon sitting alone in an ugly, empty house, and anybody's company was better than none at all.

But then he'd gone and shot off his mouth about her fiancé. She had jumped to Campton's defense, as she should if she was bent on marrying the guy.

But, dammit, Dodge knew he was right. Petite as she was, Caroline King had a steel I-beam for a spine. He'd sensed it the moment he met her, when she'd been smarting inside and out but was too proud and obstinate to cry in front of him. Losing her parents at a relatively young age had no doubt forced her to be self-assertive. Or maybe she'd been born with that stiff backbone and circumstances had only reinforced it.

Whatever, the upshot of it was that she was mule-headed, and, in large part, that was why she was going through with her marriage to Roger Campton.

Dodge refused to accept that she loved the rich, handsome son of a bitch.

Once again, she'd been mad as a hornet when she left him. He cursed himself for being a goddamn idiot. Why was it that he could talk any other woman out of her clothes, out of information, but he couldn't communicate with the one woman he wanted most to communicate with? Around her, his glibness deserted him.

He'd gone home and drunk a six-pack, slept badly for having to get up to pee every hour on the hour because of the beer, and arrived at the tire plant in a truculent mood, which is probably why, when he spotted Crystal beside a souped-up truck with oversize tires and semi-obscene mud flaps, engaged in deep conversation with her felonious boyfriend, he wended his way through the parking lot toward them.

Practically issuing an engraved invitation for a confrontation, he moved up close behind her and said, "Hey, Crystal."

She spun around, looking like a terrified rabbit caught in headlights, except that her eyes were swollen and red from crying. Her eyelashes weren't so spiky when wet with tears. "Oh, hi," she said nervously. "This is, uh, this is Franklin. My boyfriend."

Albright looked him up and down. "Nice uniform." He leaned forward and read the make-believe name stitched in red lettering on Dodge's left breast pocket. "Marvin," he added, smirking when he said it.

Dodge ignored him and addressed Crystal. "How come you're crying? Can I help?"

Franklin Albright gave Dodge's shoulder a hard shove. "You can help by minding your own fucking business."

Dodge, who'd been spoiling for a fight when he arrived, wanted to dive into the ex-con, but he settled for shaking off the hand on his shoulder. "Watch your language in front of the lady."

"It's okay," Crystal said quickly. "I wasn't crying. I've got allergies. A Sudafed should fix me up." She gave her boyfriend a worried glance, then nodded Dodge toward the plant's entrance gate. "Don't be late for work on my account."

"Do you have some Sudafed? Because I'll be happy to go get some for you."

"I've got a box in my desk drawer, thanks. If you're late, they'll dock you."

"Well, you would know, Miss Payroll," he said in a teasing voice.

She gave him a tremulous smile. Franklin Albright was all but snarling.

Dodge stared him down, trying to look like a geek trying to look tough, then ambled off in the direction of the gate, shooting one final glance at them over his shoulder before entering the plant and thinking, *Hee-hee.*

"Sure enough," he told the other members of the task force during their meeting that evening, "ol' Franklin was waiting for me when my shift ended. He accosted me just outside the gate."

"Define *accosted,*" the captain said.

"Grabbed me by the shoulders and backed me into the fence. I made a stand, but not too much of one. I didn't want to let him know that I could have laid him out flat if I had wanted to."

"What did he say?"

"He told me to stay away from Crystal."

"What did you say?"

"I said I'd do what I damn well pleased."

"Then what did he say?"

"He said I could do that, sure. If I wanted my head ripped off and used as a urinal."

"Franklin's got a real way with words, doesn't he?" one of the other officers quipped.

"Did you find out why she was crying?"

"Over lunch, she told me that she'd brought up the subject of matrimony again, and Franklin had said no, no way, no way, José. I lent her a sympathetic ear, told her he wasn't just ugly, he was stupid."

"How'd she react?"

"She laughed. She thinks I'm funny and sweet and brave for standing up to him. But she warned me against waving a red cape. She said he has a temper, as well as a knife. I told her I wasn't afraid of him." He shrugged complacently. "I'm her hero."

"But your cover is blown."

"By playing Sir Galahad? Hardly."

"But now you're in Albright's sights."

"As a complete schmuck who has designs on Crystal. If he gets wind of my prying now, he'll figure I'm just trying to move in on his girl. If I was prying for no apparent reason, *that* would have bleeped on his radar screen and caused him to be suspicious."

"So where'd you leave it?" the captain asked.

"Yeah, you haven't explained how your face got messed up," another officer observed.

"Franklin thought we'd reached an understanding. He poked his finger in my chest and said, 'You're not going to talk to Crystal anymore, right, Marvin?' And I said, 'Sure, okay, because I can screw her without talking.'"

"Holy—"

"You didn't."

"Dodge, I swear."

"You asked for it."

"Of course I asked for it," Dodge told the group. He would have grinned, but his split lip hurt when he did. His eye was the color of an eggplant and swollen nearly shut. "I'll show up at work tomorrow with Franklin's handiwork on my face, and Crystal will be full of remorse and apology. But underneath her big tits, her little heart is going to be pitter-patting at the thought of me standing up to big, bad Franklin on her behalf. I'll have won her heart and her loyalty."

"But he'll tell her what you said about screwing her."

"And I'll deny it. I'll pretend to be crushed and offended that she could even *think* I'd say such a thing. My feelings toward her are honorable and pure."

"I'm gonna puke," one of the group said drolly.

"What makes you think she'll believe you over Franklin?" the captain asked.

Despite his busted lip, Dodge spread his grin around the room. "Because she wants to."

And then Caroline King crossed his mind, and his grin dissolved. Almost to himself, he said, "Even when the bad is staring a woman in the face, she wants to believe her man is good."

CHAPTER 15

WHAT WERE THE CHANCES?

That was the question Oren had been asking himself for most of his life. Whenever Fate pulled a nasty practical joke on him, which was with unfair frequency, he had asked himself what were the odds of that happening, whatever *that* was in any given situation.

Obviously the odds of shit happening to Oren Starks were very good because the bad luck just kept coming.

Friday night had been a fiasco. The "lake house incident," as it was being referred to by the media, had been a disastrous personal failure, but to an outside observer, its absurd outcome must appear almost laughable. It had been like a bad farce, with the villain making his exit by falling down the stairs no less.

Given its comic elements, the shooting of Ben Lofland possibly could have been written off as a squabble among former co-workers. No one had died. Lofland's condition wasn't even all that serious. There would have been some unpleasant legal ramifications to plow through, but after all was said and done, the incident would soon have been forgotten.

But now, *now,* Oren Starks was wanted for the fatal shooting of a sixteen-year-old boy. Which was another kettle of fish altogether.

What were the chances?

Sneaking into a room in a disreputable motel had seemed like a good idea at the time. After all, there was a one-in-eight chance that room number eight would remain vacant. There had been seven others to choose from, for crying out loud!

But no, that particular room had been given to Davis Coldare and his female companion.

What were the chances that the Coldare kid would turn out to be an honor student, an all-star baseball player, a beloved son, friend, and student? If someone had to walk through that motel room door, why couldn't it have been a drug addict, a thief, a pedophile? Had that been the case, Oren Starks might have been hailed a hero for ridding the community of a menace.

Instead, the citizenry and every law enforcement officer in the state were on the lookout for the heartless killer of a golden boy.

What were the chances that the unnamed young woman who'd witnessed the shooting would remain levelheaded enough to later identify the shooter? It had been reported that she had picked out—unequivocally—Oren Starks's photo from a group. To add insult to injury, it had been that damn Delray Marketing employee photo that he'd always hated! The photograph on his driver's license was more flattering than that one. In it his forehead looked too high, his eyes too closely set, his chin undefined and weak.

What were the chances that he would be forced to deal with a disaster that had been totally unforeseen and for which he had no contingency plan?

The odds of all that happening were as slim as the odds for Mike Reader's neck to snap when Oren pushed him off the merry-go-round. The summer Oren turned nine years old had been a hot one in Beaumont, Texas. The wilting, record-breaking temperatures were keeping most kids indoors during midday. That's why Oren and Mike Reader were alone at the playground that fateful afternoon.

When Oren parked his bike, he approached the other boy with caution and awe. Mike was a bully who outweighed Oren by thirty pounds and was a head taller. But for all his wariness, Oren welcomed this chance encounter, seeing it as an opportunity to make a good impression on a popular classmate. If Mike and Oren forged a friendship during the summer break, then in the fall, when school reconvened, Oren would be accepted into Mike's wide group of friends.

But Mike was happy to see Oren there in the park only because he then had someone to torment. He invited Oren to join him on the merry-go-round. Oren cheerfully climbed on. But immediately Mike hopped off, gripped one of the metal bars, and, running full-out in the beaten-down track of the circumference, pushed the merry-go-round to go faster and faster until the landscape was a blur to Oren, who was holding on for dear life and whimpering in terror.

Mike jumped back on and began mocking him. He made fun of him for not having a daddy, and when Oren yelled to him that his daddy had died, the boy laughed and jeered and said he was a mama's boy. He called him a queer, a weirdo, a wimp, a sissy who probably peed like a girl, like his mother, sitting down. Oren blubbered denials, but Mike Reader persisted and began chanting the taunt. He made a little song of it.

The crude ditty was silenced when Oren mustered all his strength and, letting go of the bar he'd been clinging to, gave Mike Reader's chest a mighty push with both palms. Mike, caught off guard by Oren's courageous defiance, toppled backward off the spinning merry-go-round and landed in the hard-packed dirt. Oren heard the sound, like that of a stick being broken over someone's knee.

Catching intermittent glimpses of Mike Reader, Oren stayed on the merry-go-round as it spun round and round until it came to a full stop. Only then did he get off and walk over to the boy lying lifeless on the ground. His bladder and bowel had emptied the instant he died, which Oren saw as poetic justice, considering the nature of his recent jeers.

Oren wanted to linger over the boy's still body and gloat, but he quickly removed his shirt and used it to rub off any fingerprints his hands might have left on the merry-go-round. He brushed it over the imprints that the soles of his sneakers had made in the dirt. Satisfied that he'd eliminated all evidence of his having been there, he got on his bicycle and pedaled home as fast as he could before anyone saw him, keeping to the pavement so as not to leave tread tracks.

To this day it was believed that Mike Reader's death had been a tragic childhood accident.

Ever since that summer afternoon, Oren had wanted to kill all the other people in his life who treated him cruelly. He'd longed to give anyone who persecuted him the just deserts that Mike Reader had got. But he'd always talked himself out of it because most offenders weren't worth the risk of getting caught.

But Berry Malone's treachery was in a league of its own. Therefore his reprisal must be.

He had vowed to see her dead, and he would. But his original plan had gone awry, and, now, if he wasn't very clever, he'd be arrested for shooting that Coldare kid and Berry would go on living with impunity. Which was untenable and unacceptable.

There was one fortunate aspect to this catastrophe: Oren Starks was accustomed to coping with bad luck because he'd had so much practice at it. For instance, he knew to avoid panic. Hand-wringing over something gone wrong was a surefire way to expose one's guilt.

The day Mike Reader died, Oren had returned home, watched TV, ate his dinner of fish sticks and mac-and-cheese, had his bath, behaved normally, and no one, not even his own mother, had ever guessed that he'd been the cause of the tragedy that had taken place only two blocks from his house. When he'd heard the sirens of a police car and an ambulance screaming through his neighborhood, his only reaction had been to adjust the volume on the TV.

The Coldare kid was dead, and he would remain dead. Oren had no choice but to accept it and handle it. He must remain calm.

He must not act rashly. Problem solving was his forte. The more complicated a puzzle was, the better he liked it. It took patience and ingenuity to work oneself out of an intricate maze.

There was a way out of this muddle. He simply had to find it.

Of course, if the worst-case scenario came about, he had a fail-safe escape hatch already in place. But for the present, he was facing an unexpected wall. His only recourse was to backtrack. Bitterly, he accepted that, to ensure success, sacrifices must be made.

To that end, it wasn't absolutely necessary that Ben Lofland die.

The man had had the bejesus scared out of him and had been made to look like a fool for being caught with his pants down, literally. While this wasn't the severe punishment Lofland deserved, Oren resolved that it was satisfaction enough.

Berry, however, must die. There was no other option. He'd be satisfied with nothing less than death for her.

But how to bring it about? Everyone near her was on high alert. Oren's name and face had been widely broadcast. Any man even remotely resembling him would be arrested on sight if not shot outright by a trigger-happy vigilante. In which case, hiding was an acceptable course of action.

But hiding was unproductive and, frankly, boring. And the worst effect of hiding and taking no action whatsoever was that Berry remained alive. On the other hand, if he was seen—

And with that thought, the solution came to him suddenly.

Create confusion. Yes, yes! He would confound them. With cleverness, good timing, and a little luck—and wasn't he due some?—Berry and those protecting her would soon be scratching their heads, trying to make sense of the impossible.

The prospect of that filled Oren with glee.

CHAPTER 16

KISSING BERRY.

The world was going to hell in a handbasket—Ski Nyland's corner of it was in the express lane—and he couldn't concentrate on how to slow down that descent for thinking about kissing Berry. Elbowing their way to the forefront of his mind were thoughts of how well her long, lean body had fit his, how delicious her mouth had tasted, and others much more stirring.

He couldn't indulge them any more than he could take off and go fishing today, or catch up on two nights' worth of sleep.

From Caroline's lake house, he drove directly to his. He shaved, took a cold shower, and by the time he'd dressed in fresh clothes, his coffeemaker had brewed him a full pot. He poured the coffee into a thermal container with a drinking spout. He spread a thick layer of peanut butter onto a piece of stale bread, folded it in half, and consumed it as he left his house and got back into his SUV. The coffee tasted good and acrid, so hot it scalded his tongue.

His tongue, which had mated with Berry's.

Working the case would act as a shock absorber to the erotic sensations assailing him. He doubted they would disappear, but keeping his mind focused on catching Oren Starks would prevent them from being as jolting as they'd been there in Caroline King's kitchen.

And, anyway, personal concerns seemed obscenely selfish today, when the Coldare boy's killer was at large.

As he drove toward the motel, where he intended to grill the owner again, he called Sheriff Drummond at home. Mrs. Drummond answered, told Ski the sheriff was in the shower but said she would give him the message as soon as he was available.

He called the office. Andy was manning the phone. Ski told him where he was headed and asked to be notified immediately if anyone checked in with an update.

By the time he had drunk all the coffee left in his thermal mug, his cell phone was ringing. He answered without checking the readout. "Good morning, Sheriff Drummond."

"Not the sheriff, Ski. It's Stevens. I found the car."

The motel sign with the raccoon on it was in sight, but Ski executed a tight U-turn, which caused his tires to smoke on the pavement. He was five miles from where Deputy Stevens had discovered a maroon Toyota. Ski drove the distance with the lights behind his grille and on his light bar flashing. It was Sunday morning, so there weren't too many other vehicles on the road, which helped put him there in a matter of minutes.

The other deputy was standing beside the driver's door of the Toyota. As Ski got out of his SUV, he called to him, "You're sure there are no footprints?"

"None on this side, Ski, or I wouldn't be standing here."

The deputy had fifteen years' seniority over Ski, but he was a laid-back guy and seemed not to have taken offense when, during their brief cell phone conversation, Ski had urged him repeatedly to avoid destroying tracks or compromising evidence.

"Wish I could have told you I'd found him asleep behind the wheel," Stevens said when Ski reached him.

"Wish you could have, too."

"I'd like a piece of this sum'bitch."

"Get in line."

Placing his hands on his knees, Ski leaned down and looked through the driver's window into the car. He saw nothing either on the front seats or in the back, and nothing on the floorboards. The key was still in the ignition. Starks hadn't planned on coming back.

"How'd he get out without making a footprint?"

"Other side," Stevens said.

Ski walked around the hood in order to avoid stepping on the tire treads imprinted into the soft soil of the shoulder behind the car, which Stevens had had the good sense not to disturb when he approached in his patrol car. They'd need those to compare with the ones found near the lake house and the motel.

Ski studied the footprints. Starks had left a full right one when he stepped out, then a full left that was slightly deeper and more distinct than the right, then a partial right footprint where he'd walked into tall weeds.

From there, the trail became decidedly more obscure. Starks had had endless options for places in which to hide and directions in which to go. Directly ahead was an open field fifty yards deep that was railroad frontage. It stretched along the tracks in both directions for as far as one could see.

Across the tracks was a similar open area that bled into an industrial section on the outer edge of downtown Merritt. There were assorted warehouses, a trucking company, a distribution center for paper products, a work glove factory.

More worrisome to Ski than the businesses in daily operation were the abandoned buildings of failed enterprises. Several multistoried, sprawling structures stood in various states of disrepair, providing countless nooks and crannies in which a man could hide. Beyond that industrial area were the middle school campus and a city park with a municipal swimming pool and athletic fields for soccer and baseball.

Davis Coldare had played his final game on that diamond last Monday night.

Ski swore, using a particularly foul phrase he'd learned in the

Army. Stevens stood by, wisely saying nothing, shifting his chaw from one cheek to the other.

Behind them, on the other side of the street from the deserted Toyota, was a row of houses. Basically on the fringe of a lower-middle-class, blue-collar neighborhood, the frame houses were seventy years old at best, owned by breadwinners who toiled hard to make ends meet. One of the houses had a log-hauling rig parked in the front yard.

"Talked to any of the residents?" Ski asked.

Stevens shook his head. "Didn't want to leave the car, have somebody come by and screw up the tracks. But nobody's come or gone since I got here."

By now three other deputies had converged on the site. As they approached, Ski cautioned them to watch where they stepped so the scene wouldn't be corrupted. "I'll shoot any one of you who compromises a trace of evidence." He was only half joking.

He assigned one of them to conduct a door-to-door of the houses, to ask if anybody had seen the man who'd left the Toyota parked on their street. If anyone had information, they were to be brought to Ski immediately.

Then he went to stand in the center of the street and, hands on hips, did a slow three-sixty survey of the entire area, hoping to see something that would give him a clue as to where Starks had gone when he'd hobbled from the car. Was he miles away by now, or close? Chances were he was watching Ski from his hiding place, perhaps from the cloudy window of one of the vacant warehouses.

Ski wondered if Starks had abandoned the car here for a specific reason, but he was betting not. There were no other tire tracks indicating that Starks had been met here and picked up. Ski figured he'd driven this far from the motel before being struck with the full impact of what he'd done. He'd feared his car might have been seen, possibly by someone driving past the motel when the fatal gunshot was fired. Maybe he thought Lisa Arnold had seen the direction he'd taken when he fled.

Whatever had gone through Starks's mind—and God only

knew—he was rational enough to realize he had to ditch the car and take his chances on foot. He probably thought this was as good a spot as any. There were no streetlights in this part of town. It was a street traveled by only the handful of families who lived on it, and it was doubtful they had a neighborhood crime watch.

Starks had walked away from the car in stocking feet. That was something to Ski's advantage.

He turned to Stevens. "You're the best print man in the department. Get what you can from the car. Go over it with a fine-tooth comb."

"Sure thing, Ski," he said and walked toward his car to get his fingerprinting kit.

Addressing the other deputies, Ski said, "I'll call in more reserves, but start without them. Stay with Starks's trail through the field as far as you can. See if you can pick it up on the other side of the railroad tracks. All those abandoned buildings, start at the bottom of each one and work your way up. Look for anything recently disturbed. I want every inch of them searched. If anyone finds something, they're not to touch it. Call me immediately. Tell the others when they get here."

They nodded.

"Andy's on phone duty. I'll get him to track down the owners of those businesses and secure permission for you to go inside. I want them checked for break-ins, jimmied alarm systems, anything and everything out of the ordinary. Same goes for the middle school campus. I want frequent updates. Anything seen, heard, or discovered, I want to know immediately. *Anything,* got it?"

"Sure, Ski. Where are you going?"

"To talk to the boss."

His phone had rung twice, but he'd ignored it, knowing it was probably Sheriff Drummond returning his call. Now, he depressed the button to dial the sheriff's home number. Drummond picked up on the first ring. "Ski?"

"Morning, sir. I need a minute of your time."

"Is it about the Coldare boy? His granddad and I are in Rotary together. Terrible thing. Tragic. You're sure it was Starks?"

"Yes, sir. I've got a positive ID. I can be at your house in five minutes."

"We're trying to make the eleven o'clock worship service."

"I promise not to keep you long."

Ski didn't give him a chance to argue before disconnecting. When he arrived at the sheriff's home, Mrs. Drummond was already sitting in the front seat of their Lincoln Town Car with the motor running. The sheriff was waiting at the end of his driveway, dressed in his Sunday best, Bible in one hand, Stetson in the other.

Ski pushed the gearshift into Park but left his SUV idling as he got out. "I hate to hold you up, sir, so I'll get straight to the point."

"No apology necessary, Ski. Starks shot a good kid in cold blood. That goes beyond wounding a man in a love triangle showdown. What do you need?"

"Your authorization."

"For?"

"Dogs."

"Hey, it's Andy, right?"

Dodge, who had exchanged names with the young deputy the night before, strolled into the sheriff's department and over to the desk where Andy was seated. Fortune was with him. Andy was the only one there, and since he'd seen Dodge in Ski's company the night before, he didn't question Dodge's walking in like he owned the place.

Dodge set a white box on the desk. "What I like about small towns, they always have a doughnut shop where they're made fresh every morning."

"The Donut Hole," Andy said.

"Help yourself."

"Thanks." Eagerly the deputy raised the lid and surveyed the selection.

"Don't thank me," Dodge said. "Wasn't my idea. Ski sent me to pick up that evidence on Starks he got last night. Since you're stuck here while everybody else is out, he thought you deserved a treat."

Andy, frowning, licked strawberry frosting off his fingers. "I just talked to Ski. He didn't say anything—"

"How old's that coffee?"

Andy glanced over at the stained coffeemaker sitting on a table against the far wall. "Uh, an hour or two, I think."

Dodge grinned. "Then it should be just about right." Holding a blueberry cake doughnut in his mouth, he went over to the coffeemaker and filled a foam cup, then added two packets of sugar. Looking over at Andy, who hadn't moved, he asked, "Got that stuff for me?"

Andy looked unsure. "Ski's on his way out to the motel to question the owner again."

"That's right. He wants to confront her with that evidence."

"He . . . I'm sorry, Mr. Hanley, but when I talked to Ski . . . wasn't but a couple of minutes before you got here . . . he—"

"He didn't say anything over the phone about it, did he?"

"No, that's why—"

"Whew, good," Dodge said, pretending to be vastly relieved. "The man's got a lot on his mind. I thought he might've slipped."

"Ski? Slipped?"

"You know, slip of the tongue. Tired as he is—I don't think he's slept since Friday night—he might have forgot that he was holding that evidence in abeyance."

"Abeyance?"

"You know, from the media."

"Media?"

"The radio station, son. Where've you been? Ski's got the local station broadcasting bulletins about Oren Starks every ten minutes or so."

"I know that, but—"

"Well, the media can be useful to us, no question. Puts Joe Q. Public on the alert. But we don't want the evidence we've got on Starks broadcast to every yahoo in East Texas, do we?"

"No, sir, but—"

"And Starks is listening to the radio, too. You can bet on it, son. Ski doesn't want him to know the goods we got last night."

The young man's eyes brightened. "So when he's caught, we can use those photos of Ms. Malone to trip him up."

Dodge's stomach dropped. It took every deception skill he possessed to look happy as he slapped the young deputy on the shoulder and said heartily, "There you go." He stuffed the remainder of the doughnut into his mouth and checked his wristwatch. "Ski put me on a deadline."

Andy got up and disappeared into a cubbyhole of an office, emerging a few seconds later with a Ziploc bag with a manila folder inside. "You gotta sign—"

Dodge snatched the plastic bag from him. "Ski said not to stand on ceremony. No time for it today."

Dodge thanked him and, with the evidence bag tucked under his arm, got the hell out of there.

The desired nap didn't pan out as Berry had hoped.

She had deserted the scene of the kiss with a cowardice equaling Ski's, fleeing the kitchen and leaving Dodge and her mother without an explanation. Upstairs, she showered, slid naked between the cool sheets, closed her burning eyes, and willed her mind to shut down and allow her body to fall asleep.

But neither her mind nor her body cooperated. Thoughts of Ski Nyland persisted. Images of them in sexual scenarios flitted through her mind, making her body restless, actually feverish in places impossible to ignore, places where she wanted to feel his eyes and hands and mouth on her.

Considering the tragedy that had taken place the night before, her lust seemed particularly ill-timed. Disgusted with herself, she threw off the covers, got up, and dressed.

When she went downstairs, she found her mother seated at the dining table, sorting through her MLS directory, making notes, cell phone within reach. "You're working?" Berry asked.

Caroline removed her reading glasses. "It's Sunday. People house-shop on Sundays. I've delegated scheduled showings to other agents, but I'm checking just to make sure all my bases are covered."

"You should try and sleep for a while."

"Waste of time."

"Well I know," Berry admitted with chagrin. "Where's Dodge?"

"I have no idea. He said he didn't have time for breakfast after all, that he needed to follow a hunch. He left almost as abruptly as Ski did."

"Hmm." Berry hoped the topic of Ski would end there. But her mother was too intuitive.

"What happened between you?" she asked. "When Dodge and I came in, we could practically smell the ozone. Were you in the middle of an argument, or . . . something else?" Just then her cell phone jingled, saving Berry from having to answer. Caroline checked the caller ID. "It's my office."

"Take your call. I'm off."

"Where are you going?"

"It's Sunday. Day of atonement."

Twenty minutes after leaving the lake house, she was standing outside Ben Lofland's hospital room. She bolstered herself for whatever might come of this visit and tapped lightly on the door. Amanda Lofland opened it. When she saw Berry, her expression turned petulant and hostile.

Berry didn't give her an opportunity to speak first. "I'd like to see Ben."

"What for?"

"To apologize for his getting shot."

Startled by the blunt admission, Amanda regarded Berry with mistrust but then stepped aside and allowed her to enter the room. Ben was awake, half sitting up with pillows behind his back.

Berry smiled as she approached the bed. "You're looking a lot better than you were the last time I saw you."

"I feel worse," he grumbled. "I was unconscious when you last saw me, and wasn't feeling a thing."

Amanda went to stand opposite Berry on the other side of the bed, her expression sour.

Berry asked Ben, "Is the pain bad?"

"Only when I breathe."

"Don't the drugs help?"

"Put it this way, I'd hate to be without them."

She said softly, "I tremble when I think how much worse it could have been."

"Yeah. That's occurred to me—to us—too." He reached for Amanda's hand and squeezed it. Husband and wife smiled at each other, although Amanda's smile was somewhat strained.

"I blame myself for underestimating Oren's mental state," Berry said.

"Who'd have thought he could do something so crazy?"

"I was forewarned," Berry admitted. "I'd seen him lose it completely."

"Before Friday night?"

"Yes. But only once. I thought it was an isolated incident, a reactive outburst. Obviously I misjudged." She took a deep breath. "That's why I saw no harm in phoning him."

Ben's pale face registered his surprise. "You phoned him? When?"

"Thursday afternoon."

Still gaping at her, he said, "Had you lost your mind?"

"It was a mistake. I see that now, but I had said things to him that I regretted and wanted to apologize for. I also felt he should know the project he'd worked on was being completed and that it had turned out well. I felt that we—that *I*—owed him that."

Ben wet his lips. His gaze shifted several times between Berry and his wife, finally landing on Berry. "I wish you'd consulted me first."

"So do I. If I had, you might have talked me out of calling him, and none of this would have happened."

"I cannot believe you," Amanda muttered. "This is *so* all your fault."

Berry had acknowledged as much, but she reacted defensively to Amanda's indictment. "I thought Oren would thank me for the call, and that would be the end of it. But apparently the only aspect of our conversation he heard was that Ben and I would be spending the day together. I'm terribly, terribly sorry."

"You've got a lot of reasons to be sorry."

"That's true, Amanda. But adultery isn't one of them. There's been nothing except friendship between Ben and me for a very long time, since before he even met you."

"I've told her that," he said. "She believes me."

Berry digested that, then, holding the other woman's judgmental glare, she said, "But you don't believe *me*?"

"I believe that Ben was faithful to me and his marriage vows. But I don't trust that you sent for him with only the campaign in mind. You left Houston, your daily office routine, your work, which by all accounts you thrive on. You left your friends, your social life, and came here to the boondocks.

"Last week you got bored and restless, so you invented a reason for Ben to come here and spend the day, and then the night, with you. You knew he would come because that campaign is so important to both your careers. But I think that was just the bait you used to lure him here. You needed some amusement, a diversion, a break from the humdrum of rural life. You needed sex, and you chose my husband to provide it."

"You're wrong," Berry said with emphasis. "I didn't lure Ben to the lake house for any prurient purpose." She paused for several beats, then added, "But I might have a few months ago."

The admission shocked them. Berry was shocked by it herself, but she continued. "Before I came to Merritt, if I had deemed it professionally beneficial or expedient to sleep with Ben, more than likely I would have devised a way to do so."

Ben was still staring at her, slack-jawed. Amanda looked smug and wrathful at the same time. "So you admit it."

"I admit that my priorities were out of whack," Berry said. "In order to move up the ladder at Delray, I was doing things I didn't like. To the point where I could no longer stand myself. I got out of Houston to avoid Oren, yes. But I also came here to get a new perspective. I'm as ambitious as ever. I still want to reach the top of my trade. I'm just no longer willing to sell my soul for it."

She gave Ben a long, measured look, which he avoided by staring at the tent in the covers formed by his toes at the foot of the hospital bed.

Neither of the Loflands had accepted her apology, at least not out loud. They, especially Amanda, would probably continue to harbor resentment against her, and she couldn't really blame them. Ben had come close to losing his life.

However, short of groveling, she could do nothing more to make reparations, and she wouldn't further humble herself to these two, who were too ungracious to accept her apology.

"I'm going to Houston tonight, so I can be at the office the first thing in the morning to present the campaign on schedule."

Amanda's whole body jerked. "Without Ben?"

"He'll get equal credit."

"Oh, I'll bet."

"I'll see to it that he does, Amanda. I promise you."

The woman dismissed the value of Berry's promise with a haughty sniff.

Berry looked down at Ben. "I'll do right by you, Ben. You'll receive equal credit."

He bobbed his head. "Sure. Thanks."

Berry had hoped for a better outcome. She was disappointed with the note on which the visit was ending, but she'd said what she had come to say. The couple remained mute with animosity. Without another word, she left them.

Out in the corridor, a hospital worker wearing a hairnet and green scrubs was pushing a rattling metal cart stacked with lunch trays. She fell into step beside Berry. "You're Ms. Malone, aren't you?"

"That's right."

"Your friend is going to be fine."

"Yes. He seems to be improving."

She hurried on, but the staff member kept pace. "Shame about that Coldare boy. My son played baseball with him."

"It was tragic."

"That guy who shot him . . ." She tsked. "He needs to be caught. And soon."

"I couldn't agree more." Having reached the elevator bank, Berry punched the Down button.

The woman pushed the rattling cart past her. "The reward ought to help."

Berry looked after her with puzzlement. "Wait. There's a reward? Since when?"

Over her shoulder the woman said, "I heard it on the radio about a half hour ago. Your mother put up the money."

CHAPTER 17

Waste of money if you ask me."

"Well, I didn't."

Caroline's calm retort served to make Dodge edgier, if that was possible. Every time he lit up a cigarette, she frowned in silent disapproval, which robbed him of the pleasure of smoking it, which was creating a drastic shortfall in his minimum daily requirement of nicotine. He figured he was running at least a quart low. His system was craving it. His skin was itching from the inside. His piss factor was high.

But they were in her car, so even if he wanted to defy her objections and smoke, he couldn't. Soon as they got to where they were going, though, he'd smoke one down to the filter, and if she didn't like it, that was just too damn bad.

He'd volunteered to drive because that at least kept his hands busy. "Is there only one Walmart in town?"

"Yes. Do you need directions?"

"Nope. I spotted it yesterday."

"Before or after your chat with Grace?"

It pleased him that his conversation with the bartender still rankled Caroline, but he took it no further than to shoot her a wicked grin. "Twenty-five grand?" he said in reference to the reward she had offered the sheriff's office. "They'll have every nearsighted redneck in southeast Texas playing I Spy with Oren Starks."

"I'm sure Ski will have trained personnel filtering out the crank calls that come into the hotline."

"For all that'll help," he said under his breath. "The task force set up a hotline for information on the bank robber. Know what we got?"

"Reports of a Russian submarine in the shipping channel, UFO sightings, the Second Coming, a pack of rabid wolves running amok in the medical district, and a woman who called nightly offering free sex to whoever was interested."

"I told you that already?"

"Thirty-one years ago, you ranted about it whenever you got frustrated over the case."

"Then you must've heard it a lot."

"At least a thousand times."

"Huh."

"I'm sure Ski expects to get a number of kooks calling in," she said, "but he might also get a useful tip. Besides, putting up the reward made me feel like I'm contributing to Oren Starks's capture, rather than sitting around and doing nothing."

Dodge mumbled something.

Caroline looked at him. "What?"

"Nothing."

"Something about money. What did you say?"

"I said you won't miss the pocket change."

"You said more than that."

"I left out the expletives."

"Why were you using expletives?"

"Would you rather I'd've repeated them to you?"

"Why were you using expletives in regard to my money?"

He recognized her tone. She wasn't going to let the matter drop, which was fine with him, because her financial status had been eating at him, and he'd just as soon air his grievances.

"You wouldn't know a financial problem if it bit you in the butt, because you've never had one." Seeing her angry expression, he added snidely, "Well, have you?"

"I've been fortunate."

"I'll say. Fortunate enough to marry the rich, successful boss." Because he was feeling particularly fractious, he'd pushed, and he knew immediately he'd pushed too far.

Coldly she said, "Don't you dare criticize me for marrying Jim."

"I didn't."

"Not in so many words, but it was implied."

"You're hearing implications that aren't there because you're supersensitive on the subject of your marriage."

"I have no reason to be supersensitive on the subject."

"No?"

"No. I had a good marriage that lasted for twenty-six years. Up till the day Jim died, we were happy together."

"Congratulations."

His sarcasm didn't escape her. "You wish I'd been unhappy?"

Raising his voice, he said, "I wish you'd been happy with *me*."

"Whose fault is it that I wasn't?" she fired back.

He swore. Neither said anything for a while, then he asked, "How'd Malone die?"

She took so long to answer, he thought she might refuse to. Finally she said, "He had a stroke. Sitting at his desk in his office. It left him in a coma. He died two days later without ever waking up, which was actually a blessing. The neurologist told me that Jim had sustained extensive brain damage."

Dodge drove in ponderous silence. Then, "So you loved the guy."

"Yes, Dodge, I did. Mostly I loved him for loving me and Berry. She was almost a year old when Jim asked me to marry him. He'd been a confirmed bachelor for forty years but was willing to take on a wife and baby."

"He wanted you. You had a baby." Dodge gave an eloquent shrug.

"He didn't view Berry as a sacrifice he had to make in order to marry me. He accepted her without explanation or qualification.

He loved her dearly and reared her as his own. Which was good, since he and I never had any children together."

"Why not?"

"No reason. Just one of those things. It never happened. We didn't let it become an issue. Both of us were very involved in expanding the business. We worked long and hard. And we were satisfied with the daughter we had."

Either his nicotine deficiency or this discussion about another man loving and rearing his daughter was making his chest hurt. But Dodge couldn't stop giving voice to the questions that had bedeviled him for three decades. "What kind of kid was Berry? Was she happy?"

Caroline looked across at him and smiled. "Very. Completely. She was exuberant. Smart. Precocious. Athletic. Competitive. Willful at times, but not bratty."

"Stubborn like you."

"Cunning like you."

"Did she have your redhead's temper?"

"I don't have a redhead's temper."

He laughed at her tart response, then she joined him. His laughter was the first to falter. "Did you ever tell her?"

"What?"

"Do I have to spell it out, Caroline?"

She turned her head away to gaze through the windshield. She was doing that thing with her hands, clasping and unclasping them, a habit familiar to him. She did that whenever she was organizing her thoughts, particularly distressing ones.

"Yes, I told her. Jim had adopted her and given her his name, but I thought she should know that he wasn't her birth father. I didn't want that to be a big, dark secret lurking in the background of our lives, just waiting to spring and inflict damage on our relationship."

It cut Dodge to the quick to be reminded that he'd signed away all parental rights to his daughter. It had been a sanitary procedure, handled by lawyers. At the time, he'd been angry and had thought he'd been given little choice.

He couldn't help but wonder what would have happened if he had raised a stink. Would the outcome have been different if he'd refused to relinquish the upbringing of his daughter to another man?

But now, as thirty years ago, he couldn't see any benefit arising from a tug-of-war that would only have prolonged the inevitable and created more hostility and heartache for everyone involved, particularly for Caroline and Berry.

"When Berry was old enough to know where babies come from," Caroline continued, "I told her that Jim wasn't the man who'd planted the seed in my tummy. Something to that effect," she said, smiling gently. "But I assured her that Jim was her daddy. She accepted it."

Dodge braked for a traffic light, touched his breast pocket where the packet of cigarettes beckoned to him, worked his bottom more comfortably into the driver's seat, and muttered deprecations at the driver in front of him who didn't know to pull into the intersection so he could hook a quick left when the light turned yellow, allowing Dodge to hook an even quicker one before it turned red.

He cleared his throat. "Wasn't she ever curious to know who the sower of the seed had been? She never asked what had happened to her real daddy, why he'd left her and didn't come back?"

"She brought it up only once," Caroline said. "She was of an age when I felt I should caution her against the pitfalls of having sex in the heat of the moment without using common sense or, if that failed, protection. And she asked if that's what had happened to me. She wanted to know if she'd been a mishap, an unwanted responsibility that a man had run away from."

She looked across at Dodge, and he looked back at her.

Caroline went on. "It broke my heart to hear the vulnerability in her voice when she asked that question. Apparently she'd been haunted by the thought that her conception had been an unhappy accident. She'd yearned to know the truth but hadn't asked for fear of having her supposition confirmed."

"Jesus," Dodge groaned miserably.

"I relieved her of the notion. I emphasized that she'd been

conceived during a happy time, and that neither her father nor I had regretted the pregnancy. I told her that there had been issues between us that didn't relate to her, but that were serious enough to prevent us from being together, and that you—he—had seen the advantages of her staying with me." She looked down at her hands, still clasping and unclasping them in her lap. "She believed me. At least I suppose she did, because she never raised the subject again."

"And now?"

"Now?"

He gave her a dubious look. "She's a smart cookie, Caroline. How could she not have a clue?"

"Maybe she does. She hasn't asked outright, but she's pressured me for information about you."

"So she suspects that I'm not just a referral from a friend."

"Possibly. But it's quite a leap from expressing curiosity over your credentials to determining that you're her father. She might be putting two and two together, but it hasn't added up to four yet." After a moment, she added softly, "One thing, though."

"What?"

"Even if she is deliberating it, she won't reveal her hand until she's good and ready."

"Plays her hand close to her vest?"

She shot him a smile. "In that way she's like me."

Walmart came into view. The massive parking lot was in a state of barely controlled pandemonium. A few sheriff's office and state trooper cars were there with their colored lights flashing. Dogs were running in circles, sniffing the ground near a row of garbage receptacles. Onlookers were being held back by uniformed officers of various agencies, including the Merritt city police.

And in the thick of it was Ski Nyland.

Dodge understood why the deputy's telephone summons had been so abrupt. Presently he and several other badges were clustered around a potbellied, middle-aged guy wearing a blue Walmart employee vest. When Ski spotted Dodge pulling into the parking lot, he left the group and jogged toward them.

Dodge said, "He wants to jump our daughter."

Caroline said, "If I'm reading the vibes right, the feeling is mutual."

The moment Ski reached them, he asked, "Where's Berry?"

"She went to the hospital to see Ben," Caroline told him. "I couldn't reach her on her cell."

"Try again. Get her over here." As an afterthought he added a "please," although Caroline seemed not to have noticed his brusqueness. Responding to his sense of urgency, she immediately had accessed her cell phone and was speed-dialing Berry.

Dodge got out of the car and lit a cigarette.

Ski bore down on him, growling angrily, "What the hell, Dodge?"

Dodge clicked his lighter closed and blew smoke toward the sky. The deputy's anger needed no explanation. "I had a hunch, I acted on it."

"You tampered with evidence."

"Sue me. And, by the way, I didn't *tamper* with anything. I know how to handle evidence."

"Where is it now?"

"Safely stored. So what do you want to do? Slug out our difference of opinion on protocol and chain of evidence in front of God and everybody? Or talk about the significance of those pictures?"

Ski removed his sunglasses and wiped his sweating forehead on his sleeve. He glanced into the car at Caroline, who was still talking on her cell phone. Coming back around to Dodge and keeping his voice low, he said, "Best I can tell, they were taken with a telephoto lens."

"But close enough to be scary."

Ski gave a solemn nod of agreement. "Close enough. They're a whole friggin' photographic study of Berry's life here. He got shots of the lake house from every angle. He's got her coming and going all over town."

"Wearing different clothes," Dodge said. "Which means he followed her on numerous occasions."

"He got up close and personal, too."

The deputy's square jaw hardened, and Dodge knew he was thinking about the series of shots taken of Berry through her bedroom window, and when she was sunbathing on the pier, blissfully unaware that a man who'd vowed to kill her was watching, perversely violating her in a way that made Dodge's blood boil.

"Careless of him to leave them in the motel room."

"He didn't," Ski said. "I found them in a trash barrel on the side of the road behind the motel, near where he'd hidden the car."

"So even after killing the kid, he had the presence of mind to take them with him and try to unload them."

"He didn't want to be caught with something that would implicate him."

"Careful bastard."

"Berry told me he works puzzles. He's methodical. He won't stop."

"Which means we gotta stop him," Dodge said, tossing away his cigarette butt.

"He's on foot. At least he was."

"Fill me in."

"We found an abandoned maroon Toyota. Just by eyeballing the tire tracks, I'm almost certain it's the same car that was at the lake house and behind the motel. Starks left it on foot, shoeless."

"You used the dogs to track him." Dodge motioned to the trio of German shepherds, which were leashed but still moving in frenzied circles, their noses to the asphalt.

Ski said, "Army buddy of mine has this canine search and rescue outfit out of Tyler. He called up one of his best trainers and his dogs, got them down here in a hurry. We had Starks's shoes. The dogs picked up his scent, followed it along the railroad tracks till they crossed Highway 287 at a point a half mile from here."

Caroline got out of the car and joined them. "I caught Berry just as she was leaving the hospital. She'll be here within minutes."

"Then what?" Dodge asked, turning back to Ski. "After Starks got here."

"Then nothing. The trail goes cold."

"Shit."

"Tell me," Ski muttered. "All the dogs converged on the area just over there by the Dumpsters. Either he stole a vehicle, which I doubt since none has been reported, or he hijacked one, or somebody picked him up."

"You've ruled out that he was sucked up by space aliens?"

Ski snuffled. "At least then I'd know where to start looking. As it is, the trail ends here." He motioned toward the Walmart employee who seemed inflated by all the attention he was receiving. "Store manager. He's got Starks on several security camera videos. At least I'm fairly certain it's Starks. That's why I want Berry to take a look."

"Here she comes," Caroline said.

The parking lot was swarming with law enforcement personnel and onlookers, including a van full of elderly people from an assisted living facility, but Berry spotted the trio she sought the instant she turned off the highway.

She pulled her car to a stop near them and got out.

Ski said, "Thanks for getting here so fast."

She responded with matching formality. "Mother said Oren has been here."

He gave her a bullet-point rundown of the events that had taken place since the discovery of the abandoned car. "I thought you might look at the videos, confirm it's Starks."

"Of course."

"I'll get the manager and meet you inside the main entrance." He left them and, in his long-legged stride, walked over to the group of peace officers huddled around the man in a blue vest.

As she, Dodge, and Caroline made their way toward the store entrance, Caroline asked after Ben.

"He's glad he has drugs for the pain."

Berry had no more to say on the subject and was relieved when they didn't press her for details. The AC inside the store was a welcome relief from the heat of the parking lot. Ski and an older deputy, whom she remembered simply as Stevens, came in accompanied by the store manager, who said importantly, "This way," and busily jangled a cluster of keys attached to his belt.

Before they fell into step behind him, Dodge motioned toward the store's snack bar, where a young man was slouched in a booth. Across from him was a woman wearing a Merritt County sheriff's deputy uniform. The young man's posture and expression conveyed boredom and bad attitude. The deputy looked angry and dour as she tapped a pen against her blank notepad.

"Who's that with the deputy?" Dodge asked.

"The cashier who rang up Starks's purchase. We haven't been able to shake much out of him."

"Mind if I give it a shot?"

Ski shrugged. "Be my guest."

Stevens looked at Ski with surprise but didn't question his decision to give Dodge a turn with the witness.

Dodge strolled over to the booth. Ignoring the young man, he said something to the deputy, who looked over her shoulder at Ski. Ski gave her a nod. She shrugged, slid out of the booth, and left the store through the exit. Dodge took her place in the booth, facing the young man across the table.

Berry said, "I thought women were his speciality."

Caroline smiled faintly. "He can be persuasive with men, too."

Ski said, "I gotta get back outside, so I'm turning you over to Stevens."

He left, and the store manager ushered Berry, Caroline, and Stevens to the rear of the store and into his office. He seemed disappointed when Berry identified Oren Starks within seconds of watching the first security video he put into the player.

"That's him. Definitely." On the monitor Starks could be seen entering the store. "He's even wearing the same clothes." The video was in black and white, but even though the pants and shirt were rumpled, they matched those he'd had on when he came to the lake house.

"He's limping, too," she observed. He appeared benign, an average-looking man without a single sinister aspect. But seeing him again made Berry shiver with revulsion and fear.

"Didn't anyone notice that he was in stocking feet?" Caroline asked.

"The store is open twenty-four/seven." The deputy pointed at the digital time readout at the bottom of the screen. "He walked in at three-twelve A.M. That time of morning, only a skeleton crew is manning this huge store. There were a handful of other customers, but you can tell Starks avoids going down aisles where there were other shoppers."

Oren had made short work of picking out a pair of sports shoes and paying for them. He was in and out of the store within minutes. Caroline asked, "Why didn't he just put on the shoes and walk out? Why risk being recognized by the cashier?"

"Why risk being caught shoplifting?"

"And it wouldn't have been gaming," Berry said. The others looked at her. "He knew security cameras would be recording his movements. He's saying to us, 'I may be a killer, but I'm not a thief.'"

Stevens said, "You're positive this is our guy?"

"Positive."

"Ski was, too, but he wanted it corroborated anyhow. He's careful that way."

They filed out of the office and made their way through the aisles of the store toward the exit. There was no sign of Dodge and the young man in the snack bar, but when they emerged from the store, they saw him standing with the female deputy who'd been questioning him before Dodge took over. He now appeared much more talkative; the deputy was taking rapid notes.

"Guess your guy got him to open up," Stevens remarked as he guided Berry and Caroline over to where Ski and Dodge were conferring. Dodge was pulling hard on a cigarette. As they got near, Berry heard him say through a foggy exhale, "It's amazing how cooperative a guy can get when his dick is the bargaining chip."

Berry couldn't help but smile. "Dare I ask?"

Dodge grinned, but it was a chilling expression. "The cashier. I told him his attitude needed some readjustment, like right fucking now, or else. I made myself understood and believed."

"What did he say about Oren?"

Dodge was grinding out one cigarette and lighting another, so Ski answered for him. "He'd never heard of Oren Starks. He just moved here from Fort Worth to live with his grandmother, and all she watches on TV is the Weather Channel. Since he didn't go to school here, he didn't know Davis Coldare, either. He hates his job, hates the manager, hates the hours, but needs the money."

"For dope," Dodge provided. "He smoked some weed during his break about half an hour before Starks showed."

"You got that out of him?" Ski asked.

Dodge shrugged. "As I said, we reached an understanding."

Ski resumed. "Starks came up to the counter with the shoebox. The cashier scanned the bar code. Starks paid cash. The cashier gave him change for three twenties and a ten. He remembered because every other customer had paid with a credit card. He asked if Starks wanted a sack. Starks said no and walked out carrying the box, which we found along with his receipt in one of those containers. I'm assuming that's where he put on his new shoes."

"Then pulled a Casper and disappeared," Dodge said with finality.

"That was the extent of his exchange with the cashier?" Berry asked. " 'Do you want a sack?' 'No.' That was it?"

"I'm afraid so," Dodge said. "I asked him if Starks was acting funny. He said no. I asked was he acting weird or furtive. He asked me what *furtive* meant, so I described furtive behavior, and he said, 'Well, yeah, I mean, dude, I guess, maybe.' Make of that what you can."

Before they could make anything of it, Berry's cell phone rang. She took it from her handbag and touched the screen. "Hello."

"Hello, Berry."

Her heart nearly leaped from her chest. Even through the phone, despite the noise in the parking lot, there was no mistaking Oren's voice.

"Surprised to hear from me?" he asked.

Caroline and Dodge were bickering over his cigarette, but Ski's gray gaze was fixed on her. Reading her shocked expression correctly, he waved for the others to be quiet and moved to stand within an inch of her, a silent question in his eyes.

She nodded, wet her lips, said into the telephone, "Yes, Oren. I am very surprised. Where are you?"

He laughed, the awful sound causing goose bumps to break out on her arms. "Wouldn't you like to know?" He hummed a few bars of a tune.

Berry turned the screen of her phone toward Ski so he could read the number displayed. He scribbled it into his palm with a pen and held it out for Dodge to read. Dodge dropped his cigarette and ran toward a group of sheriff's deputies.

Ski was making a rolling motion with his hand, indicating to Berry that she should keep talking. But it was hard for her to hold a thought with all the commotion going on around her. She thought of switching over to speakerphone but was afraid that Oren would detect that others were listening in and hang up.

"Tell me where you are, Oren, so I can come and help you."

"Help me?" He dismissed that with a snort. "As if."

"You need help. You're hurt."

"Clumsy of me to fall down your stairs. It put my aim off, or you'd be dead."

It was difficult to ignore that, but she did. "Is your leg broken?"

"I'm not sure." He answered nonchalantly, as though she'd asked him whether or not he thought it would rain. "It's black and blue. Very swollen."

"Painful, I'm sure."

"Nothing I can't handle with some ibuprofen."

"You should get it examined. You might have developed an infection that could be fatal."

"Oh, I won't die that ingloriously, Berry. And I won't die without taking you with me."

She shuddered. Ski took her arm in a firm, reassuring grip that fortified her enough to continue. "Please listen to reason, Oren. You're in a lot of trouble. Ben is going to be okay. But the boy you shot last night died."

"That wasn't my fault."

"That's what we think, too."

"We? Meaning you and Deputy Nyland?"

At the mention of his name, Ski's eyebrows shot up, and she realized that he could hear Oren's voice through the phone.

"How do you know Deputy Nyland's name?"

"He's been mentioned in all the news reports."

"Yes, well, he believes you didn't mean to kill the Coldare boy." Ski nodded approval of what she'd said. "He thinks that shooting was an accident."

"Oh, I'll just bet he does."

"He does. He told me so himself. He's giving you the benefit of the doubt, Oren, but you're making yourself look guilty. Turn yourself in and—"

"He's there with you now, listening in."

"No, he isn't. I'm alone."

"Liar. There's too much background noise."

"I'm at a fast-food place waiting for my order."

"Which fast-food place?"

"What difference does it make?"

"Which fast food-place? I've become rather familiar with Merritt. Are you at the Chicken Shack or The Smokehouse?" Then he laughed. "Don't bother answering. Whatever you say, I know differently."

"Oren—"

"Shut up and listen to me, Berry. I'm going to kill you. I'm going to kill you slowly. I'm going to watch you die, and I'm going to enjoy it. Turn around."

"What?" she asked hoarsely.

"There's a lot of confusion at Walmart this morning. Why, I'll bet a person could be in plain sight but remain unseen."

She spun around, her eyes rapidly scanning every face, searching for his.

"Boo!" He laughed his high-pitched giggle, hummed another few notes of a song, and then the phone went dead.

The hand holding her cell phone fell to her side. Caroline stepped forward and took it from her before she dropped it. Ski remained standing in front of her, as solid as a pillar, his hand still around her biceps.

Dodge came huffing up. "They've got the cell phone on GPS. Somehow, some way Starks made it back to Houston from here 'cause that's where he's at."

"He can't be," Berry said weakly.

Dodge gave her an odd look. Ski said to him, "He intimated that he could see her, that he's here."

"Here? Un-uh. He's just trying to spook you."

"Well, it's working. He said he knew Ski was with me. He said there was a lot of confusion at Walmart. How would he know that if he wasn't here, watching?"

"Easy guess," Dodge said. "He would know that, by now, he'd been tracked to the store, and that the first thing checked would be the security cameras to confirm that he was here. He's playing you."

Going back to Ski, he continued. "His location hasn't been pinpointed, but the GPS coordinates have been passed along to HPD and Harris County S.O. Officers have been dispatched and are running hot. Damn, I wish we'd had these toys when I was a cop."

Berry didn't doubt that Ski had registered everything Dodge had told him, but his eyes had remained on her. Softly he said, "You did great."

She gave him a weak smile and nodded. "Thanks."

"How'd the son of a bitch sound?" Dodge asked.

"Smug," Ski replied.

"What did he say?"

"That he was going to kill her. Slowly. That he was going to watch her die and enjoy it."

Dodge muttered an obscenity. "Give you any clues where he was?"

"The parking lot of Walmart," Berry said dully.

"He ain't here," Dodge insisted. "He called from a Houston location. Was there any background noise?"

Ski said, "I didn't hear anything distinctive. Did you, Berry?"

She shook her head.

Ski moved his hand onto her shoulder, squeezed it gently and repeated, "You did great." Then to the group in general, he said, "If he called from Houston—"

"He did," said Dodge emphatically.

"Then I'm going down there. Dodge, do you still have your pistol?"

"What do you think?"

"Will you stay with Berry?"

"I want to be there when they book this asshole," Dodge said.

"They don't have him yet."

"When they do."

"You're still hoping for a crack at him."

"That, too. That *especially.*"

Ski shook his head. "Sorry, Dodge. You're unofficial. Besides, if Starks eludes capture again, I trust Berry with you more than I trust her with anybody else."

Dodge swore, looked at Caroline, then at Berry. "All right," he said to Ski. "I won't let her out of my sight."

"Thanks."

"But I'm still gonna shoot the bastard if I get a chance. I know an excellent defense attorney."

Ski grinned, then turned and started jogging away.

"And, Ski, something else." Ski stopped and turned back. Dodge said, "That number that Starks called her from?"

"I'm sure HPD is running down the records on it."

"No need to," Dodge said. "Didn't you recognize it? It's Sally Buckland's cell phone."

CHAPTER 18

IT DIDN'T AMOUNT TO ANYTHING," DODGE SAID AS HE POURED a shot of whiskey into a highball glass and passed it to Berry.

"No, thanks."

"Take a couple of sips. It'll help steady you."

"I can't drink. I'm leaving for Houston soon."

He pushed the glass into her shaking hand. "Couple of sips."

Dodge had followed Berry and Caroline back to the lake house, staying on Berry's bumper for the duration of the trip. When they reached the turnoff to the house, he lowered the window on his car and told the reserve deputy on guard that if he saw somebody on the property who didn't belong to shoot first and ask questions later.

"What's Ski say?"

"He says to shoot twice," Dodge lied. "Pass it on to your buddy on the pier."

Once inside the house and satisfied that its security hadn't been breached, he'd asked Caroline if she had any liquor. When she pointed him to a cabinet in the living room, he took out a bottle of bourbon and poured the shot for Berry, which she now sipped as advised.

"Thanks."

"What about Sally Buckland?" Caroline asked.

Dodge sighed but knew she would persist until he gave her a full explanation. "As I said, my one conversation with her didn't amount to anything. I called her—"

"Why were you calling her?"

"Because I thought maybe I could get more information out of her than Ski had. He's good, but his bedside manner needs some work."

"And yours has been perfected."

"Mother, please," Berry said wearily. "Let him tell us what he knows." To Dodge she said, "How did you obtain Sally's phone numbers?"

"I'll get to that. The point is, I called her cell phone several times. Got no answer but finally reached her on her landline. She was as evasive with me as she had been with Ski. The shooting here was none of her business, she hadn't seen any of the people involved since she left Delray Marketing, yada yada."

Berry asked, "Did she say I was lying when I called Oren a stalker?"

"Almost word for word what she'd told Ski."

"Incomprehensible," Berry murmured.

"I got the same runaround from the lady that Ski did. I decided to let her sleep on it, then tried calling her again this morning, hoping to catch her in a more cooperative mood. No answer on either number."

"She would have recognized your number on caller ID," Berry said. "She didn't want to talk, so she didn't answer."

"Figured that," Dodge said. "So I planned to drive down today for a face-to-face, see if I could get a better read, but you know what it's been like around here today."

She didn't know about the photos he'd tricked the deputy into giving him, and, for the time being, he wasn't going to tell her. Apparently Ski was of the same mind, or he would have told her about them. Oren's telephone call had knocked her on her can.

Caroline was looking none too steady herself. Ski had put him in charge of protecting them, and that included withholding information that wasn't absolutely necessary for them to know. Knowing about the photographs would only add to their fear.

Dodge picked up the topic where he'd left off. "Yesterday Sally Buckland defended Oren Starks. Today he's using her cell phone."

Berry pulled her lower lip through her teeth. "That doesn't bode well, does it?"

"Not at all."

"I'm worried about her."

"You should be."

"You think she's in danger?"

Dodge frowned. "That wasn't what I was going to say."

"You're thinking something," Caroline said. "What?"

"Starks and Sally Buckland could be in cahoots."

"I refuse to accept that," Berry said.

"Then give me something better."

"I can't, Dodge. But I know with certainty that Sally loathed Oren. Maybe even feared him just as I came to."

"Even antagonists can team up against a greater foe," Dodge said.

"Me? I'm the foe?"

"Don't get your panties in a wad. I'm just bouncing around some ideas. Is it even remotely possible that they teamed up to get back at you for something?"

Berry took another sip of the bourbon. Dodge noticed that her hand was shaking as she raised the glass to her mouth.

The silence stretched out. Eventually Caroline said, "I trust Ski to wring some answers out of Sally Buckland."

"First thing he's going to ask her is about Amanda Lofland."

Dodge deliberately dropped that statement like a lead weight and then watched closely for Berry's reaction to it. Her astonishment seemed genuine, even to his keen eye. "Amanda and Sally? What's the connection?"

"You don't know?"

"I wasn't aware they knew each other."

"Well, they do."

"How do you know?"

"I pinched Amanda Lofland's phone yesterday."

"You *what*?" Berry said. "Why?"

He shrugged. "Curiosity. I checked her contacts and call log."

"And found Sally Buckland's number among them," Caroline said.

"Yep. Calls going back and forth for several weeks—the lady must never wipe her log clean. Later I gave the phone back to Ski. If he's done his homework, and I think we can assume he has, he'll see those same calls and wonder what those two ladies, along with Oren Starks, have in common. Astute boy that he is, he'll come up with the same thing I did." He looked at Berry. "You."

Berry didn't comment. Instead she lowered her head and stared into the contents of her glass.

Caroline said, "But Ski hasn't specifically talked to you about Amanda Lofland?"

"No, but he called while I was in the car, following you here. His mind is following the same track as mine. He asked if I thought it was possible that Sally Buckland and Oren are working together, that maybe she scooped Starks off that Walmart parking lot."

"What led him to think that?" Caroline asked.

"He'd already heard back from Houston PD. Officers dispatched to Buckland's house report there's no one there. Garage is empty. They've put out an APB on her car. Her cell phone goes straight to voice mail. Which isn't surprising. After calling Berry, Starks would know better than to leave it on."

"Which brings me to another question," Caroline said. "Why did he use that phone to call Berry? Why call her at all?"

"Ski and I gnawed on that, too," Dodge admitted. "Doesn't make good sense. Starks would know we could track him that way, except that he picked a damn good location to call from. Guess where." Before either could venture a guess, he told them. "Minute Maid Park. He called just as the Astros game was ending. HPD was all over it, but nobody knows what Starks is driving."

"Sally Buckland's car?" Caroline said.

"Best guess. But no one knows with absolute certainty that's what he's in. Even if he is, it took a while to get her license plate number into the pipeline, so he could have escaped before anyone was looking for that car. Adding to the confusion, there were thousands leaving the ball game. Traffic was snarled." Grudgingly, Dodge added, "Couldn't have been smarter of the son of a bitch."

Berry said huskily, "What you're telling us is that he's escaped again."

"Yeah," he said heavily. "That's what I'm telling you. But I gotta add that signaling the authorities to his location seems like a stupid thing for a man on the run to do."

"He's not stupid. Far from it. He used Sally's phone for a reason. He called me for a reason. We don't know what those reasons are, but I assure you that everything Oren does is part of his master plan." She set the unfinished glass of bourbon on the coffee table and stood up. "I'm going up to pack."

Dodge said, "You'd just as well finish that whiskey, because you're not going to Houston tonight."

Her chin went up a notch. "I most certainly am."

"No, ma'am. Get that plan right outta your head."

"I've got to be at Delray Marketing tomorrow morning to make my presentation."

"Did you clear that with Ski?"

"I'm not obligated to."

"He'll have a shitfit."

"He's got his work, his career, and I've got mine. The deadline for that campaign is tomorrow. It was assigned to me. It represents a whole year's work. It's my baby. I'm presenting it on schedule."

Caroline said, "Berry, I know how important that commitment is to you. But given the circumstances, everyone at Delray, as well as the client, would understand if you asked for a postponement."

"Would you postpone an important closing?"

Caroline seemed about to answer one way, changed her mind and said softly, "Probably not."

"Then you can understand why I have to be there tomorrow. Ben can't be. I made a promise to be there on his behalf. The client expects me to come through, and so does Delray."

"Screw Delray, screw Lofland, the client, and every-damn-body," Dodge exclaimed. "Have both of you forgotten that a freaking lunatic has threatened to kill you?"

"If I hide here, put my life on hold, Oren's won," Berry argued. "I'm going." She left the room and started up the stairs.

Dodge placed his hands on his hips and fixed a baleful stare on Caroline. "Are you just going to stand there? Do something. Stop her."

"How? I tried. I'm open to suggestions."

"I don't know *how,* just do it. Reason with her."

"Impossible, Dodge."

"Right. Because she's just as bullheaded as you."

She brushed past him on her way to the staircase. "And as ambitious as you."

Berry was determined to keep her appointment the next morning, and Caroline was equally determined not to be left behind. Dodge had pledged to Ski not to let Berry out of his sight. Bottom line: all of them were going to Houston.

Dodge put up credible objections and grumbled about the long drive facing them, but he was secretly glad the trip was on. Berry's stubbornness gave him an excuse to go where he wanted to be anyway. He wanted to confront the son of a bitch who'd been terrorizing his daughter. Once Starks was in custody and behind bars, it would be more difficult for Dodge to tell him how lucky he was to be intact and breathing.

And if Dodge was fortunate enough to catch Starks before the authorities did, the man wouldn't live to see the inside of a jail cell.

It was decided that they would take Caroline's car, which had a roomier and more comfortable interior than his rental. Knowing he couldn't smoke in it, he inhaled as many cigarettes as he could while waiting for the two women to gather up what they would take with them.

Berry was the first to join him outside. As she came down the back steps carrying a large leather portfolio and a small suitcase, she eyed the cigarette butts he had extinguished in the pot of caladiums. "Do you think those will sustain you till we get there?"

"Do I have a choice?"

His querulousness caused her to smile. Together they stashed her things in the trunk. She was about to get into the backseat when she hesitated. "I know you consider this assignment glorified babysitting. You'd much rather be in on the action. But, for what it's worth, I'm glad you have my back, Dodge." She reached out and touched his hand. "Thanks."

He had ridiculed people who got mushy over their kids. He'd believed them to be goddamn fools, bores, and probably liars. But when Berry smiled at him, touched his hand, he understood the absurd, inexplicable, boundless scope of parental love.

It was several minutes before he recovered his breath and the tightness in his chest relaxed.

Once they were under way, he tried to reach Ski but got his voice mail. He left a message, briefly apprising him of their plans. There was no response until they were halfway to Houston and had stopped to take a break at a large service station. Dodge was standing guard outside the ladies' room when his cell phone rang.

He checked the caller ID, sighed, and braced himself for what he knew was coming. "I swear I tried." He let Ski rant profanely for a full thirty seconds before butting in. "She's damned and determined to make that meeting tomorrow."

Ski expelled his breath, and along with it another series of swearwords. "I want her back in Merritt as soon as it's over."

"I hear you. What's going on at your end?"

Ski talked for several minutes, then asked, "How's Berry? I mean besides being a massive pain in the ass."

"Abnormally quiet."

"Scared?"

"Yeah. And she doesn't even know about those pictures."

"You haven't told her or Caroline?"

"No."

"Good." He paused before continuing. "I had a deputy return Amanda Lofland's cell phone to her. Let's not pretend that you didn't dig into it."

"You saw Sally Buckland's numbers?"

"Hard to miss."

"Berry wasn't aware the two women even knew each other."

"You asked?"

"Yeah, and she looked surprised to learn they'd been in contact. What do you suppose they had to talk about?"

Ski refrained from answering. Tersely he said, "Drive safely," and clicked off.

Caroline and Berry came out of the restroom as Dodge was replacing his phone in the holster on his belt.

"Who was that?" Berry asked.

"Ski."

"Any news?"

"We'll talk about it in the car." He waited until they were back on the road before passing along Ski's update. "He's outside Buckland's house, waiting for a search warrant so he can go in, but this is Sunday. They're having to track down a judge."

He glanced at Berry in the rearview mirror. "He also asked me what the *expletive deleted* you think you're doing running off to Houston. He wasn't happy about it, let me tell you. He thought you were tucked in safe and sound at the lake house with his heavily armed guys, including me, guarding you."

"I didn't need his permission."

"I'll buy a ticket to watch when you tell him that. But between now and then, he's nixed us staying at your place overnight. Even with HPD officers posted as guards, which he thinks he could get, he's not comfortable with you being where Starks could so easily find you."

"So where are we staying?" Caroline asked.

"Ski's gonna book us rooms at a hotel. Says since you and Sheriff Drummond are such close personal, social friends, he's sure he can get him to approve the expense." Ski had said nothing of the sort regarding Caroline and the sheriff, but Dodge threw it in out of jealous spite.

"Soon as Ski's got the rooms reserved, he'll let us know where to go. He'll try to get a hotel close to Delray. And, Berry, he wants your, uh, *rear end* back in Merritt tomorrow as soon as your meeting is over. I promised to get you there. No argument. Understood?"

"Loud and clear. And I can see the advisability of staying in a hotel, but I've got to stop at my house first."

"How come?"

"I've got to pick up something to wear."

"What's wrong with what you've got on?"

She and Caroline both looked at him like he was an imbecile.

Resigned, he said, "Five minutes tops. Deal?"

"Deal," Berry said.

"Tell me how to get there."

Traffic increased as they approached the city. Seemingly half the population of Houston was pouring back into town after being away on weekend excursions. Dodge was itching to smoke and was relieved when Berry finally told him to take the next exit off the clogged freeway.

The neighborhood into which she directed him was well tended and bespoke affluence, and, when she pointed out her house to him, he was even more impressed. He could never have provided his daughter anything as grand as what she had acquired on her own. Of course, Caroline could have finagled a good deal for her on the house, but still.

He felt humbled, intimidated, and inadequate as he followed the two of them up the walkway to the front door. Needing to reassert himself, he slid his handgun from the holster at the small of his back. "I'll go in first."

"I need to disengage the alarm."

"Remember what happened to Davis Coldare."

Without further argument, Berry gave him the code, then she and Caroline waited on the porch while he went in, disengaged the alarm, and, following his nose from room to room, flipped on switches and flooded the one-story house with light. Satisfied that Starks wasn't lying in wait for Berry's return, he replaced his pistol in its holster and gave them the all clear to come inside.

"Make yourselves at home." Berry headed down the hall toward her bedroom.

"Five minutes," Dodge called after her.

If circumstances had been different, he would have liked to explore his daughter's home. You could tell a lot about a person—things he would like to know about Berry—by the stuff in her house, how it was maintained, how it was arranged. Just this brief exposure to her place indicated that, when it came to neatness and home decor, she took after Caroline a whole lot more than she did him.

He was about to remark on that to Caroline when Berry screamed.

CHAPTER 19

IN THE STREET IN FRONT OF BERRY'S HOUSE, SEVERAL EMERGENCY vehicles were causing other cars to detour. The lawn had been cordoned off with yellow tape. Onlookers were standing in groups outside the barricade, speculating on the nature of the emergency.

Ski waded through it all, showed his ID to the uniformed cop standing sentinel at the front door, and was told to go on in, that Detective Rodney Allen of the Houston PD was expecting him.

He stepped into a foyer that had a limestone tile floor and a tall, healthy ficus tree in the corner. Ordinarily it would have been an inviting entry. But now, with the discovery of Sally Buckland's body in the master bedroom closet, the house had become a crime scene, its warm domesticity destroyed by everything the term entailed.

CSU personnel and a photographer were milling around in the living area. Upon seeing Ski, one of the men wearing latex gloves asked, "You looking for Detective Allen?" and when Ski nodded, he hitched his head. "In the kitchen."

"What are you doing?"

"Waiting for the coroner to finish in the bedroom so we can have it."

Ski glanced down a short hallway from which came the murmur of voices, then went in the direction the man had indicated and found his way to the kitchen. Dodge was standing with his back propped against the granite countertop. Beside him was a good-looking black guy with a shaved head and well-defined pectorals, a bodybuilding type.

Alert, every muscle in his compact body contracted, the black guy looked ready for anything.

Dodge looked ready to kill somebody.

Caroline and Berry were seated on one side of a rectangular dining table with a rustic finish, making it look like it had been salvaged from a French farmhouse after World War I. Caroline's arm was protectively draped over Berry's shoulders.

Sitting across the table from them was another man. When Ski entered the room, he looked at him from over his shoulder, then scraped back his chair and stood up, extending his right hand.

He was tall and middle-aged. His slight paunch was the only soft thing about him. He had the world-weary eyes and toughened bearing of a large-city homicide detective. Years of seeing the worst of mankind's handiwork had left an indelible stamp on his face. His handshake was strong and dry, his palm as hard as a hoof. The white squint lines extending from the corners of sharp blue eyes contrasted with his sunburn, which Ski figured was perpetual.

"Rodney Allen."

"Ski Nyland."

"That's Detective Somerville."

The black guy bobbed his sleek head to acknowledge the introduction but didn't say anything.

"Have a seat," Allen said.

As Ski sat down, Berry met his gaze only momentarily before lowering her head. To the detective he said, "Thank you for inviting me to sit in."

"He was your guy before he was ours. If in fact the individual who killed Ms. Buckland was the same man who shot the kid in Merritt last night."

Ski said, "Oren Starks certainly should be a person of interest to you."

"Person of interest, my ass," Dodge muttered. "He's a fucking woman killer and kid killer."

He had called Ski immediately after notifying 911 of the gruesome discovery in Berry's closet. Ski had been waiting for a judge to grant a search warrant for Sally Buckland's house, which was on the other side of Houston from Berry's place. Despite the flashing emergency lights on his SUV, and the speed at which he'd driven, it had taken him over half an hour to get here.

During that time, Allen and Somerville had arrived to investigate the apparent homicide of Sally Buckland. During preliminary questioning, Dodge had apprised them of Ski's investigation in Merritt. Allen hadn't invited him here strictly out of professional courtesy. The detective was after information about the suspect he and Ski had in common.

Ski knew to be concise. He recapped the shooting at the lake house on Friday night. "He was facing felony charges for that. But after last night, he's in much deeper."

"The kid," Allen said brusquely.

"Davis Coldare was fatally shot at a motel. Oren Starks has been identified by an eyewitness. He fled the scene, then abandoned his car several miles away and went on foot to a Walmart store. We've got him on security cameras." He explained the shoe purchase and the reason for it.

Allen asked, "What time was he in the store?"

Ski told him. "But from there, he vanished. It's like he was raptured off that parking lot, so he must've been picked up and driven back to Houston, possibly by Ms. Buckland."

"What makes you think that?"

"Because he used her cell phone to call Ms. Malone this afternoon, around four o'clock. The call originated near Minute Maid Park. Local officers were dispatched. But Starks knew to turn off the phone, the baseball game was just letting out, there was lots of traffic, and we don't know what he's driving. Could be Sally Buckland's car, or not. The trail's gone cold again." He paused to take a breath. "That's where we are."

Allen said, "Well, it wasn't Sally Buckland who picked him up from the Walmart and drove him back to Houston, because at three-something this morning she was long dead. Coroner's best guess, she's been dead at least twenty-four hours, probably longer."

Ski's mind backtracked with the speed of a rewinding video recording. "I talked to her by phone yesterday afternoon."

"So did I," Dodge said.

"Then she must have been killed shortly following those conversations," Allen said. "The autopsy might help nail down the time of death more precisely, but the guy in there now is a competent man, been in the ME's office for years, sees bodies all the time. He estimated she died sometime yesterday afternoon."

Dodge cursed under his breath. "She sounded edgy, nervous, in defense of Starks. I thought she was standing up for him because they were working together. I realize now she was scared." He locked gazes with Ski. "Starks was with her when I called."

Berry hunched her shoulders and hugged her arms closer to her body.

"You're guessing," the Houston detective said.

"I think he's right," Ski said. "My conversation with her was off somehow. I couldn't put my finger on it before, but now I get it. Either Sally Buckland was being coerced or she was saying what she knew Starks wanted to hear. She was trying to save her life."

"She was shot in the left temple," the Houston detective said. "Practically at point-blank range. But not here. She was killed in another location and her body brought here."

"How'd he get the body in here without setting off the house alarm?"

"We were getting to that when you arrived," Allen said.

They all turned to Berry.

Speaking in a thready voice, she said, "Oren had a habit of being here when I got home from work or after an evening out. I'd come in and turn off the alarm. He was always . . . close. Hovering.

Maybe he saw the sequence of numbers. I kept meaning to change the code, but then I moved to Merritt, and it seemed pointless."

"He took a chance of being discovered by transporting the body here," Ski remarked.

"The risk was worth it to him," Berry said. "He wanted me to find Sally. That was part of my punishment."

After a short silence, Allen said, "The murder scene will give us more to go on, but we gotta find it first."

"We have," said Somerville, whose bass voice was in keeping with his muscular build. He held up his cell phone. "Just got a text. Detectives at Sally Buckland's house found blood in her bed. Lots of it. Soaked into the pillow. Also residue that looks like semen on the sheets. Which is consistent with what the coroner saw on the remains, on and around—"

"Thanks, Detective," Allen said, cutting short the chilling report from his subordinate.

But enough had been said to make Caroline King go pale. Berry pressed her fingertips into her eye sockets. Dodge muttered under his breath, then said, "I gotta smoke," and left through the back door.

As Ski stared at the top of Berry's bowed head, he thought about what Somerville had told them and related it to the photographs taken of Berry in her bedroom and while sunbathing, how beautiful and unaffected she'd looked, how unaware and defenseless. He struggled to maintain a professional detachment, but it was impossible. He wanted to hunt down Oren Starks and hurt him. Bad.

He said, "Detective Allen, when you get the ballistics report on the bullet that killed Ms. Buckland, I'd like to compare it with the one that killed Davis Coldare."

"You'll have it as soon as I do."

Berry said, "Don't forget to tell him about the message."

Ski looked at her, then at Allen. "Message?"

The detective said, "The body was zipped into a garment bag. One of those like my wife stores winter coats in. Rod inside, big hook attached to the top."

Ski nodded.

"On the outside of it, there was a message printed in blood, apparently Ms. Buckland's."

"What'd it say?"

Ski had addressed the question to Detective Allen, but it was Berry who replied in a bleak voice. " 'Sally has you to thank.' "

Shortly after that Sally Buckland's body was removed from the house to be taken to the morgue, and the CSU team went into Berry's bedroom to do their scavenging for evidence. Somerville excused himself to take a telephone call, and, when he returned to the kitchen, he informed them that Sally Buckland's car had been found in a vast multilevel parking lot in Houston's famed medical district.

"The entry ticket was in the console, stamped seven-seventeen yesterday evening."

"Several hours after I talked to her," Ski said.

"Security videos have this man—" Somerville held out his cell phone so Ski could see the freeze-frame photo that had been texted to the detective.

The image was grainy and blurred, but there was no doubt that the man behind the steering wheel was Oren Starks. "That's him."

Somerville then held his phone so Berry could confirm the identity. She rolled her lips inward and nodded.

"This was taken as he entered the parking garage," Somerville continued. "But Starks wasn't picked up on cameras inside any of the buildings in the complex."

"He'd left another car parked nearby," Ski said. "Presumably the maroon Toyota."

Somerville said, "The patrolmen who discovered the car said there are traces of blood on the driver's seat and in the trunk. Looks like Starks killed Ms. Buckland at her house, brought her here in her own car, drove it to the garage, and abandoned it there, where it could have remained for a while without causing suspicion. Patients and family members sometimes stay for days in those treatment centers."

"Starks made the swap inside the garage and drove the other car out," Allen said.

"They don't take photos of cars as they're leaving," his partner added. "More's the pity."

Allen noticed Ski's frown. "What, Deputy Nyland? You don't like that scenario?"

"Yeah, I do. Except, that would mean that Starks had parked a car in the garage in the medical district, walked to Sally Buckland's house, where he killed her and picked up her car. Right?"

"I reckon."

"Okay. From the medical district to her house is a distance of what? Two miles at least?"

Somerville gave a negligent shrug. "Thirty-minute walk."

"For you and me," Ski said. "But not for a man with an injured leg."

"He told me it was black and blue and swollen," Berry said.

"A limp wouldn't have attracted much attention in that area," Somerville said. "Lots of rehab clinics. Day surgery places. People on crutches, wheelchairs. A guy with a limp wouldn't have attracted attention."

"I guess," Ski said, but still with doubt. "That's a lot of walking for a man with a bum leg." He explained that Starks had walked almost a mile from the abandoned Toyota to Walmart in Merritt. "Part of that was over rough ground and in the dark. If you're right, he did that *after* walking from the medical district to Sally Buckland's house. Not only that, why did he make the car switch? Why use Ms. Buckland's car to move her here? Why not the Toyota?"

"He didn't want the Toyota to be seen by any of her neighbors, who could later identify it," Somerville said.

The detective's explanation was thin but logical, and Ski didn't have a better one.

"What's the skinny on that Toyota?" Allen asked.

Ski said, "The VIN has been scratched off. The license plate belongs to a blue 2001 Taurus in Conway, Arkansas. One of our deputies talked to the owner. He was recently in Houston, had his license plate lifted while he was here, but he's not sure where or when the theft took place."

"Starks was laying his groundwork."

"Apparently. But it wasn't too smart of him to return to Merritt last night after killing Sally Buckland," Ski said. "He had to know that every peace officer in deep East Texas was on the lookout for him with a warrant for his arrest for the lake house shooting. Yet after stashing Buckland's body here, which seems another reckless thing to do, he went back to Merritt and hid in a ratty motel. What the hell for?" He shook his head in frustration. "Doesn't make sense to me."

"He had unfinished business in Merritt," Berry said softly. "*Has,* that is. I'm still alive."

Caroline hugged her closer. "Is that all for now, Detective?"

They wrapped up with Allen and Somerville. As they congregated at the front door to exchange contact information, Ski noticed Berry staring down the hallway toward her bedroom. When she came back around, there were tears in her eyes. It would be a long time, if ever, before she could go into that room and open the closet door without remembering the gruesome discovery she'd made. Oren Starks had contaminated her home, too.

As Caroline and Berry went through the front door, Detective Allen detained Ski. "Another sec, please, Deputy?"

"Sure."

"Who's the character?" Allen nodded through the open doorway toward Dodge, who was standing just inside the yellow crime scene tape, smoking and chatting with a uniformed Houston police officer.

Ski replied, "He's a private investigator, working for Ms. King."

"He's packing."

"He's licensed to carry."

"So he said."

"Then what's the problem?"

The detective shrugged. "I don't know. Is there one?"

"No. He's sound. He was a former cop here in Houston. When did you join the force?"

" 'Eighty-six."

"You missed each other. He left in 'seventy-nine."

"Any particular reason why?"

Ski glanced beyond Allen and saw Somerville propped against the entryway wall, intent on his cell phone. "Have you got your man there checking?"

"I do, yeah." Allen smiled, but not with humor.

"Dodge had some insubordination issues, but he wasn't fired. He left by choice."

"Good. A police department doesn't need a man like that."

Ski locked gazes with him and, in a steely voice, said, "You're right. It needs a thousand." He let that sink in, then said, "Excuse me."

By the time he rejoined Caroline and Berry, Dodge was also walking toward them. Ski could tell by his expression that he had acquired new information. "What?"

Dodge glanced warily at the women. Caroline said, "Don't spare us weakhearted females, Dodge. What did you learn?"

He took a final drag on his cigarette and flicked it into the gutter. "That officer was one of the first responders. Talkative guy." He looked at Berry and asked a question that seemed out of context. "Did Sally Buckland have any boyfriends?"

"Not that I know of. Another man wasn't the reason she rejected Oren. Why?"

"Because this cop told me that the only thing on her body was one piece of jewelry. A silver link bracelet."

Berry's face drained of color. "With a heart-shaped charm."

Dodge looked hard at her, then at Ski, who answered his silent query. "Starks gave Berry a bracelet like that."

He didn't expand on it. He didn't need to. They all realized the significance of the bracelet. Oren Starks was fixated on two women to whom he'd given identical pieces of jewelry. Both had rejected him. One was dead.

"By the way, Berry, you called it," Dodge said. "You were afraid for her. I'm sorry I read it wrong."

"Same goes for me," Ski said.

"Neither of you could have saved her," she said sadly. "She was long dead before Oren used her cell phone to call me."

Before more could be said, Caroline intervened.

"Berry needs to be put to bed. What hotel have you booked us into, Ski?"

"A Sheraton only a couple of miles from Delray. Busy hotel. I wanted you where there'd be a lot of people."

Caroline placed her arm around Berry's waist and guided her toward her car. The men fell into step behind them.

"I'll lead you there, but stay close," Ski said to Dodge, who would be driving Caroline's car.

"Put your cherry on the roof. That'll make you easy to follow."

"I don't want to be followed." Ski hitched his chin.

Dodge looked in the indicated direction and saw what Ski had: a TV news van trying to nudge its way between the emergency vehicles.

CHAPTER 20

Caroline hadn't expected Ski to accompany them to the hotel, but she was glad that he did. She was so fatigued she could barely put one foot in front of the other. Berry looked ready to drop. Ski's authority cut through the tedious process of checking in. Once he introduced himself to the manager, the man personally escorted them to their rooms, where he assured Ski that Berry would be safe.

"They're checked in as 'special guests,' Deputy Nyland. No names."

"If someone finds her here, media included, media *especially*, I'll know where the tip came from." The message was subtle but effective.

The man quailed and became even more anxious to please. He filled the ice bucket in each of the connecting rooms and readjusted the thermostats to suit them. Noticing the pack of cigarettes in Dodge's breast pocket, he said tentatively, "These are nonsmoking rooms."

Dodge gave him a drop-dead look and deliberately removed his jacket so the man could see that he was armed. Quickly the hotelier wished them a good night and scuttled out.

Berry actually jumped when her cell phone rang. All of them tensed as she read the caller ID. "It's not him," she said, her shoulders slumping with relief. "But I need to take the call. Excuse me." She went into the bathroom for privacy. Caroline noticed that Ski stared hard at the closed bathroom door for several moments before turning away.

With each passing hour since Berry had been told about Davis Coldare, Caroline had watched her becoming more withdrawn. On the drive down to Houston, she'd been unusually quiet and contained.

Caroline supposed her daughter's disassociation was due to the series of traumatic events. But she wondered if there was more to it. Berry was entitled to her privacy, but harboring something for too long was often detrimental. Caroline questioned how long she should wait before inviting Berry to confide what was so obviously troubling her.

Ski and Dodge examined all the door locks to make certain they were adequate, then stepped out onto the balcony, ostensibly to check the connecting rooms' level of security, but Caroline could hear them in whispered conversation.

When they came back inside, she was standing with her hands on her hips and greeted them with a demand to know what they'd been whispering about. "Tell me. Neither Berry nor I wishes to be cosseted."

"What's that mean?"

"You know what it means, Dodge," she said irritably. "What's going on?"

"Media's on the story," Ski said.

Caroline groaned.

Dodge said, "Bloodthirsty jackals."

"According to people in my office, Sally Buckland's murder was a break-in headline," Ski told her. "Viewers are being promised they'll have the complete story on the ten o'clock news. They showed exterior shots of Berry's house. The CSU van. Allen and Somerville looking stone-faced as they left the scene. We got Berry out of there just in time. The reporter at the scene said she was un—"

"Unavailable for comment." Berry stepped through the bathroom door and tossed her cell phone onto the bed. "Which, of course, makes it sound as though I have something to hide. No one *asked* me to comment, not that I would have *wanted* to comment, but the phrase certainly has a negative connotation, doesn't it?"

"How'd you hear about it?" Ski asked.

She pointed at her cell phone as she sat down on the edge of the double bed, put her elbows on her knees, and her face in her hands. "God, is there no end to this nightmare?"

Ski waited a few beats, then said, "You're identified as the daughter of the real estate moguls, that's a quote, Caroline King and the late Jim Malone, which gives you a sort of celebrity status because their names are so familiar. The shooting at the lake house was referenced."

"As the result of a love triangle," she said without raising her head.

"Implied."

Dodge hissed something foul. Caroline sat down on the other double bed. She wanted to go to Berry but judiciously restrained herself.

Ski said, "What really pisses me off—excuse me, Caroline—is that the love triangle aspect is what they're exploiting."

Berry raised her head, saying angrily, "There was no love triangle."

"I get it, Berry," he said, matching her tone. "My point is that Davis Coldare's murder is being glossed over like it hardly mattered. It's a footnote. The media are playing up how Sally Buckland might have fit into a sordid little ménage, while the important factor is that Oren Starks is a cold-blooded killer who's still at large."

Berry wilted a bit. "It's the juicy stuff that has viewers staying tuned until ten. Sex and scandal turns them on. Or off." She tossed back her head and used both hands to hold her hair away from her face. Caroline saw dried tear tracks on her cheeks. "Certainly my boss at Delray was concerned about my involvement."

Caroline glanced at the discarded cell phone. "That's who you were talking to?"

Berry nodded. "My days at Delray are no more."

"What!" Caroline shot to her feet. "He fired you?"

"Don't be ridiculous, Mother," Berry said with a bitter laugh. "If they had fired me over this, I would have sued them, and they know it. However—and it's a big *however*—Delray's position is that the company takes the mental health of each employee very seriously. In light of the succession of traumas that I've experienced in recent days, wouldn't it be in my best interest, and, by extension, that of the company, if I took an extended leave of absence? When I assured my boss that my mental health would be fully restored once Oren was in police custody, he insisted that I give myself time to recuperate from these disturbing events. In other words, he and everyone at Delray wish for me to make myself scarce."

"What about your presentation tomorrow?"

"Oh, yes, that. Regarding my participation in that campaign from here forward, the client wouldn't dream of being a source of additional stress during this difficult time. Therefore, they've agreed to wait until Ben has adequately recovered from his injury so that he can present the proposed campaign *as well as* assume total responsibility for its implementation."

Caroline was seething. "Wait a sec. Are you saying . . . Am I to understand that you're considered mentally *impaired* by all this, but Ben Lofland isn't?"

"It would seem so, yes. And just in case there's any doubt of Ben's fortitude, emotional and/or physical, Amanda, in a lengthy and enlightening telephone conversation this afternoon, assured our boss that Ben is ready to take the lead and run with it. I rather imagine she painted me as a scarlet woman who's suffering the slings and arrows of my own treachery."

"That little bitch!"

"She had her claws out, all right." Berry gave another dry, mirthless laugh. "I wonder. If Oren had shot me instead of Ben, would I have been considered a heroine? Or would I still be looked upon as the attempted home-wrecker who got her comeuppance? That's a good topic for debate, don't you think?"

"What I think," Dodge said, "is that your bosses at this outfit are lily-livered assholes. You're better off never darkening the door of that place again."

"I agree with you, and I'm sure that's the position Delray predicted and hoped that I would take," Berry said. "The concern for my well-being that the boss so effusively conveyed was in actuality his safety net. He wants my resignation. He just needs the decision to be mine so that his hands can stay clean. I left it open-ended for now. Let them sweat it for a few weeks. But I already know what my final decision will be."

"My two cents' worth," Ski said, "you're too good for them."

She looked up at him with watery eyes and said hoarsely, "Thanks."

"You're welcome."

For several seconds they seemed to forget that Caroline and Dodge were still in the room, then Ski pulled himself into the here and now. Duties awaited him.

"I'd better shove off."

"There's an extra bed in my room next door," Dodge said. "You're welcome to it."

Ski thanked him but declined the offer. "Sally Buckland's murder case belongs to the Houston detectives. I've got Davis Coldare's to deal with."

"Last we heard from Starks, he was here in Houston."

"Yeah, Dodge, but I can't help thinking . . ."

"What?"

Ski ran his hand around the back of his neck. "Oren wanted to thumb his nose at me and everyone else who was searching for him. That's why he came back here to place that call to Berry today. He knew we'd beat it here, try and chase him down. He wanted to cause confusion and make us look and feel inept." He smiled crookedly. "He succeeded."

"'Spinning Wheel.'"

All of them looked at Berry, who'd whispered the words.

"Blood, Sweat and Tears," she said. " 'Spinning Wheel.' That's the tune he was humming during our phone conversation."

"Dammit, you're right," Ski said.

"Well, ain't our boy cute?" Dodge said. Then he dropped all traces of humor, sarcastic or otherwise. "I gotta kill this son of a bitch. I really do."

"He raped Sally, didn't he?" Berry asked, directing the question to Ski.

"I don't know about penetration," he said evasively. "Maybe he just . . ." He let the statement trail off, for which Caroline was glad. "I won't know till I get the autopsy report from Detective Allen."

Thoughts of what that young woman might have suffered subdued them for several moments; then Caroline addressed Ski. "You were theorizing on his motive for calling Berry."

"Yeah. What really worries me is that he might have had something else up his sleeve when he got us out of Merritt."

"Like what?" Dodge asked.

"I don't know. That's why I need to get back." He looked down at Berry. "I assume you're returning in the morning?"

"I've got nowhere else to be."

"Okay. I'm going to keep the guards at the lake house. But I'm going to make it appear I've pulled them off. They'll still be there when you get back. Just invisible."

"Laying a trap for him?" Dodge asked.

"Oren won't fall for it," Berry said.

"I don't think so, either," Ski said, "but it doesn't hurt to keep some people in place, just in case."

He commissioned Dodge to remain vigilant, then looked down at Berry. "Are you going to be all right?"

The question was softly spoken, personal, and effectively excluded Caroline and Dodge. Berry nodded, but it was a tentative motion. Their gazes held for what seemed like a long time, then, without another word, Ski strode to the door and left.

The instant the door closed behind him, Berry jumped up and

charged across the room. But at the door, she stopped. Caroline watched as that one burst of energy deserted her. She leaned into the door, pressed her forehead against it, and remained that way for several seconds before decisively flipping the dead bolt and securing the chain.

When she turned back around, she went directly into the bathroom, saying, "I'm going to soak in the tub for a while."

She didn't come out for almost an hour. When she did, she was wrapped in a towel; another was around her hair. Her skin was rosy. Her eyes were red.

"You've been crying," Caroline said.

"I got it out of my system." She whipped off the towel turban and shook loose her wet hair. "But I don't know what I've got to cry about. Not when I think of Sally's last hours. She, Davis Coldare, they're the real victims, not me." She unzipped her small suitcase and took out a tank top and boxer shorts.

Caroline said, "I waited to order a room service supper."

"You should have gone ahead. I'm not hungry. Where's Dodge?"

"In his room. He thought you and I needed some time alone."

Berry removed the towel from around her and pulled on the sleepwear. "Anything more from Ski?"

"He called Dodge about fifteen minutes ago. Nothing to report. He just wanted to make sure you were okay. He didn't look happy to be leaving."

"He shouldn't be driving back to Merritt until he's slept. He looked exhausted. Did you notice his eyes?"

"He can't keep them off you." Berry turned her head and looked at Caroline, who added softly, "I noticed *that.*"

Berry lay down on the bed, stacking two pillows beneath her head and hugging another to her chest. Nervously she plucked at the corner of the pillowcase. "It could never work between him and me."

"Why do you say that?"

"For a thousand different reasons."

"Name a few."

"So you can shoot them down?"

"One by one."

She looked across the narrow space separating them. "You like the idea of him and me becoming an us?"

"Only if you do, Berry. But you would have my approval."

"Don't get your hopes up. We're two entirely different types."

"Um-huh. He's male, you're female."

Berry smiled. "You know what I mean. We want different things."

"But do you want each other?" Berry gave her another sharp look, and Caroline laughed. "Don't bother answering. You just have. And, anyway, it's palpable every time you're near each other."

She smiled at Berry with affection. "You and Ski may want different things, you may be different types, but all that has little to do with attraction. He's fighting it as hard as you are, but it's obvious that he likes you."

Berry turned her head and looked toward the ceiling. A tear trickled from the corner of her eye and slid into her wet hair. "He won't."

"What do you mean?"

"Not now, Mother, okay?"

Caroline hesitated, then said, "Okay."

She'd invited Berry to open up to her, but if she wasn't ready to do so, they'd just as well try to rest. She put her suitcase on the bed and unzipped it, then reached in and pulled out the nightgown she had hastily stuffed into it before they left the lake house. That seemed like a long time ago, much longer than the several hours it had been.

During those rushed minutes before their departure, Berry had been checking the contents of her portfolio to make sure she had everything she would need for her presentation, which now wouldn't take place.

Dodge had been waiting for them by the car, puffing cigarettes for all he was worth, unaware that Caroline was watching him from her bedroom window and wondering why his face, for all its cynicism and signs of unrepentant abuse, was the one in all the world that could still make her heart trip. Thirty years' time hadn't diminished its appeal to her.

She could speak to Berry about attraction, because she knew well the dominating ferocity of it. Even when it made no sense, when it was just plain wrong, one was powerless against it.

"I always thought it was Roger Campton."

Caroline, lost in her reverie, didn't immediately grasp what Berry had said. When she did, she froze momentarily. Then slowly she came around, clutching her nightgown to her chest like a shield.

"I thought my birth father was Roger Campton."

Caroline, rendered speechless by surprise, said nothing.

"I was in middle school," Berry continued. "Eighth grade to be exact. Roger Campton died in that plane crash down in Mexico. One of the girls at school told me that her mother had told her that you were engaged to him before you married Daddy. And she asked me if you were sad that he had died.

"I'd never heard of Roger Campton. Neither you nor Daddy had ever spoken that name within my hearing. I told the girl she was wrong. But she insisted that her mother wasn't a liar. Why would she make that up?

"So the following morning, I got Daddy's newspaper and read about the plane crash. There was a whole story about Roger Campton, his growing up in Houston, joining his father's company after graduating from SMU's business school. Wealthy, influential family. Socially prominent. His picture showed him to be very handsome.

"Because he wasn't married when he died, I spun this romantic fantasy. His heart had been so severely broken when you married Daddy instead of him that he remained single. But I figured that you, sensible as you are, would have had a very good reason for choosing Dad over him.

"I was happy with the way things were. I loved Dad with all my heart. I couldn't very well grieve for a man I hadn't known. Nevertheless, I was glad that I'd uncovered the secret of who my real father was." She held Caroline's gaze for ponderous seconds, then said, "But it wasn't Roger Campton, was it, Mother?"

Caroline shook her head.

"After Daddy died, and I encouraged you to get back into circulation, you told me you weren't interested in dating, or having a relationship, none of that. You told me that you'd had a good marriage to a wonderful husband. You told me that you'd had the love of your life. I assumed they were one and the same man." Berry gave her a rueful smile. "But they weren't."

Caroline sank down onto the edge of the bed.

"My birth father was the love of your life."

Caroline nodded.

"Dodge."

Tears spilled over Caroline's lower eyelids and rolled down her cheeks.

CHAPTER 21

Houston, Texas, 1978

DODGE WAS WAITING FOR CAROLINE WHEN A NURSE WHEELED her out of the hospital. The wheelchair was unnecessary, but it was a nonnegotiable hospital policy.

His car was illegally parked at the curb. An eight-by-ten card behind the windshield had the Houston PD logo stenciled on it, making the car look official enough to ward off parking monitors.

He was leaning against the passenger door, ankles and arms crossed. As the nurse guided the chair through the automatic door, he pushed himself off the car and walked toward them.

Caroline looked up at him through the dark lenses of her sunglasses. "I called a taxi."

"I gave the driver ten bucks for his trouble. I'm taking you home."

His voice brooked no argument. He motioned the nurse to roll the chair to his car. Hesitantly, she said, "Ms. King?" and waited for Caroline's nod before complying with Dodge.

Caroline was leaving in the clothes she'd had on when she was admitted three days earlier. She had nothing with her except her handbag. Dodge took it off her lap and placed it in the backseat of his car, then offered her his hand and helped her out of the wheelchair. She thanked the nurse for her assistance. The nurse wished her good luck and good health before wheeling the chair around and heading back into the building.

Dodge asked Caroline if she wanted to lie down in the backseat.

"No, I'll ride up front."

He looked like he might argue, especially when he noticed how stiff and tentative her movements were, but he helped her get situated as comfortably as possible, then went around and got in the driver's side. They covered three blocks without either of them saying anything.

When he stopped for a traffic light, he turned toward her. "How do you feel?"

"Weak. Like I've been lying in bed for three days."

"They didn't feed you?"

"I didn't have much appetite."

"Can't blame you." He made a face. "Hospital food."

"When were you in the hospital?"

"Never. But I've heard."

She smiled, but her lips were tremulous, and he noticed.

He asked, "Does it hurt?"

"Not as bad as it looks like it should. It looks pretty awful. One of the nurses felt sorry for me, I guess. She brought me the sunglasses."

He was trying to see past the opaque lenses so he could assess the damage, but the driver behind him tooted his horn when the light turned green, forcing him to return his attention to driving.

"How did you find out?" she asked.

"Jimmy Gonzales."

"He wasn't one of the responders."

"His night off. But it's still his beat. He heard about it the next morning. I've been out of touch the last couple of days, so he didn't reach me till late last night. I called the hospital this morning and was told they were releasing you."

"Don't you have to work today?"

"I called in sick."

They rode in silence for a time, then she said, "Did you go after Roger?"

"I wanted to. Still do. I'd like to kill him." His fingers were wrapped so tightly around the steering wheel the skin had turned white. "But I won't."

She said nothing, waiting for him to finish.

Finally he braked for another traffic light and turned his head. "The only reason I haven't killed him is because you begged me not to. That means more to me than the promise I made him the night I beat him up."

Nothing more was said until they reached her house. He assisted her up the front walkway to the door. She went in. He followed. A broken vase and dying roses were lying on the living room floor. The water had left a damp stain on the carpet. A picture on the wall was hanging askew. A floor lamp had been overturned, the lampshade was dented.

These mute testimonies of Roger's violence no longer embarrassed her. They made her furious. But she was just as furious with herself for excusing his abuse for as long as she had, which had been way too long. Feeling in defiance of it now, she removed her sunglasses, exposing her eyes to Dodge.

He clenched his jaw and rocked slowly back and forth on the balls of his feet as though he could barely contain the wrath that surged through him. "I might change my mind about killing him."

"Don't. He's not worth it." He seemed on the verge of saying something but didn't. She said, "I appreciate the ride home. Thank you."

"You're welcome. I'll wait while you throw some things together."

"What things?"

"Your things. Whatever you want to take. You're staying at my place for a while. It's no palace, but—"

"What are you talking about? I can't stay with you."

"Can and will."

"Forget it."

"Get your stuff."

"What entitles you to order me around?" she asked angrily. "Your policeman's badge? Being right about Roger's true spots? You accused me of staying with him out of stubbornness. Well, *fine*. I concede. I should have ended the relationship long ago, but out of pride, I didn't. I didn't want to admit how mistaken I'd been about his true character. So, okay, you were right. That doesn't give you license to take over where Roger left off."

She drew herself up to her full height, which was still far beneath his. "I've been bullied for the last time, Dodge. I won't be pushed around again, emotionally or physically or any other way."

He expelled a short breath. "Look, when it comes to expressing myself, I'm crap. I always sound like I'm bullying even when I'm not. And I'm not. I swear. I'm trying to be nice . . . a friend. You need a hand, I'm offering one. But no matter how I put it, or how deep you dig your heels in, the fact is that I'm not leaving you here alone. End of discussion."

"That sounds like bullying."

"Sue me."

She smiled, but it wavered after a moment. "I'll be perfectly safe. Roger's in jail."

"He got out. Last night. His family posted bail."

"He won't be coming back to me."

"How do you know?"

"He told me so. He was livid. He said he was done with me."

"He'll change his mind, and I don't want you here when he does. In fact, you should relocate. You're a realtor. Put this house on the market. Find a new place."

She laughed without humor. "That would be poetic justice."

"What do you mean?"

"That's what set him off. I was excited over a pending contract. If it closes, it will be my largest sale to date. I was babbling on about it, then Roger said he hoped for me that it would close before I had to quit.

"I thought I'd misunderstood, but when I asked him what he meant by that, he stated unequivocally that I would no longer be 'a working girl' when I became Mrs. Roger Campton. It just wouldn't do for us to be a two-income family. What would people think? That he couldn't support his wife? I would have plenty to do, he said, taking care of him. He promised to keep me busy.

"I actually laughed. I told him that he'd taken leave of his senses if he thought for one moment that I planned to quit my job, forfeit my career, just because I was getting married." She raised her hands at her sides, adding sarcastically, "That didn't sit too well."

"The son of a bitch nearly knocked your eye out."

It had felt as though he had. The ophthalmologist who was summoned to the emergency room told her later that she was lucky her vision hadn't been impaired by one vicious blow.

Dodge said, "Gonzales told me the cops who responded to your call said you couldn't even stand upright."

"Roger hit me in the ribs, too. I thought some were cracked. They turned out not to be, but the bruise was very painful. Still is when I move too quickly or take a deep breath."

"Jesus," Dodge whispered. "That guy . . ." He placed his hands on his hips and walked a tight circle in the center of the room, again looking like a man who wanted to throttle somebody. When he came back around to her, he said shortly, "Pack your things."

"All right. I'll pack. You can drive me somewhere. But be reasonable, Dodge. I can't stay with you."

"How come?"

"We barely know each other."

He dismissed that. "We'll get to know each other. If you're afraid I'll cross a line—"

"I'm not."

"Well, good. But if you are, you can always call Jimmy Gonzales. If I laid a hand on you, he'd have my ass."

"I could go to . . . to . . . a friend's house."

"Doesn't Roger know who your friends are? You don't think he'll look for you among them? I'll bet you haven't shared with them that he hits. You'd have to explain your bruises. Besides, you know the downside of that plan or you would have already called a friend, and you wouldn't have stammered when you suggested it."

"An extended-stay motel then."

He folded his arms across his chest, considering it. "I've made plenty of arrests at those places. They're for shiftless transients. Whores. Drug dealers. Fences."

"Not all of them are disreputable. Some are actually very nice."

"Okay. Say you got into a good one with a decent clientele. It would require a lot of wear and tear."

"Wear and tear?"

"On me. I'd be going back and forth, checking on you several times a day, making sure you were all right."

"I wouldn't require that."

"*I* would. And who's to say Campton wouldn't hunt you down until he found you?"

"He could find me at your place."

"Yeah, but he'd have to kill me to get to you. Now," he said, "we've wasted enough time arguing over it. Go get your things."

He lived in a condo, one of a unit of four, in a complex made up of ten identical units. These were connected by landscaped grounds and lighted walkways. There was a common swimming pool, a tennis court, and a clubhouse for owners' use. It was a place where single professionals resided, not people who were investing their time, labor, and money creating a lasting home.

Before leaving for the hospital, Dodge had cleared out two bureau drawers and half his closet for her, much more space than she required. "I won't need any work clothes," she'd told him when he commented on how little she was taking from her house.

"Yeah, what about that?"

"I talked to Mr. Malone from my hospital bed the day after the incident. I hinted that I'd suffered some minor female ailment that required surgery. He didn't ask for details, which I knew he wouldn't. I asked for a month off to give myself time to recover and regain my strength. He told me to take all the time I needed."

"You need a *month*? Your injuries must be more serious than you've led me to believe."

"I won't need that long to recover. As I told you before, I bruise easily and deeply. This," she said, pointing to her eye, "will take weeks to fade. It'll go through a spectrum of colors. To avoid questions from clients and co-workers, I don't want to go back until it's completely gone."

Her explanation relieved his alarm, but he was a little jealous of the glowing terms in which she referred to her mentor, Jim Malone. At the same time, he was glad she wasn't working for a demanding, impatient asshole who was stingy with sick leave.

After her things had been put away, he forced her to eat some mashed potatoes, which he made himself from scratch. He admitted that he wasn't a gourmet but told her he hadn't starved, and he wasn't going to let her starve, either, even though she was already well on her way to emaciation.

After she'd eaten all she could hold, she took one of her pain pills, and he tucked her into bed. She slept for sixteen hours, waking the following morning barely in time to see him off to the tire plant.

"Marvin?" she asked, squinting at the embroidered patch on his shirt.

He frowned. "Believe me, you don't want to know."

He told her to keep the doors locked, not to leave, to stay in bed all day if she felt like it, and she promised she would. He told her to keep his pager number handy and to page him if she needed anything. He said he would avoid calling for fear of disturbing her rest, but if he did, he would call and let it ring once, then call back. That way she would know it was him.

Despite these safety precautions, he left her reluctantly.

After his shift at the plant, he went to the daily meeting of the task force. He reported that there was still no love lost between him and Franklin Albright. Albright had punctured one of his tires.

"Stupid thing to do since my car was in the parking lot of a tire plant, for crissake." He'd had the tire replaced in no time.

He couldn't be sure Albright was the culprit, but he didn't have any other enemies at the plant, and Albright had given him a smirking grin when he reclaimed Crystal as she and Dodge came through the exit together after their shift. And Dodge knew about Albright's fondness for his knife.

Playing nerdy whipping boy to the violent ex-con was getting real old, real quick, but this was the role he'd started with, so it was the one he had to stick to. In the meantime, Crystal was becoming more affectionate. Recently she'd stroked his hand and wistfully told him she wished she'd met him first.

Dodge had told her it was too bad she didn't know something about Franklin that would land him back in the penitentiary for a long, long time and save her the hassle of having to break up with him so she and he—Marvin—could be together.

Her smile had faltered, and she'd quickly changed the subject. Her reaction raised Dodge's suspicion that something about Albright definitely made her uneasy, but she was a long way from blurting out that he was planning an armed bank robbery.

Dodge felt like he was marking time while accomplishing nothing, but no one else on the task force had anything cooking, so he had to keep his janitorial job and continue putting the make on Crystal in the hope of either getting something on Albright that would identify him as their robber or eliminating him from the suspect roster. And in the process, to avoid getting murdered by Franklin Albright, jealous lover. Staying alive was now a top priority with Dodge. He really wanted to live.

With Caroline.

When he got home that first evening, he caught her napping on the sofa. Embarrassed, she sat up, clasping and unclasping her hands self-consciously, apologizing for her tousled hair and disheveled clothing. Her shy uncertainty made his heart do cartwheels.

"How was your day?" he asked.

"Lazy."

"Perfect."

He'd brought home a carton of rich, creamy tomato basil soup, a speciality of a café where he often had his meals. They sat at his kitchen table and ate the soup with hunks of French bread he tore off the loaf and buttered with a heavy hand.

When he gave Caroline a second piece of it, she asked, "Are you trying to make me fat?"

"I'm trying to get you to where I can see you in profile."

After their supper, which included vanilla ice cream and fudge sauce, they watched television for a while, but by ten o'clock, Caroline was yawning. "I'm sorry. It's not your company, I promise."

"No apology necessary. I'm beat, too."

As she had the day before, she put up an argument for giving him back his bed and sleeping on the sofa. "I'm smaller. I'm the interloper. I don't mind."

"But I do."

In the end, he wouldn't hear of relegating her to the sofa, and she relented. Dodge spent his second wretched night on the damn hard and unforgiving thing, but relishing every single minute of his torturous insomnia because Caroline was under his roof and snug in his bed.

That first day set the pattern for those that followed. She got up each morning in time to see him off and was there waiting when he returned. At her insistence, he'd stocked the pantry and fridge with more groceries than they'd ever had in them. She wanted foodstuffs and spices on hand so she could prepare dinner each night.

"It's the least I can do to repay your hospitality."

He permitted it, conditional upon her eating half of everything she cooked, and promising not to overexert herself.

He watched the bruise around her eye fade from eggplant to violet, then to avocado green. Natural color returned to her cheeks. Her tiny frame fleshed out a little more each day until she no longer looked dangerously underfed.

She groused about her idleness, but to Dodge she seemed industrious. Daily, she studied the real estate sections of newspapers. She lamented the listings she'd missed and strategized how she was going to make up for lost time when she returned to Jim Malone Realty.

She made endless notes in a spiral notebook she'd brought with her, jotting down ideas as they occurred to her. Her ambition was undiminished by this temporary setback. In fact, because of it, she was even more determined to make a name for herself. Dodge supposed she wanted to succeed in order to spite Roger Campton and his family of untouchables.

She discussed with Dodge the career path she had plotted, as though he could offer valuable advice on how she could achieve her goals in the time frame she'd set. He had little to offer, but she didn't seem to realize that. He was flattered that she often asked for his unlearned opinion.

She was more cultured than he was. She'd read more books, heard more symphonies, listened to more lectures, and toured more museums. Hell, in his whole life, he'd been inside one museum, and he'd gone then only because he'd heard it had an exhibition devoted entirely to paintings of naked women.

Caroline was way above him intellectually. But the way she listened when he talked made him feel smarter, like she thought anything he said was worth hearing.

"I bet you got straight A's in school," he teased one night.

She blushed, which was as good as an admission.

He laughed. "I got my degree by the skin of my teeth."

"But you've got common sense."

"Street smarts."

"Don't dismiss the importance of that," she said earnestly. "In your line of work, that's vital to keeping you alive."

He couldn't talk to her about his present duty, but he told her about previous cases he'd worked, some amusing, some tragic. She seemed fascinated by even the most mundane story.

On one of his days off from the tire plant, they ventured out together for the first time. He took her to the movies. She wore her dark glasses until they got into the theater and the houselights went down.

They shared a box of popcorn. Occasionally their hands reached in at the same time and they had swatting contests. Once when she crossed her legs, her foot bumped his calf, but she excused herself and moved it away.

It was a movie about two brothers, one good, one bad, both of whom hated their tyrannical father but loved the same woman. There was a scene where the leads made love—sexy, hungry, forbidden love. Dodge had never been so turned on by a film sequence, and it wasn't because he got flashed by a celebrated pair of tits that were probably insured for a million dollars by Lloyd's of London. It was because he was sitting next to Caroline, whose breasts were small but the objects of fantasies that each night left him sweaty and fretful on his damn sofa.

He wanted her. God, did he. But he didn't touch her. For damn sure not during that movie scene. Even the slightest move in that direction would've shattered the trust she'd placed in him. Anyone who knew him would never believe their relationship was chaste, but to take advantage of her situation would be to abuse her worse than Campton had.

Dodge didn't think about the future when she wouldn't be there to welcome him home after his workday, when he would no longer hear her humming in the kitchen, or catch the scent of her shampoo in the bathroom. He pretended it would go on like this forever. Except for his raging, confused, and chaotic libido, he was wonderfully content.

Up till the day he was upended by a stupid, senseless, unnecessary calamity that made him want to pick up a baseball bat and attack God where he lived.

That day, after his grind at the tire plant, Dodge called Caroline and told her it would be another hour or so before he got home. He went to task force headquarters for a scheduled briefing.

He should have noticed the subdued atmosphere in the building immediately upon entering it. But he was thinking about Caroline and the pot roast dinner she had said was waiting for him. Pot roast was such an evocative dish. It connoted hearth and home. Permanence.

His daydream of pot roast dinners for years to come was swaddled in such a rosy haze that he didn't pick up on the funereal mood among his fellow officers until he realized that they were all avoiding eye contact with him.

He asked the room at large, "What'd I do?"

No one said anything.

"What's going on?"

Silence.

"Jesus. There's been another robbery? Did somebody else get killed? *Goddammit!* Was it Albright? What bank? When?"

One brave soul cut off his tirade. "It's not that, Dodge. It's, uh, it's . . ."

"What? *What?*"

"It's Gonzales."

It took a moment for Dodge to switch his thoughts from their elusive, clever bank robber to his former partner and best friend. But from there he made an instant connection between the glum mood in the room and Jimmy's name.

His heart came to a sudden, thudding halt. He stopped breathing. He swallowed convulsively, but his mouth had gone dry, he had no spit.

"There was an accident," one of his cohorts said. "Gonzales was . . . He didn't make it."

"Sorry, Dodge."

"Hey, man, I'm sorry."

"Goes with the territory, but . . . shit."

"Anything I can do, Dodge, just ask. Okay?"

The murmured words of consolation barely registered. He turned his back to the other men and tried to assimilate what they were telling him. He couldn't. He came back around. "Jimmy's *dead*?" When that was affirmed with solemn nods, he started hyperventilating.

"Take it easy, Dodge."

"Where is he?"

"The morgue. His folks are there."

"I gotta—"

"Dodge, you can't!"

He made a dash for the exit but was grabbed from behind, and he began struggling savagely to shake off restraining hands. "You can't go to the aid of a cop, Dodge."

"Think, man!"

"You'll blow your cover."

"Fuck that!" he yelled. "And fuck you. Let go of me."

He continued to scream obscenities, but eventually he exhausted himself, and the reasonableness of what the other officers were saying sank in. He ceased struggling, and they released him. He dropped into the nearest chair and sat there for the longest time, trying to collect himself, wishing he didn't believe the unbelievable. Finally he looked up. "You said it was an accident. What happened?"

A rock star had flown into Hobby Airport for a concert to take place that night at the Astrodome. Gonzales, wanting the overtime, had volunteered to ride in one of the squad cars providing police escort for the singer's limo. Word had leaked out of his arrival time. From Hobby Airport, the limo was chased by paparazzi and carloads of crazed, dope-fueled, fanatical fans.

Gonzales and another officer were in the car directly behind the limo. One of the cars chasing the motorcade, trying to get between them, clipped the front bumper of the squad car. They were going so fast that the officer behind the wheel lost control. The car spun out and was slung into a telephone pole, hitting it broadside with such force, it was almost cut in half.

Jimmy Gonzales was.

Cut in half.

The captain asked Dodge if he wanted to talk to a chaplain, a counselor, a psychologist. Dodge told him to fuck off. He didn't stay for the briefing.

For a while, he drove around the city looking for someplace

in which to vent his roiling anger but soon realized that his erratic driving was a danger to innocent motorists and their passengers. Where would be the sense in his killing somebody in a car crash? No one would appreciate the irony. Least of all Jimmy Gonzales, who would rebuke him from the cold slab in the morgue on which the halves of him lay.

He wound up at a batting cage. It felt good to have something hard and potentially lethal in his hands, taking whacks at something as defenseless as Gonzales had been against the laws of physics and that goddamn telephone pole.

He didn't go home until hours later. By then the pot roast had been put away. Caroline's eyes were soft with sympathy when she greeted him at the door. "It was on the ten o'clock news. I'm so sorry, Dodge."

He nodded and walked past her into the kitchen. He opened the refrigerator but didn't know what he was looking for, so he just stared into it sightlessly.

"I want to do something to help you," she said with feeling. "But I don't know what to do."

He slammed the refrigerator door, rattling glass containers inside. "You can't do anything to help. I can't do anything. I can't even go to his funeral. I've been ordered not to. I can't go see his parents. Nice folks, by the way. Proud as punch of their son Jimmy, the cop." His throat seized up, and he groaned, "Jesus."

Caroline took a step toward him, but he rebuffed her. "There's nothing you or anybody can do, all right?" he shouted. "Don't you get it? The dumb asshole should have been off duty. Instead, he's dead! And for what? He died protecting that flaming fairy with pink hair and green satin pants, whose singing, frankly, sounds to me like a cat getting fucked in the ass.

"And the person who caused the wreck fled the scene. Didn't even have the decency to own up to taking out a good cop and a great guy. Probably some cokehead. If I ever find out who . . ." He raised his hands, curled his fingers toward his palms. "If I ever find out who was driving that car, I'll kill him with my bare hands."

"Dodge, you're—"

"You don't think I mean it, do you?"

"Dodge."

"Think again, nice girl. I beat up your fiancé, didn't I? Have you forgotten that?"

"You're not yourself."

"I'm exactly myself." He sneered. "This is me, Caroline." He pounded his fist against his chest. "Take a good look. This is the *real me.*"

He could feel the angry blood throbbing through the veins in his head and neck. He knew that his eyes were glowing with fury, that he was spraying spittle with each word, that he probably looked feral.

That he probably looked like his old man.

But even knowing that, he couldn't stop himself from saying what his father used to shout at him. "Just leave me the fuck alone, will you?"

With remarkable calm, Caroline sidestepped him and left the room.

Then he had no one on whom to direct his rage, so he threw himself down into one of the kitchen chairs, put his head on the table, and sobbed till his throat was raw.

He stayed there until dawn, benumbed by grief, steeped in self-loathing.

When he realized the sun was coming up, he stirred. He toed off his shoes and tiptoed through the house to the bathroom, where he splashed his face with cold water. His shirttail was out, his hair standing on end, he had a full day's growth of beard. He looked like a derelict after a weeklong binge, but he was too weary in body and soul to make repairs.

As he left the bathroom, he looked down the hallway toward the bedroom. The door was ajar, not quite an invitation, but she hadn't barred herself against him, which, after the way he behaved, she'd had every right, practically an obligation, to do.

He went to the door and pushed it open. Its hinges creaked, but that didn't waken her because she was already awake. He sensed she was even though she was facing away from him, lying on her side, her knees pulled up nearly to her chest. She lay on top of the covers, fully dressed except for her shoes. The pads of her toes, perfect dots of flesh, were lined up against the balls of her small feet.

The sight of her caused the bitterness that he had nursed through the night to disintegrate, and all he was left with was emptiness.

He walked to the bed and lay down, close to her, but without touching. He expected her to tell him to get away from her, that she couldn't stand the sight or sound or smell of him. But she didn't. She lay perfectly still, and that silent acceptance of his presence emboldened him to speak.

"I was wrong last night," he said in what, for him, passed as a whisper. Even so, his voice sounded abnormally loud. He tried lowering it another decibel. "When I said there was nothing you could do to help me, I was wrong. There is something."

"What?" Her voice was muffled by the pillow beneath her cheek.

"You're doing it."

"I'm not doing anything."

"Yes you are. You're . . . you're *being*." He moved his head closer to hers, closed his eyes, and pressed his face into her hair.

"Just being?"

"That's enough. Actually, that's a *lot*."

She turned over until they were face-to-face. She didn't rebuke him for rubbing his face against her hair, which he was afraid she might. Her regard wasn't judgmental. More like tender.

"I'm sorry for flying off the handle." Then he snuffled with disgust. "That's an understatement. I went way beyond that."

"You were upset."

"I was. Am. But nothing excuses the way I acted and the things I said."

"I didn't take them personally."

"Good. They weren't directed at you."

"I know. I understand." Her sweet expression said she did.

It made his throat tight. "Do you think you can forgive me?"

"I saw you at your worst, and I'm still here."

He shook his head sadly. "That wasn't my worst, Caroline. Not by a long shot."

"I'm still here," she repeated softly.

Gazing into her calm, sherry-colored eyes, he felt little cracks forming in his mean ol' heart. It had been toughened early by the loss of his mother, who'd loved him, hardened by his father, who hadn't, then made stony by the man's ceaseless cruelties.

But his callous heart didn't stand a chance of remaining so when Caroline looked at him as she was doing now. Little fissures in it opened, allowing trickles of her gentleness, kindness, and goodness to get inside.

He was nearly suffocated by yearning. "Caroline." He stopped, swallowed noisily, tried again. "Caroline, a few weeks ago, you were engaged to another man." Again he paused, at a loss for how to express himself. "I'm bungling this, dammit. What I'm trying to say—"

"I know what you're trying to say." Her voice, unlike his failed attempts at whispering, was a perfect whisper. It was little more than a breath, a vibration of air that was felt more than heard.

She leaned forward and touched his lips with hers. When she withdrew, her eyes skated over his face, taking in his features, which he knew weren't classically handsome. Not even close. He'd never minded his looks until now. Miserably he wondered if there was anything in his off-center face that she could possibly find appealing.

Her hand came up, and he felt her fingertips, as soft and cool as flower petals, touching his scruffy cheek and chin. Then, she leaned forward and pressed her lips to his again. And this time they stayed.

He made a sound that, had he been a woman, would have scared the hell out of him. It sounded like something you'd hear in the darkest heart of the jungle. But Caroline didn't flinch. Instead her lips relaxed invitingly, and his tongue did what tongues seem to do by instinct. A few heartbeats later, he couldn't remember what it had been like to kiss any other woman because he was kissing

Caroline. The word *kiss* was suddenly, wondrously redefined. It became an act of love, an engagement not merely of mouths but of souls.

Even more miraculous, she was kissing him back with a boldness and fervor that stunned and thrilled him. It was she who first left off mouth kissing for other parts. She pushed aside the collar of his shirt and pressed her open lips to his neck. If she was doing that, then surely she wouldn't mind if he slipped his hand under the back of her shirt and touched her skin. She didn't. When he splayed his hand against her delicate spine and applied pressure, she scooted closer to him, until her body was flush with his, and their middles started rubbing against each other.

He wasn't sure how a guy went about getting a decent woman out of her clothes. He had no experience with that. But Caroline solved the dilemma for him. She began gracefully peeling off her garments. He tore at his as though they'd caught fire.

When she lay beside him on her back, fully naked, he was struck with a terrible case of stage fright. She was so beautiful, he felt like he was about to defile a national treasure or a religious icon. Some might think her nose too pert and her lips too narrow, but he thought hers was the most beautiful face he'd ever seen. Her spare frame didn't represent the ideal of womanhood, but he had never desired a body with the passion he felt for hers.

The sunlight coming through the slats of the blinds painted peaches-and-cream stripes across her pale skin, which was adorably sprinkled with freckles. Her nipples were virgin pink, and the hair over her sex was a soft, golden red.

She smiled up at him. "Are you ever going to touch me?"

Gingerly, he placed his hand on her torso, and it almost spanned her rib cage. He felt burly. Hairy. Huge. "You're so . . . pink. And little. I'm afraid I'll hurt you."

"You won't."

"Your ribs—"

"They hardly hurt at all anymore." She put her hands on his shoulders and pulled him down to cover her. "You won't hurt me, Dodge."

They began kissing again, and his inhibitions were soon abandoned. One brush of his tongue, and her nipples went from sweet to wanton. She sighed his name and moved restlessly beneath him. Her small hand closed around him and guided him. He nudged her with the tip of his erection, and she was soft and wet and receptive, so, with a low groan he claimed her.

His fingers threaded through her hair to cradle her head. He put his lips directly against her ear. "The first time I saw you, I wanted this. I wanted to be up you like this. Inside you. I wanted to feel your . . . your . . ." He knew all the crude words and phrases to say, none of the sweet and romantic ones. "I don't know how to say it right."

She turned her face toward his and rubbed her lips across his jaw. "You're saying it just fine."

Pressing deeper, he groaned. "God, you feel good."

"So do you." Folding her legs around his hips, she arched up. "Stay as long as you like."

He didn't, he couldn't. Not that first time. Months of pent-up passion drove him toward a quick completion. But the next time lasted longer, and the time after that . . .

Dodge didn't know that happiness like this was possible. He'd never experienced it before. In the days and weeks that followed, he was saturated with a soul-deep peace and contentment that even his sadness over Jimmy Gonzales couldn't reach.

He didn't think he could be any happier.

He was wrong.

Six weeks after the morning they first made love, Caroline shyly informed him that they had made a baby.

CHAPTER 22

"WAKE UP, LADIES. SKI JUST CALLED FROM MERRITT." Dodge whisked aside the blackout drapery.

Berry came up on her elbows and blinked against the sudden light.

Caroline sat bolt upright. "What's happened?"

"Starks has been at it again. I'll give you the scoop on the way."

He disappeared through the door connecting his room to theirs. Caroline and Berry looked at each other, each taking a moment to remember where they were, why they were there, what had happened to Sally Buckland, and what they'd talked about long into the night.

Then, as if a starting pistol had been fired, both flew into motion. Dodge returned within five minutes to find them dressed, suitcases packed, ready to leave. Because Ski had checked them in, and the sheriff's department was handling the bill, they were able to skip the checking-out process.

Dodge was curt with the valet parking attendant, who didn't retrieve their car as quickly as he wished. Berry couldn't help but be amused by his impatience, because she could relate to it. Like father, like daughter. The thought made her smile.

She wanted time to reflect on everything that her mother had told her last night. Caroline had talked until she was exhausted and Berry was too sleepy to retain any more information about the unorthodox love affair that had brought her into being. She and Caroline had agreed to wait for morning to continue, but the situation in Merritt had evidently become imperative. The rest of her parents' story, specifically why they'd been apart for thirty years, must keep for now.

Dodge snarled imprecations at Houston's rush-hour traffic. Caroline insisted that he allow time to get coffee at a fast-food drive-through. "You'll be unbearable until you have some."

"I guess a cigarette is out of the question."

She didn't even deign to answer, asking instead, "When are you going to tell us what happened? Has Oren Starks been captured?"

"No."

"Then what?"

"When I've had my coffee."

"You're just being mulish because I won't let you smoke."

"Sue me."

The drive-through line at McDonald's seemed interminable, but when they'd been fortified with steaming cups of coffee, Berry spoke from the backseat. "Now, Dodge. Start talking."

His summary of events was inadequate. Berry and Caroline began firing questions. "That's all I know," he said, talking over them. "Ski was called away before he could give me the details. He just said to get you back to Merritt, so that's what I'm doing. Besides, I want to get back there myself."

"You're tired of playing my babysitter."

He met Berry's eyes in the rearview mirror. "No. I just want to be there when this son of a bitch is captured. I didn't get face time with Creighton Wheeler, and I had a personal grudge against that guy for what he did to Maggie."

"Who's Maggie?"

"Derek's dog."

He told them the story of the Atlanta playboy who was now

serving a life sentence in prison. "They've got him in a section for the really scary psychos, which is still too good for him. Kinda sad for his folks, though. For rich people, they're okay. Because of Creighton, most of their friends have abandoned them. Julie's good to them."

He rambled on. Berry realized he was doing so to keep her and her mother diverted during the drive to Merritt, but she didn't really mind. She now had a special interest in anything he said.

Having had her suspicion confirmed that he was her father, she'd found it hard to behave as though she was still in the dark about it. Even while rushing from the hotel, she had wanted to pause and study him. She was seeing him in a new light and wanted to learn everything she could about his life.

So she listened to his digressive monologue without interrupting, enjoying the sound of his gravelly voice, clinging to every word from his mouth, most of which were colorful, irreverent, or profane. Even though he talked largely about Derek and Julie Mitchell, Berry was able to piece together, from hints he inadvertently dropped, a few facts about his life. The picture that began taking shape in her mind was rather depressing.

As they approached their destination, he said, "Ski said we can join him at the scene if you can keep out of the way. Can you?"

She and Caroline promised not to do anything that would impede the investigation. Dodge rolled to a stop at the entrance gate of an RV park. A car with the sheriff's office insignia on the door was parked horizontally, blocking the road. A deputy got out and walked over to them, leaning down to address Dodge. "Mr. Hanley?"

"You got it."

"Follow this main road to the first fork. Go left. You'll see the commotion."

The deputy returned to his car and pulled it onto the grass long enough for Dodge to drive through the gate. The park was well maintained and pretty. Berry, thinking back on what Dodge had told them earlier, asked, "How old did Ski say they were?"

"Seventy-something."

"Lord," Caroline said. "Who could harm people that age?"

"Same person that could shoot a woman in the head, then zip her into a garment bag."

A hundred yards beyond the road fork, the tranquil RV park took on the appearance of an armed bivouac. Double the number of law enforcement agents were here as had been at the Walmart store the day before, and also twice the number of spectators, campers who had been awakened with shocking news.

Uniformed officers were questioning them in groups or singly. Others were speaking into walkie-talkies or cell phones. Some appeared to have nothing to do but were trying to look as though they did. A helicopter circled overhead, adding its noisy clapping to the scene.

Dodge got as close to the yellow crime scene tape as he could, parking next to an ambulance. Through its open rear doors Berry saw a man, who was much younger than seventy-something, being examined by an EMT. Dodge got out of the car and whistled shrilly. "Deputy!"

The young deputy named Andy turned, and, when he saw Dodge, his apple-cheeked face grew even redder with anger. He stalked toward them. Berry lowered her car window so she could hear what was being said.

Without preamble, the deputy said, "You got me in a heap of trouble with Ski."

Dodge didn't apologize for whatever the nature of the trouble had been. "Serves you right for being such a gullible bonehead. You'd be smart to learn a lesson from it. Where's Ski?"

"In the RV." Andy nodded toward a large gray RV with a bright blue wave painted on its side. All its doors were open. "Texas Rangers' CSU just finished in there. Ski's talking to them, but he told me to let him know when y'all got here." He reached for the walkie-talkie attached to his belt.

Dodge asked, "That the victim?" He was looking into the open ambulance.

The deputy shook his head. "They already transported the old folks to the hospital. That's the guy who found them. He had a spider bite. The ambulance was here, so—"

Ski's voice interrupted him through the walkie-talkie's speaker. "Go ahead."

"Hey, Ski. Andy. They're here."

"Five minutes."

They waited. A little more than five minutes later Ski stepped out of the RV. He spotted them immediately and came toward them, looking thin-lipped and grim. Berry got out of the car along with Caroline and joined Dodge just outside the yellow tape.

Ski ducked under it. His eyes searched Berry's for several seconds, then he said, "We know how Starks pulled the vanishing act from Walmart."

Talking in choppy phrases, he explained that Starks had hijacked the RV at gunpoint. "Elderly couple, Mr. and Mrs. Mittmayer. They'd just rolled in from Iowa. Planned on spending a couple days here before going down to Corpus Christi. They wanted to see Padre Island."

"What the hell were they doing at Walmart at three A.M.?" Dodge asked.

"They had planned to spend the night at a park in the Ozarks, but when they got there, it was overcrowded, no choice spots left, so they decided to drive on down here, their next scheduled stop. They pulled into the Walmart parking lot to pass the rest of the night until the check-in office here in the park opened the following morning.

"According to Mrs. Mittmayer, Starks limped up to their RV. He looked like he was in pain, in distress. Her kindhearted husband opened the door for him, despite her cautioning him against it.

"Starks lunged inside, hit the old man in the head with the butt of a pistol, knocked him out cold. He backhanded Mrs. Mittmayer and told her if she didn't stop screaming, he was going to shoot her husband first, then her. He bundled both of them into the back, tied them up, and gagged them."

Dodge dragged his hand down his face. Caroline was looking into the surrounding trees, shaking her head over the unnecessary cruelty. Ski locked eyes with Berry and held, then continued.

"At nine A.M. yesterday, Starks drove the RV here and forced Mrs. Mittmayer to go into the office and check in, as though nothing was wrong. He threatened to drive away and kill her husband if she gave him away."

"Where had they been in the meantime?" Berry asked. "Between Walmart and here?"

"Mrs. Mittmayer doesn't know. She was in the back, couldn't see out. Besides, she's unfamiliar with the area. All she knows is that they left Walmart, drove for about half an hour, then parked. Starks rummaged through their pantry, ate some bread and a can of tuna, drank two Diet Cokes.

"His leg was giving him a lot of pain, she said. When he raised his pants leg to examine it, she saw that it was grotesquely swollen and discolored. He took a handful of Advil he got from their medicine cabinet. Then he dozed."

"They didn't try to—"

Ski interrupted Dodge, shaking his head. "She was scared out of her wits. Worried about her husband. He was in and out of consciousness. His head was bleeding. She was afraid Starks would kill him if she so much as moved.

"Starks roused himself at dawn. Ate some peanut butter crackers, drank another Diet Coke, took more pain reliever. Then he asked her where they'd been headed, and told her he would know if she was lying. She gave him the name of this park. He drove the RV here."

"Where it looked right at home," Berry observed out loud.

"They had a reservation and arrived as expected," Ski said, "so nobody was alerted to trouble. Once inside the park, Starks tied up and gagged Mrs. Mittmayer again. He dozed awhile longer, then washed up, exchanged his clothes for some of Mr. Mittmayer's, then locked them inside, unhitched their car, and drove away in it. This was about noon yesterday, while we were tracking him to the Walmart parking lot."

"He drove to Houston in their car. Made that call to Berry from near the stadium."

Ski agreed with Dodge's theory. "That's my best guess. We've got an APB out on the Mittmayers' car."

"How are the Mittmayers now?" Caroline asked.

"Your deputy told us that man there had found them," Dodge said.

The man with the spider bite was now talking to Andy. His arm was wrapped in gauze. "Neighboring camper," Ski said. "It took most of her strength, but Mrs. Mittmayer finally managed to worm her way over to a wall. She hammered on it with her fist. That guy had got up early this morning to go hiking, heard the pounding. He'd seen Starks unhitch the car and drive away yesterday, so he was curious as to who was inside the RV doing the knocking. He checked it out. Found them. She's basically okay, severely dehydrated. She's getting treated at the hospital."

Berry, along with Caroline and Dodge, looked at him expectantly.

He looked down at the ground, expelled his breath. "Her husband's skull was fractured. He didn't make it. He was seventy-six years old."

Dodge cursed. Caroline gave a sorrowful moan. Berry just stood there staring at Ski, futilely wishing none of this was happening.

"Mrs. Mittmayer identified Starks by his picture," Ski said. "The only good thing to come out of this is that he left indisputable evidence. Prints, DNA, an eyewitness. Add kidnapping to his other felonies. He'll be charged with a capital crime."

"Not if I catch him," Dodge muttered around the cigarette he was lighting, despite the bans against smoking in the area.

Ski said, "I wanted you to hear this firsthand, not on the news, not in snatches with rumors mingled in." Addressing Dodge, he said, "Take them home. There's a female deputy inside the lake house. Two outside patrolling the grounds and watching the lakefront. They're in constant touch with me and everyone else in the department."

Berry said, "For all we know, Oren is still in Houston."

"For all we know," Ski admitted. "But this indicates that he's going for broke. I'm not taking any chances."

"I'll drive them home," Dodge said, "but I'm coming back and joining the hunt."

Ski hesitated, then grudgingly agreed. Eager to get into the fray, Dodge hustled Caroline around to the passenger side of the car. Ski opened the back car door for Berry. "You okay?"

"Not at all okay."

"Since Friday night, you've received one shock after another."

Berry glanced over at Dodge and said softly, "They haven't all been bad."

Ski's cell phone rang. It was already in his hand; he raised it to his ear. "This is Nyland."

Instantly Berry could tell the call was urgent. He began talking rapidly. "Yeah. Yeah. Say again? Okay." He began walking quickly toward his SUV, then jogging. He ended the call and shouted back at Dodge. "They found the Mittmayers' car."

"My daughter says it's a sizable *re*-ward."

"Twenty-five thousand dollars."

The man smiled broadly, affording Ski a repugnant view of uneven, gapped teeth stained by chewing tobacco. "When can I collect?"

"Soon," Ski promised. "We're all a little busy right now."

"Trying to catch a fugitive from the law," the man said, nodding sagely.

"That's our priority, Mr. Mercury."

Ski had his cell phone to his ear. He'd been put on hold by his friend with the search dog business, otherwise he wouldn't be giving Ray Van Mercury-like-the-car this much of his precious time. The man was like a pesky flying insect, buzzing with seeming aimlessness but repeatedly coming back to the topic of Caroline King's reward like a housefly to a sugar cube.

"Ski, you still there?" his Army buddy asked into the phone.

"Give me some good news."

"Still trying to track somebody down. Instead of holding, want me to call you back?"

Ski impressed upon him the urgency of the situation.

"I hear ya."

His friend clicked off. "He has to call us back," Ski told Dodge, who'd had all of Ray Van Mercury-like-the-car he could stomach and had moved several yards away to smoke.

"Every minute we waste standing here, Starks is getting farther away," Dodge grumbled.

"Not if he's in there."

Ski looked into the forest. Footprints of athletic shoes, like the ones that Starks had bought at Walmart and that had been described by Mrs. Mittmayer as the kind of footwear he'd been wearing, led from the elderly couple's abandoned compact car into the densest part of the Big Thicket. No-man's-land.

The Big Thicket National Preserve had countless legends and mysteries associated with it, everything from a resident Sasquatch to capricious lights with no traceable source. Famous outlaws of Texas lore had eluded capture in its endless bogs and dense forests.

It was a popular destination for outdoor activities. There were campgrounds, marked trails, and waterways navigable by fishing boats and canoes, but many of the preserve's vast, off-limits acreage was composed of twisting bayous, monotonous swamps, and forests too dense for a gnat to wiggle through, much less a human being. It was a teeming habitat for poisonous snakes and other reptiles, biting insects, and carnivorous predators.

Dodge said, "I don't see why we can't just—"

"I've told you why," Ski snapped. "You don't know what it's like in there. We'd lose his tracks, and then I'd have men going in circles, getting lost, getting tangled up in brambles, getting bogged down—literally—looking for a needle in a haystack. Worse than that, actually."

Ray Van Mercury piped up. "Lucky for y'all I found the car. Or he'd've got clean away."

He was a tough, spry old man. Ski estimated he weighed no more than 130. He had a greasy gray braid that hung down his back to his waist. His lined skin was as brown and wrinkled as a walnut shell, and a lot of it was exposed because all he had on was a pair of grimy jeans unevenly cut off at his knobby knees.

"Yep, lucky for y'all I decided to go fishing this morning. You know," he said, lowering his voice to a confidential pitch, "you ain't s'pposed to go wandering off the trails in the Thicket. You ain't s'pposed to fish 'cept in designated areas. Them park rangers'll get you good, they catch you at it. But I ain't never got caught and I ain't gonna. I've been in the Thicket all my life. I've slithered through parts of it a pissant couldn't get through.

"My mama was one of the Alabama-Coushatta tribe. I know, I know, I don't look like one of them people. I took after my daddy. So Mama said. I never laid eyes on the man myself. He was an oil man. Weren't no good at it. Dry holes was all he ever drilled. Got on the fightin' side of some of his investors. One night under cover of darkness, he took off, leavin' my mama with me still in her belly. So anyhow . . ." He paused to spit some brown stringy stuff into the underbrush, then wiped his mouth with the back of his hand. "Where was I?"

"At the part where I'm gonna kill you if you don't shut the hell up," Dodge growled.

Mercury tilted his head at Ski like an inquisitive bird. "What's the matter with him?"

"He's worried that our fugitive will escape capture. Why don't you wait over there, Mr. Mercury, so you'll be handy if we need any further information."

"Over there?" he asked, pointing to the row of official vehicles parked along the ditch.

"*Way* over there," Dodge said.

"My daughter give you our phone number, right? So's you can call and let me know where I can pick up the *re*-ward?"

Ski patted his shirt pocket. "Right here."

He grinned at them again and set off in a bowlegged trot.

"Oil man, my ass," Dodge said. "His mama screwed her brother."

Ski's phone rang. He answered it, listened, then said, "I owe you one," and immediately hung up. "He's got a trainer on the way. Twenty minutes at the outside. I'll let the others know."

At the RV park, a deputy had been assigned to follow Caroline and Berry to the lake house and to see them safely inside, where the female deputy waited. In the meantime, Ski and Dodge had clambered into Ski's SUV and sped to the spot several miles away where Ray Van Mercury had found the abandoned car.

Mercury-like-the-car lived with his daughter and her three children in a mobile home less than a quarter mile outside the perimeter of the Thicket.

He'd been on his way to his favorite fishing hole when he discovered the car. Had his eye not been so keen and familiar with the Thicket, he might have walked right past without seeing it. It had been left in a jumble of brambles and dense foliage. Not one to interfere in other people's business, Mr. Mercury had continued on, fished until he had a plentiful catch strung onto his rope belt, then returned to the trailer, where he'd mentioned the car to his daughter as she was gutting the fish.

He'd told Ski she "flew into a tizzy." "I don't pay no attention to news shows because the only thing on TV fit to watch is Vanna White and old-timey westerns," he'd said. But his daughter caught the news each morning. She'd heard about the fugitive and the elderly couple he had left tied up in their RV when he'd stolen their car. She'd called the sheriff's office, and when Ski arrived at her trailer, Ray Van Mercury had shown him and Dodge to the car's hiding place.

Within an hour, Ski had mustered a sizable search party that included a number of reserve deputies, DPS officers, one man from Merritt's municipal police department who was a notch above the rest, two agents from the nearest FBI office, and several Texas Rangers.

Now he made his way over to the line of vehicles parked along the shoulder of the road where the men were assembled and waiting. The DPS helicopter, which had been circling above the RV park, had followed the parade to the new location and had set down in a clearing near the Mercurys' trailer.

Some of the peace officers had arrived with saddled horses, ready to mount. Others had brought four-wheel ATVs. But Ski doubted their usefulness. The only possible way to get through this part of the Big Thicket was on foot, and even then there were sections that were impenetrable. In addition to the impassable terrain, they'd be subjected to the dangerous wildlife, biting insects, and the sweltering heat. The search wouldn't be a picnic.

Ski got everyone's attention and announced that the search dogs were on the way. "One of the best and most experienced trainers, I'm told." He urged them to use the downtime to check their gear, apply sunscreen and insect repellent, and make sure their water bottles were full.

Then he rejoined Dodge where he stood in the shade of a tree. Dodge took a last pull on his current cigarette, then conscientiously ground it out against the tree trunk and rubbed it between his palms until it had shredded and posed no threat of igniting a fire.

"I can't figure it," he said.

"What?"

"Starks."

"Be more specific."

"Everything. All of it. Nothing he's done fits a pattern."

"I'm with you," Ski said. "Yesterday, after tying up the Mittmayers, he drove all the way to Houston just to place a call on Sally Buckland's cell phone. Why?"

"Maybe that's when he moved her body. He wanted to draw us down there, scare the daylights out of Berry. He wanted to cause us to scratch our asses, just like we're doing. Don't forget his little hummed song."

"Okay. But then he came straight back here. What kind of sense does that make?"

"Fuck if I know. He'd eluded capture. He was driving a car we didn't know about. Why come back?"

Ski thought on it for a moment. "Refuge? He was relatively safe inside the RV. He had a well-stocked pantry. Refrigerator. TV, so he could keep track of what we were doing."

"Advil," Dodge said, picking up Ski's thought.

"He had all the comforts of home at his disposal. The Mittmayers had the camping spot reserved for three nights, and they posed no threat to him. Starks could have holed up there, got some rest, allowed his leg to heal."

"Or rot off."

Ski smiled grimly. "Neighbors are temporary and constantly changing. The inactivity around that RV could have gone unnoticed. He could have stayed hidden until he felt it was safe to make another run at Berry."

Dodge frowned. "Okay, let's say that was his plan. What was he doing out here in Mercury-like-the-car's backyard?"

"He got lost."

Dodge shot him a dubious look.

Ski shrugged. "On his way back from Houston, he missed a critical turn. It could be that simple."

"It could," Dodge said, "but not for a guy who's an expert on mazes."

"Shit." Ski removed his sunglasses and wiped at the sweat dripping off his forehead into his eyes. "We're missing something."

"Or somebody."

Ski gave him a sidelong look. "That's what I'm thinking, too. He's had help."

"I figured Amanda Lofland," Dodge said.

"So did I. But she hasn't left the hospital since she arrived. She's even spending the nights in her husband's room."

"You checked?"

"Early this morning, before the Mittmayers were discovered," Ski said. "I went to the hospital to talk to the Loflands about Sally Buckland's murder. I brought up the calls to and from her on Amanda's cell phone."

"And?"

"She said she barely knew Sally Buckland. Had only met her a few times at company parties."

"Then how'd she explain all those calls?" Dodge asked.

"They'd played phone tag. She'd been calling to get Buckland's address so she could mail her an invitation to a fortieth birthday party she's throwing for Ben in the fall."

"How did she react when you brought this up?"

"Pissed. The party was supposed to have been a surprise."

Dodge's laugh sounded like he was gargling phlegm. "She's a piece of work, that one. But she couldn't have been two places at once. So if she's not Stark's partner in crime, then maybe it was Sally Buckland."

"She'd served her purpose? He killed her to tie up a loose end?"

"Maybe. Hell, I don't know." Dodge reached for his cigarettes.

"Put them away," Ski said. "Dogs are here."

He and Dodge made their way over as the trainer alighted from a pickup truck that had dog crates in the back. "I'm supposed to be meeting Ski," he said to the group.

Ski threaded his way through the other lawmen and shook the man's hand.

"I brought an extra trainer." He introduced Ski to the man accompanying him. "Also two extra dogs. Just in case."

"Thanks. We may need them. How many do we start with?"

"Three. They're my best."

The dogs were released from their crates and put on heavy-duty leashes. The trainer took two black Labs, the other guy got a bloodhound. The dogs were eager. Ski let them smell the filthy clothes that Starks had left behind in the Mittmayers' RV.

"Okay, they're good to go," the trainer said.

One of the FBI agents said, "Let her roll."

Ski hid his smile. If there was one word that inaccurately described how one navigated this part of the Thicket, it would be *roll.*

Which they soon discovered. They hacked and clawed and slogged their way through. Within half an hour those who hadn't heeded the advice to apply strong insect repellent were fighting their way back to escape thick swarms of biting species. Even sturdy boots were sucked into mud the consistency of tar.

Clothing and skin were ripped by thorns that were as thick as thumbs or as fine as human hairs. While searching for Oren Starks's tracks, they also had to be on the lookout for alligators, mountain lions, razorbacks, cottonmouths, copperheads, and rattlesnakes that didn't like to be disturbed.

Ski couldn't imagine more hostile terrain anywhere in the world. After an hour, they had progressed no farther than a hundred yards. The strong men were made weak by the brutal heat. Those who had stamina in the gym were left gasping for breath. Even the energy of the search dogs began to flag. But they had Oren Starks's scent, and instinct and excellent conditioning made them determined. They strained at their leashes, pulling their trainers into bramble bushes that had to be hacked down with machetes.

Ski kept pace with the dogs, and when the assistant trainer stepped into a hole and twisted his ankle, he passed the leash to Ski. "She should do all right with you if you keep praising her."

Ski managed the dog. He was more worried about Dodge, who'd had difficulty keeping pace the night they walked through the woods at the lake house. That had been a stroll in the park compared with this. But the older man remained close on Ski's heels, wheezing heavily, cursing elaborately, but plowing purposefully forward.

"Changed your mind about deputizing me?" he asked when they paused to drink from their water bottles.

"You can't shoot him, Dodge."

"Hell I can't. My aim's excellent."

"That's not what I meant."

"I know what you meant." He recapped his bottle and pushed aside a thorny branch that was in his path. "But when we find him, he better have his hands on top of his head, praying out loud for mercy."

"Or what?"

"Or I'm gonna consider him a fugitive in flight."

The afternoon wore on. The temperature rose, and water bottles emptied. One by one searchers surrendered to the elements until only a few diehards continued on, and then that number dwindled.

When the remaining troop stopped again to rest, Ski sidled up to Dodge, who was laboring over every breath. "You've gotta call it quits."

"When hell freezes over." He mopped his florid face with a handkerchief. "Which sounds pretty damn good right now."

"Look, Dodge," Ski said angrily, "I don't want you dying on me."

"Have you developed a crush?"

Ski didn't take the gibe. "You croak on my watch, and those two women in your life will never forgive me."

Dodge seemed on the verge of making a stinging retort when he thought better of it. He replaced the handkerchief in his pants pocket. "I'm not quitting."

Ski gave him a level look, then said tightly, "Have it your way."

The going got even rougher. One of the dogs on the trainer's leash began to limp. "She's picked up a thorn," the trainer told Ski after an inspection of the dog's front paw.

"Can she make it back?"

"She'll have to. It'll be slow going."

"You see to her. I'll take the other one."

The trainer transferred the second dog's leash to Ski. "Those two usually don't like each other. But maybe they're too tired to give you any trouble."

By now the group had decreased to only a handful. Dodge was still with them. When one of the FBI agents suggested they call it a day and resume tomorrow, Dodge said scornfully, "You can puss out. I'm not going to."

Ski told them he was in for the long haul, too. "The dogs haven't quit. They're still on Starks's trail."

The Rangers wouldn't quit, either, although one was regarding

Dodge with concern. It was almost painful to watch him breathe. Ski made another attempt to get him to stop. "I know you want to be in on the capture, but—"

"Lead on, Deputy."

"I could order you to go back. I could get one of these Rangers to take you back."

"You'd have to kill me first."

"You're about to save me the trouble."

He motioned Ski forward. "I'm right behind you."

And he was, even when others couldn't keep up. Ski's threat to have him escorted back seemed to have imbued Dodge with strength. But the elements and the terrain were more powerful even than his fierce determination.

He and the few remaining fell farther behind until Ski was alone out front with the two dogs, whose past differences seemed to have given way to their common goal. They continued to thrash through the underbrush. They dragged Ski through marshes.

And finally they caught up with their quarry.

Oren Starks didn't have his hands on top of his head, praying out loud. He was sitting on the edge of a swamp among the knees of a giant cypress tree that jutted out of the murky water. His back was against the main trunk of the tree. He was slumped to one side, his forehead almost touching his thigh.

The dogs, barking in wild delight over their achievement, splashed through the water, separating the duckweed that covered the surface like a film of pea soup. When within a few yards of Starks, Ski reined them in and securely wrapped their leashes around a tree branch. He fired his pistol into the air three times to signal those men behind him that the search had ended, then waded through the knee-deep water, stumbling over tree roots concealed by the opaque surface, until he reached Starks.

There was a bullet wound just above his cheekbone at the outside corner of his eye. Obviously self-inflicted. The pistol was still in his hand, submerged in three inches of swamp water.

Ski went down on his haunches to get a closer look. The blood around the flyblown wound was congealed but not completely dry. His face was crisscrossed with scratches and swollen from numerous insect bites.

He'd lost one of his new shoes. Burrs were embedded in his sock. He was wearing the clothes of the man he had killed. Ski recognized them from the description Mrs. Mittmayer had provided. The gray Dockers were almost black with grime. The green and blue striped shirt was torn, covered in filth, and stank of body odor.

The remaining searchers gradually caught up and began collecting in a semicircle behind Ski, who remained squatting beside the body. Each murmured a comment on the grisly sight.

Ski heard Dodge's wheezing as he came near. He said, "Well, shit." Ski supposed he was disappointed that Starks had robbed him of the satisfaction of killing him.

Birds, whose primal environment was being disturbed by the barking dogs and interloping human beings, flapped their wings and squawked noisily in the treetops. The dogs were happily panting, their tongues hanging from their mouths, dripping slobber.

The first of the Texas Rangers to arrive was talking to the pilot of the DPS helicopter through a transmitter. Shouting to make himself heard, he was telling the pilot to watch for a flare that would mark their location and advising him that they would need a stretcher lowered so they could strap the body onto it and lift it out.

Ski was taking all this in subconsciously. His focus remained on Starks. He watched a large ant crawl across the bridge of Starks's nose and down his cheek. A small fish was nibbling at a finger on his submerged hand.

The Ranger on the radio was saying, "To get the body out of here—"

"It's not a body," Ski said suddenly. "He's still alive."

CHAPTER 23

THE DEPUTY ASSIGNED TO GUARD BERRY AND CAROLINE INSIDE the lake house was the woman who'd been questioning the recalcitrant Walmart cashier before Dodge took over. She introduced herself as Deputy Lavell, and she was all business.

Never more so than when she came into the living area, where Berry and Caroline had been killing time while anxiously awaiting news, and announced that Oren Starks had been apprehended and was in custody.

The two assailed her with questions, but she remained as starchy as her uniform. "I don't have any details. Ski said for you to sit tight, and he'd be in touch."

Berry wanted to leave immediately for the sheriff's office, but Caroline kept the cooler head. "What could we do except get in the way? The important thing is that the man is in custody and you're safe. We'll hear more from Ski when he has a chance."

"Why hasn't Dodge called? He must know we're going nuts here."

"I'm sure he's caught up in the maelstrom, too. This is a police matter, Berry. Show some patience."

"I'll give them an hour."

They were fifty-three minutes into that hour when they heard a car approaching. Berry rushed from the living room, Caroline right behind her. They squeezed through the front door together just as Dodge brought an unfamiliar car to a stop and got out.

"What in the world?" Caroline exclaimed. She started down the steps at a run.

He held up a hand to halt her. "Don't come too close. God only knows what I picked up in that godforsaken place."

"Where have you been?"

"To hell and back. A.k.a. the Big Fucking Thicket."

Berry was astonished. "That's where you found Oren?"

"At the edge of a swamp in a grove of cypress trees with a self-inflicted gunshot wound." His last four words silenced them. "Same place he shot Sally Buckland. Apparently he favors the temple."

Berry was too stunned to speak. Caroline said, "He's dead?"

"Good as. Broken tibia from when he fell down your stairs had caused massive infection. Until the swelling in his brain goes down, they can't really assess the level of damage there. In bad shape is our friend Oren Starks."

No one moved or said anything for several seconds, then Caroline waved Dodge up the porch steps. "Get cleaned up. What is that smell?"

"Swamp gas. Dog shit. Armadillo shit. God only knows. I'd be a lot worse off if Ski hadn't loaned me these boots." When he got to the porch, he worked his feet from the rubber hunting boots, then, without any ceremony, undid his pants and shucked them. He took off the rest of his clothing, dropping it to form a stinking heap on the porch. He went into the house wearing only his undershorts.

Standing in the entry was Deputy Lavell, not a hair out of place, staring at him with stern disapproval.

"Ski said for me to tell you to return to the sheriff's office."

"How come he didn't tell me himself?"

Dodge held their eye contact for fifteen seconds, then repeated what he'd said word for word. She shrugged, then walked out without a backward glance.

Berry was indifferent to the deputy's rudeness. She wanted to pump Dodge for information, but he insisted on taking a hot shower first. "Before any bugs can lay eggs on me. Pour me a bourbon, please," he said over his shoulder as he climbed the stairs.

He was back down in ten minutes, scrubbed and smelling of soap, his wet hair combed back off his face. He was carrying his sport jacket and was wearing a pair of Dockers and a short-sleeved shirt. With all the muck now washed off, the scrapes and scratches on his exposed skin were visible.

"Did you put some antiseptic on those?" Caroline asked as she passed him the requested drink.

"No." He took a gulp of the whiskey.

"Don't say anything till I get back."

"It better not sting," he called to her as she rushed toward her bedroom.

He sat down in the bentwood rocker that he'd sat in the day he arrived. That had been Saturday. This was Monday. Berry was amazed at how familiar to her he'd become in that short span of time, how many monumental events had occurred, how much she had shared with a father she hadn't known until forty-eight hours ago.

"Is Ski all right?"

"What, the hero of the day?"

"He is?"

"Last man standing. Made even the Texas Rangers look like little girls." He took another slurp of whiskey. "He's worse for wear, but fine."

"Where is he now?"

"Last I saw him, he was at the entry to the hospital emergency room, fielding questions from reporters. All the Houston stations. One from Tyler. Lafayette, too, I think. People still like hearing about a posse running the bad guy to ground. Especially in the Thicket. Adds to its mystique."

Berry shook her head in wonderment. "I can't imagine Oren venturing into a wilderness."

"I can't imagine him doing a lot of the things he did." He warily eyed the bottle of antiseptic that Caroline carried in along with a plastic sleeve of quilted cotton pads. "Is that gonna burn?"

"It won't hurt as much as an infection would," she said. "You probably should get a tetanus shot."

"Don't hold your breath."

Frowning at him, she knelt down beside the rocking chair and doused a cotton pad with the liquid, then applied it to a nasty puncture wound on the back of his hand.

Between curses over the stinging antiseptic, he talked the women through the previous few hours.

When he finished, Berry asked, "What are Oren's chances?"

"Of surviving? He won't. He'll die now or he'll face three counts of murder and die courtesy of this sovereign state. Either way, his goose is cooked."

Berry got up and walked to a window that afforded a view of the lake. The sun was setting. A flock of birds was reflected on the surface of the water. Pines cast long, straight shadows on the pebbled shore. The setting was picturesque and tranquil, exactly as it had been last Friday evening when she and Ben finished their work and, innocently, decided to cook steaks on the grill and celebrate the completion of a yearlong project. The memory caused her to grimace.

She turned to face her parents. Funny that she automatically thought of Caroline and Dodge now as a unit. A pair. Her *parents*.

"I want to see Oren."

With a decisive thud, Dodge set his glass on the cocktail table at his elbow. "Goddammit."

"What?"

"That's exactly what Ski said you would say. He *bet* me that's what you would say. I just lost five bucks."

"Whose car is that?"

He retrieved the glass and slammed back the last of the whiskey. "Belongs to the deputy who's guarding Starks's room at the hospital. Ski said I could borrow his car to come here, get cleaned up."

"Well, now that you're clean, you can drive the loaned car back. We'll follow in Mother's."

• • •

Berry was anxious to talk to Ski, or just to *see* him, if only from a distance.

She was also anxious to see Oren. She desperately wanted this episode of her life concluded, and it wouldn't be completely over and done with until she had acknowledged to Oren the part she'd played in all the egregious things he'd done.

He must have been mentally ill all along, but perhaps she had tipped a precarious balance that had plunged him into insanity. Perhaps if she'd been kinder and more tolerant, his innate impulses would have remained dormant until he died of natural causes at a very old age.

In any case, until she owned up to her culpability, she wouldn't have peace.

If his condition was as critical as Dodge had said, time was running out for her to meet that obligation. Unfortunately, as she was crossing the hospital lobby on her way to the ICU floor, she was intercepted by Ben and Amanda Lofland.

"So that's Ben," Dodge said out the corner of his mouth, his tone indicating he wasn't impressed by what he saw.

"You two go on up," Berry said. "I'll be along."

Reluctantly, Dodge ushered Caroline toward the bank of elevators, leaving Berry to confront the couple alone. Ben was in a wheelchair being pushed by a hospital orderly. He looked pale, drawn, and thin. Amanda was at his side. She was brimming with malice.

Berry said, "Hello, Ben, Amanda."

Speaking over his shoulder, Ben asked the orderly to give them a minute. As soon as he was out of earshot, Amanda launched her attack. "Why did you sic that deputy on me?"

"Ski?"

"Ski?" she repeated in an unflattering imitation of Berry. "You're on a first-name basis with him. No shocker there."

"I don't know what you're talking about, Amanda."

"He was here first thing this morning, questioning me about Sally Buckland. *Questioning me.* He found some calls to her on my cell phone. Why would he be investigating my call log if you hadn't poisoned his mind about me?"

Had the subject of Sally's death not been so serious, Berry would have rolled her eyes over Amanda's melodramatic phrasing. "All I ever said about you in connection with Sally was that I wasn't aware that you two knew each other."

"We didn't. But we both knew *you*. We both knew the treachery you're capable of."

"Let it go, Amanda." Ben sounded weary. Berry figured he'd been listening to her ranting about this for hours. "What does it matter now that Sally is dead and her killer is in custody?"

"So you've heard about Oren?" Berry asked.

"The TV in my room was on," he said. "Hell of a thing, this whole mess. And Sally." He ran his hand over his pasty face. "Jesus."

"You have no idea. It was quite awful, finding her that way. They're thinking that Oren abused and tortured her for hours before he killed her."

"I hope the creep dies," Amanda said. "He almost made me a widow."

"Mrs. Mittmayer wasn't as lucky as you," Berry said quietly.

"Like I said, I hope he dies." She gave Berry a hard look. "Are you here to see him?"

"I want to, yes."

"What for?" Ben asked, looking genuinely flummoxed.

"You know what for, Ben. For the same reason I called him on Thursday afternoon."

Under her meaningful stare, he squirmed in the seat of the wheelchair. "What purpose would it serve to talk to him now?"

"Maybe none. But I still want to say what I feel I must."

Amanda looked impatient and made an event out of checking the time on her wristwatch. The woman really was too self-centered and mean-spirited to deserve Berry's notice.

Addressing Ben, she said, "Good luck with the campaign. It's all yours now."

"He had nothing to do with that."

Amanda was so quick to make the point, Berry was certain the opposite was true. Her expression must have conveyed her feelings, because Ben came in right behind his wife with a denial of responsibility.

"Swear to God, Berry, I never thought Delray would take such a hard stance. Not with you, you of all people."

Berry actually laughed. "Me of all people? The scarlet woman of the company? Isn't that what Amanda implied to them?"

"That's not how it was, Berry. They drew their own conclusions about what went down in the lake house, and why. I swear I . . . we . . . didn't—"

"Don't work yourself into a lather, Ben. Whatever you or Amanda told them or led them to believe, whatever explanation or apology you're about to sputter now is meaningless to me. You let me take the fall, and that was dishonest and disloyal.

"But I'm not all that broken up over it. I don't want to work for a company that has so little regard for me as to believe the worst without even extending me the courtesy of a defense." She drew herself up. "The portfolio with everything in it, from the first sketches to the final mock-ups, is at the lake house. I'll have it sent to you by courier."

"He doesn't need your largesse," Amanda said. "And you can keep the portfolio. Ben has made copies of everything all along."

Berry looked from Amanda back down to Ben, whose expression bore the imprint of guilt. "Oh. I see." Berry held his tortured gaze for several seconds, then, without shaking hands or even saying good-bye, she walked away.

She'd been outside Oren's ICU for almost an hour when Ski arrived, looking recently showered and dressed in fresh clothing. Upon seeing him, her heart kicked up its pace, but his demeanor was suitably professional, so she curbed the impulse to fling her arms around him and, instead, greeted him with a reserve that was appropriate.

After they'd exchanged hellos, he turned to the deputy sitting in a formed fiberglass chair, who'd been assigned to guard Oren's room. "Do you need a break?"

Either he took the hint or he really did need a break, because he thanked Ski, left his chair, and walked away, leaving them alone.

Berry, speaking quietly, said, "Dodge told me about your heroic efforts to bring Oren in."

He waved off her compliment. "I should have caught him sooner."

"I shouldn't have called him on Thursday. I shouldn't have invited Ben to come here on Friday. I shouldn't have treated Oren so unkindly. His parents and teachers should have recognized his psychotic tendencies." She gave him a wan smile. "The blame extends a long way back, Ski."

She glanced into the ICU, where Oren's vitals were being monitored by softly blipping machines. "They let me go in. There were things I wanted to say to him, and I did." Regretfully, she shook her head. "But I don't think he heard me."

She could feel the weight of Ski's contemplative gaze on her. "Why did you want to talk to him, Berry? Why are you still here?"

"I really can't explain why. I just feel I should be. Is it macabre of me to stand vigil, waiting for something to happen?"

"It's macabre to have restraints on him." In addition to all the tubes and wires attached to Oren, there were bands around his wrists and ankles that secured him to the bed. "But he killed three people. Ruthlessly. We shouldn't feel sorry for him."

"I don't. Not really. I don't know how I feel, Ski. I'm relieved that he's no longer a threat to me or to anyone else, but my emotions are mixed. I don't know what to think about anything." Her eyes coming back to his, she added helplessly, "About *that.*"

He knew exactly what she was talking about. His voice dropped in volume. "Right. *That.* The kiss that rocked my world. I don't know what to think about it, either. I just know that I do. Constantly." Inclining a fraction of an inch closer, he added, "I didn't want to leave you last night."

"I almost came after you."

"You did?"

"I made it as far as the door. I knew you had to go, but I didn't want to be away from you."

The hungry stare they exchanged was interrupted by a commotion at the end of the long corridor. The deputy, returning from his break, was arguing with Lisa Arnold.

"I want to talk to Ski Nyland."

"It's okay," Ski said. The deputy moved aside. The girl's flip-flops made slapping sounds as she walked toward them.

"How are you, Ms. Arnold?" Ski asked politely.

She hooked a hank of overprocessed, raven-colored hair behind her ear, from which several silver rings dangled. "I'm okay. I mean, I guess. You know, I'm still sad over Davis."

"Of course."

Her gaze slid to Berry. Ski made the introductions.

"I know who you are," the girl said. "It started at your house. He shot your boyfriend, too, right?" Before Berry could correct her, she turned away from them and looked into the ICU. For several moments, she stared at Oren. Finally she said, "I saw on TV that you'd caught him. The deputy that's been parked outside my house came up to the door and told me that he was leaving, that there was no reason for him to guard me anymore."

Ski asked, "Is that the man you saw in the motel, who shot Davis Coldare?"

"That's him, all right. The son of a bitch." But her sneer gave way to rising emotion. "I talked Davis into taking me to that motel. If we'd've stayed at the drive-in, he would still be alive."

"You aren't responsible for what happened, so don't blame yourself," Ski said kindly.

She came around and gave Ski a watery, grateful smile. "Well, I just wanted to come and thank you for catching him."

"I had a lot of help."

"And something else? Thanks for being so nice to me the night it happened."

"You're welcome."

"I'm sorry my stepmother was such a bitch."

Ski smiled. "That's okay."

"Don't take it personal. She's a bitch to everybody." She cast one final, malevolent glace at Oren, then said good-bye and headed down the corridor toward the elevator. Dodge and Caroline stepped off as she got on.

Ski's cell phone rang, and he stepped aside to take the call.

"Any change?" Dodge asked Berry as they approached.

"No."

"Waste of time, just standing here, staring at him."

"Probably, but . . ."

Ski rejoined them, holding the cell phone against his chest. "We've got a situation at the sheriff's office. The man who found the Mittmayers' car—"

"Jesus. That inbred?" Dodge said with distaste.

Ski smiled. "Mr. Mercury is demanding his reward, accusing everyone in the department of trying to cheat him out of it. I hate to bother you with this now, Caroline, but would it be too much of an inconvenience—"

"Of course not," she said, not even letting him finish. "I'm happy to write him a check."

It was decided that they would go together and get that matter taken care of. They immediately departed for the courthouse. Dodge looked at Berry. "Guess that leaves us at loose ends, and, frankly, I think you should cut bait on this guy. The sooner you do, the better off you'll be."

"Perhaps you're right."

"Trust me. I'm hungry. You hungry?"

"I am," she said, just now realizing she couldn't remember when she'd last eaten. She glanced at her watch. "But it's late by Merritt's standards. I don't know what's open."

"I do."

"Hi, Grace."

"Hi, Dodge."

The bartender's smile dimmed a bit when she saw that he had Berry with him. "This is Berry Malone."

"We met once," Berry said, smiling at the other woman.

"You must be awfully relieved that that Starks character has been caught."

"I am."

"Is he still alive?"

"Hanging on by a thread," Dodge said. "Are you serving food this time of night?"

She nodded toward a row of booths along the far wall. "Claim a table. I'll bring menus over. What would you like to drink?"

Dodge ordered a bottled beer. Berry said that sounded good and ordered the same. They sat opposite each other on faux leather benches. The tabletop between them was made of heavily shellacked wood. Providing light was a red glass holder with a flickering candle inside. Grace brought their drinks. After a quick review of the laminated menu, they both ordered cheeseburgers and fries.

Grace returned to the bar. They were alone. Dodge watched Berry take a sip from her bottle of beer. He chuckled.

"What?" she said.

"Nothing."

"You're surprised that I'm drinking beer from the bottle."

That was precisely what he'd found amusing, but he remained noncommittal.

"Mother wouldn't be caught dead," Berry said. "She thinks it's unladylike." She took another drink, watching him down the length of the chilled bottle. When she lowered it to the table, she said quietly, "But you know that, don't you, Dodge?"

He leaned back against the tufted leather and studied her for a moment, knew that she knew. Gruffly, he said, "That's just one of your mother's prissy taboos."

"But you loved her in spite of them."

He reached for his own bottle, but, although his mouth had gone dry, he found he no longer had a thirst for the beer. He rubbed the condensation between his fingers as his gaze stayed fixed on the familiar beer label. "So you know. About me. Us." Although it took all the courage he had, he lifted his eyes to those of his daughter.

She nodded.

"When Caroline finds out, she'll be furious."

"She knows."

"She does? Since when?"

"Last night. I had figured it out. She confirmed it."

"She didn't want you to know."

She gave him an arch look. "Oh no? Then why did she involve you in this?"

Grace brought their burgers. After serving them and asking if they needed anything else, she left them to their meal. Berry wasn't shy. She dug in. Dodge had lost his appetite.

"How'd you guess? I treated you no differently than—"

"It wasn't how you treated *me,*" she said, licking a smear of mustard from the corner of her lips. "It was how you and Mother treated each other. First of all, she's been a nervous wreck. She's never nervous. I'm the one who's high-strung and impatient. In my life, I've never seen her so tightly wound. At first, I thought it was because of the crisis situation. But then I became aware of how she was with you. She was never like that with Daddy."

Dodge's gut was tied in a knot. He craved a cigarette, but not as much as he craved to know how Caroline's behavior toward him was different from what it had been with Jim Malone. He hated himself for asking, but he did. "What was she like with him?"

"They had a very solid marriage. They loved each other. I'm convinced of that. But they were unfailingly reserved and polite. She and Daddy never fussed over each other the way the two of you do. They never fussed *at* each other the way you do. Their relationship . . . well, it didn't spark. I never knew any differently, so I didn't think anything of it until I saw how the two of you are with each other. There's no polite formality."

"We spark?"

She laughed. "Yeah. You do." She was reflective for a moment, then said, "Looking back on Mother's relationship with Daddy, I think she was always trying to ensure his approval of her. She doesn't strive for yours."

"My standards aren't as high as his."

Berry smiled. "No. She knows she has your approval. Unconditionally."

Grace appeared at the end of the booth. "Something the matter with the burger, Dodge?"

"No. Guess I wasn't so hungry after all."

"I'm going on a smoke break in a minute. Want to join me?"

"Check back."

Looking disappointed, she removed their plates. Berry's eyes followed her. When they came back to Dodge, she said, "She likes you."

He shrugged and reached for his beer.

"All women do."

"That's an exaggeration if I ever heard one."

"I don't think so. Mother hinted as much."

"Did she?"

"Was that the problem?" Berry asked.

He looked across at her but said nothing.

"You're popular with the ladies, Dodge. Is that why you didn't marry my mother?"

CHAPTER 24

Houston, Texas, 1979

If work hadn't sucked so bad, Dodge's life would have been perfect.

Roger Campton's family had trundled him off to South America, ostensibly to oversee their oil interests in Venezuela. Good riddance to everyone except the Venezuelans, Dodge thought.

"I hope they know to lock up their daughters," he told Caroline when they read the notice in the business pages of the newspaper.

Her tummy had a bump that he thought was adorable. "I can see you in profile now."

He couldn't keep his hands off the slight protrusion, sometimes to her annoyance.

"Dodge, you're in my way."

"When's it supposed to kick?"

"A while yet."

"It'll feel weird, won't it? Something moving around inside you."

She winked at him. "You've moved around inside me."

"Hmm, talking dirty comes with pregnancy. I like it."

She swatted aside his wandering hands. "The first time I feel the baby move, I promise to let you know. In the meantime, it wants to be fed, and I can't get dinner on the table if you're going to continue feeling me up."

He grinned wickedly and covered her swollen breasts with his hands. "Now, about these . . ."

Dinner was late being served that evening.

She listed her house and his condo with Jim Malone Realty, and they sold within days of each other. She had found what she referred to as a "doll house" in an older, established neighborhood. Dodge donated his furniture to Goodwill, since it was nothing to brag about, and they moved Caroline's into their shared residence.

It took Dodge four evenings to paint the spare bedroom a soft unisex yellow and three evenings to assemble the crib. "I hope the kid likes it, because I'm never doing this again," he informed her.

"Stop calling my baby the kid."

He grabbed Caroline's hand and pulled her down beside him onto the nursery room floor amid the tools he'd used during the project. "*Our* baby. And what do you want to call it?"

"My mother's maiden name was Carter. What do you think? Carter Hanley?"

"What if it's a girl?"

"I'm thinking."

"You're pretty when you're thinking." He kissed the tip of her nose, and they wound up making love on the rug.

They were complacent about a wedding date. "A piece of paper isn't going to make me any happier than I already am," he told her. "But I want to make this union official."

She agreed. "Before the baby gets here."

But a date was never set, and they were content with the way things were, so neither dwelled on that technicality. Days turned into weeks, then months, and still they felt no urgency to have their pairing solemnized.

She had returned to work as soon as the bruises around her

eyes were no longer detectable. To make up for lost time, she'd doubled her efforts to become the top salesperson in the company. Often she worked late into the evenings, showing houses when it was convenient for clients, hosting open houses on weekends.

Her erratic schedule was okay with Dodge since most nights he had to go to the task force jam sessions after his shift at the tire plant. He was beginning to think the whole thing was a waste of his time and the taxpayers' money. Had a promotion to detective not been the carrot, he'd have asked to be removed from the special unit. He hated having to spend every workday at that damn plant. Mopping floors and replacing burned-out lightbulbs didn't seem like police work.

But had he quit the task force and gone back to patrolling a beat, he would have felt that he was letting down not only his new family but himself, and especially Jimmy Gonzales. So he stuck with it, even though cultivating Crystal's confidence had lost all its allure. The only woman Dodge desired was Caroline, and his desire for her was so fierce, so all-consuming, it was damn near impossible to work up any enthusiasm for his quasi romance with Crystal.

But his pursuit must have been convincing, because one day as they ate their lunch together, she became weepy. "I'm worried about Franklin."

"In what way?"

"The way he's acting." She pulled her lower lip through her teeth. "I shouldn't talk about it. It's probably nothing."

Dodge appeared suitably worried about her. "But what if it is something? What if his rehabilitation in prison didn't take?"

She smiled weakly. "He's promised me that he won't break the law, ever again."

"Do you believe him? Can he keep a promise to anybody about anything?"

She crumpled against him, resting her head on his shoulder. He placed his arm around her. "You're so good to me, Marvin."

He bent his head over hers and kissed her lightly on the cheek. "I just want to take care of you."

The other members of the task force were excited when he reported this to them. "Albright's planning another robbery, and she knows it," the captain said, rubbing his stubby hands together with exhilaration.

"That's what I think, too," Dodge said. "I need to get into their house. It's a rental. A duplex. Crystal told me the other side is empty, and Albright is using it for storage, without the landlord's knowledge or permission."

"What's he storing?"

"Crystal doesn't know."

"You believe her?"

"Yeah, I do. It's a bone of contention between them. I need to find out what he's got in there."

"Anything you find would be inadmissible in court," the captain reminded him.

"Yeah, but if I saw something suspicious, we could put him under constant surveillance. And if it was something incriminating, I could use it as leverage to get Crystal to turn state's witness against him."

"You'd have to tell her you're a cop."

"Not necessarily. Not at first. I could still be the concerned friend persuading her to do as her conscience dictated."

"I doubt she would ever agree," one of the other cops remarked. "Not if it meant betraying her boyfriend."

Dodge looked at him with disparagement. "If it was easy, *you'd* be doing it."

The captain sided with Dodge. "Can you get in and out of their place without Albright knowing?"

"I'll do my best. But if I go missing, look there first."

"This is serious, Dodge. Cover your ass. Don't get yourself killed over this. It would make us look bad," the captain said with cruel candor.

"Let me work on Crystal, see what I can do."

Dodge seized upon the additional risk. By taking on the responsibility of going into Franklin Albright's lair, he was raising the stakes for himself. But the reward would be greater, too. If he came through, and delivered Franklin Albright, he'd get that detective's badge he so wanted.

Several nights later, he returned home particularly tired after a long, grinding day. Caroline met him at the door and hugged him close. He leaned in to kiss her, but she pushed him away and sniffed his shirtfront. "Is that Tabu?"

"What?"

"The fragrance."

And he thought, *Oh, shit.* He unbuttoned the top two buttons of his tire plant shirt, then pulled it over his head. He held it to his nose and took a deep breath. "Sorry. I didn't realize it was so strong."

He went to the closet that housed the washer and dryer and tossed the offending shirt into the hamper. When he came back around, Caroline was staring at him, her head angled, waiting for an explanation.

"A woman at the . . . at work. At Marvin's workplace. She hugged him today."

"She hugged you?"

"She hugged *Marvin.* It had nothing to do with me." He went to the refrigerator and got a beer. He opened it and took a long swallow. Caroline was still looking at him, obviously waiting for further explanation. "I can't discuss it, Caroline."

"What does she look like?"

"I can't discuss it."

"Why were the two of you hugging at work?"

He gave her a look that warned her to stop with the questions. But either she didn't recognize the look or she defied it. "This is one of those situations that Jimmy referred to, isn't it?"

"That *Jimmy* referred to? Jimmy Gonzales?"

"The night he came to dinner."

Shortly after Dodge had brought her from the hospital to his place, but before they'd become a couple, she had urged him to invite his partner to dinner. "Officer Gonzales has been very kind to me on several occasions. I'd like to repay him by cooking him a meal."

So, on his next night off, Jimmy had come to dinner. He arrived before Dodge got home. When he got there, Jimmy and Caroline had been companionably chatting.

Now, he asked her warily, "What did Jimmy tell you?"

"He must have assumed that we were already sleeping together, because he told me that you'd been smitten with me from the get-go."

"Which came as no surprise to you."

"But then he said, 'I guess he'll be relinquishing his title of department Romeo.' When I asked him what he meant, he rapidly backpedaled. But the gist of it was that you have a reputation for easily getting information out of women." Caroline forced him to look her in the eye. "Is that true? Were you, *are* you, the police department's Romeo?"

"Guys talk, Caroline. Mostly it's bullshit."

"Mostly?"

She continued to look at him levelly, and he knew she would persist until he gave her something.

"Okay, I'll tell you this much. The girl at work was upset over something her boyfriend did. I'm her pal. I extended her a listening ear, a kind word, a shoulder to cry on. She expressed her gratitude by hugging me. That's all it amounted to, and that's all I can tell you."

She appeared to be mollified, but even if she wasn't, that was all he was going to tell her. He wasn't about to give her a physical description of Crystal and start her thinking that he was interested in the girl for any reason except as a means of trapping Albright. He wouldn't tell Caroline about the threat Albright posed, either. He'd minimized the danger of the undercover work in order to prevent her from worrying every time he left the house.

He excused himself and went to take a shower. Although the heady scent of Tabu no longer lingered, Caroline was abnormally quiet over supper, and later, when they went to bed, they lay with their backs to each other.

After an hour of tense wakefulness, Dodge knew she was still awake, too. He turned onto his side, so that he was addressing her back. "Everything I do, I'm doing for us."

She said nothing.

He placed his hand on her shoulder. "I'm trying to make detective, Caroline. If I do a good job on this special assignment, I'll have a much better shot at getting the promotion. It would mean a pay increase. I wouldn't be patrolling a beat. And, besides all that, it's what I've wanted since I signed on with the department. Before that. Since I was a kid."

She turned to him then and laid her hand on his cheek. "I know you want that, Dodge. And I understand why you can't talk about the case. I do."

"But?"

"But I wouldn't be a woman if I didn't question your coming home smelling of drugstore cologne."

He could think of a thousand ways in which she was all woman, but he knew better than to begin listing them. She wasn't in the mood to be charmed. "Everything I do now is for us. You, me, the baby."

"Hugging the Tabu woman?"

"Part of the job. I swear."

She thought it over for several moments, then said, "You're her pal? That's all?"

"That's it."

"She has a boyfriend?"

"Yes. And so do you." His hand moved to her breast and caressed it lovingly.

"I feel fat and ugly. Don't laugh!"

He pecked her lips with his. "You're pregnant, not fat. And you couldn't be ugly, no matter what."

"You still love me?"

"You have to ask?"

The discussion ended there, and for seventy-two hours nothing more was said about Crystal.

Then he came home one night looking like an extra from *The Texas Chain Saw Massacre*.

Twelve hours earlier that day, during their morning coffee break, he'd caught Crystal chatting with one of the other women who worked in payroll. "He's an asshole," Dodge overheard her say.

"Not me, I hope."

She smiled up at him. "Hey, Marvin. No, you're not the asshole."

"Let me guess. The chief among them. None other than Franklin Albright. What's he done now?"

"The kitchen sink has been clogged up for a week, and he's promised to fix it. But every night he's had another excuse, and tonight he's going over to a buddy's house to play poker."

And Dodge thought, *Bingo!*

He offered to repair her sink, and she accepted his offer. It was almost too easy.

"Franklin said he'd be leaving around eight-thirty or nine." She warned him not to arrive before then. "He wouldn't like you and me being there alone."

"I'll make sure his pickup is gone before I come to the door."

On his lunch hour he called his captain, who agreed to the plan Dodge outlined but warned him again to be careful. "Learn what you can, but don't get killed doing it."

"You don't have to tell me twice."

The captain offered to place undercover officers in the vicinity in case there was trouble. "Not necessary," Dodge said. "I'll be okay." Besides, if this turned out well, he didn't want to share the credit. He wanted it to be a one-man show. *His* show. "But one thing you can do, sir."

"Shoot."

"Square it with my boss here at the plant that I need to leave early today. There's stuff I gotta do."

The captain made the call. Dodge clocked out early, leaving him time to run some necessary errands. His first stop was at the

7-Eleven store where Doris worked. He walked in just as she was beginning her shift.

Her face lit up with her smile. "Dodge! Come to take me dancing?"

"Came to do some business."

Her tone changed dramatically. "Let's go out back."

She asked a stock boy to cover the register and led Dodge through the storeroom and out the rear door. In the alley, amid the trash receptacles, they lit up cigarettes. She exhaled. "I heard about Jimmy Gonzales. I'm sorry."

"It sucked."

"I liked him."

"So did I. He was a great partner. The best."

"But he never caught on, did he?" she asked, looking at him askance. "He never knew that you and I had our side thing going, did he?"

"No, he never did. He wouldn't have approved. He was a straight-up cop, as honest as they come." Several times, Dodge and Doris had swapped favors, and the services they exchanged weren't always within the law. They certainly weren't ethical.

They smoked in silence for a while, then she asked what he needed.

He told her.

"By when?"

He told her.

"Tonight! Jesus, you don't ask for much, do you?"

"Can you get it?"

"It'll cost you more than a night of dancing." She bobbed her eyebrows suggestively.

"Sorry, but no can do."

"You've gone queer?"

He smiled. "Just the opposite. I've got a lady in my life."

"For real?"

"The real thing."

"Well, hell. What else have you got to barter?"

"What's your little brother's status?"

"Still languishing in jail awaiting trial while the greenhorn ADA, his half-assed court-appointed attorney, and the judge dick around with bigger cases."

"He's charged with B and E, right? Who were the arresting officers?"

She told him, and he said they were buddies of his, and maybe if she could get him what he requested in a timely fashion, he could talk his buddies into a memory loss convenient to her little brother when his case eventually came to trial. "For a coupla fifths of Scotch, your brother would probably get off with time served."

"Which the little jerk deserves just for being stupid."

"Before you agree, I gotta tell you, Doris, if he ever gets busted again, he's on his own. You do this for me, I do that for you, we'll be square."

"Deal."

By dusk, she had what he'd asked for. It was secondhand and looked the worse for wear. "Will it work?"

"You want a guarantee, you go to Radio Shack."

Before he left, he asked, "How's the A-rab treating you these days?"

"Still suspects me of stealing from him."

Dodge laughed. "I can't imagine why."

He called Caroline from a pay phone and told her not to wait dinner on him. She asked if he would be working, and he said yes. She asked if he would be in danger, and he told her no. She didn't ask if he would be with the woman who wore Tabu, and he wasn't sure what he would have told her if she had, but it probably would have been an extremely loose variation of the truth.

At nine o'clock, he drove past the duplex shared by Crystal and Franklin Albright. There was no sign of his redneck pickup, but Dodge thought it prudent to kill a little more time and make sure the criminal wasn't at home. At nine-fifteen, he parked at the curb and started up the walk, carrying with him a bag of plumbing implements he'd bought at the hardware store that afternoon.

The front door was open. He peered through the screen door into a living room that had been furnished and decorated by someone who had done the best she could with the little she had. His heart went out to Crystal. The kid deserved credit for trying.

He knocked. "Anybody home?"

She appeared in an open doorway across the room. She was wearing a pair of short denim cutoffs and a red shirt tied under her braless breasts. Her hair was loosely piled on top of her head. She was barefoot. She looked like the porn-flick farm girl who incited a hillbilly gang bang.

Her bare feet making soft pats on the hardwood floor, she came quickly to the door and unlatched it. "Thanks for this." She was a bit breathless as she motioned him in. "The darned thing is still stopped up. It's disgusting."

He held up his sack of plumbing supplies. "I'm no Roto-Rooter, but I'm still your man."

"Come on back."

As he followed her into the kitchen, he casually said, "I wouldn't have known which side of the duplex you live in if the front door hadn't been open." He motioned with his head. "Next door. Is that where Franklin keeps his stash?"

"His stash?"

"He won't let you go in there." Looking as sappy as he possibly could, he shrugged. "I immediately thought drugs."

"He's never used drugs around me." She chewed her lower lip nervously, then pointed to the sink. "You see the problem."

He whistled. The sink was full of viscous, opaque water that was, indeed, disgusting. She moved to the refrigerator and took out two beers, uncapping one for each of them. They toasted to unclogged drains, then he went to work with a plunger.

She hopped up onto the countertop so she could face him while he worked. Her bare heels rhythmically tapped the cabinet door. She rolled the rim of the beer bottle across her lower lip.

She was laughing at something Dodge had said when her breath caught and she strangled out the name "Franklin!"

CHAPTER 25

THE SON OF A BITCH HAD BEEN AS SILENT AS A PANTHER. Dodge hadn't realized Albright had returned until he was *there.* But in fairness to himself, the oscillating movement of Crystal's unfettered breasts beneath the bright red shirt had been a distraction.

Albright snarled as he grabbed her messy topknot and yanked her off the counter. He pulled the bottle of beer from her hand and hurled it into the wall. Broken glass and beer showered them. Still holding Crystal by her hair, Albright shook her like a terrier with a rat and called her a cunt, then sent her reeling into the table, on which lay a wrench, purchased just that afternoon. Albright snatched it up and applied it to Dodge's head.

Or tried. If not for Dodge's excellent reflexes, honed even sharper by years of street fighting and police training, he'd probably have been brained with the wrench. Instead he ducked just in time to catch the tool on his shoulder bone, which hurt like bloody hell but wasn't a lethal blow.

Albright threw down the wrench and attacked Dodge's face with his bare fists.

Ordinarily Dodge would have fought back and probably killed the guy, but he was role-playing. Marvin wasn't supposed to have deadly fighting skills. It was hard to take a beating and do nothing. Dodge's restraint was really tested when Albright flicked open a switchblade, grabbed Dodge by the hair—he must like hair—and pulled Dodge's head back, exposing his throat and nicking the thin flesh over his Adam's apple with the tip of the blade.

"You ever come near her again, I'll slit your throat. You *sabe* me, Marvin?"

Dodge had no doubt the felon meant what he said and wanted to take him out right then and save the taxpayers of Texas a lot of expense. Because this guy was bad, and eventually he'd wind up convicted of killing somebody, possibly this misled girl, who had bad judgment but didn't deserve to die for it.

However, they didn't have solid evidence against him yet, so Dodge rolled his eyes wildly, whimpered, and stammered that he understood the warning.

Albright released him, spun him around, and kicked him in the kidney, which sent him flying out the back door. He fell facefirst onto the driveway and skidded a few inches, leaving a trail of his skin on the concrete. Then he crawled to his car.

He made it home without passing out. But by the time he got there, every cell in his body was throbbing in agony. Upon seeing him, Caroline actually screamed and dropped a folder of paperwork. Real estate documents scattered unheeded across the living room floor. Moving with as much alacrity as her eighth month of pregnancy would allow, she rushed toward him.

Words tumbling off her lips, she demanded to know what had happened, how badly he was hurt, if he'd seen a doctor. When he told her no, she said, "I'm taking you to the emergency room."

"I don't need to go to the emergency room. Some squirts of Bactine, a few aspirin, I'll be fine in the morning."

"Please let me call an ambulance," she pleaded, practically weeping as she examined his flayed face.

He refused by adamantly shaking his head, which made him

dizzy. He figured one of Albright's blows had given him a slight concussion.

"It was the Tabu woman's boyfriend, wasn't it?" Caroline asked as she helped him undress.

"Caroline, I—"

"Can't talk about it. I understand. But I know this beating has something to do with her. Her boyfriend didn't like you hugging her any more than I did. He's a criminal, isn't he? No, don't tell me. I know you can't say, but I know he did this. He could have killed you." She began to cry in earnest.

Dodge drew her to him and held her close, painful though it was. "Shh. He didn't kill me. He won't."

"Please don't get killed. If anything were to happen to you—"

"Nothing's going to happen to me."

"How do you know?"

"I know."

"You can't be sure."

"Shh. This crying can't be good for you or the baby."

"I'm scared."

He kissed her hair. "You don't need to be scared."

She set herself away from him and looked up into his swelling eyes. "What good will making detective do you if you're dead?"

He chuckled at her logic, but it hurt all over when he laughed. "I know how to take care of myself."

"I know that. I saw what you did to Roger that night outside his gym. You could have defended yourself tonight, but you didn't."

"No."

"Why?"

"Because I've gotta be convincing in my role. A lot is riding on it."

"Getting detective."

"And getting the bad guy."

"One and the same thing."

"Right. So this is a small price to pay."

"Not so small, Dodge," she cried. "Look at you!"

He dropped his flippancy and cradled her face between his

hands. All seriousness, he said, "You gave up a rich guy for me, Caroline. I gotta do this and I gotta do it right. I can't let you down."

"Or Jimmy Gonzales."

He said nothing.

"I know this is important to you," she said in a quavering voice. "How important, Dodge?"

Matching her tone, he said, "This isn't just important. This is everything."

Dodge was sore, swollen, and bruised for days after Albright's attack.

However, the discomfort was worth the reward.

The mission hadn't been as successful as it would have been if he'd been able to get into the attached apartment and discovered what Albright was hiding. But while Crystal had been getting their two beers from the fridge, Dodge had successfully planted a listening device, courtesy of Doris, on the underside of the kitchen table.

Even on short notice, Doris had provided him a whole setup. He'd had with him several more bugs, which he'd hoped to put in key areas of the duplex, but having successfully placed one was better than nothing.

The surveillance had not been sanctioned by his superiors. Officially, their strong hunch that Albright was their culprit didn't amount to "just cause." Not yet. But it was enough for Dodge. If anyone found out that he'd planted a bug without authorization, he would be removed from the task force, if not drummed out of the Houston PD altogether. But if it paid off the way he predicted it would, it was worth the risk.

The day following the beating, he called in sick at the tire plant. As soon as Caroline left for work, he drove to within a block of Crystal and Albright's duplex and gave the equipment a test run. He was able to pick up snatches of their breakfast conversation. Most of it consisted of his yelling at her and calling her ugly names. Crystal tearfully denied that anything sexual had transpired between her and Marvin.

Dodge couldn't catch all of Albright's response to that, but he picked up the word *eunuch,* which pissed him off. He lived for the day when the ex-con realized he'd been had, not by the nerd infatuated with his girlfriend but by Dodge Hanley.

When he returned to work at the tire plant, his brutalized appearance shocked co-workers. He fielded questions about what had happened to him and created a fender bender, saying it had been severe enough to push his face into his windshield and teach him a hard lesson about wearing his seat belt.

Crystal avoided him. At lunch, she joined a table of other women, and, after giving him one shamefaced, sympathetic smile, she steered clear. It went on like that each following day. They made eye contact, but she never gave him an opportunity to get close to her.

His captain was on his ass about it. Other cops on the task force considered his attempted penetration of Albright's duplex a complete bust.

In the evenings, after dinner, he contrived reasons for leaving the house. He drove to the duplex. He parked near enough for the receiver to pick up any transmissions from the bug, but not so close that he risked being spotted by either Albright or Crystal.

Only once did he hit pay dirt. He heard Crystal asking Albright what he was doing next door. Why was it such a big secret? Why couldn't she go in there? If the landlord found out that he was using it for extra storage, they'd be kicked out of the apartment. She asked if he was dealing drugs. If so, she threatened to move out.

Albright told her that she would move out when he ordered her out and not before. Then he shouted for her to shut the hell up and not to meddle in his business.

Having heard that exchange, Dodge returned home pumped, only to become alarmed when he caught Caroline sitting on the edge of their bed, stroking her mounded stomach with one hand and massaging her lower back with the other.

He rushed to her side. "Oh, God. Is the baby coming?"

She affectionately ruffled his hair. "Not for another couple of weeks at least. I'm having Braxton Hicks contractions."

"What the hell is a . . . what you said?"

"They're perfectly normal. Really just twinges."

"Looks like more than twinges to me."

"The doctor says to expect these contractions until the real thing comes along."

"How will you know it's the real thing?"

She laughed lightly. "Oh, he says I'll know."

For the rest of the night, even while she slept, he kept his hand on her belly, wondering how she could possibly sleep with so much activity going on inside her womb.

Worry gnawed at him. If her uterus was in proportion to the rest of her, it was tiny. He thought it was a miracle that a frame as small as hers could carry a child of any size, but what if their baby was extraordinarily large? He couldn't remember if he'd ever been told how much he'd weighed at birth, but even if he had been told, he didn't know what the standard was. He'd have no gauge of comparison. What if he and Caroline had conceived a giant? His offspring could bust something up inside her. She could be ripped apart.

He lay awake all night, fearing an anatomical catastrophe. Consequently, he was out of sorts the next morning when he reported for work at the tire plant. His mood didn't improve when he realized Crystal hadn't clocked in that day. Was she sick? Had Albright made her leave the job because of her friend and co-worker Marvin? Had he started thinking about the plumbing episode, got angry all over again, and taken his abuse to a new level?

At the end of his shift, Dodge quickly made his way toward the employee exit. He was anxious to get home, reassure himself that Caroline was all right, and then see if he could pick up anything untoward going on in the household of Franklin Albright. He practically mowed down a female co-worker who planted herself in his path.

"Hi, Marvin."

"Hi. Excuse me. I'm in a hurry."

"I have a message for you from Crystal."

He stopped in his tracks.

Crystal's friend passed him a slip of paper. "She wants you to call her at this number."

"Is she okay?"

Either the co-worker didn't know or she wasn't saying. "First chance you get, she said."

"Okay. Thanks."

He called from a pay phone. Crystal answered on the second ring. Her hello was faint, hesitant. "It's Marvin. Are you all right?"

At the sound of his voice, she began wailing. "No, no, I'm not! I'm scared."

Dodge cooed and consoled and finally got out of her that she'd left Albright.

"More like escaped," she sobbed. "He's . . . he's . . ."

"Where are you?"

She told him, and, twenty minutes later, he was at the motel, knocking on the door, glancing over his shoulder and hoping that Albright didn't have a bead on the back of his head.

Crystal looked a fright. Her face was splotchy and bloated from hard crying. She was also a mess emotionally. Sitting beside her on the bed, Dodge held her until she stopped shaking. Brushing the hair off her damp cheeks, he urged her to tell him everything.

"I can't help you if I don't know what's going on." The first thing he wanted to know was if he had to worry about Albright crashing in on them again, wielding his switchblade and making good his promise to slit Dodge's throat. "Does he know you've left him?"

"I'm sure he does by now," she said, hiccuping. "He went out and said he'd be gone for a few hours, but I didn't trust him not to come right back. Not after the other night when he tricked me. As soon as he left, I called a taxi. I packed only what I could carry, and all the time I was waiting for the taxi, I was frightened he'd come back and catch me before I could get away."

"You didn't leave a note or anything telling him where you were going?"

"No! I've left for good, and I'm not going back. Oh, Marvin, if he catches me, he'll kill me."

"No he won't, because I won't let him."

She clutched him tighter and said she didn't know what she would do without his friendship and protection. Out of gratitude, she kissed him on the lips.

"Listen, Crystal," he said, setting her away from him. "Do you have any other reason to be scared of Franklin?"

She blinked the gummy eyelashes. "Like what?"

He cautioned himself not to blow it, to go easy. "Like . . . I don't know. Do you think he's planning another crime?"

She averted her eyes. "Maybe. He's up to something."

"Jesus."

"He's been on the phone a lot. With the cousin in Mexico. Remember I told you about him?"

Heart racing, Dodge nodded.

"I think they're planning something." Here her eyes began to leak again. "And if they go through with it, I'm afraid the cops will think I'm an accomplice." She sniffled and wiped her nose with the back of her hand. "My parents tried to warn me. Why didn't I listen?"

"Maybe you ought to talk to the police."

She raised her head and looked at him with alarm.

"Yeah," he said, pressing her hands between his. "If you tip them to what Franklin's planning, then they'll know you're not in on it. See?"

He kept at her for half an hour, trying to worm out of her the nature of the criminal plot, but she wouldn't say anything specific, nothing useful that he could convey to the task force. Her eyes continued to produce fresh tears, and she bewailed the day she'd ever become involved with Franklin Albright. Why hadn't she been fortunate enough to meet Marvin first? Her parents would have approved of him. If only she'd met him before becoming involved with Albright, she wouldn't be living in fear of the police, in fear of reprisal from a jealous, violent ex-convict.

"Oh, God, my life is in such a mess! You're the only thing in it that's good, Marvin. You're the only person I can trust."

The second time she kissed him, it wasn't out of gratitude, and Dodge knew enough about women and kisses to recognize the difference. She pushed her tongue into his mouth, and, when she fell back onto the bed, he let himself be pulled down with her.

As she nuzzled his neck, he said, "Franklin is all talk and bluster, Crystal."

"You're so sweet to me." She took his hand and placed it between her thighs.

"Albright will land in prison again as soon as he's caught, and then we can be together without any fear of him. The sooner the better. You should help the police catch him in the act of committing a crime."

She arched up, into his palm. "I want to be with you."

"Then let's go to the police together. I'll be right there with you."

She demurred. "I'll think about it."

"I think we should go right now. Before Franklin has a chance to do whatever he's planning."

"Maybe tomorrow." She unzipped his pants.

"You promise?"

"I promise to *think* about it. But I don't want to talk about it anymore."

So they didn't talk.

Not until after, when she was curled up against him like a kitten, making mewling sounds in admiration of the hair on his chest, which was damp with their combined sweat.

Only when she was drowsy and mellow from sex would she be led into further conversation about Franklin. Then she spoke freely. Because if a woman will trust you enough to share *that,* she'll trust you with her deepest, darkest secrets. That had been Dodge's experience, anyway. That tenet was what his reputation in the department was founded on.

Crystal spilled all she knew. It was terrific insider information gleaned from overheard conversations between Franklin and his cousin in Mexico that included buzzwords like "getaway car" and "semiautomatic" and "popping anybody who gets in the way" and "the twenty-fifth," a date that was only two days away.

Eventually she fell asleep.

Dodge stretched the motel room phone cord as far as it would go, taking it into the bathroom and closing the door. He called his captain at home, woke him up, and reported what Crystal had told him.

To his surprise and irritation, the captain was skeptical. "How reliable is she? Maybe she's onto you, feeding you bullshit to throw you off. Saying stuff just to get you to sleep with her."

Dodge opened the door a crack and peeked through. Crystal was sleeping the peaceful slumber of the unburdened. "I don't think so, sir. She's scared of Albright. I'm certain of that. She also said she was afraid she would be considered an accomplice because she's been living with him while he plotted the crime. Besides, she didn't tell me anything of substance until . . . later."

When his superior said nothing, Dodge plowed on. "She's not tooling me around. She's using lingo she wouldn't know unless she'd heard it from somebody like Albright. I know I'm right."

After a thoughtful pause, the captain sighed. "Okay. I have to trust your instincts, Hanley. As well as your experience," he added drolly. "You've had your last day at the tire plant. Report to task force headquarters first thing in the morning. The twenty-fifth is only two days away, which doesn't give us much time to plan the sting."

Dodge thanked him for the confidence he'd placed in him, then, as quietly as possible, he washed up and put on his clothes. He left a note on the bureau for Crystal, telling her not to report to work again until she'd heard directly from him. He told her that he would take care of everything. All she had to do was trust him and stay where she was until he got back to her.

He drove through the empty, predawn streets, wondering how he was going to explain to Caroline why he'd stayed out all night without calling. Even when the task force briefings had kept him late—and never till five o'clock in the morning—he had called to let her know so she wouldn't worry.

He'd just have to say, truthfully in fact, that something urgent had come up, they'd got an unexpected break in the case, and he hadn't had an opportunity to call until it was too late for him to do so without disturbing her sleep.

He had it all sorted out in his mind, which went into a tailspin when he reached their house and saw that her car wasn't in the garage.

"Oh, Jesus."

He didn't even take the time to turn off his car's engine. He shoved it into Park and left it idling as he bolted for the back door, where he fumbled his key, then, when he managed to get the door unlocked, practically fell across the threshold.

He ran through the house, crashing into walls, stumbling on the rug in the hallway, barreling through the door of their bedroom, then drawing up short when he saw the blood-tinged stain on the bedsheet. It was still damp.

He was breathing so hard, his lungs actually hurt. His heart was pounding. He went to the closet and flung open the door. Her suitcase, the one they'd packed together a few weeks ago so it would be ready when needed, was gone.

He retraced his path through the house, moving even more recklessly than before. He plopped the cherry on the roof of his car, uncaring of his undercover status. With the red light flashing, he sped to the hospital.

He left his car in a loading zone and raced inside. He pounded the call button for the elevator with his fist until it finally arrived. When he reached the nurses' station on the maternity floor, there was no one there.

"Where the hell is everybody?" His shout echoed off the sterile surfaces of the deserted corridor as he ran down it.

Each door was decorated with either a blue or a pink wreath and a complimentary stuffed bear. Finally, a nurse came out of one of the rooms. He almost collided with her. "Can I help you?" she asked.

"Caroline King?"

"You are?"

"The . . . the father."

She smiled. "Congratulations. You have an awfully sweet baby."

He felt like he'd been turned upside down and slam-dunked into the tile floor. "It's here?"

"*She's* here," the nurse said, laughing. "Would you like to see her?"

Dumbly, he nodded and followed her along the hallway to a window blocked with drawn blinds. "Wait here and I'll bring her over." She was about to enter the nursery when he said, "Wait. Where's Caroline?"

"Room four eighteen."

"Is she okay?"

"She had a short labor and easy delivery. I'm sorry you didn't make it in time."

He'd been tupping Crystal when Caroline's water broke, when she went into labor, when she had to carry her carefully packed suitcase to the car and drive herself to the hospital, when she'd given birth to their daughter.

His breath hitched until he was actually gasping. He couldn't imagine self-loathing more wretched than what he felt for himself. He stood staring at the slats in the blinds until they were opened, and there stood the nurse on the other side of the window, holding up the tiniest human being he'd ever seen.

Her face was red, her nose was flat, her eyes puffy. She was wrapped up like a papoose. A pink knit cap was on her head. The nurse removed it so he could see the red peach fuzz covering her scalp. Her pulse was beating in the soft spot on the top of her head.

Tears came to his eyes, and, if he'd found it difficult to breathe before, it was impossible to do so now.

He gave the nurse a thumbs-up and mouthed *Thank you* through the glass, then he turned away and went in search of room

418. When he reached it, he smoothed back his hair and dragged both hands down his face. He took a deep breath.

The door was heavy. He opened it only partially before slipping into the room. The light above the bed was on, a mere glow, but enough to see by. Caroline was lying on her back, her face turned away from the door. Her tummy was flat, and that looked strange now. When she heard the soft swish of the door, she turned her head toward it.

She looked at him with full knowledge of his transgression.

He made the long walk to her bedside. He, always the smooth talker, didn't know what to say. Words failed him completely.

She was the first to speak. "When you didn't come home, and I didn't hear from you, I called the police department. I told the man I spoke to that it was an emergency, that I needed to reach you right away. Since you're on a special task force, working undercover, he told me he would try to get word to you to call me.

"But you didn't. So I called a second time, more frantic than when I'd called before. The man said he'd been unable to reach you but told me that, if it was any comfort, you hadn't been reported killed or wounded in the line of duty."

Both her voice and her eyes were expressionless. "You slept with her, didn't you? To catch your crook, you had sex with his girlfriend."

He would have preferred screamed invectives and tears. He wished she would reach up and slap him. That kind of fury he was prepared to handle. This controlled rage terrified him.

He opened his mouth to speak but still couldn't think of anything to say. He didn't even consider denying it. He wouldn't heap lying onto his betrayal, adding insult to her wound, and, in any case, it would be futile.

"I want you out of the house before I bring the baby home."

Panic shot through him. "Caroline—"

"I mean it. I want you gone. Out of our lives. Hers, mine. You're to have nothing to do with either of us. Ever again, Dodge."

"You can't—"

"Yes I can. I *am*."

"I—"

"You ruined it."

"I did something stupid."

"Label it any way you like. You abused me worse than Roger Campton ever did."

Those words were like a lance straight through his heart. "How can you say that?"

"How could you *do* it?" Her voice cracked, and that was telling. "How could you do it?" she asked again, emphasizing each word.

He was asking himself the same thing. He could offer her no excuse, because there was none.

She turned her face toward the ceiling. "You've seen me for the last time, Dodge. I want nothing to do with you. Our daughter will never know you, or you her. Enjoy being a detective. Have a good life. Now get away from me."

He stood there beside the bed for a full two minutes, but she didn't look at him again. He left the room, and then the hospital, because he really would be a brute to stay and hassle a woman who'd just given birth. He didn't want to cause a scene and further humiliate Caroline in front of hospital personnel and other new mothers whose partners had been with them when their babies came into the world.

He went out to retrieve his car and practically came to blows with the hospital parking Nazi who accused him of impersonating a police officer. Because he couldn't carry ID around Crystal and Albright, Dodge couldn't prove the guy wrong. So he shoved him out of his way, gave him the finger, said "Sue me," then sped away with the guy threatening legal repercussions.

In the house he'd been ordered out of, he stripped the soiled sheets off the bed and replaced them with fresh. He vacuumed the living room rug. He emptied all the trash cans and scrubbed the bathroom fixtures till they were sparkling. While carrying out these chores, he planned what else he could do to win back Caroline's favor.

On the day she was due to come home, he would put flowers in the bedroom. In the baby's room, too. Pink ones. He'd stock the fridge and pantry with Caroline's favorite foods. He'd leave chocolates on her pillow every night. He'd get up with her each time she had to nurse the baby. He would fetch and carry. He'd give her back rubs. He'd buy the baby stuffed toys and lacy outfits that Caroline would call extravagant but would secretly adore. He'd do anything and everything, whatever it took to change her mind.

He had to have her in his life, or his life wouldn't be worth shit. It was as simple as that. He must convince her to take him back. But first, he must prove himself worthy.

When the house was as perfect as he could make it, he showered, shaved, dressed, and drove to the task force office. There was only one guy in the large room, and he was on the phone. Seeing Dodge, he hung up. "Where have you been? Why didn't you answer your page?"

"I—"

"Doesn't matter. He hit a bank at eight oh seven this morning. Right after it opened."

"Jesus! You're kidding. Crystal told me the twenty-fifth. Albright must've—"

"Albright? Forget Albright. Our guy's some dickweed executive for a pharmaceutical company. No priors. We never would have looked at him. Not in a million years. Can you believe it?"

CHAPTER 26

DODGE CAME TO THE END OF HIS LONG STORY.

"This pharmaceutical executive thought he was smarter than everybody else. He robbed the first bank as a lark, just to see if he could get away with it. When he did, he tried it again. And again. He said it got addictive.

"I guess that young guard he killed gave him an extra-special rush. I wonder how much fun he had on death row. I'm sure he's been executed by now, unless he received a pardon. When I moved to Atlanta, I lost track." He shifted on the faux leather bench and, in a lower tone, added, "But for you, that's probably the least interesting part of the story."

Berry had been listening for almost an hour without speaking a word. She cleared her throat and took a sip from the water glass that Grace had refilled without her even noticing. "What happened to Franklin Albright?"

"ATF caught him and his so-called cousin conducting a lucrative business in automatic weapons. They were selling them to drug cartels across the border."

"Crystal?"

Dodge sighed and shook his head ruefully. "I guess she finally figured out that Marvin wasn't coming back to rescue her from the motel. I lost track of her, too."

"You never saw her again?"

"No. Marvin vanished from her life."

Berry hesitated, then asked in a quieter voice, "And Mother?"

"I'd failed to uphold every promise I'd made her. So I did as she ordered and was out of the house by the time she brought you home. I didn't see her again until last Saturday. Or you, either." He gave her an appraising look. "Your hair's still red, but your nose is no longer flat."

She returned his wistful smile. Her moods had shifted a dozen times while he'd been telling his story. She'd gone from curiosity to anger to heartache. She wasn't sure which emotion she should land on, so she let them ebb and flow as they would without making a conscious effort to claim one.

She said, "The task force was disbanded."

"Yep."

"And you made detective."

"No. My reputation with HPD fluctuated somewhere between a laughingstock and a fuckup. I was assigned to another beat, another partner. Actually, I had a series of partners because I was a shit-heel to all of them, and nobody wanted to ride with me.

"I got sloppy on the job. Bad attitude. Surly to my supervisors." He tapped his shirt pocket. "Started smoking because I was searching for something, anything, to occupy my thoughts and dull the pain of losing Caroline and you, and nicotine wasn't as risky as cocaine or booze.

"About six months into this self-inflicted purgatory, I went on a screwing spree. See, the self-blame phase had worn off, and the I'll-show-her one had set in. So I went on a sex binge. After months of one-night stands, all I'd proved was how much I loved your mother.

"One morning I woke up and realized I'd never get her back if I stayed on that rail, so I switched. I turned over a new leaf. I cleaned up my act and began trying to salvage my job, which I was on the brink of losing. The cigarettes I was hooked on, but I went cold turkey on women. I lived like a freaking monk." He stopped, and the lines in his face settled heavily into an expression of abject sorrow.

Berry asked softly, "The reform didn't last?"

"Not past the day Caroline's marriage to Jim Malone was announced."

"You read it in the newspaper?"

"Yeah. Came like a bolt out of the blue. Shows how cruel Fate can be. I had no idea she'd even been seeing him. Not that way, I mean. And then there it was in black and white. She was married to him."

Berry could tell by the ragged sound of his voice that, even after all this time, it hurt.

He sat for a moment, staring into near space, then said, "Through lawyers we settled on Malone adopting you and giving you his name. I caved on that without really putting up a fight. I had nothing to offer. You had a new daddy who seemed a decent sort, who would give you a good life, one I couldn't come close to providing." He paused a beat, then said, "I left, and never went back."

After a time, his gaze refocused on her. "That's it, Berry. Not a very pretty bedtime story for a man to be telling his daughter, is it? Not exactly Goldilocks."

"It's a sad story. Particularly for you."

"I didn't tell you so you'd feel sorry for me. Last thing I want you to do is make me out as some kind of woebegone hero, a tragic figure. I made bad choices and paid for them. The only reason I told you is so maybe you'll take a life lesson from it. That's the best I can do for you. God knows I haven't done anything else."

They exchanged a long look, which was interrupted only when Dodge's cell phone rang. He pulled it from his belt and checked the number calling. "It's Caroline." He answered, listened, then said, "Okay, we'll be right there."

When he disconnected, he told Berry that Caroline and Ski had finished their business at the sheriff's office. "That Mercury cretin got his check. She says Ski needs to stay there. Everybody wants him for something. Caroline asked if we could pick her up."

Berry grabbed her handbag and slid from the booth. "You can drop me at the hospital."

"Wrong. I'm taking you home. No argument," he said sternly, cutting off her protest. "Like it or not, I'm your old man, and I'm telling you now that you're going home and getting some rest."

On the drive out to the lake house, Dodge watched his daughter in the rearview mirror. Her expression blank, she stared through the window into the night without making a movement or a sound. He would have given a thousand dollars to know what she was thinking. About him? About Starks? About her lost job? Maybe she was just pining after Ski. Who the hell knew?

Whatever was on her mind, he wanted to help her with it. But this parenting thing was tough even when your child was an adult. Possibly it was even more difficult because Berry was an adult. He'd put his foot down about her standing vigil over a felon who was already brain-dead. But after that, he couldn't think of anything to say that wouldn't sound stupid, banal, unnecessary, or a combination of all three, so he hadn't said anything. Caroline must have been of the same mind, because she was subdued when they picked her up at the courthouse and remained silent for the duration of the drive.

Once inside the house, he followed them upstairs. When they reached the gallery, the two women went one way, he went the other. He showered in the bathroom where it all had started. He even turned down the bed. But he couldn't rest until he knew Berry was okay, so he put on fresh clothes and went back downstairs to wait for Caroline to come down.

He'd been waiting almost an hour when he heard her light tread on the stairs. She didn't notice him sitting there in the dark living room as she passed it on the way to her bedroom.

He gave her a couple of minutes, then went to the door and tapped softly. "It's me."

When she opened the door, he could tell by her expression

that she immediately assumed another tragedy had befallen them. "What now?"

"Nothing's wrong. Before I cashed in for the night, I just wanted to make sure that Berry's okay. She looked pretty ragged."

Caroline motioned him into the room and closed the door behind him. He looked around. It wasn't a fussy room, but it was totally feminine all the same. There were an unnecessary number of pillows piled against the iron headboard of her bed, and gathered fabric framed the three windows. The walls were painted what looked to him like the same color of pale yellow that he'd painted Berry's nursery all those years ago. Most everything else in the room was white, including the terry-cloth robe wrapped around Caroline's slender body.

"Berry's exhausted," she said. "Upset."

"Over? Not Starks, I hope. He's getting what he deserves. Unless he dies peacefully, in which case he's getting better than he deserves."

"As cruel as that sounds, I agree. He continues to torment Berry even as he's dying. She's carrying the burden for everything that happened."

"Know what I think?" Dodge said. "I think Starks played her like a fiddle. He kept her feeling sorry for him."

"I'm sure of it," Caroline said. "He's a manipulator."

Dodge went across to one of the windows and looked out across the back of the property, at the dark forest, the swimming pool and terrace, the lake beyond. It was a pleasing view. The moon was sparkling on the water that gently lapped the lakeshore. The reserve deputies had been withdrawn, returning the landscape to serenity.

Thinking out loud, he said, "I still don't get why he went into that frigging swamp. Ski's confounded by it, too."

"I suppose we'll never know. I'm just glad he's where he is now."

"I'll feel better when he's in the ground," Dodge said with feeling.

He gave the rear of the property one final, searching survey, then turned back in to the room. Caroline had sat down on the end of the bed. He hesitated, then said, "Berry and I talked." He backed up to an upholstered chair and sat down. "Over cheeseburgers, while you and Ski were dealing with Mercury."

"She figured it out."

"I don't think it took her too long."

"What did you tell her?"

"Everything. The whole ugly truth."

"You didn't have to, Dodge."

"Yeah, I did. Not for her, but for me. I needed her to know everything."

"Why?"

"First off, so she would never blame you for splitting us up. Not that she would ever have a mind to, but I wanted to ensure she wouldn't. Secondly, so that whatever she feels for me is grounded in the cold, hard facts, not some fantasy daddy. I didn't want her view of me to be romanticized.

"By telling her the truth, I took a risk on her despising me. But maybe she'll see some redemption in my not trying to pass myself off as anything other than what I was. What I *am.* I hope she'll at least give me credit for being honest."

"I believe she will. She's always been fair. She's not one to hold grudges, either. Besides, she's told me she likes you. She thinks you're cute."

He guffawed.

"In a scruffy sort of way."

"See, that's what I'm talking about," he said crossly. "She's seeing me better than I am." He looked at Caroline and, for the millionth time, felt a shark's bite of regret. "Not you, though. You saw me for exactly what I was."

"And loved you anyway."

A long silence stretched between them. Neither moved or looked away. Eventually she said, "You didn't knock on my door only to talk about Berry."

Dodge took a deep breath and expelled it, looked aside, and then came back. "I never told you I was sorry, Caroline. Talking about it tonight brought back to me . . ." He stopped, sighed. "As soon as it was done, it was too late to make it right. Fucking Crystal was the least of it. I know that sounds like a cliché, but I swear to God, it meant nothing. I went through it mechanically, the whole time planning what I was going to do as soon as it was over.

"I didn't betray you with my dick. I betrayed you with my ego. Nothing I said then, or say now, will make any difference. I did it. But I want you to know how sorry I am about it all. When you told me I'd hurt you worse than Roger Campton had, I hated what I'd done. Hated myself for doing it to you and destroying what we had." He paused, took another soughing breath. "I've wanted to say this to you for thirty years. I'm sorry for the pain I caused you."

Her chest stuttered a little when she inhaled. "Apology accepted."

"Thank you." Before he made an utter fool of himself, he slapped the tops of his thighs and stood up. "I'm beat. I can't even remember this morning."

"You came into our hotel room in Houston and woke us up."

"That was today?"

"It's been a long one. But at least Oren Starks was caught. We can rest without worrying over our daughter's safety." As he made to move past her, she reached for his hand and pressed her fingers around his. "Thank you, Dodge."

"I didn't do all that much."

"You answered my call for help."

"I'm glad you asked for it."

"You were the first, the only, person I thought to ask."

A moment ticked by, then another. She didn't release his hand. Instead, she studied the back of it and traced the ropy veins with her fingertip. Then slowly she turned it over, raised it to her lips, and pressed a kiss into his palm. She held his hand against her mouth for a long time, then looked up at him with eyes he could drown in.

"All these years," she said huskily, "and you're still so familiar to me. I would know this hand out of every other hand in the world."

He just looked at her, not daring to move, or to believe that this was really happening.

"You've had a lot of women since me. Two wives. And many others."

He made a motion with his shoulder.

"Do you . . ."

"What?"

"Do you remember anything about me?"

Gruffly, he said, "Only everything."

She smiled with uncertainty and a trace of sadness. "I'm not young and lithe anymore."

He'd restrained himself for as long as he could, for as long as he was willing to. He pulled her up and clutched her to him. No hug had ever been tighter. He rubbed his face in her hair and poured out the words he thought he'd never have another chance to say.

"You're the only thing I ever loved. God knows." Placing his finger beneath her chin, he tilted her head up. "I made such a goddamn mess of it, Caroline, but I wanted you the minute I saw you, and that's never changed."

She lay across his chest, her cheek pressed against his heart, his chin propped on the top of her head. "You're quiet," she whispered.

"I'm old. You wore me out."

She nudged his crotch with her knee. "You're a stud."

"You think?"

She came up on her elbow to look into his face. "Um-hmm." He smiled, and she smiled back. She ran her finger across his chin, her eyes moving lovingly over his face. "Until tonight, you hadn't told me you were sorry. And, until now, I never thanked you."

"Thanked me?"

"For Berry."

His throat grew tight. He combed his fingers up through her hair. "Yeah, you have. Every time you look at her, I can see how much you love her. That's thanking me, Caroline."

They kissed. She was the first to pull back. "When are you going to tell me?"

He kept his expression blank. "Tell you what?"

"What's on your mind."

"On my mind? Right now, you. You naked. What a turn-on your freckles are. I'm especially fond of the ones on your tits."

She laughed but wasn't dissuaded by his joking. "You're not going to tell me?"

"Nothing to tell."

She searched his eyes for a moment, then murmured, "Okay," and returned her head to his chest. Except for a few whispered endearments, their conversation ended there. Occasionally Dodge would say something coarse that caused her to sigh, laugh, or blush. Or they used no words to express what they were feeling, and that was the most meaningful communication of all.

Finally she nuzzled his throat and mumbled sleepily, "I don't want this to end, but I can't hold my eyes open any longer."

He kissed her lips softly, then turned her away from him, pulling her hips up against his lap. "I know you like to spoon."

"And I know what you like." She drew his hand to her breast and covered it with her own. "They're not as pert as they were."

"Pert is overrated. Now sleep."

She did, falling quickly under. Dodge lay awake for a long while. He was bone tired, but, like Caroline, he didn't want to miss a nanosecond of this night together. He wouldn't waste a moment of it sleeping when he could be holding her, feeling her soft warmth, and listening to every dear breath she took.

And then there was that other thing, that niggling discontent that she had sensed in him, that unidentified something that lurked unseen at the back of his mind, gnawing at his subconscious like an insidious rodent, denying him physical repleteness and making peace of mind impossible.

In spite of her emotional turmoil, Berry had slept deeply and dreamlessly. However, she woke up at sunrise. She showered, dressed, and went downstairs to make coffee. Just as it finished brewing, Dodge joined her, looking sheepish and defensive at the same time. She looked past him toward the direction from which he had come—her mother's bedroom.

She curbed the temptation to tease him and instead offered him a cup of the fresh coffee. "Thanks." He added two spoonfuls of sugar, sipped, then said, "That bracelet with the heart charm. Tell me about it."

"It was one of several gifts Oren gave me over time." She told him what she'd told Ski and Sheriff Drummond about Oren's refusal to take back his unwanted gifts. "To avoid seeing him, I gave up trying to return them. Why do you ask now?"

"It crossed my mind that we never talked about it once we determined that Sally Buckland was wearing one identical to it. You didn't know that he'd given her one, too?"

She shook her head.

"Do you have yours here?"

"Upstairs. I brought everything Oren had given me when I came to Merritt."

"Seems like you had an intuition. Like you might need this stuff for evidence."

"Maybe that's a trait I inherited from you."

The remark seemed to please him immensely. But he kept to the subject. "Mind if I take a look at the bracelet?"

She went upstairs. When she returned a few minutes later, her mother was in the kitchen pouring herself a cup of coffee. She was disheveled but positively aglow. She gave Berry a shy smile and a mellow good morning, but rarely did her eyes wander from Dodge.

Berry had collected all the items Oren had given her into one small duffel bag. She unzipped it and dumped the contents onto the kitchen table, then sifted through the articles in search of the bracelet. When at first she didn't see it, she sorted through everything more carefully.

Then she looked at Dodge and Caroline with misapprehension. "It's not here. How could it not be here? The last time I saw it, it was with all this other stuff."

"When was that?" Dodge asked.

"I don't remember exactly."

"Before you moved here, or since?"

"Since. I was trying to talk myself into making a clean sweep, getting rid of any reminders of him. I changed my mind, but the bracelet was here, I'm sure of it. It was the most personal of the gifts."

"Maybe you removed it at some point and just don't remember."

"Of course I would remember!" Then, immediately sorry for taking out her rising anxiety on her mother, she reached for her hand and gripped it. "I would remember, Mother." Sinking down into one of the chairs at the table, she moaned, "You don't think—"

"That it was your bracelet on Sally Buckland's wrist?"

Dodge had finished the awful thought for her. She wanted to nullify it before it could become fact. "It couldn't possibly have been. When would Oren have taken mine?"

Dodge cleared his throat. "It's possible—just possible—that Starks was here."

"Here? You mean, in this house?"

Berry and Caroline listened with incredulity as he told them about the photos that had been discovered in a trash can not far from the motel where Oren had been hiding until Davis Coldare walked in on him.

"Looked like he was getting the lay of the land, so to speak. There are shots of the house from every angle. Some of you," he said uneasily. "To get them, even using a telephoto lens, he had to be fairly close to the house. Maybe he was ballsy enough to have come inside when you weren't here and made himself at home."

"He knew where to find your bedroom the night he shot Ben Lofland," Caroline said.

Berry hugged herself, rubbing her hands over the goose bumps that had broken out on her arms. "He went through my bureau drawers? Pawed through my things?" The thought made her physically ill.

"We don't know that he did. But it's possible."

"I want to see the pictures," Berry said.

"No you don't. Trust me."

"I want to see them, Dodge."

He cursed under his breath. Berry caught words of self-chastisement for telling her about the damn pictures. "You'll have to ask Ski," he said. "He made me give them back to him."

Just then his cell phone rang. He checked caller ID. "Speak of the devil." He answered, listened, then said, "On our way." He disconnected. "Starks is showing signs of coming around."

"It's an ugly scene," Ski told them as they joined him outside the ICU.

Inside it, the hospital bed was surrounded by an attending physician and several nurses, all doing something different, moving with a sense of urgency while trying to give assurance to their patient, whose agitation was obvious. Oren was struggling against the restraints securing him to the bed.

A nurse, noticing them, came to the door. "You can wait down the hall, Deputy Nyland. I'll come and get you if he starts to speak coherently." It was a subtle suggestion for them to relocate.

They moved as a group to a small waiting room. Berry and her mother sat down on a love seat. "This whole ordeal . . . ," Caroline whispered, shaking her head remorsefully. She never finished the thought. Those words said enough.

Dodge took a chair. He removed a pack of cigarettes from his shirt pocket, fiddled with it, replaced it. Ski stood near the door, his back to the wall. He was watchful and tense, like a soldier waiting for the shot that would end a short cease-fire.

No one spoke for a time. But the pressure on Berry's chest became such that she finally blurted out, "I stole from him. From Oren."

The three looked at her with bewilderment.

Before they could speak or she lost her nerve, she plunged on.

"You know that Oren had worked on the campaign that Ben and I finished on Friday." They nodded in unison. "That was when things with Sally were coming to a head. She resigned, and it was understood that Oren was the reason."

She hesitated, then lowered her head. "No, that's not quite accurate. I *made it understood* that Oren was the reason."

"What do you mean, Berry?" Caroline asked.

"Management consulted me about Sally's leaving. I told them that she'd left because of Oren."

"Which was true."

"Let me tell this, Mother, please." She paused to collect her thoughts. "I led management to believe that the company had narrowly escaped a costly sexual harassment suit, when actually Sally had never suggested such a thing. I went further, intimating that other women in the office were considering taking matters to that level. This rattled them. They asked 'How bad is it?' In my opinion, as a female employee, what should be done with Oren Starks? Should they give him a warning and probation, or fire him outright? Was he or was he not redeemable, dispensable?

"It should be obvious to you what I told them. I remained silent about the excellent work Oren was doing. I didn't tell the bosses that his original idea had been the best, and that Ben and I were designing the entire campaign around it. Instead, I fed their paranoia and made them fear the worst if Oren remained an employee.

"He got his pink slip the following day. He wasn't allowed to take any of his work with him. He was escorted from the building by security guards and treated like a criminal." In a voice barely audible, she added, "He became one."

No one spoke for a long moment, then Dodge said, "Wait a damn minute here. You can't blame yourself for what Oren *became*. People get fired from jobs. They don't start killing. He was what he was before he got fired."

"He's right, Berry." Ski spoke more quietly than Dodge, but he was just as adamant.

"But that's not the end of it. After his dismissal, he asked me repeatedly to intercede on his behalf. I kept stringing him along, telling him that I had tried to get him his job back but that Delray's decision was firm. It was a lie. I never spoke up for him. Not once. Quite the contrary. After he was gone, I took credit for his work. Ben did, too, just by remaining silent. He knew how I'd played it, and, tacitly, he went along. He never acknowledged to anyone

Oren's valuable input." In an undertone, she added, "I've since learned that he never really trusted me after that."

She paused to take a breath. "As for Sally, I encouraged her to leave the company. I told her she would never shake free of Oren as long as she remained at Delray."

"Also true," Caroline said.

"In all probability," Berry agreed. "But I had a selfish reason for urging her to resign. She was good. Clients liked her unassuming manner. Management did, too. She posed a threat to my advancement. I wanted her gone. So I pressured her into leaving. I played both ends against the middle. I manipulated Sally into leaving, and I saw to it that Oren got fired. All for my self-gain."

She turned her head and spoke directly to Caroline. "No one is prouder of your extraordinary success than I am, Mother. But it's a lot to live up to. I'm equally ambitious, but when it comes to achieving goals, I don't have your patience, your style, or your grace. I'm wired differently, I guess," she said, glancing at Dodge.

"In any case, the pressure and guilt I was feeling over what I'd done intensified. That's why I launched into you that day, and then later had the scene with Oren on my porch. I came here to Merritt to get my head straight, my priorities readjusted. During that process, I realized I must acknowledge my underhandedness and rectify it. When I called Oren last Thursday night, I told him that his name would be on that campaign when it was presented." She paused, then added softly, "It wasn't enough."

The silence among them was heavy, then Dodge heaved a sigh. "You ask me, that's all bullshit. Okay, so maybe your ambition got a little out of hand. Sally Buckland had free will. You may have nudged her, but she made up her own mind to resign.

"As for Starks," he continued, making a face of distaste, "behind this guy's smarts was a weird little creep with violent tendencies just begging for a chance to get out." He pointed a stern finger at Berry and said, "Now, you've fessed up. Drop it."

She felt a rush of affection for him and would have expressed it out loud if the doctor treating Oren hadn't suddenly appeared in the open doorway. "Any of you named Berry?"

She stood up.

"He's saying your name over and over."

"Should I . . . ?"

He gave a pragmatic shrug. "Up to you." Then, as abruptly as he'd appeared, he vanished.

Caroline reached for Berry's hand. "Don't go in there. We shouldn't have even come."

Berry looked over at Dodge, silently asking for his opinion. "I wish he'd've died out in the Thicket, spared you this."

When she met Ski's eyes, he said, "If you go in, I'll go with you. I need to hear what he has to say."

She went to him. He placed his hand on her elbow, and together they left the waiting room and walked down the corridor.

Oren's ICU was a scene from a horror show. She approached the bed with trepidation. His eyelids were wildly fluttering. He was murmuring her name, like a chant. His hands were moving restlessly, his fingers plucking at the bedding while his wrists pulled against the restraints around them.

"Can he hear me?" she asked.

"You can try," one of the attending nurses replied.

Berry swallowed her misgivings. "Oren?" When he didn't respond, she cleared her throat and said more forcefully, "Oren? Can you hear me? It's Berry."

His eyelids blinked open, but his eyes were rolled back into the sockets, unfocused. He spoke her name in a thin, raspy voice.

"Yes. It's me." She groped for something to say that wouldn't sound entirely inane. "You're in the hospital. The doctors and nurses are trying to help you."

"Berry." Again her name passed through his lips as he blinked rapidly to bring her into focus. "Berry."

"I'm here."

"You're alive."

"Yes."

"You should be dead."

She sucked in a quick breath and recoiled. Ski put his hand on her shoulder. "Let's get out of here."

But before she could move, Oren managed to twist his hand, enabling him to grab her wrist. She looked down in horror at his cold, moist fingers clamped around her wrist. His eyes were now wide open and focused on her. The madness in them caused her to sob in fright.

"You will die," he said with malice. "You will *die.*"

She wrenched her wrist free and stumbled backward, coming up against Ski but remaining transfixed by Oren's maniacal gaze. Then suddenly his eyelids fluttered again. His throat bowed hideously. His head slammed back into the pillow, knocking askew the gauze that had been covering the hole in the side of his skull and the brain matter bulging out of it. His body began to buck uncontrollably.

"He's seizing," one of the nurses said in an urgent voice.

Ski turned Berry away and propelled her from the room. Outside in the corridor, she fell into his arms.

CHAPTER 27

SKI KNEW THAT IF HE'D RETURNED TO THE SHERIFF'S OFFICE immediately following Oren Starks's death, he would have been beset by reporters and other deputies, all salivating to know the grisly details. He needed some downtime before returning to the fray, so he was making calls from his kitchen table.

Besides, he could better handle outstanding matters here, where he wouldn't be constantly interrupted. He had his cell phone, a carafe of strong coffee, and a checklist of people to call. First was Sheriff Drummond, who expressed appropriate concern over the wasted life of Oren Starks, then commended Ski on his capture.

"It was a coordinated effort, sir."

The sheriff dismissed his humility, then asked about Caroline and Berry, and after Ski had assured him that they were as well as could be expected, the sheriff stunned Ski by telling him that he'd decided not to run for reelection.

"It's time I passed the baton." He paused, then added, "I'd be pleased to endorse you as my successor. There'd be nobody better. And I don't say that just because you're the hero of the moment."

"I appreciate the vote of confidence."

"You've earned it. Think about it. We'll talk it over soon."

Ski was flattered and excited, but he couldn't indulge in thoughts about the future when duties in the present were so pressing. Doggedly he continued down his list, next calling the nursing home where Oren Starks's mother was a patient. The administrator reminded him of the extent of her illness. "She's unresponsive, Deputy Nyland."

"I understand, ma'am. I just thought she should be officially notified of her son's demise."

Since no power of attorney documents had been found among Starks's papers in his Houston house, and his mother was incapable of making decisions regarding his interment, Ski made arrangements with a funeral home in Merritt.

Last, he called the Houston detective Rodney Allen and gave him a rundown of the capture. "He had very little chance of surviving the head wound. He died early this morning, in distress, still wishing Ms. Malone dead."

"Be glad you got him."

"I am."

Allen asked for the paperwork necessary to close his case on Sally Buckland's murder, and Ski promised to get it to him as soon as he'd signed off on it.

After a slight pause, the detective said, "I checked out Hanley's record."

"He's a good man to have on your side."

"If you say so."

"I say so." Before more could be said, Ski disconnected. And just then someone knocked on his back door.

Berry looked at him through the panes of glass that formed the top half of the door, hoping to gauge his reaction to her unannounced visit. But before she could get a good read on it, he opened the door. He was wearing a pair of jeans and a white T-shirt, the tail out. He was barefoot.

"Hi."

"Hi."

He stood aside. She took the last step up and crossed the threshold into a kitchen that smelled like fresh coffee. She noticed the items on the table, including a legal tablet with scribbles and lines made in a firm, masculine hand. "You're working?"

"Just finished up making some official calls. How are you holding up?"

"Fine." Shortly after Ski had propelled her from Oren's ICU, the doctor had pronounced him dead. "Still a bit trembly."

"It was a bad scene."

"Yes."

He slid his hands into the back pockets of his jeans, then removed them. He nodded toward the counter. "You want some coffee?"

"No, thanks."

"When you left the hospital, you said you were going home to sleep."

"I was. But when we got there, Mother said we all should eat. Dodge volunteered to go to the store and get things for brunch. I volunteered to come and extend you an invitation to join us." She took a breath, knowing she was going for broke but willing to take the risk. "But inviting you to brunch was just an excuse. The real reason I came is because I want you to hold me."

It took him only one wide step to reach her. He pulled her against him and wrapped his strong arms around her. And for the longest time, that was enough, just being held. Then he tipped her chin up and kissed her with surprising gentleness. When he pulled away, he searched her eyes as though asking permission and must have seen in her gaze what he was looking for.

Dipping his head, he rubbed his lips against hers, then their open mouths fused hungrily. She slid her arms beneath his. Her hands met at his spine and held him fast against her. They shifted the angle of their heads several times but didn't break the kiss until he pulled away and pressed his lips against her neck just beneath her ear.

"Can we continue this with our clothes off?"

She made a humming sound that he took for a yes. Reaching for her hand, he led her from the kitchen, through the house, and into a spacious bedroom. She was impressed that the bed was made, but it wasn't for long. He flung back the covers, then returned to her and immediately began undoing the buttons on her blouse. He unclasped the front fastener of her bra and pushed aside the cups. He took her breasts in his hands as he kissed her again.

Lips, tongue, fingertips. They made her breathless, helpless, until she didn't even realize that the small sounds filling the quiet room were coming from her own throat. He continued caressing her with his mouth while his hands reached beneath her skirt. One splayed over her ass, the other slid into the front of her panties.

She whimpered, because he knew exactly what to do and how to do it well. The slip-slidey play of his fingertips soon had her gasping. "Stop. Ski. Stop."

"No," he murmured, his lips moving against her nipple.

It felt too good. The pressure of his fingers, the barely-there caress of his thumb. She began rocking against his hand, riding it. Urged on by his fervently whispered encouragement, she let go of all control and allowed the pleasure to surge through her. Tidal waves of it battered her until she was limp and clinging to him.

He eased her back onto the bed and smoothed the hair off her face. He kissed her lips softly, then removed each article of her clothing. Never breaking eye contact, he stood at the end of the bed and peeled off his T-shirt. He unbuttoned his jeans with a practiced hand, then pushed them down and stepped out of them.

He'd been wearing nothing underneath them, and that incredibly sexy sight caused a purling sensation deep inside her. He crawled over her until he was levered above her, bracing himself on stiff arms. His frank study of her body made her feel hot with shyness, but she wanted to touch him, so she did. His eyes closed and his breath became rough and loud, then hissed through his teeth when her thumb glanced the most sensitive spot and came away damp.

When he pressed inside her, she bit her lower lip to keep her moan fractionally contained. His arms relaxed. She welcomed his weight all along her body. Instinctually she pulled her knees back to take more of him, and he responded not only with his body but with a rumbled litany of vulgarities—the blunt, elemental language of a man totally absorbed in the moment, in mating.

Ski was on his back, holding Berry close. They lay with legs entwined. He was relaxed, but his body continued to buzz with sensations that occasionally sparked and sizzled along his nerve endings. No wonder. The object of his lust was naked, in his bed, and she was incredible.

"I love that you kissed me."

Her husky voice sent a dart of renewed desire through him. He turned his head to look at her.

"During it, I mean. That was very nice. Sexy, absolutely. But also"—she lifted her face to look at him—"awfully sweet. Special."

It had been meaningful to him, too. Never before had he kissed a woman, really deeply kissed her, while actually fucking her. Berry probably wouldn't believe him if he told her that. It was too soon to be telling her things like that. For that matter, it was too soon to be feeling things like that for a woman he'd met only four days ago. But that's how it was.

Looking at her now, he realized how goddamn great it would be to wake up every morning for the rest of his life and see her face on the other pillow. Thinking about it gave him an ache deep in his gut. Felt like yearning.

"Tell me," she said, "did you learn that wicked language in the Army?"

"Oh hell," he groaned. "What'd I say?"

"You don't remember?"

"I was preoccupied. If my language was offensive, I apologize."

She gave him a naughty smile. "I kinda liked it."

"Hmm?"

"Hmm."

They kissed lazily. Eventually she was the one to pull back. "Did you also get your scar from the Army?"

He looked down at the raised, jagged line along his thigh. Well-trained surgeons had tried to clean it up, make it less unsightly, but it still looked like his flesh had been pried open with a rusty, old-fashioned can opener and then sutured with barbed wire. "I should have warned you."

"Are you all right talking about it?"

He rubbed her earlobe between his fingers. It was incredibly soft. "Afghanistan. We'd been ordered to police, render aid where needed, not to engage the enemy. The Taliban didn't get the memo, I guess. My unit went into the house of a guy who'd been acting as our interpreter. We went there to discuss security at the local school.

"It was a trap. He was Taliban, and those guys are fighting to win. Or fighting for us to lose. Either way, it was a bloodbath. We killed all of them. Two women. One kid who looked about thirteen. I and one other guy were the only two of our unit to survive. Last I heard of him, he's still messed up psychologically." His eyes slid from his study of her earlobe to her soft gaze. "I got lucky."

"Does it hurt?"

"Sometimes it reminds me it's there. Not too often." He smiled crookedly. "Rubbing it helps."

"How about kissing it?"

And without waiting for a reply, she moved down. She ran her fingertip delicately along the scar that ran from knee to groin, then followed that same course with her lips, touching it with feather-light kisses. He placed his hand on the back of her head, not in the least bit forcefully. Lightly. Just to acknowledge how damn good it felt, how sweet it was of her not to be repelled.

Then she kissed his penis, took the tip of it into her mouth, and every cell in his body jangled. "Christ." He took a handful of hair and pulled her up. "Stop, Berry." He kept tugging on her hair until they were once more face-to-face. Hers wore an uncertain expression. She looked a bit wounded.

He ran his thumb across her lips. "I want you to, God knows. It felt amazing, and five minutes from now I'll probably be weeping because I stopped you. But you've gotta know some things."

"What things?"

"I'm not going anywhere from here."

She shook her head in confusion. "What?"

"From Merritt. I'm here to stay. People wonder why I settled here. It's rumored that I lack ambition, that I'm wasting myself in a backwater place. Maybe all that's true to some degree. But the fundamental truth is that, when I left the Army, I was sick to death of seeing blood and watching people die, and die in ugly ways. I wanted to be a cop, I've wanted that all my life, but I didn't want the job in a big city, where violence is an everyday event."

"Violence can occur anywhere. Case in point," she said of Starks.

"Yeah, but not on a daily basis. The last few days excluded, my main job here is keeping law and order. I do some good. Sure, I haul the lawbreakers to jail. I've busted up meth houses, and sometimes bloody wounds come out of those raids. But I haven't had to kill a woman before she could kill me. I haven't had to blow away a boy who was too young to shave."

"But that was—"

"War. On the other side of the world. I get it. But read the papers, Berry. Listen to the news. I want to be where there's less chance of me having to kill somebody. I might—*might*—consider running for sheriff when Drummond retires, but that's as high as I'll go. I don't want you to get in too deep, only to find out that I'm not who you thought I was, or who you'd wish me to be."

She smiled, but not particularly with humor. "It's funny."

"Somehow I don't think so."

"No, it is. Dodge said practically the same thing to me last night."

"Jesus, I'm starting to sound like Dodge?"

She turned toward him and nestled closer. Speaking in a near whisper, she said, "He and Mother slept together last night."

"Not for the first time, I think."

"He's my father."

"How long have you known?"

She looked at him with surprise. "You knew?"

"Guessed."

"How?"

"The way he looked at her, at you, didn't match the rest of him. Everyone else on the planet he barely abides. He cares for the two of you, and it shows. Wasn't too hard to figure out why."

She related the story that Dodge had told her the night before. When she finished, she said, "I'm sad for him. He made a terrible mistake, but he's been paying for it for thirty years. That's an awfully long penance for one sin. I'm sad for Mother, too. He was the love of her life. She's lived without him."

"What about you?"

"What about me?"

"Dodge left. Caroline let him go. Do you forgive them for those choices?"

"Yes. They were both right, and both wrong."

"Hmm."

She propped herself up on her elbow so that she was looking down into his face. "That was a very eloquent *hmm*. What?"

"You and Dodge are a lot alike."

"We're both flat-chested."

He grinned but didn't let her distract him from his point. "That wasn't what I was thinking."

"Were you thinking that he and I are manipulative? That I followed his method of trying to get ahead professionally unethically and at all costs?"

"What I was going to say," he said with exaggerated patience, "is that you two are willing to forgive everyone but yourselves."

She stared deeply into his eyes, her brow furrowed. "Possibly. Because I don't think I'll ever forgive myself for what Oren did to those people."

"You're not to blame for his meltdown. When someone goes postal, once his background and behavior are analyzed, the only thing that's surprising is that he didn't flip out sooner. What happened wasn't your fault."

"I appreciate your saying so."

"It's not just pillow talk, Berry. I mean it. The issue at Delray, your self-incrimination exceeds the crime. What's the company policy on retaining an employee's work when that employee leaves before a project is finished?"

"That employee's input stays with Delray," she answered quietly.

"When Sally left, did she take her work?"

"I see your point," she said with some asperity, "but still, what I did didn't feel right. My motives certainly weren't."

"Okay, maybe your ambition went into overdrive. You cheated a bit. Took some unethical shortcuts. Just as Dodge said, drop it. Let it go. If you don't it'll eat you alive."

"I don't know how to forgive myself."

"It's an acquired skill."

Her focus sharpened. "Is it?"

"Yes. You have to practice it every day."

She touched his cheek. "Is this the voice of experience speaking?"

Looking directly into her eyes, he said, "I convinced the guys in my unit that we could trust our interpreter."

Understanding the implications, she laid her head on his chest and hugged him close. He went one further and pulled her on top of him until they were belly to belly. She lay perfectly still while he strummed his fingers along her spine. He stroked her ass and as far as he could reach down the backs of her thighs. Because she lay so still, he thought she might have fallen asleep. And that was okay. He would have lain with her like that for hours, days, but eventually she stirred and moaned with pleasure, and the tenor of his caresses changed.

"That night at the lake house," he whispered as he worked his hand between their bodies and cupped her sex. "I caught a flash of this."

"I thought you might have."

"I did. And I wanted it. I've wanted it every breathing moment since." He stroked her, felt her quick, hot breaths inside his mouth. "And now . . ."

"Ski . . . ," she gasped.

"I want *you*."

CHAPTER 28

Berry and Ski entered the lake house through the back door, feeling chagrined but without regret. The kitchen was empty. The house was silent. "Knock, knock," Berry called.

"In here." Caroline's voice wafted from the dining area.

Ski leaned close to Berry as they crossed the kitchen. "Thank God. It occurred to me we might've caught them doing the same thing that kept us from brunch."

"Shh."

Both were snickering as they entered the other room and found Caroline sitting at the dining table all alone. Her forlorn expression instantly alarmed Berry.

"What's wrong?"

"Dodge left."

"What do you mean by left?" Berry asked.

"What part didn't you understand?" Her snappish tone surprised them all, especially Caroline herself. Her shoulders slumped forward, and she raised a hand to her forehead. "I'm sorry."

Berry took the nearest chair and looked at Ski inquisitively as he sat down across the table from her. He shrugged, letting her know that he didn't know what to make of this startling turn of events, either.

Berry asked, "When did he leave?"

"He never returned from the supermarket." Caroline lowered her hand, clasped it with her other, twisted her fingers, released them. "After half an hour and he still wasn't back, I called his cell phone. When he didn't answer, I got a feeling . . ." She hiccuped a sob. "I went up to the guest room. His things weren't there." Miserably she said, "He left."

Tears began to overflow her eyes. Angrily she brushed them off her cheeks. "For thirty years I did without that man. I did fine. Better than fine. Then, I saw him and . . . In only four days' time he became essential. And now . . ." She buried her face in her hands, rubbing the heels of them into her eye sockets. "I hate myself for crying over him again."

Nobody said anything until she lowered her hands from her face.

Berry spoke first. "Your reunion wasn't one-sided, Mother. You spent last night together."

Caroline smiled through her tears and gave a small nod.

"And it was . . . good?"

She burbled a soft laugh. "Like we'd never been apart."

"Then he wouldn't have just up and left without saying something."

"He did."

Ski asked, "He gave you no indication that he was going to split?"

"Something was troubling him. I asked him about it last night, and again this morning, but he put me off, told me it was nothing, made jokes. But I think . . ."

"What?" Ski prompted.

"I think he'd done what he came here to do. The bad guy had been caught." She shrugged with helplessness. "He dreaded a prolonged good-bye."

Ski pushed his chair back, stood, and moved to the window. He slid his hands, palms out, into the back pockets of his jeans, a habit

Berry was coming to recognize and find endearing. After a moment, he turned back to them. "With all due respect, Caroline, I don't think that's it. Not entirely anyway. He was bugged."

"About what?"

"As we were leaving the hospital after Starks died, he told me about Berry's missing bracelet. He hated that he would never get an explanation for that. Was it or was it not the one on Sally Buckland's wrist?

"He was complaining that this case had been wacky from the start, that Oren Starks had never followed a pattern, which was odd for a methodical guy so into solving puzzles. It wasn't just the dread of an emotional parting that was bothering Dodge."

"Then why would he leave without a word? Why won't he answer his phone?"

"He's a coward," Berry declared.

"When it comes to situations like this, yes, he is." Caroline reached for Berry's hand and pressed it between hers. Smiling sadly, she said, "Even if he wasn't going to say good-bye to me, I thought he would want to say something to you."

It's better this way, Dodge told himself for the hundredth time.

He'd got in, he'd got out. He had done what he'd come to do. He'd helped get his kid out of a scrape. The culprit was history. Mission accomplished.

Personal issues that were decades old also had been resolved. He'd met his daughter. They'd established a good rapport, far better than he'd had any right to hope for.

As for him and Caroline, he'd have thought the world would end before she shared a bed with him. Last night . . .

Stop it!

If he let himself think about that, he would turn the car around so fast, he'd give himself whiplash. Loving her, having her love him, had been a bonus, a gift he hadn't expected and didn't deserve. To his dying day, he would be grateful for it. Leave it at that.

Why spoil all the good stuff with a tearful farewell scene? It was better to make a clean break.

Without him, their lives would return to normal. He would be no more missed than a hand that's removed from a bucket of water. That's what his old man used to tell him whenever he threatened to run away from home.

"You know what happens when you take your hand out of a bucket of water? Instantly, it's like it was never there. So go! See if I care. See how long you're missed."

That's how this would be. Caroline had her work to sustain her. Berry was strong-willed and talented. She would recover from the trauma of the last few days and do just fine. And if she needed support, Nyland was there to lend it with his big broad shoulders. Big cock, too, probably.

But if the deputy ever did wrong by her, and Dodge learned about it, he'd come back and kill him.

His phone rang for the umpteenth time. "Why won't that damn woman give up?"

But he saw Derek's number on the readout. He was calling for the second time this morning. Dodge hadn't answered the first time, but, thinking that he might just as well get this conversation over with, he yanked the phone from his belt and barked into it, "Yeah?"

"Dodge?"

"Isn't that who you called?"

Derek chuckled. "Hello to you, too."

"Hello."

"How are you? Are you okay?"

"Why wouldn't I be?"

"Julie and I have been worried. You said you were going to call. You haven't."

"I've been busy."

"How're things going down there?"

"Fine."

"Then why do you sound so out of sorts?"

"Because I'm probably going to be charged a fine for smoking in this rented car."

"Well, you should be."

"That's discrimination. What I need is a good trial lawyer to fight my case in court. Except I don't know one."

"Ah, hitting below the belt. That means you're good and pissed over something. What's going on?"

"Nothing. I'm coming back."

"This soon?"

"I'm flying out tonight. Maybe tomorrow morning. Depending."

"On what?"

"I may hang around tonight and eat some decent Mexican food. God knows you can't get it in Atlanta."

"The problem that took you there, did it get solved?"

"Yeah."

"Good. That's good. Hold on." Dodge could hear whispering in the background, then, "Julie says to ask how your daughter is."

"She's all right."

"So you saw her?"

"Yeah."

"It went okay?"

"It went fine."

"What's she like?"

"Her mother."

"Is that good or bad?"

"Look, Counselor, you're exceeding the minutes on my calling plan. Are you going to reimburse me?"

"Come on, Dodge, talk to me."

"I thought that's what I was doing."

"If there's a problem, and you need my help—"

"There's no problem, and all I need your help with is this phone bill."

After a couple of beats, Derek said, "Stop this and tell me what's going on."

"There's nothing to tell."

"I find that hard to believe."

"Sue me."

"You told us that your daughter was in a jam. A police matter."

"You got a remarkable memory, Counselor. Anybody ever tell you that?"

"Has the police matter been resolved?"

"Yeah. I mean, for the most part."

"For the most part?"

"The culprit's dead, and she's safe."

"So why aren't you happy?"

"Who said I wasn't?"

"You don't sound happy."

He was tempted to lay it all out there and get Derek's opinion. Because he really did value it, although he'd deny it with his dying breath. But the personal aspect of his dilemma was a sad tale, and he was the ogre of it, and he didn't want to lessen Derek and Julie's regard for him, which couldn't be all that great to start with. As for his misgivings over the "police matter," they were just that. Unsubstantiated, unidentifiable, and, at this point, irrelevant.

Crossly, he said, "You don't have enough drama in your life, Counselor, you gotta borrow from mine?"

Derek sighed with resignation. "Have a safe flight."

They disconnected. Supremely agitated and in need of a cigarette, Dodge pulled onto the shoulder of the freeway and lit one. He was at a crossroads. Literally. Up ahead the freeway divided. The right fork would take him to the airport, where he could probably get on a flight to Atlanta this evening. The left fork would almost certainly lead him on a wild-goose chase.

Why was he even debating the choice? Why didn't he just go? He'd made a clean break.

But that was bullshit, and even he was no longer buying it.

He hadn't made a clean break, he'd sneaked out.

He'd run away because he was too chickenhearted to say goodbye. The two women he'd left behind would be furious, frustrated, maybe a little heartbroken.

And even without taking their feelings into account, there was this other thing nagging him, holding him back when he should just get the hell out of the freakin' state of Texas.

"Shit." He drew hard on the cigarette one final time and tossed it out the window. Cursing himself for being every kind of fool, he put the car in Drive and shot across four lanes of traffic in order to take the left fork.

"You're not supposed to be in here now. Didn't you read the sign? Visiting hours are over."

Dodge turned away from the bed. The nurse filling the doorway was maybe four feet, eleven inches tall and almost that wide. Her scrubs had clown faces on them. Her hair had been plaited into dozens of cornrows with multicolored beads that dangled against her shoulders.

He gave her his most engaging smile. "I like your hair."

She propped a ham-size fist on her ample hip.

Instantly he switched tactics and became repentant. "I must have missed the sign."

"Um-huh," she said, like she'd heard it all before. She waddled into the room and looked down at the tiny form on the bed. "How you doin', sweetheart? You gonna sit up and talk to your gentleman caller here?"

With obvious compassion, she stroked the patient's cropped white hair. The woman who'd given life to Oren Starks showed no sign of awareness even though her eyes were open.

"Is she always like this, Glenda?" Dodge asked, reading the name on the tag clipped to the nurse's top.

She looked him up and down. "You a relative?"

"Friend of the family."

"You know the son who got himself shot? We got the news this morning."

"Actually, he shot himself. I hadn't had the misfortune of meeting him, but I know a lot about him. He did some bad stuff." Dodge, feeling a rare urge to tell the truth, said, "I was in on his capture."

"Huh." He was subjected to another once-over. "You look like a cop. You got a gun?"

He turned his back to her and raised the hem of his jacket.

She harrumphed. "You're not supposed to have firearms in here."

"I must have missed that sign, too."

She tsked and shook her head as though he was a hopeless case, then returned her attention to the patient. "I can't see her boy's dying making much difference to her."

"How long has she been like this?"

"It came on gradual like, you know, the way it does. But she's been unresponsive for more than a year. Some of the sorry help in this place just ignore the poor little thing. Never talk to her. But I take good care of her, and we have our chats." She plucked a tissue from a box on the nightstand and used it to wipe a string of drool off Mrs. Starks's slack lips. "Don't we, sugar? You feel free to chime in now anytime you get a mind to."

"You're a saint, Glenda."

"You're full of shit."

"No, I mean it."

"So do I." But she was grinning.

He laughed. "Guilty."

"What are you doing here, Mr. Cop?"

"I don't know."

"You don't know?"

"No. And that's no shit." He looked thoughtfully at Mrs. Starks. "I guess I hoped she would enlighten me."

"Like how?"

"Like tell me something about Oren that would explain why he whacked out, killed a woman, a sixteen-year-old boy, and an old man, then wished another person dead with his dying breath."

"Lord o' mercy." The nurse shook her head again, causing the beads to clack together. "I'm sorry, sir, but she can't help you. Last few times that Oren came to see her, she didn't know him, didn't even know he was here."

Dodge asked how often Oren had visited his mother and when the last time had been.

"A while back," Glenda told him. "Several months, at least. Frankly . . . and this is just between us, I wouldn't say it if this poor soul could understand."

"My lips are sealed."

She leaned toward him and spoke in a stage whisper. "I didn't like him."

"No one did. I didn't even know him, and I didn't like him."

"He wasn't right in the head, you ask me. Made you uncomfortable just to talk to him, you know?"

Dodge nodded.

"I was never happy to see him coming but was always glad to watch him go." Glenda's giant hand, with its surprisingly gentle touch, stroked her patient's arm. "Poor lady. I wouldn't wish her condition on anybody, but I'm kinda glad she doesn't know what her boy sunk to. After all that other sad business, she didn't deserve this."

Dodge's heart hitched, and the hair on the back of his neck stood on end. "Glenda, darlin'?"

"Hmm?"

"What other sad business?"

"Do you have to go?" Berry asked when Ski kissed her good-bye at the back door of the lake house.

"Duty calls. I've got to make an official statement to the media. Dot i's, cross t's."

"Will you come back for supper? I think it will make Mother feel better if you're here." She rubbed against him. "It'll make me feel better, too."

He nuzzled her ear. "You couldn't possibly feel any better."

Laughing with self-deprecation, she said, "I'm being shamelessly easy."

"I haven't exactly played hard to get." He pecked her lips with his. "Save my place."

She waved him off, watching like a lovesick puppy until his SUV was out of sight, then she climbed the stairs and went into the guest room that she'd occupied since last Friday night.

Upon entering the room, she spotted the bag of Oren's gifts sitting on the bed. Seeing it made her shiver. She had retrieved it this morning from the closet in her bedroom, the one Dodge had been sleeping in until last night. After getting Ski's call that Oren was regaining consciousness, they'd rushed from the house, leaving it and its contents on the kitchen table.

Who had brought it up to this room? She didn't want to look at it but was loath to touch it, so for the time being, she left it where it was. In an attempt to banish all thoughts of Oren's dying moments from her mind, she was eager to feel the heat of the sun on her skin, the embrace of the cool lake water.

After quickly changing into a swimsuit, she jogged downstairs and went to her mother's bedroom. She wanted to ask her about the bag, but when she opened the door, she saw that Caroline was curled onto her side, hugging the pillow that would have been Dodge's. Probably she had cried herself to sleep. Berry decided to leave her in peace.

She walked to the edge of the pier and dove into the lake. She swam underwater for as long as she could hold her breath, then surfaced and began swimming a vigorous crawl. The tension in her muscles gave way to a burn that felt good.

When she tired, she rolled onto her back and floated, expending just enough energy to keep herself afloat as she gazed at the white puffy clouds overhead and thought about the bizarre events that had taken place since the last time she'd gone for a swim.

So many bad things.

But good things, too.

She'd met Dodge, and, despite what her mother believed, she refused to accept that he would abandon them again. He loved her mother. Berry would bet her life on that. And he liked her. She knew that to be equally true.

No, she thought decisively, Dodge wasn't out of their lives yet.

Even if he was operating under that delusion, she wasn't going to let him go.

And Ski. They'd got off to a rocky start, but sexually, they weren't merely compatible, they were combustible. He left her as hungry as she was satisfied, and the same seemed to be true for him. They'd pleasured each other until they were weak, but still they'd wanted more.

Aside from the marvelous sex, she also liked his solidness, admired his practical viewpoint of things and his unmitigated honesty, even regarding his own shortcomings. He appealed to her physically, cerebrally, and emotionally. He was as close as she'd ever come to *the one*.

With enticing possibilities in mind, she flipped onto her belly, then did a surface dive and swam back to the pier. When she reached the ladder, she grabbed the top rung and was about to pull herself up when a head popped over the edge of the pier.

"Boo!"

CHAPTER 29

OREN STARKS LEERED DOWN AT HER. "SURPRISE!"

Berry screamed and tried to push herself off the ladder, but Oren grabbed her wrist, clamped a handcuff on it, and jerked hard. "Get out of the water!"

Her only thought was *Escape*. She kicked and thrashed. She tried to pull her wrist free, but the metal cuff cruelly gouged into skin and bone.

"Berry, if you don't get out of the water, I'll kill your mother." He tapped the barrel of a handgun against the edge of the pier. "Bang-bang, she's dead."

Instantly she stopped fighting.

He smiled beatifically. "Thank you, sweetheart."

She gaped up at him with horror and stupefaction. Her teeth were chattering with terror. She couldn't speak.

"You look like you've seen a ghost. Thought I was dead, didn't you?"

Her head wobbled an affirmation.

"Well, clearly you were wrong." He yanked on the cuff. "Get out of the water."

"I . . . I can't."

"Ber-ry," he said in a singsong voice, "I'm going to count to three. One. Two."

"All right." She gulped a breath. "I'll get out. But you'll have to let go of my hand or I can't climb the ladder."

He aimed the pistol at the bridge of her nose. "With those long, shapely thighs of yours, I'm sure you'll manage."

"I need both hands to pull myself up."

"Let me make myself clear. Either you'll make do with one hand or I'll blow your brains out, then go into the house and do likewise to your mother. But only after fucking her in every orifice. If you don't think I'll do it, remember Sally."

If he could rise from the dead, he was capable of anything. Seeing no option available to her, she placed her foot on the bottom rung of the ladder, but she was trembling so bad it slipped off. She fell forward and banged her chin on the metal rung.

"Hurry up!" Oren hissed.

Apparently he had had the same thought she had, that a boat might come near enough for her to scream for help. He alternated between charting her progress up the ladder and scanning the lake for an approaching craft. Unfortunately, this being a workday, there weren't many boaters out, and none on this inlet of the lake.

Berry hauled herself up onto the pier. She thought of lowering her head and plowing into him, surprising him with an aggressive action. But he could still shoot her, and then her mother would be helpless.

Besides, she wasn't sure she could muster the strength. She was shivering with fright and with cold now that the air was hitting her wet skin. Her teeth continued to chatter.

Oren grinned evilly and nudged her raised nipple with the barrel of the pistol. "I took a picture of you like this. Have you seen it? You were stretched out here on the pier. The wind must have kicked up." He stuck out his tongue and waggled it obscenely.

Berry ignored that, focusing instead on how this could possibly be happening. She'd seen his brain bulging out of his cranium, his body convulsing. The doctor had pronounced him dead. Yet now he looked completely healed and whole. Gone were the scrapes and scratches on his face and arms that he'd got during his chase through the Thicket. He didn't have a broken tibia.

The only difference between him now and his sudden appearance in her bathroom last Friday night was that his head had been shaved. It was as slick as a billiard ball.

He spun her around and pulled her arm behind her back, then linked her wrists together with the handcuffs. He pushed her forward, forcing her to stumble ahead of him along the pier toward the house.

"Who are you?"

"I'm Oren, silly, who do you think?"

"You're dead."

"Wrong. Dead men don't have boners like the one I've got from seeing your stiff nipples."

"You must be Oren," she said. "That's the kind of juvenile, off-color remark that's typical of you."

He hammered the butt of the pistol against her temple. She hadn't seen it coming, and the pain was intense. It caused her to drop to her knees. They landed hard. She crumpled forward. Her stomach heaved. She tasted bile in her mouth and had to spit it out in order to gasp in pain. He grabbed her hair and pulled her head back. Blood ran into her eye.

"Now see what you made me do?" he cooed. "It's that snotty attitude that got you into this situation in the first place, Berry. You've got only yourself to blame."

He hauled her to her feet. She swayed, half blinded with the pain in her head as well as the blood that trickled into her eye. All her loathing and hatred for him and the things he'd done boiled over. "Fuck you."

He laughed, unfazed. "Possibly. I haven't decided yet. You look like the very devil just now. No temptation at all. But I'll think about it. I promise I will. In the meantime, your mother will do nicely. You can watch," he said, as though he'd just thought up a fun, new game. "Then you can watch me kill her. Only then, Berry, will I begin to deal with you."

"He's a twin!"

"What?"

"A twin. Identical twin."

Ski sat bolt upright in his desk chair.

Through the phone, Dodge's breathing sounded like he'd been heaving hay bales. He was gasping each breath, but he made himself heard. "I went to that place where his mother is at. Nurse there told me Mrs. Starks had twin sons. Bookends."

"Fuck!"

"Tell me. The guy we pulled outta that swamp is Oren's twin brother, Carl. I'd stake my balls on it."

"Shit!"

"Something was hinky. I knew it, just didn't know what."

"We thought it was off. The Oren that Berry described didn't fit with somebody who'd hide in the Thicket."

"Makes sense now. It wasn't Oren."

"But he was the mastermind."

"That's what I think."

"Which means—"

"He'll come after Berry."

"I'm on it." Ski rounded his desk. "Where are you?"

"Blasting through Houston. I'll be there quick as I can."

Ski didn't waste time thanking him. He disconnected and began shouting the names of other deputies who were in the squad room. Simultaneously he punched in the telephone number of the lake house. Caroline answered.

"Caroline, Ski. Where's Berry?"

"Uh . . . you woke me up. I—"

"You need to find her."

"She mentioned earlier she might go for a swim."

"If she's out, get her in. Stay inside the house and set the alarm. Keep the pistol on hand." He covered the mouthpiece and said to the men who'd assembled around him, "Stand by. New development in the Starks case." Then he addressed Caroline, who, fully awake now, was demanding to know what was going on.

"Oren Starks is alive."

"What?"

"The man who died was his identical twin."

"What!"

"Dodge went to Houston, to the facility where his mother is a resident. He talked to a nurse and she told him. That's all I know."

"Where's Dodge?"

"Racing back. Alert Berry. Okay?"

"Of course, yes."

"And, Caroline?"

"Yes?"

"Call me as soon as you're both safely inside. I've got some calls to make, but if you beep in, I'll answer. Don't forget."

"I promise."

Ski clicked off and addressed the deputies grouped around him. "I want one of the launches on the lake ASAP, patrolling that inlet where Mrs. King's house is."

"I thought the asshole was dead."

"His twin brother is dead. He's still unaccounted for, still considered armed and dangerous."

He assigned special tasks and ordered the dispatcher to put out the word. "City police, DPS, Rangers, FBI, everybody, got it?"

"Got it."

He personally placed calls to the detectives in Houston. Rodney Allen was unavailable, but Ski talked to Somerville, who was no more gregarious than before. He listened to Ski's remarkable update without emotion or comment, then said, "I'll inform Detective Allen. We'll check out Oren Starks's residence, put out an APB."

"One more thing."

"Yes?"

"Tell Allen it was Dodge Hanley who cracked it."

After breaking off the connection, Ski unlocked the department's gun cabinet and took out a high-powered rifle with a scope. Stevens, who was on the phone, raised his eyebrows as Ski walked past his desk, the rifle on his shoulder.

"Bringing out the heavy artillery, Ski?"

"You bet your ass."

Caroline came racing into the kitchen just as Oren shoved Berry headlong through the back door. Caroline screamed and rushed forward to help her daughter, who had fallen hard, banging her shoulder against the floor.

Oren thrust the pistol into Caroline's belly. "Drop the phone! Drop the phone!"

"Mother, do it! I'm okay. Do as he says."

Caroline let go of the cordless phone. Oren moved it along the floor with the toe of his shoe, then kicked it out the back door before slamming the door shut.

Berry worked herself into a sitting position. She shook back her hair and tried to blink the blood from her eye as she looked up at her mother. Caroline cried out in shock at the sight of her bleeding head. "What did you do to her?" she screamed.

"Shut up! You scream again, I'll shoot you."

"I'm okay, Mother." Berry tried to stand up, but Oren placed his hand on her shoulder and shoved her back down. "Did I say you could get up?"

"Don't hurt her," Caroline pleaded.

"Oh, she's going to hurt. So are you."

"My mother's done nothing to you. It's me you want. Let her go."

He laughed. "As if. Carl had my permission to kill her, too, if she should happen to be in the house on Friday night."

Berry looked up at him with bewilderment. "Carl?"

"My twin."

"Twin?" she echoed faintly.

"Twin?" he repeated, mocking Berry's tone.

Berry's blood-filled eye sought her mother to gauge her astonishment, but Caroline was staring at Oren, her face devoid of expression, probably due to the shock of seeing him alive when she'd thought him safely dead.

"Carl was the millstone around my neck my whole life," he was saying. "I couldn't have friends because Carl was such a psycho. No one wanted to play at our house, and I couldn't go play with other children because I had to play with *him*.

"Finally, my stupid excuse for a mother put him in a mental institution, where he stayed for years. *Shh!* Dirty family secret. We moved from Beaumont to Houston. 'Let's not tell anybody about your brother and his mental illness, Oren.' As if I wanted to advertise that my brother, my womb mate," he said, giggling over his play on words, "was a lunatic.

"Thank God I'm finally rid of him. Stupid son of a bitch. Couldn't even kill himself without botching it." Suddenly his voice changed. "Where the hell do you think you're going?"

He'd caught Caroline inching toward the door that led into the dining area. Berry remembered that her mother's cell phone was on the dining table. She'd been using it to try to call Dodge.

Dodge, why aren't you here?

Ski, where are you?

She couldn't depend on their rescue, on anyone's. This was her fight. It was up to her to keep her mother and herself alive.

Ski was speeding toward the lake house when his cell phone rang. He answered without reading caller ID. "Berry?"

"Sheriff Drummond. Am I understanding correctly that Oren Starks is still at large?"

"I'm afraid so, sir."

Ski gave him the shorthand version. Drummond was in midsentence when call waiting beeped. "Excuse me, sir. I'll fill you in on details as I get them, but I need to take this call."

He didn't even wait for his boss to acknowledge before clicking over. "Berry?"

Another deputy identified himself. "Ski, we've got a problem."

"Go ahead."

"Somebody's horses got out of their pasture."

Ski's mind was so fixed on the crisis, it took him a moment to process. "Horses?"

"They're running along the highway, going haywire. Motorists are having to dodge them. You told us to check out all the boat rental places, which is what Andy and me were doing. But we can't split up, and if somebody hits one of these horses . . ."

Ski didn't need to be told what could happen. The animal could die, but anyone inside the vehicle could also be seriously injured or killed. "You're together in one car?"

"Yeah, Stevens was gonna take—"

"Never mind. Get the horses back where they belong. Then get on those boat rentals. Keep me posted."

"Ten-four."

Ski checked his phone for recent calls, thinking he might have missed one. There had been none. He hit speed dial for the lake house. It rang until voice mail picked up. Swearing, he dialed Berry's cell number. It went straight to voice mail. He checked the time. It was seven minutes since he and Caroline had talked. He rang the house phone again and, when he got no answer, called Dodge.

"Talk to me."

"Can you call Caroline's cell for me? I don't have her number programmed into my phone." He told Dodge about instructing her to call him. "Caroline promised me that one of them would as soon as they were safe inside the house. I haven't heard from them."

"You're on your way there now?"

"Turning onto Lake Road as we speak. I'll try Berry's cell again. You call Caroline's."

"Roger that."

Ski called Berry's cell. Then the house. Got voice mails. Eleven minutes had elapsed. Ample time for Caroline to have called Berry indoors. Unless, he thought with a modicum of relief, she wasn't swimming in the pool.

When Caroline had mentioned her taking a swim, he'd automatically thought *pool,* which was right outside the back door off the terrace. But Berry could have gone swimming in the lake. In which case, it would be taking longer for them to get inside.

Caroline would have had to walk to the end of the pier. Maybe Berry had been far out. Maybe it had taken a while for her to notice Caroline signaling from the shore, then several minutes for her to swim in and for them to walk back to the house.

His phone rang. "Berry?"

"Me," Dodge said. "She didn't answer."

"Christ. I should have told Caroline to take the phone with her when she went to get Berry."

"She ain't stupid, Ski."

He was right. Caroline didn't need it spelled out for her. She would have immediately grasped the implications of Starks's being alive. She would have taken every precaution, and that would have included keeping a telephone in her hand.

Dodge's thoughts were running parallel. "The only reason she wouldn't call you back is if she couldn't."

Ski's stomach dropped. He started swearing, started praying, stamped the accelerator.

Oren forced the two women at gunpoint into the living area. He motioned toward the sofa and ordered Caroline to sit. Berry he kept standing in front of him, the pistol against her temple. "This is a lovely room," he said pleasantly, looking around.

"You've been here," Berry said. "When you took back the bracelet."

He laughed. "So you noticed it was missing? I wondered. I thought you might check for it when it was found on Sally. And I was right."

"You also came into the house this morning when we weren't here."

He laughed. "You discovered the bag in the guest room? I guess I can't blame you for switching rooms. Imagine my surprise when

I saw my gifts on the kitchen table. I replaced them in the bag and even added some duplicate prints of the photos I took of you. The close-ups." He licked his lips obscenely.

Berry looked away in disgust, but he placed the pistol along her cheek and forced her to look at him. "It was Carl who came here last Friday night. I had laid the groundwork, showed him the photos, and drew him the layout of the house. I had told him a thousand times to wait until you and Ben were cozy in bed. He was to shoot you both and get out. No fuss, no muss. But, the best-laid plans . . ." He sighed.

With his free hand he picked up a picture frame from an end table and looked at the photograph. To Caroline he said, "You're very photogenic. Just like Berry."

She merely glared at him.

"You said Carl was in an institution," Berry said. "When did he get out?"

"Couple of years ago. The state declared him cured. He got dumped on me because of Mother's condition. He'd been the bane of my childhood, now I was responsible for him for the rest of his life. Wonderful. Fabulous.

"But then," he said, his inflection shifting, "when I started thinking about how I could get revenge on all you hateful people at Delray, I saw a way to put the head case to use. I began brainwashing him on how evil you were, how you must be killed, how it was up to him to do it if he wanted to go to heaven and live with Mother forever and ever." His giggle sent chills down Berry's spine. "It worked."

"It didn't work very well," Caroline remarked coolly.

Berry was surprised and grateful for her composure. Her mother had to be every bit as afraid as she was, yet she gave the impression of being calm. "Mother is right, Oren," Berry said. "Carl made mistakes. Ben survived. He panicked and couldn't shoot me. He—"

"Shut up!" Oren barked. "I know all about it."

"From Carl? You saw him after he left here on Friday night?"

"He's the idiot, Berry, not me. Of course I didn't see him. But I'd given him a cell phone, so we could stay in touch. He was to call me as soon as it was done. When he did call, he was blubbering, crying, telling me he'd failed, wailing because now he wouldn't go to heaven. I got the details from news reports. Oren Starks was a wanted man, so I had to get Carl out of sight. I told him to find a place to hide."

"The motel."

"It seemed like a good idea," he said defensively. "That goof-up was a—"

"It was a fatal shooting of an innocent boy."

Oren shrugged. "It was that kid's time to die."

"And Mr. Mittmayer's, too, I suppose."

"I was furious with Carl over that. Hijacking the RV was smart, but it was careless of him to hit the old man hard enough to kill him." Oren thoughtfully tapped his lips. "Although, it actually worked out for the better. His killing spree, as they called it on TV, made him look all the crazier."

"He began to unravel."

"You have no idea," he said, rolling his eyes.

"You told him the only way to heaven was to kill himself."

"Precisely. I told him to go into the Big Thicket."

"That was an elaborate choice. Why there?"

"Because the more difficult his capture, the more fatigued everyone would be afterward. Your friend Nyland would breathe a huge sigh of relief and relax his vigilance. You see?"

When she said nothing, he continued. "Carl was instructed to throw away the cell phone, somewhere where no one could find it, then to use the pistol on himself. I promised him it wouldn't hurt, and he'd go straight to heaven. He could wait there for Mother, who would join him soon. You should have heard him. He was so relieved and happy, he sobbed. But"—he gave another dramatic sigh—"the moron couldn't even do that correctly."

"Is that why you killed Sally yourself? You wanted to make sure it was done right."

He chortled a laugh. "That, and I didn't want Carl to have all the fun."

Berry swallowed with difficulty.

"She came home to find me inside her house." He smiled as though fondly recalling the scene. "She'd heard about the shooting here the night before. She knew what my being in her house implied. She had an inkling of what I had in store for her. But only an inkling." Chuckling, he added, "I had some surprises for her."

Berry tamped down another surge of nausea.

"I told her that if she was convincing when the authorities called, which they were sure to do, and if she threw them off track, I'd let her live. She actually believed me!" he said around a laugh. "We spent a lot of quality time together, but by the time I actually killed her, I think she was relieved."

Berry looked over at Caroline. Their eyes met, communicating that Sally Buckland's fate would be their own if they didn't prevent it. While he'd been talking, Berry had been surveying the room, searching for something that would serve as a weapon. Fireplace tools? Brass candlestick? Crystal vase?

Nothing looked lethal, and even had there been something to use as a weapon, her hands were manacled behind her. Her mother was too petite to overpower him. She'd be shot the instant she attempted it.

Berry reasoned that the only way to escape would be to continue stoking Oren's ego by asking questions. Meanwhile she'd watch for him to relax his vigilance, and then she must be poised to act. As he'd noted, she had long, strong legs.

She said, "You certainly had this well planned."

"Didn't I just?"

"It was risky for you to call me from Houston on Sally's cell phone, after being spotted in Walmart."

"Well, that was Carl in the store, of course. Meanwhile, I was at Sally's place trying to decide how I was going to dispose of her body. Oren Starks was at Walmart buying shoes at three o'clock in the morning. He's at the Astros game in Houston hours later. That call *was* risky, but it added to the confusion and suspended the search for Carl in and around Merritt. That is, until those old people were found in their RV the next morning. But by that time, I had persuaded him to go into the Thicket and finish this thing."

"Why did you take Sally's body to my house?"

"Because you'd told me that Monday was the day you were making your presentation to the Delray client. Knowing you, I didn't think the crisis in Merritt would keep you from that. And I was right, wasn't I? I figured you would be in Houston Sunday evening to prepare, and thought that extra little surprise would really leave everyone scratching their heads. And it did! By the way, I've been meaning to ask, did you catch the song I was humming when I called you? 'Spinning Wheel.' Get it?"

Berry refused to give him the satisfaction of an answer. "You're still a long way from getting away with this, Oren."

"Would I leave a stone unturned, Berry? No. This past weekend, I lined up several alibis. Early Saturday morning, I drove over to Louisiana, where I'd rented a cabin for the entire summer. Backwoods. Cajun country. Everybody's kin to everybody else, and outsiders are noticed. I had my head shaved at the local barbershop. The barber will remember, believe me, because I was squeamish about making such a drastic change in my appearance.

"In the supermarket I created quite a scene over some spoiled milk I'd bought several days before, and I had the receipt to prove it. People in the store at that time will remember me. I made sure of it.

"If the authorities inspect the cabin, it will appear that I've been there. Trash dating back several weeks. Fresh produce in the fridge. There's no TV, no radio, no computer with Internet, so I was completely out of touch with the outside world. I'd heard no news.

"Only when I returned to Texas did I learn that my demented brother had murdered three people during my absence! And he's dead, too! Oh, woe is me! I'm devastated!" He smiled smugly. "You see? I've got it all covered."

"It seems you do. Except for one thing. I'm still alive."

"Not for long."

"If you kill me now, the authorities will know Carl didn't do it."

"Random act of violence," he said flippantly. "Two women left alone in a lake house. A deviant comes along." He shrugged, leaving the rest unfinished.

"That would be awfully coincidental, Oren," Berry said. "I don't think any peace officer would believe that."

"Any peace officer like your brawny Deputy Nyland?" he sneered.

"If anything happens to Mother and me now, you'll naturally be the prime suspect."

"Nyland might suspect, but—"

"Nyland knows."

They all jumped at the sound of the voice coming from the open doorway that connected the kitchen to the dining area. Berry nearly fainted with relief. Dodge stood there, his hands raised high above his head.

Oren squealed as he jabbed the barrel of the pistol against Berry's temple. "I'll kill her!"

"No!" Dodge kept his hands in the air but frantically waved them. "Please don't."

He was red in the face and short of breath, as if he'd just run a mile before stepping through the doorway. His shirt was sticking to him with sweat. Berry shifted her eyes to her mother, who didn't seem all that surprised to see him, and, in that split second, she realized that, somehow or another, Caroline had known he would appear when they most needed him.

He said, "I just want to talk to you, Oren."

"Who are you?"

"Berry's father."

Oren sputtered. "That's not true. Jim Malone's dead. Do you think I'm stupid? You're a cop they sent in here to—"

"I'm not a cop, Oren. I'm Berry's father. And I don't think you're stupid. I know you're smart. Too smart to pull that trigger. Because as soon as you do, Nyland's going to take you out. He's former Army. Special Forces. The best of the badasses.

"And right now, he's got a rifle aimed at you that looks like it could blow your eye out from a mile away. If you kill Berry, he'll do it. The only reason he hasn't pulled the trigger yet is on the *outside* chance that he'd miss you and hit her. But if you kill her, he'll have nothing to lose. He'll squeeze that trigger, and your head will disintegrate, and I bullshit you not."

Oren wet his lips and gripped the pistol more tightly. "You're trying to trick me."

"While you've got a pistol aimed at my only kid's head? No way."

"She's not your kid."

"She is. I left her in the hospital nursery the day she was born and only just reunited with her. Don't take her from me now. Please."

"You're breaking my heart," Oren said.

"All right. You don't care about us, think about yourself. Don't be foolish enough to think Nyland sent me in here to bargain with you. The man's a cowboy. He wants you dead. I had to fight my way past the son of a bitch to get in here. Thought I might get a bullet in the back at any second."

"You're a cop."

"I swear I'm not."

"It's true, Oren," Caroline said. "He's Berry's birth father. He abandoned her just as he said."

"I don't believe you."

"Who else besides a desperate father would defy Nyland, huh?" He looked at Berry and changed the tone of his voice. "You're bleeding. Does it hurt too bad?"

"No. I'm okay."

"Shut up! Shut up!" Oren said shrilly. "I'm not falling for this."

"Please," Dodge implored. "Don't harm my baby." Suddenly, he grimaced and sucked in a wheezing breath. Exhaling it slowly, he said, "Nyland is so pissing mad at me right now, he'll probably shoot me, too. But if you kill my daughter and Caroline . . ." His gaze shifted to her and stayed for several seconds. Then, back to Oren, he said, "If you harm them, I'd just as soon die."

Out the corner of her eye, Berry could see Oren in profile. His face was greasy with sweat. She could feel his nervous tension, his indecision. His bravado had vanished. She could smell his fear that what Dodge was telling him was true.

Dodge took a few steps toward them, but Oren dug the barrel of the pistol into her temple, and Dodge halted immediately. "Okay, okay," he said quickly. "I won't come any closer. But if you want to live, Oren, you gotta surrender."

"No!" He gave his head a stubborn shake, like a child refusing to eat his vegetables.

"Now's not the time to get stupid, Oren. Nyland found out about your brother, figured you'd come after Berry. He's got this place . . ." Dodge winced. His breath caught.

"Dodge?" Caroline stood up abruptly. Oren shouted for her to sit back down, and she did, but remained perched on the edge of the sofa, her eyes worriedly fixed on Dodge.

"I'm all right," he said, patting the air. "Just winded from fighting off Nyland." Looking back at Oren, he said, "The house is surrounded. Nyland was the first here. He saw you through the windows. Saw you holding that gun to Berry's head. He's got the whole sheriff's department, Texas Rangers, every uniform he can think of, in position and armed to the teeth. All of them want a crack at you so bad, they're hyperventilating."

He cast a guilty glance toward the front windows. "Of course, I'm not supposed to be telling you that. Just hear this, Oren, and hear me good. You can't possibly escape. Come on. Let Berry go. Release her and Caroline. Give yourself up."

"I told you no!"

"All right. Don't surrender. I'll be your hostage. I'll help get you out of here in one piece. I'll negotiate—" He broke off as he gave a sharp cry and clapped his right hand over his left shoulder. Bending double, he staggered several feet forward. As he did, he pulled his pistol from the holster at the small of his back.

But it was of no use to him. When he pitched forward and fell to the floor in obvious agony, the pistol dropped from his listless hand and slid across the hardwood.

Caroline, ignoring Oren's warning shout, launched off the sofa and flung herself down over Dodge, calling his name repeatedly.

Berry screamed, "Mother! Dodge!"

Oren, frantic at having lost control of the situation, pushed Berry aside and kicked Dodge's pistol out of reach, then bent over Caroline and struggled to pull her off Dodge. "Shut up! Get back over there!"

Berry gave the side of Oren's knee a vicious kick. It buckled and he howled, but he didn't release Caroline, who held on to Dodge, still wailing his name.

Oren doubled his efforts to haul her up.

Berry bicycled her legs against him, striking him as hard as she could with her bare feet.

He let go of Caroline, spun around, and aimed his pistol down at Berry's face. "I said I would kill you!"

Then there were two loud claps in rapid succession. Before Berry could even register Oren's surprised expression, he dropped to the floor with two bright blooms of red on his chest.

Ski burst into the room, pistol drawn. Other officers rushed in behind him and swarmed over Oren's prone form. Ski bent over Berry, who was struggling to stand up. "Help me."

He pulled her up, supporting her as she stumbled over to the couple huddled on the floor. Hands still manacled, she awkwardly dropped to her knees beside them, joining her mother's mournful chant of her father's name.

One of the deputies called out, "Starks is dead, Ski."

Berry barely registered that. Her concern was channeled strictly to Dodge. She released a sob of relief when he eased Caroline off him and came up on his elbows. In his right hand was a small, blunt-barreled pistol.

Caroline threw her arms around his neck and held on tight. She was openly weeping. "You scared me half to death!"

Looking up at Ski, he wheezed, "Motherfucker was resisting arrest."

"You had no choice. He would have killed Berry." Ski gave him an arch look. "You failed to tell me about the second pistol. Ankle holster?"

Dodge, still struggling for breath, nodded.

"Well, you faked him out," Ski said. "Especially with the heart attack."

Caroline, who had been anxiously studying Dodge, suddenly realized the truth of the matter and gave a startled cry.

Dodge gasped, "I wasn't faking that."

EPILOGUE

I'M CALLING ABOUT DODGE HANLEY," SKI SAID TO DEREK Mitchell's polite but firm personal assistant who had told him that Mr. Mitchell was unavailable. "If he's there, put me through. If he's not, tell me where I can reach him."

Ski was asked to hold, and seconds later the attorney came on the line. "Deputy Nyland? This is Derek Mitchell. Marlene said you were calling about Dodge. What is it? Is he all right?"

"I'm afraid not, Mr. Mitchell." Ski delivered the news forthrightly, which he figured the attorney would appreciate. "It was a bad one. He arrested twice in the ambulance on the way to the hospital. CPR kept him alive. Barely.

"I didn't call you sooner because I didn't have anything solid to report until just a few minutes ago, when the cardiac surgeon came out to give us the lowdown. Dodge held on through the surgery, but the doctor used words like *infarct* and *friable,* and he didn't sugarcoat the prognosis."

"Which is what? How bad?"

"Chance of survival, fifty-fifty. And the surgeon said that's optimistic. Dodge is at risk to suffer another heart attack or a stroke. The surgeon said he'll feel a lot more confident of his survival if he's still alive forty-eight hours from now."

The silence on the other end was ponderous. Derek Mitchell's concern was palpable. He cleared his throat twice before he was able to speak. "You said 'us.' The surgeon came out to talk to 'us.'"

"How much do you know about the situation here?"

"Only that Dodge went down there to help out his daughter, whom he hadn't seen since the day she was born. I talked to him today, asked how it was going, and all he would say was 'fine.' He was crotchety and evasive, but that's typical."

Ski had to smile. "Yeah, I know." He gave the attorney a brief summary of the events that had led up to Dodge's going into the lake house to negotiate with Oren Starks. "Dodge insisted. Said he would go in with or without my sanction. Said I couldn't stop him with a team of wild horses or a Sherman tank. Said he would save those two women or die trying."

The grim irony of his vow hadn't escaped Ski. "Berry had the presence of mind to keep Starks talking, but Dodge and I were wasting precious time arguing over his plan, so I agreed to it. He was confident that he could play Starks and get him to release Berry and Caroline and then to surrender. He almost pulled it off. He faked everything except the heart attack.

"When I saw him lose his pistol, topple, I almost had a heart attack myself. I thought it was over. And it was for Starks. Dodge hadn't told me he was packing an extra handgun." Wryly he added, "He played me, too, I guess."

"Ankle holster?"

"How'd you know?"

"He's never without it."

"I know that now."

Ski glanced over at Berry, where she sat with Caroline at a table in the hospital cafeteria. The surgeon had said it would be a while before anyone could see Dodge, so they had come down for coffee. But he noticed that their cups had been left untouched. On the tabletop, their hands were tightly clasped, as if they were both dispensing and deriving comfort from the contact.

Sharing a common urgency, the two men wrapped up their conversation. "What did he say?" Berry asked when Ski rejoined her and Caroline at the table.

"Thanked me profusely for notifying him. He's going to charter a private jet to fly him and his wife here. Soon as he knows where they'll be landing, he'll text me. I'll dispatch somebody to pick them up, bring them straight here. It'll be the wee hours, probably, but he didn't want to wait until tomorrow."

None of them questioned the reason behind Derek Mitchell's haste.

Berry said, "Dodge will be glad they're here. He talks about them all the time. He loves them."

"Gauging by Mitchell's reaction, I think the feeling is mutual."

"In Dodge's mind, he doesn't deserve to be loved."

They looked at Caroline, who'd spoken in a soft voice, made even gruffer from crying. Up till then, Ski hadn't been sure she was even following their conversation. Berry leaned across the table. "What makes you say that, Mother?"

"His father told him so, by the way he treated him if not in actual words. Dodge believed him. Up to the day you were born and I ordered him out of our lives, he'd been trying to earn everyone's respect and acceptance. Everyone's love." She looked down at her hands, which she was twisting together. "Ever since that day, he's been trying to kill himself for being unlovable."

Ski agreed with Caroline, and he figured Berry did, too, although they weren't going to say so, because that would lay unfair blame at Caroline's doorstep. Dodge had willfully cheated. By doing so, he had thrown away the best thing that had ever happened to him. Caroline had taken a position and refused to back down. Neither had won.

The loss to both had been enormous, and it had defined the paths their lives would take for the next thirty years. Years that could have been happier for all of them. If only he'd been faithful. If only her rejection hadn't been absolute.

Caroline's cell phone rang. Knowing that she'd given her number to the ICU nurse, they all reacted with alarm. Bracing herself for the worst, Caroline answered.

She listened for several seconds, then said, "I'll be right there," and disconnected. She was trembling as she pushed back her chair and stood up. "He's regaining consciousness."

"Thank God," Berry whispered, obviously sharing Ski's relief that the news hadn't been what they feared.

"She said if I come right now, I can see him for five minutes."

"Go," Berry said, making shooing motions with her hands. "Run. We'll be right up."

Caroline gave her a grateful look, then dashed toward the cafeteria's exit.

Berry was none too steady as she stood up. She looked at Ski through watery eyes. Then her face crumpled, and she began to cry. He reached for her and hugged her close.

"I've been holding myself together for her sake, but I can't any longer."

"Go ahead and cry."

Oblivious to the other people in the cafeteria, he stroked her back and continued to hold her as sobs shook her entire body. She might lose the father she'd just found. That was bitter. She also bore the guilt for everything that had happened, and she would carry it for a long time.

He admired her for taking up that mantle. A more shallow individual would have made self-serving excuses and shrugged it off. His admiration was also tinged with pity. He had firsthand knowledge of how heavy a burden guilt could be. Only by sheer force of will would she carry on with her life and, eventually, forgive herself. He was confident she had the fiber to do it. She was, after all, a combination of two determined, hardheaded people.

Having cried herself out, she pulled away from him, plucked a napkin from the dispenser on the table, and used it to blot her eyes and face. "Well, that was a spectacle."

"Not really, and anyway, who cares?"

She gave him a wavering smile. "Thank you."

"You're welcome."

"We'd better get upstairs. Mother may need me."

With his hand curved around the back of her neck, Ski guided her from the cafeteria and across the lobby toward the elevator bank. One was available, and they were alone as they rode up to the ICU floor.

He bent down and gently kissed the butterfly clip above her eye. It had been required to close the gash caused by the butt of Oren Starks's pistol.

She leaned into him. "I know you have duties, responsibilities. But if you can, I'd like for you to stick around."

"I'll stick around."

She looked up into his face. "Think before you commit, Ski. It might be for quite a while, and the outcome is unsure."

Knowing that they were now talking not only about the vigil at Dodge's bedside but also about their future together, he cupped her face between his hands and touched her lips tenderly with his. "I'll stick around."

It surprised the hell out of Dodge when he came to. He had a good buzz going. Everything within his field of vision was blurry around the edges, and his overall feeling was one of languor. It felt like he had a fifty-pound weight sitting on his chest, but that was only mildly uncomfortable. The best part, Caroline was there, bending over him, stroking his hair.

So even if he was dead, his afterlife wasn't half bad. He wondered if smoking was allowed. If so, this really was heaven.

Or maybe this was just a staging area, and it could still go either way.

In fact, the weight on his chest was steadily turning into a dull ache. He had a lot to account for. He'd better get started before he was escorted to the next level. Down.

He blinked Caroline into better focus. "I skipped out."

She smiled and placed her hand on his cheek.

"Didn't say good-bye." He tried to swallow, but his mouth was dry. Worse than dry. It was pasty, and his tongue kept sticking to the roof of his mouth, so it was difficult to form words, not that he could think of that many. "Nothing to offer you. Then. Now. Never."

She shushed him and continued to smooth his hair off his forehead.

Dammit, he needed her to pay attention. He shook his head, only then realizing that there were tubes in his nose. *Jesus!* How undignified was that? He reached up and pulled the cannula away. Or tried. Caroline replaced it, and there was nothing he could do about it because he didn't have enough energy to raise his hand again.

The dull ache had worsened, and now he remembered being wheeled down a corridor, blinding overhead lights flashing past with dizzying speed, people running alongside the gurney talking in loud, excited voices. Had a guy with a goatee actually been straddling his chest and pounding on him, or had that been a weird dream?

Had those extra-bright lights been on the ceiling of an operating room? Probably some asshole with a trophy wife, a golf club membership, and a healthy six-figure annual income had been digging around inside his chest, and that's why it felt so tight and achy.

He heard a soothing voice as if it was coming from the end of a tunnel. It said, "Only another minute, Ms. King. Then you'll have to leave."

He hadn't realized his eyes had closed until he pried them open again. Caroline was still there. He gazed into her face and thought how lucky he was to be seeing it one more time, and marveled over how beautiful she was. He felt the warm, wet trickle of his own tears. Well, this was just super. Here he was, about to die, and there were tubes in his nostrils, and he was crying like a complete puss.

He forced his thick tongue to move before his final minute in this staging area was up, and Caroline would be lost to him forever. "Sorry I was . . ."

Shit. Sixty seconds wasn't enough time to list all the things he was sorry for. He just needed to tell her how much he loved her, had always loved her and always would. But he had to hurry because the stranger with the soothing voice was injecting something into the tube in his arm. Instantly he felt a rush of honeyed heat and sublimity. It was great fuckin' stuff, but as good as it was, he fought its effects.

He must say what needed to be said to Caroline, and he must say it in a way that would encompass the immensity of his love.

He groped for her hand, found it, squeezed it with all the strength he had. "I'd die for you all over again."

She turned his hand and pressed his palm against her heart. It beat steadily, strongly against his hand. She bent down and kissed his lips. Not gently. But with ardor, the way she used to when she was either really aroused or really pissed off.

When she pulled back, she whispered, "I know you love me enough to die for me, Dodge. Do you love me enough to *live*?"

Damn the woman! He couldn't leave now. Now that she'd given him something more to prove.

ACKNOWLEDGMENTS

THANKS MUST GO TO . . .

My longtime friend Barry Hanson, who provided me with information on Big Thicket National Preserve. Without his input, I really would have been lost in the wilderness.

And to Sheriff J. B. Smith of Smith County, Texas, who corrected all my misconceptions about those who wear the tin star. Well, most of them anyway.

And to Dodge Hanley, who's a fictional character, but one with enough forbearance and fortitude to live with me through the writing of another novel. It's my hope I did him proud.

—Sandra Brown

SMASH CUT

SANDRA BROWN

Available in paperback
from Pocket Books

Turn the page for a preview of
Smash Cut . . .

CHAPTER 1

Creighton Wheeler stormed across the bluestone terrace, whipping off his sun visor and making a swipe at the sweat streaming down his face, then without breaking stride, angrily tossed the damp towel and visor onto a chaise. "This better be damn important. I was about to break his serve."

The housekeeper who'd summoned him from the tennis court was unfazed by his temper. "Don't you take that tone with me. It's your daddy wants to see you."

Her name was Ruby. Creighton didn't know her last name and had never bothered to ask, although she'd been in the family's employ since before he was born. Any time he got out of sorts with her, she reminded him that she'd wiped his butt and his nose, that both had been nasty, and that she hadn't enjoyed doing either. It rankled to think of her being that familiar with his person, even when he was a baby.

He brushed past her three-hundred-pound bulk and crossed the industrial-size kitchen to one of several refrigerators, yanking open the door.

"Right now, he said."

Ignoring her, Creighton got a can of Coke from the Sub-Zero, ripped off the tab, and took a long drink. He rolled the cold can across his forehead. "Take one of these out to Scott."

"Your tennis coach's legs ain't broke." She turned back to the counter and slapped her large hand on the hunk of beef she was preparing to go into the roasting pan.

Something ought to be done about her sass, Creighton thought as he pushed through the swinging door and made his way toward the front of the house, where his father had a study. The door was ajar. He paused outside it, then knocked once on the doorjamb with his Coke can, nudged the door open, and strolled in, twirling the tennis racquet against his shoulder. He looked every inch the aristocrat called away from a session of healthy exercise. It was a role he was perfectly suited to play.

Doug Wheeler was seated behind his desk, which was presidential in proportion but much more pretentious than anything inside the Oval Office. The desk was flanked by mahogany flagpoles, one for the Georgia state flag, the other for Old Glory. Ancestors glared from oil portraits hanging on opposite walls, which were paneled in stained cypress meant to last till the Second Coming.

"Scott's time is money, and the clock is ticking," Creighton said.

"I'm afraid this can't wait. Please sit down."

Creighton took a seat in one of the cordovan leather chairs facing his father's desk and propped his tennis racquet against it. "I didn't know you were here. Weren't you scheduled to play golf this afternoon?" He leaned forward and set his Coke can on the polished surface of the desk.

Frowning, Doug placed a coaster beneath the can so it wouldn't leave a moisture ring. "I dropped by here to change before going to the club," he said. "But something urgent—"

"Don't tell me," Creighton interrupted. "The paper clip audit exposed an embezzlement. Damn those sneaky secretaries."

"Paul is dead."

Creighton's heart gave a bump. His smile collapsed. "What?"

Doug cleared his throat. "Your uncle was shot and killed in the Hotel Moultrie about an hour ago."

Creighton continued to stare at him, then finally released his breath. "Well, in the immortal words of Forrest Gump. Actually his mother. 'Life is like a box of chocolates. You never know what you're gonna get.' "

His father lurched to his feet. "Is that all you can say?"

"I think that says it fairly well."

Creighton had never seen his father cry. He wasn't crying now, but his eyes looked suspiciously moist and he was swallowing too often and too hard. In an attempt to hide the emotion about to overwhelm him, he stepped from behind his desk and moved to the wide window. He looked out over the grounds of the estate, where Mexican laborers were hand-picking weeds from colorful beds of impatiens and caladiums.

Quietly Creighton asked, "Did I hear you correctly, Father? Uncle Paul was *shot*?"

"In the forehead. Almost point-blank range. During an apparent holdup."

"A holdup? Like a robbery? At the Moultrie?"

"As unheard of as that seems."

Doug ran a hand through his hair, which was thick and gray like that of his brother—now late brother—who had been his senior by only eleven months. He and Paul went to the same barber and used the same tailor. Of almost identical height and weight, they were often mistaken for each other from the back. Their sibling relationship had been almost as close as that of twins.

"I don't know any details," Doug continued. "Julie was almost too distraught to speak."

"She was notified first?"

"Actually, she was with him when it happened."

"At the Hotel Moultrie. During the middle of a weekday."

Doug came around and gave his son a hard look. "She was almost hysterical. According to the policeman. Detective actually. He took the phone from her when she could no longer speak. He told me that she had insisted on calling and telling me herself. But she managed to get out only a few incoherent words before she began crying to the point that I could no longer understand her." He paused to clear his throat.

"The detective, Sanford I think he said his name was, seemed decent enough. He extended his condolences and told me I could come to the morgue if I . . . if I wanted to see Paul's body. There'll be an autopsy, of course."

Creighton looked away. "Christ."

"Yes," Doug said on a weighty sigh. "I can't come to terms with it either."

"Did they catch the guy?"

"Not yet."

"Where in the hotel?"

"The detective didn't say."

"One of the shops?"

"I don't know."

"Who would rob—"

"I don't know," Doug snapped.

A taut silence followed. Doug's shoulders settled heavily on his tall frame. "I'm sorry, Creighton. I'm . . . not myself."

"Understandably. It's astonishing."

Doug massaged his forehead. "The detective said he would give me a full account when I get there." He glanced at the open door but made no move toward it, clearly reluctant to leave on that errand.

"What about Mother? Has she been told?"

"She was here when Julie called. Naturally she's upset, but there are arrangements that must be made. She's upstairs making preliminary calls." Doug went to the bar and poured himself a shot of bourbon. "Want one?"

"No thank you."

Doug tossed back the drink and picked up the decanter again. "As difficult as this tragedy is to absorb, there are practical matters that must be addressed."

Creighton braced himself. He disdained anything with the word *practical* attached to it.

"Tomorrow morning, I want you to go to the offices and make a personal statement to our personnel."

Inwardly Creighton groaned. He wanted nothing to do with their personnel, which amounted to several hundred people, each of whom held his uncle Paul in the highest esteem while most demonstrated nothing but contempt for him whenever he graced the corporate headquarters with his presence, which was as seldom as possible.

Wheeler Enterprises manufactured and sold building materials of some kind. Whoopee. Fascinating.

His father looked over his shoulder at him. Obviously a response was expected.

"Of course. What should I say?"

"I'll write something out tonight. I'll call for a companywide assembly in the auditorium on the third floor at ten o'clock. Deliver your statement, then perhaps a minute of silence should be observed."

Creighton nodded solemnly. "Most appropriate."

Doug downed the second drink, then decisively set the empty tumbler on the bar. "You may be required to take up some of the slack while we're sorting through all this."

"All of what?"

"The funeral, for starters."

"Oh, of course. That'll be an event."

"No doubt," Doug said with a sigh. "I'll keep it as dignified as possible, but your uncle was involved in—"

"Bloody everything. He was the undeclared king of Atlanta."

Doug pressed on. "Yes, and now the king is dead. To complicate matters, his death was a homicide." Thinking about the brutality of it, he winced and dragged his hand down his face. "Jesus." He glanced toward the bar as though considering pouring one more shot of Kentucky's finest, but didn't. "The police will need our full cooperation."

"What can we do? We weren't witnesses."

"But Paul's killer must be apprehended. You will cooperate and do so willingly. Do we have an understanding?"

"Of course, Father." Creighton hesitated, then said, "Although I hope you'll act as the family's official spokesperson. The media will flock to us like vultures to carrion."

Doug gave a brusque nod. "I'll see to it that you and your mother are sheltered. Although I'm compelled to make the funeral a public observance, I'll insist on it being as low-key as possible.

"We must set an example to our employees, and keep the company running smoothly, which is what Paul would want us to do. To that end, I want you to be prepared. I've left some materials in your room. You should review them tonight, bring yourself up to date on new products, where we rank in the market, our projections for next year."

"All right." *As if.*

His father seemed to read his mind. He gave him the full-on, American eagle, hard-ass treatment. "It's the least you can do, Creighton. You're almost thirty years old. I've been remiss and take partial responsibility for your lack of interest in the company. I should have given you more responsibility, involved you more in the expansion of the business. Paul . . ." He stumbled over the name. "Paul encouraged me to. Instead, I've spoiled you. No more. It's time you stepped up to the plate. Now that Paul's gone, you'll take over when I retire."

Who was he kidding? Himself maybe, but certainly not Creighton. His father was delusional if he thought Creighton planned on jumping into the corporate cauldron. He knew nothing about the business or management thereof, and didn't want to know. All he wanted out of the family business was revenue. He loved his life exactly as it was and had no intention whatsoever of changing it by taking on responsibilities that any yes-man could do.

But now wasn't the time to replay the scene he and his father had played a thousand times before, when his shortcomings and misplaced priorities were paraded for his review, when he was reminded of duty and what it meant to be a grown-up, a man, a Wheeler. Bullshit like that.

Changing subjects, he asked, "Has it made the news yet?"

"If not yet, it will soon." Doug moved to his desk and picked up a sheet of paper, passing it to Creighton. "Would you please call these people and notify them? They deserve to be told by a member of the family, rather than hearing it on the news."

Creighton scanned the typewritten list, recognizing most of the names as personal friends of his uncle Paul, stockholders in Wheeler Enterprises, city and state officials, other prominent businessmen.

"And would you also break the news to Ruby?" Doug asked. "She knows something's up, but I didn't have the heart to tell her, especially considering the horrible circumstances. You know how much she loved and admired Paul."

"Yes, I'll do that." *And I'll enjoy it,* Creighton thought. That was one way to get back at her for sassing him. "Would you like me to go to the morgue with you?"

"Thank you, but no," Doug said. "I wouldn't ask that of you."

"Good. I can't think of anything worse." Creighton pretended to ponder it a moment, then shuddered. "Maybe a Carnival cruise."

SANDRA BROWN is the author of numerous *New York Times* bestsellers. Her most recent novels include *Smash Cut, Smoke Screen, Play Dirty, Ricochet, Chill Factor, White Hot,* and *Hello, Darkness*. She and her husband live in Arlington, Texas. Visit her website at www.sandrabrown.net.